FOR THE SAKE OF HAPPINESS

MEL THORN

ISBN: 061591361X
ISBN-13: 978-0615913612

For James. You never stopped believing in me, and your support made this possible.

For Ray. You've taught me more than I thought I could learn.

1. Letter

Cory Anderson always got the feeling he was being watched, and in spite of his best efforts, could never shake the notion that someone was following him.

Late that October afternoon, a low fog had clung to the surface of the ground as summer limped into its final days of existence, bringing an already bitter, wet autumn, one of which Michigan was famous for. An abnormal fog had coated the air since earlier that morning, and had dropped all possible visibility. Ever since he had left work, he was forced to turn on his headlights in order to cut through the thick mist. He didn't yet look into his rear view mirror, but he knew someone was behind him.

The fact that someone drove behind him wasn't the odd thing. Not everyone that joined him on the same road was following him. The strange thing was that even in the thick clouds of smoke, they weren't using lights. He tried not to let it get to him, and didn't want to jump to any conclusions. It was possible that their lights didn't function, or maybe they didn't need them, for whatever reason. When he saw the bright green sign labeled "Hunter St," He veered onto it without using a turn signal. The car behind him slowed when he pulled into the subdivision, but continued on its journey after Cory had gone around the corner. After taking a breath of relief, he traveled toward his destination: the house where he currently lived, along with his mother and two younger sisters.

As his speed limit dropped while he crawled along the looping road and he looked at each of the houses lining the occupied street, he still felt as though eyes were on him, like the entire neighborhood could see and hear him, and that no matter what he did, he would never truly get a sense that he was alone. In the twenty-four years he had lived his life, never had he experienced a sensation that unsettled him as much. Where this feeling originated, he might never find out.

When he parked his car in the driveway of his mother's house, he was waved to by Denise Ballard, his neighbor, as he walked up the cement path to his front door. She was preparing her garden for the upcoming winter, tending to her magnolia bush. Cory tossed her an amiable wave back, but he wasn't in the mood for small talk. He walked into the two-story, grey and white split-level before she could speak to him, hanging his keys on one of the series of hooks on the wall.

A pile of mail was stacked on the kitchen table, and on top of it, a clock radio. He took this as a sign that his mother was already home from work. The radio was meant for him to repair, a sentimental item of hers that once belonged to his father, who divorced her two years ago. He would fix the radio for her (again, for the third time), but not until he had filled his stomach. He prepared himself a microwavable frozen dinner, and nibbled on it while he grabbed some tools to remove the outer cabinet from the radio's chassis. While he checked the capacitors and coils for damage, he heard footsteps behind him, descending the stairs.

"Hi, Cory," squeaked a saddened young voice.

Cory turned halfway toward her while seated, peering at the juvenile visitor. His youngest sister at fourteen years of age, Erica, was shambling toward the living room, cradling her ten pound, rambunctious calico cat, Missy, in her arms, which she then released when it fidgeted. It scampered over to its food bowl and gnawed. "Hey, Erica," he greeted with a drawn-out sigh. He soon noticed the redness around her eyes, the wet glaze of fresh tears over her irises. "What's wrong? Everything okay?"

"Me and mom got into another fight. She doesn't like Josh."

"I'm sure she'll come around," he said while turning back to the radio's husk.

"Yeah right. Maybe you could talk to her for me?"

2

Cory stifled a threatening groan. He was always looked to as a family mediator, one that they rarely listened to, even when his advice was solid. It was simply one of those things, those responsibilities that he had to take on when moving back home, whether he accepted it or not. "She's just protective of you."

"Yeah, I know, but she listens to you better. I keep explaining that Josh is really nice." She stuck her bottom lip out in the same manner she once did after being denied a dollhouse when she was nine. "She hates him for no reason."

"Give her time," he sighed, squinting at the tiny parts inside of the radio, which he gave most of his attention. "You just started dating him. He hasn't made an impression on her yet."

Erica didn't make any more remarks on the subject, dragging her feet into the kitchen to find an afternoon snack, and he went back to his job fixing the radio. Samantha Taccetta, Cory's mother, entered the kitchen from the bathroom down the hallway. She didn't seem surprised to see him, but otherwise appeared troubled. "Oh, good, you're home," she noticed with a casual, however tired tone. "I see you're already looking at the radio. Did you fix it already? I'd like it fixed."

Cory often used his busy hands to silence his busy mind, but these serene moments were frequently vanquished by his mother's presence, who insisted that it was always a good time to use Cory as therapy. "It doesn't look good, mom," he pronounced like a surgeon to a dying patient's family, awaiting the incoming torrential sadness.

"What do you mean? It worked just fine yesterday!"

"Well, today it's not."

Samantha leaned over him and the table where the dead radio rested, and gazed upon it with her eyes growing rounder, her hand planted against her chest. "Can't you do something?"

He elucidated the situation precisely as one would when explaining the death of a goldfish to a toddler. "Mom, I just don't think it's going to work anymore. You can still keep it if you want it for sentimental value, but with all of the money I keep putting into fixing this thing, I could have bought you a new one by now."

"I see." She accepted the clock's fate, for once. "If that's what you have to do, I guess I'll get over it. Maybe I'll try to give it back to your father."

"Why would dad want a broken radio? Just put it in the attic."

"No, I don't want it up there. I'll just keep it in my room." She watched Cory reassemble the lifeless fragments of a once fully functioning timekeeper, clicking her tongue a few times. "Do you think he might like a new one?"

As he tightened the screws along the sides of the outer cabinet, he shrugged before handing the junk over to her. "I'm sure he has a new one by now. I'm assuming that's why he left this piece of crap here."

She either hadn't heard him, or didn't pay much mind to his realism. She rarely did. "I'll buy him a new one. I need to stop by his house later anyway."

He didn't lecture her, as he normally would, that they were divorced for a reason. Instead, he left the table, relieved that he didn't have to fiddle with the scrap of rubbish any longer, and could finally have some alone time. As he ascended the narrow staircase to the second floor, he checked his cell phone as he headed toward his room. He had no texts or calls from anybody. Nothing he wasn't accustomed to seeing.

When he returned to Michigan to live with his family, he left more than just his old apartment behind; he left his two closest friends, Alex and Scott. In between working, partying and bar-hopping, they would find the time to call every now and then, but Cory had recently felt like he was losing touch with them. They were too busy for him, now that he wasn't around them, and though at the start they phoned him every day, it had been a while since he had heard anything from them.

His only friend now was his childhood buddy Angie, who had lived her whole life in Lansing, and refused to move. She told him it was to stay near her family, whom she loved and respected, but also to stay near Cory, that is until he abruptly moved to New York when he was old enough to. He wasn't aware of the impact it had on her when he left Michigan when he reached nineteen, but he found out when she cried to him how much she would miss him just before he departed. It was the saddest he had ever seen her, even since their days in high school. Angie was one thing he was happy to come home to when he moved back in with his family, and despite having a busy life herself, he was usually able to convince her to spend time with him.

Once in his bedroom, he shuffled into his adjacent bathroom, giving himself and the brunette-auburn stubble growing on his chin a good look in the mirror. His straight hair was chin-length now, a style he never really desired, but one he allowed in apathy. While shaving the fuzz from his thin and pointed jaw line, he noticed one of the light bulbs above the mirror had dimmed. He frankly didn't give enough of a damn about it to inform his mother, and as long as he could see what he was doing, he might let the rest of the lights follow in its path.

Another chore knocked off of his already short list, he went to his computer to check his e-mail and networking sites. He had empty inboxes on both accounts, and no one bothered to comment on the new photos he posted a few days ago. Dissatisfied with the shortcomings of online relationships, he shook his head at the monitor as if it could understand his plight. He abandoned the Internet with a heavy heart, and instead played some music he enjoyed, resting on his bed while listening to it, hoping it would drown out the sound of the sudden bickering of his mother and Erica.

After an hour or so of random titles blaring from his shuffled play list, his phone rang. Like a mole emerging from a hole in the ground, he leapt to life, clutching his vibrating cell phone and pressing it to his ear. "Hello?" He said to his caller with hope.

Angie was on the other end, and as usual, she sounded exhausted. "Cory, you are taking me out tonight."

He was inured to her short and to-the-point personality. At times it was refreshing, and others, it caught him in the worst of moods. He wasn't particularly in a good one when she rang. "I am, huh? When is it your turn to take *me* out?"

"When I can afford it!" She exclaimed, however in amusement. "There's a new bar open downtown. It looks pretty trendy. It's a good chance for you to get out of the house."

Perhaps a game of pool would ease some of his stress, even if only temporarily, but alcohol was not something he consumed on a regular basis, or socially for that matter, and Angie was well informed on this. Not only did booze disgust him, but he was quite the lightweight, and he never enjoyed the feeling he got when inebriated. "Are you sure you're not doing this because drinks are cheaper at Happy Hour?"

"Don't be so negative. Of course I'm doing this for you. If I have a few drinks, you can't hold it against me."

It had been long, too long, since Cory "went out" just to entertain himself. Angie was a good friend in some respects, but in most, she loved attention, and nothing greater. Nevertheless, even with that in mind, Cory's desperation had reached full throttle; he *needed* to get out of the house, to change things, to do something different, and it didn't matter who he did it with. After a few moments, he let out a weighted sigh. "I'll come and pick you up."

Cory didn't mind spending his time practicing a lone game of pool while Angie ordered drinks all night and talked his ear off regarding her boyfriend, Derrick. The fact that he wasn't required to speak to her, since her mouth almost never closed, kept his concentration on the game steeled.

"He keeps asking me if I have a thing for you," she continued while gorging herself on martinis.

"We all know that you do," Cory joked, knocking a solid ball into a corner pocket.

With an affronted gasp, she replied, "What are you talking about?!"

"I'm just messing with you, you know."

"Oh. Yeah. Yeah, I knew that." She silenced herself with a swig of her drink. "I'm just tired of him asking me. If he really thought I preferred you over him, I don't know why he thinks I'd stay with him all this time. You and I have been hanging out like this since you started living here again. You'd think he would grow up by now."

"Maybe because lately, you see more of me than you do of him." With a clack, the cue ball struck a striped one.

"That's ridiculous. He lives with me, silly."

"Exactly my point."

She blocked his next shot with her arm to attract his full attention. "Wait a minute! Whose side are you on, anyway?"

Sighing, he lowered his cue while waiting for her to move. "I'm not on anyone's *side*. I think if breaking up with him is the right thing to do, maybe you should do it."

"I think I know better than anybody what the right thing is for my relationship." There were a few beats of silence, other than the sound of the chattering crowd and music. Cory rubbed chalk onto the end of the cue he was holding while averting his gaze. "Okay. I have been seeing you a lot. I didn't think there was anything wrong with that. He's just been getting weird on me, that's all. He's getting possessive, almost. He needs to respect my boundaries."

"We all have to make tough decisions, Angie. If you don't love him, maybe it's time to ask yourself some serious questions."

"I didn't say I didn't love him."

He wasn't listening to her anymore, because he felt it— eyes were on him, burning into the back of his shirt. He peered around the bar, searching for the source of his paranoia. He hoped to see someone familiar, anyone that he might recognize, but there were so many strangers mashed together in the crowd that he couldn't confirm or deny his delusions.

"Cory! You asleep over there?" Angie's voice echoed for the third time, but it was the first time Cory heard her.

"Huh?" He turned his attention, as well as his eyes, to her. "Sorry. I'm a little distracted."

Her smirk meant that she was about to get playful with him, which he already didn't appreciate. "The men in black suits after you again? They've come to check on the chip in your brain!" She then pulled aside a few strands of Cory's hair as if looking for a hidden scar.

"Stop it. Don't tease me. I'm telling you, someone really is following me. I can *feel* them. I know it sounds crazy…"

"Sweetie, you've been saying that for, what, two years now? Who the hell would keep that up for so long without saying anything to you?" She snickered and slugged him in the arm with a balled up fist, causing him to flinch and retract his upper torso from her vicinity.

"Maybe they're afraid of me? You ever think of that?"

"Who would be afraid of sweet, adorable little you?"

He endured a pinch to his cheek, which he winced at. "Never mind. If you're not going to take me seriously, I don't know why I bring it up." He knocked his cue into the white ball once again, frustrated at her condescending nature.

"Oh, come on, Cory, you know I'm just playing."

He ignored her, aloof to her taunting. He knew how foolish he sounded whenever he brought it up, and he didn't need to be reminded of that. He loved Angie, but after she had a few drinks, she was too absorbed in looking attractive to be concerned for him, and became detached from any serious conversation. It was embarrassing bringing it up to her, and having her laugh at him made him even less inclined to rely on her assistance.

After driving his intoxicated buddy home for the night, which he was rewarded for by a sloppy kiss on the cheek— one that reeked of vodka— he made his way back to his own house. Now alone in the car, which was thankfully vomit-free, he was able to wallow in his own thoughts. He was sure the person inside of the car behind him wasn't following him, but he performed routine checks into his mirrors out of habit, wanting to catch the person in the act and end this charade once and for all. Had he seen that car before? It looked familiar. Many people drove green cars, and many drove that make and model, so how could he know? He was more than certain that he never would for sure.

Upon arriving, he parked in the driveway, not wanting to wake everyone by opening the garage, and sauntered inside with his head low and his hands in his pockets, shivering in the chilled October winds. He saw his second youngest sister, Amanda (who, like him, took a more physical likeness of their father rather than their mother), standing in the kitchen, drinking a glass of water. She smiled when she saw him and waved, chain bracelets jingling as they dangled from her wrist.

"How was your night?" She asked before rinsing her cup out in the sink.

"Interesting. I usually have fun with Angie, but tonight felt different. I don't know, maybe I'm in a bad mood. I've been a little off since I woke up this morning."

"This might take your mind off of it." Amanda shuffled some papers upon the kitchen counter, where they usually kept all of their junk mail. She retrieved a white envelope from the pile and held it out to him. "This was in the mail today."

Cory glimpsed at it with intrigue, having not expected any mail. After taking the envelope from her, he saw written in fluid curves the words *For Cory*. There was no stamp, address, or return address— just those directions in two straightforward words.

"What the hell is this?" He asked after a few thoughtful seconds, looking to Amanda for answers.

"I don't know. I asked mom and I don't think she knows either. It kind of freaked her out, actually."

"Well, it's freaking me out, too. You know how I've been telling you that I feel like I'm being followed?" He held the envelope up to the light, trying to see the contents inside. "This isn't helping."

"Come on, open it," she urged, bouncing up and down on her heels. "I want to see what it is."

With a twist of the wrist, he tore open the edge of the envelope and reached inside, pulling out a few pages of loose leaf, which were neatly folded before they were inserted. Curiosity took hold of his hands as he opened and flattened the sheets. The handwriting on the letter matched that of the scratching on the front of its container, and every word seemed to be written with time and care, as if the author had considered each one for some time before jotting it down with a black fountain pen.

Dearest Cory,

For two years now, I have been preparing for this moment; the time when I finally speak to you. I thought that after all of this time, I would have the courage to approach you personally, to at least say hello. I am nothing but a coward.

I'm ashamed to admit that I have employed myself a position I didn't intend to fill. I can tell, when you look around for me, that you know deep down that I'm there. I've noticed your expressions of fear and concern. This wounds my heart so deeply, because I never intended to inflict harm or fear upon you. I only want happiness for you, and that is the reason for the letter I am writing you today.

Yes, I am the one. I am your shadow. I didn't plan to be, but it merely just happened. Call it fate, if you will. My reasons and justifications for such actions stem from too many issues that I can even speak of, let alone write here, especially without risk of sounding utterly insane, but over time, those reasons have developed into a strong and devoted fondness for you.

You see, it was an accident that I have fallen in love with you, or rather, the person I've learned that you are. You became something, someone, of great importance to me, and being near you has become necessary for me to go through my daily life.

I'm sorry I waited so long to even write you just a simple explanation. You deserve so much more than that. If only I could trust within myself that telling you to your face my reasons for my apparent insanity had some reasoning, a background, a story, no matter how wild and crazy it might be, without receiving a painful rejection. Just know that deep within the confines of my very dark and dreary heart that I know how lovely you are.

He was speechless when he came to the end of the unsigned letter, a tremble now rattling his weak knees. Amanda scooted up beside him when she saw how pale he was, and looked at the creased papers in his hands. "Someone really has been following me," Cory confirmed, and he looked at his sister, his face filled with complexity. "I have a stalker."

With bugged eyes and a gaping mouth, she softly spoke. "Who is it?"

"That's the thing, I have no idea. There's no name, no return address. It's like it was written by a ghost."

"Do you have an idea of who it is based on the way they wrote it?"

He raised a sarcastic eyebrow, his lips curling. "Please. Half of the people I talk to can barely spell, let alone use proper grammar, at least from what I understand from the way they text me. This has to be from someone I've never even met. If I've never met them, how can they think all of these things? The fact that they know where I live means they've followed me to our front door." Saying such a thing aloud made his stomach tumble.

Amanda took the letter from her brother and scrutinized it. "Maybe you've met them, but you don't remember?"

"I can't recall meeting any lunatics in the past two years."

She scoffed at him, rolling her eyes. "It seems kind of crazy, but whoever wrote it was at least a little smart. How did they manage to hide from you for that long?"

"I frankly don't care either way. I need to find out how to deal with this." He took the letter back from her, carrying it up to his room. While sitting at his desk, awake later than his intended bedtime, he read and re-read the anonymous letter. Cory had felt very alone since he moved to Michigan, even with Angie around, but he found the irony a bit too much to handle. He would have liked to have more friends, but he didn't necessarily want someone to be obsessed with him, to stalk him. He had to learn who wrote it, and soon, before he lost his mind even further.

He now had the proof he needed that he wasn't insane, that it hadn't all been in his head. He had that to be relieved of, but all the same, he wished he had learned of something less serious in nature to console him. Now the problem had gotten even more complicated and unsolvable.

For two years, his mind replayed. *For two whole years. They've been following me since I moved here, and I never noticed them. They could be anyone. They could be anywhere.*

2. Thorns

When he got out of bed the following morning, Cory didn't have much of an appetite. For the single hour he slept, he had disturbing lucid dreams, all involving many faceless onlookers staring at him with hollow eyes. His mysterious admirer certainly knew how to be discreet, and it was with this knowledge that he could not relax. He assumed that upon learning he wasn't a schizophrenic, he'd be happier, but now his safety was threatened more than it was beforehand. The letter-writer claimed that they didn't want to harm him, but to Cory, acting like a creep was enough harm in itself.

He settled on a small breakfast before work; a toaster pastry that would usually put him in a good mood at the start of the day, but its sweetness was now sickening. He threw it in the trash after two bites, and didn't bother making himself a lunch for the day.

Since he was awake much earlier than the rest of his family, he was the first to put the coffee on as part of his everyday routine, needing the caffeine. After taking a shower, dressing for work, and drinking a cup of coffee, the women of the house were awake by that point. He didn't want to talk to his mother about his stalker, knowing how panicked she'd get. Much as he expected, however, she wanted to be updated.

"Did Amanda give the letter to you?" She asked while pouring herself some java.

"Yeah," he answered with drooping eyes. "It was nothing."

"Cory has a stalker," Amanda piped up. "It was written by someone in love with him."

He hoped, deep down, that she could see the glare on his face. This wasn't how he wanted to start his day.

Samantha, stunned, choked on her beverage. "What?!"

"I'll take care of it. I'm going to take the letter to the police station after work. Maybe they can fingerprint it."

"I think you should stay home today."

"You know I can't do that. We're behind on some of the bills here, because you refuse to sell this damn house and move out." He retracted his bite, seeing how pained she was at the reminder. "I'm sorry. I'm just in a really bad mood right now."

She tucked some of her dyed blonde hair behind her ear, which was one of her many nervous ticks. "You know I can't part with this house, Cory."

"I know, mom. Forget I said anything." After finishing his coffee, he wished them all a good afternoon before slumping toward the front door. He wanted nothing more than to just get through his work day in one piece, get some information from the police, and come home to try to get some sleep, but how could he? He knew, as soon as he opened the door, the day would not be without obstacles.

On the doormat lying on the front porch rested two items. The top item was a rose, budding, and not yet fully bloomed. Beneath it was folded parchment, devoid of an envelope, but was stamped with the words, *Good Morning Cory*. Bile crept up his windpipe, and he grabbed the two objects in his fingertips like they were infested with eroding bacteria. He speed-walked to the trash bin at the end of the driveway and tossed the rose into it, and prepared to do the same with the note, but he chose to read it first, his curiosity getting the better of him.

> *You're probably leaving for work just now. If I know how things go, and I usually do, you should be the first one to notice this gift, since you're usually the first one to leave. It's a lovely morning, isn't it? Autumn is my favorite time of year.*

I brought you this rose as a humble request for your forgiveness. I apologize greatly for my behavior. I've been doing it so long now, that I can't seem to stop. I have forgotten myself. I need to be near you, to be surrounded by your constant warmth. Does this offend you? It's okay if it does. I know there's something wrong with me.

Roses are a traditional symbol of love and affection, but I believe them to be more than that, don't you? Every rose has its thorns. We can't have happiness without pain, without grief, without sadness. We wouldn't know just how lucky we are to be alive if we didn't have consequences set before us. I wonder, for all of the giving and help for others you have done, if you feel lucky. I, for obvious reasons, do not.

One day, I might work up the nerve to talk to you, because I would love discussing these things as I look into your beautiful hazel eyes. You are, as great artists say, a sight to behold, a work of pure majesty, a beauty among men, and not just in appearance.

I hope you have a lovely day. I'll be there if you need me. You just won't know it.

Cory, in revulsion, reopened the trash bin and threw the note into it, watching it drift to its grave beside its thorny companion. He slammed the lid back on, clenching his hands as he kicked rocks all the way to his car. His freedom, his home, both violated, and from the sounds of the note he just read, his privacy as well.

What else has this psycho seen me do? Can they see me through my window? Have they watched me do personal things?

As he drove to Hot Wire, he reflected on how he was going to stay in his right mind during work. He couldn't possibly imagine thinking about and discussing televisions all day with the unending thought of someone nearby, watching his every move, romanticizing a fantasy life with him in their delusional head. If he saw them, would he even know if he had? What if they pretended to be a customer? He would be none the wiser.

Hot Wire, the stylish, well-stocked electronics retail chain, was crowded full of people that day hoping to get in on a new sale for a brand of camera phone, but the store's warehouse size accommodated the capacity. Cory clocked in as soon as he found a reasonably quick and easy path to the computer system in the back, weaving in and out between customers, ones he didn't look forward to dealing with that day.

He went to work when he was able, approaching customers, as was part of his job description, that didn't look like they knew what they were doing there. He managed to interest people in some expensive TVs, which he got marks for on his review if he did it enough, but couldn't keep it up for long. Feeling a fainting spell was on the way, he slipped into the bathroom halfway through the day and splashed his face with cold water.

Every moment he was pacing the floor and speaking to customers, the feeling of being stared at never ended. At thirty minute intervals, he had to stop what he was doing to check the room to see if any eyes were fixed on him. He hadn't noticed anything all afternoon, and he was in worse shape than he was when he arrived at the store.

Where are you? Who are you? What would you do if we crossed paths? What would I do if I met you?

He took his lunch break early, as demanded by his supervisor, and he ran into another of his coworkers, Rick, a man who, in Cory's view, was way too old to be working there. He threw Cory a wave as he passed, and Cory granted him one in return, feigning a pleasant disposition. He took a moment to speak with him before taking his break in his vehicle as he always did, disliking the noisiness of the break room.

"How many customers have you taken today?" Rick asked, punching some information into a touch screen monitor.

"Enough for me to want to go home already."

"I'm on a roll, myself. I've got my fire back after my vacation!" He cackled in a thick voice, wrinkles crinkling around his eyes. He looked at Cory, and lingered on his tired face for some time. "Goodness. What's the matter, Cory?"

"Nothing. I just didn't get a lot of sleep last night."

"Maybe you should go home. You look really out of it."

"I'll be okay. I've come to work feeling worse before." He wasn't sure if he agreed with himself or not on that note.

Rick nodded, thumbing a pair of reading glasses up the bridge of his nose. "That asshole customer came in again today."

He knew exactly to whom he was referring. "Shouldn't we know that dude's name by now?" Cory achieved a full grin, the first real one he had all day.

Rick had a warm chuckle, one that cheered him up. It was just the proper medicine for his ailment. "I know his name. I just dare not speak it. He's a cursed nether-creature, I'm sure of it."

"How long has he been coming in here trying to scam us?"

"Oh, jeez, I've lost count of the days. Could be years for all I know." He finished typing in whatever it was he was working on, then removed his glasses, giving Cory, his coworker and friend, his full attention. "You should see the car he drives. He must be pretty wealthy if he can afford it. Makes you wonder why he bothers with these stupid little scam plots."

"The human mind is a complicated thing."

Rick nodded in agreement. "That it is, Cory, that it is. On your lunch break, are you?"

"Yeah. I was going to spend it in my car, but I feel too weak to move. That and I enjoy your company, of course."

"You're welcome to join me in the break room, if you'd like."

Cory wasn't lying when he said he enjoyed Rick's company. He was the only one in the building he got along with, and found his fatherly nature comforting in stressful times such as his current situation. He agreed to join him for lunch, and took the useful opportunity to have a friendly chat with someone.

When his shift ended, he couldn't wait to leave the suffocating store, away from the watching eyes. His stalker might have still been inside, waiting for him to leave, maybe taking a few minutes so that he could follow him home at a distance. His stomach turned with every step he took to his car, but he told himself it wouldn't be long now before he spoke to the police. If anyone could help him, it was them.

He stopped dead in his tracks when he reached his vehicle, noticing something stuck underneath his wiper blades: another rose with a second note. He spun in circles, looking in all directions for any signs of unusual behavior, but all he could see were customers getting into their cars. Maybe one of them was his stalker. There was no way for him to tell.

Not wanting the items to get carried away by the breeze, he ripped the flower and note from its place on his window, jumping into the safety of his car before carefully opening the letter to read it.

The Cory I happened to fall in love with gives to charity. He steps up to end arguments, before they result in fights. He looks after his mother, his sisters. He stops what he is doing to help people who have found themselves in an unfortunate situation, even if he is going out of his way. He gives servers extra in tips. He is decent, he is thoughtful, he is loyal, and he is one that some are auspicious to call 'friend.'

Knowing these things, I was beside myself to see you throw my gift away. It was heartbreaking and shocking to see you, a person of understanding, be so cold. It brought tears to my eyes, which have shed many long before they saw you. I know I'm not mistaken regarding the type of person you are, Cory. I've seen your kindness firsthand. I was compelled to believe that I had been wrong about you, but deep down, I know you're just upset, maybe even angry. And that's okay. I'm just as angry with myself for putting you in this position.

If you choose to throw away this second rose, I at least won't be around to see it, but I implore that you keep it. I picked them especially for you, and I have no other use for them. I would rather they bloomed in water instead of decay in the garbage.

Cory reviewed the letter with mixed emotions. He glanced at the rose he had tossed into the passenger seat, its petals shaken loose by his rough toss, limp and wilting like a lover scorned. It stared at him while lying sprawled and lifeless on the seat, begging mercy, questioning the reasons of his mindless abuse. He frowned, apologetic.

For now, he kept the rose, a decision he intended to be a temporary one. On the other hand, it was an attractive flower.

The policeman on the other side of the desk had been patient and quiet until Cory came to the end of his tale, and when he arrived at the conclusion, he leaned forward over his desk with a creased brow and tight mouth. "You said a couple of years, right?"

"That's right," Cory said with a nod. "Read the letter. They even confess to it."

"Who the hell would be crazy enough to do that for so long?" He shook his head, which rested on a stiff, veined neck.

"I don't know. But I want to find out and get it over with."

"Well," the officer continued, gears turning in his skull. "Since you don't know who could be doing it, we'll have the letters checked for prints, but I'm not hopeful."

"What? Why not?"

"Whoever wrote these sounds like she… or he… knows what they're doing. They might have stalked in the past. Regardless, we're going to see what we can do for you."

Cory was asked to wait, and he did, but couldn't help but fidget. He thought he saw a couple of officers snicker at him before turning their backs, but he had lived with constant paranoia for so long that he could very well have imagined it. Either way, their presence made him feel wimpy. What would they say over some beers later? That a whiny kid came in earlier crying that someone followed him, like an emotional, fearful woman? Would they embellish on it, claim that he was in tears, that he was a-a-a-afraid to go out at night? He sank lower in his chair, wishing with all of his might that he could shrink three sizes. He already felt like less of a man for living with three women. He didn't need the entire town believing he was a sissy, passing around stories that he came barreling into a police station one day with piss in his pants, especially if it ended up being a woman following him. Women were expected to be scared. Men were expected to grow a sack and take care of it themselves, whether or not there was any truth to those statements.

Finally, he was given a moment to speak with the officer again, who was shaking his head as he returned. When he asked what was wrong, he shrugged at him. "Paper, envelope, the flower... all clean. Your stalker must be smart enough to wear gloves."

"That's fucked up," he blurted without much forethought, but the officer agreed, despite the vulgarity.

"It's not uncommon. Stalkers are usually intelligent, and sometimes adequate social engineers. What scares me, though, is how arrogant this person sounds. She, or he, feels entitled to you because they're 'the only one that notices you for who you are,' or 'the only one that really cares about you.' It's a self-righteous attitude that some stalkers possess, and they use it as rationalization for what they're doing. If you were to alter their view on the type of person you were, or befriend people your stalker doesn't like, they might get dangerous. I don't want to see that happen."

"So what am I going to do?"

"Well, to be frank with you, without fingerprints, a name, or address, we have nothing to go on. You said this person doesn't call you, so they probably don't know your phone number, or they're smart enough to avoid it." He went on when he saw how hopeless Cory appeared. "But I have an idea."

"What's that?"

"What I suggest," the officer continued, "Is that we find a way to lure this person out of the shadows. They vie for you to notice them, really crave your attention, right? They're not confessing who they are because they know it could land them in jail, but also because they don't want to be rejected by you. If they were convinced somehow that you were really interested in them, they might come out, and then we can nab them."

"How the hell would I do that?"

Officer Stiff-Neck twisted his lips around in circles. "You could write them back. Tell them you're flattered, pretend you want it. I'm willing to bet that they'll pop right out of the darkness. I wouldn't normally recommend this to people, because it can make the situation worse, but if you really want to know who this person is, it's a start."

He had to admit that the plan sounded clever, but risky. "What if they want to meet in person, and they're a psycho with a gun that's going to shoot me if I don't want them?"

After a moment's hesitation, the officer sighed and leaned back in his office chair. "If they want to meet in person, you could always call us. Even if this person makes it out to sound like they won't hurt you, we always have to be cautious."

Cory mulled over the possibility that his stalker was someone he knew, a friend, or perhaps even a distant family member. What would he do then, if it was someone he cared for? He pictured this mystery pursuer in his mind, whether they be male or female, and put himself in their shoes. He imagined someone he was deeply in love with pretending to love him back, using his own weakness as a trap setup. Though he had spent two years disturbed and haunted by whoever it was, he imagined how painful that would be if he were on the other side of the fence. He almost wanted to say that he didn't want to hurt them, the very person who had been invading his life.

"All right," Cory agreed, getting out of his chair. "I'll try it." He shook the officer's hand and thanked him for understanding, and not laughing at him. He seemed confused by this added statement, but said nothing.

Cory wanted to relax. His legs were motivated by the sole thought that he would soon be home to sleep as long as possible, but as soon as he walked in the door, drama was waiting for him. The sound of shouting traveled down the hall, which was again coming from Erica and his mother, as it normally did when there was a verbal argument in his home. He stepped between them to end it before it got out of control.

"All right, guys," he interceded, exasperated. "Relax. What's going on?"

"Missy's gone!" Erica bawled. Her calico had run away again, and he didn't blame it.

"She'll come back, Erica," he reassured. "She always does."

"I told mom to ask the neighbors if they've seen her, and she won't do it!"

Samantha turned her flaming eyes to her son. "I said I'd ask Denise, but I'm not going to *his* house."

The house Samantha referred to was that of her neighbor, William Shepherd. Cory knew almost nothing about the man, save for the fact that he lived alone, and that his mother wouldn't touch him with a ten-foot pole. Regardless of the situation, she would never speak to him, but always had something nasty to say about him. "Do you want me to talk to Shepherd?" He suggested.

"Would you?" Her stress faded as soon as he offered.

"Sure. No problem." They were both silent now, no longer fighting, no longer crying. If that's what it took to kill their dispute, then he was glad he thought of it. He left them to discuss things more civilly. After heading outside, he took a moment to look over at Shepherd's yard, which was a tangled, matted mess. Weeds were overgrown, and bushes needed a good trimming, as did the uncut grass. As he crossed the threshold between both of their lawns, he took a long look at Shepherd's decrepit home, at the busted and broken window panes, the flaking paint, the missing roof shingles, and the dilapidated front door with a tarnished golden knocker. The wooden steps of the porch creaked as he walked upon them, like he was stepping onto an old man's spine.

He pressed the doorbell, a chipper tune, one that sounded out of place for having belonged to such a gloomy home. He heard shuffling and creaking from inside, and could make out every single one of Shepherd's slow footsteps as he made his way to the house's entrance.

Cory scratched at a non-existent itch on the back of his neck when he saw a young, tired face peek through one of the two front windows. He had to wait several seconds before Shepherd made any sort of action. The beaten door made a deafening creak as he pulled it, and he only opened it just enough so that he could see outside, most of his face obscured by darkness.

"Yes?" He said, just a touch above a whisper, so soft that Cory had to lean closer to hear him. Strands of unkempt hair dangled over his forehead, and he figured that he had woken him up from a nap, seeing how sleepy he looked.

Cory gazed past the lenses of his black-rimmed eyeglasses and stared directly into his half-open blue eyes. "Hi. I'm Cory Anderson. I live next door?"

"I know who you are," Shepherd replied in a deep monotone, though his eyes were widened in what looked like surprise.

"Right, of course you do." He shifted back and forth, twisting his foot onto the wooden slats of the porch, hearing them groan beneath his weight. They could snap and give way any day now if they continued to be neglected. "Listen, um, my sister is missing her cat. I was wondering if you've seen it. She's a calico, with red and black patches on her."

Shepherd pulled the door open further, revealing more of his face, his oak-tinted hair scattered and covering part of his eyes. He had a coat of dark stubble on his chin and jaw. "Her cat has run away?"

"Yeah, she does that sometimes. She's really attached to that cat, so if you see her, I'd really appreciate it if you told us."

"I'm sorry to hear that." His voice was still lower than the breeze. "I'll be sure to inform you if it crosses my path."

"Really? You will?"

"Of course."

"Oh. Well, thanks, Shepherd. It means a lot to my sister."

"What are neighbors for?" He stared into Cory's face with grayed irises and pinned pupils.

Cory slinked away from the door and toward the porch steps. "Okay. Well, see you around."

Without answering him, he shut the door, which made a soft click, and even from a distance, Cory could hear his footsteps moving down the hall.

They're right. That guy is weird. I kind of like it. It's different.

Once he had that bothersome task out of the way, he told his mother and sister that he handled it before heading straight for his room. He slept for many hours, and didn't wake up until the following morning. Feeling more rested than the previous day, he could focus better, and the first thing he centered on was the advice given to him by the police officer. He had to take his suggestion, but he wasn't sure if he was up to it quite yet. He had to ponder what to say to his stalker, and how to say it.

During work that day, he thought of Angie. Though their time together was usually spent listening to her discuss herself, her boyfriend and job, he needed to see someone other than his mother and sisters. He would have to get a hold of her, ask if she'd like to hang out with him.

He was surprised to find no letters or gifts from the romantic stranger that day, but he knew, somehow, that it wasn't over.

3. Restrain

"**D**o you remember the way we were in high school?"

Angie had downed a few beers, and after that point, she'd begin reminiscing. Cory didn't always mind it, but the subject was an awkward one, and he wasn't sure why she felt the need to bring it up.

They were sitting side-by-side on her living room couch within her and Derrick's apartment, pop music playing on a moderate volume on her stereo. She was giving him a recognizable look, one of mystery and mischievousness.

"Yes," he said with a dejected sigh. "Why would I forget it?"

"It's not that I assumed you'd forget it. I just look back on it sometimes. We were so stupid, weren't we?"

"I thought I was the stupider of the two of us. Well, naïve, at least."

"No you're not! Don't make me hit you for saying stuff like that."

"You know what I mean." He didn't look at her. He didn't want to.

She draped her arm across the back of the couch, behind his neck. "I know I hurt you back then. You don't have to tell me. And I'm sorry for it."

"Angie, it happened years ago. We were still kids. I'm over it by now.

"I know, it's just that… sometimes I wonder…" She paused to sip from another beer that Cory hadn't seen her open.

He already knew what she was going to say. This wasn't the first time she brought it up. "If things would be different now, had we gotten involved in a relationship?"

"Yeah. That."

"I don't think it would have changed anything. Maybe we just weren't right for each other, not in that way. To be honest, I'm happier having you as a friend rather than a girlfriend, so I'm glad it didn't work out the way I wanted. Besides, having a 'friends with benefits' relationship taught me a lot. About women, I mean."

Angie frowned, which confused him. He thought she'd be happy knowing that he considered her a friend, but she looked so disappointed. "Don't you think we would have made a cute couple, though?"

He wasn't sure how she wanted him to answer that. If she had asked him the same question when he was eighteen, he would have replied with a resound "hell yes." Now, he was apathetic on the matter. "I guess so."

"I still think we would now." She ended this observation with a giggle, twirling follicles of her long, brunette locks. "You were so cool back then. You always told me the funniest jokes…"

Hurt, he asked, "I'm not cool anymore?"

"Of course you are! I just miss those days, that's all." She stuck the bottle back in her mouth to shut herself up, a relieving moment for Cory, who just wanted the subject to vanish. She was teasing him, and he felt his insecurity returning.

He had never felt more grateful for an interruption to a conversation. The front door swung open, and in stepped Derrick, Angie's curly-haired, goateed confidante, carrying a plastic bag full of cigarettes and chips. It was the first time Cory had ever seen the guy, despite Angie's many dramatic stories, but from what he was told, he wouldn't value his uninvited visit.

Derrick froze when he saw Cory, a lit cigarette perched between his lips. Smoke swiveled toward the ceiling as a wolfish snarl formed on his lips. "Who the fuck are you?" He interrogated, squinting his beady, bright eyes.

"Uh, honey," Angie uttered while standing up, moving away from her friend. "This is Cory. Cory, this is Derrick."

Derrick didn't once look at his girlfriend, but instead stared Cory down like a junkyard dog ready to snap at the first sign of movement. His incisors flashed. "So you're the one she's always talking to."

Cory left the couch, only to step into the lion's den. "I've heard a lot about you." He followed rules of etiquette, taught to him at an early age by his father, by daring his hand forward for a shake. Derrick sneered at him, and not only did he refuse to shake his hand, he also walked away into the kitchen, snorting with derision.

"She sure loves spending time with you." The air was laced with ice as he spoke.

"We're friends. Friends spend time with each other."

"Yeah. So I see."

It was a very uncomfortable state of affairs, one that Angie didn't seem to get too involved in. Instead, she stood by and allowed them to work it out themselves. Cory didn't want to stick around long enough for a fight to erupt, so he bid his friend farewell.

"You don't have to go," she countered, gripping his bicep in her small hands. "I know he seems a little confrontational, but he's not so bad."

"I just don't want you two to get into an argument. We can talk later if you want to."

"But…" She gave up, setting him free. "Okay. Why don't you call me tomorrow?" She saw him out, and as soon as he left the apartment, he heard her shouting at her angry lover. Angie meant a lot to him, but he hated when she didn't listen.

Cory left feeling emptier than he did before he saw her. Why did she need to remind him of how pathetic he always felt? It had crossed his mind to bring his stalking situation to light, but he didn't want to come off as a weakling to her.

For an entire week, he didn't hear from the shadow, nor was he given any more gifts. Pleased that they might now be backing off, he could enjoy his weekend. He invited Angie over on Saturday and they watched some movies together, and enjoyed a home-cooked meal by his mother. She apologized for Cory's previous visit, and for Derrick, but he asked her not to dwell on it. He could tell that she had a lot more on her mind, but he never found out what it was.

With the stalker suddenly avoiding contact with him, even in the following week, he wondered if he should still write them back as he had planned. It was true that they had held back for now, but the thought that someone was still out there watching him never faded.

No, he vowed. *I don't want to let this go. I'm going to find out who it was. I'm not going to be able to relax until I do.*

After coming home from work, he greeted his family. Erica was still lamenting over her missing cat, which had yet to come home. She had resorted to creating printed flyers to hang around town, and Cory didn't have to heart to tell her that it might not work. Missy was probably gone for good this time, and he couldn't say he blamed her. He was going to spend the evening writing to his admirer, but he decided to instead help his sister hang the posters on some telephone poles and street lights. Lending a hand to her raised his spirits when seeing how much she appreciated it. He gave her hope that someone might spot her. She had a collar and tags with their address on it and someone would eventually call, even if he didn't believe it himself.

The following day at Hot Wire, The Asshole Customer showed up again, this time trying to deceive Rick into believing a television he bought came broken in the package. When they dismissed his efforts, he swore never to buy anything from them again.

"Yeah right, I wish," Rick muttered to Cory when they overheard him.

"Can't Larry do anything?" Larry was their heavyset branch manager, a man of integrity who seemed at times to care more for the customers than his own employees.

"We have to 'stay professional,'" mocked Rick with a roll of the eyes. "It doesn't matter if they're here every day just to annoy us. We have to treat them with respect and pretend to care."

"I wonder who sold him the TV. It sure as hell wasn't me."

"Ross, probably. He's just as much of a loser as that guy. Come to think of it, I haven't seen Ross in a while. Maybe the jackass finally quit."

"Or got fired."

Rick erupted into a devilish laugh. It was no secret which of his coworkers he despised, though he'd never come out and say so. "I hope."

When he got home that evening, after parking his car in the driveway, he didn't yet go inside his mother's house. Instead, he went straight to the Ballards' place. After doing a great amount of thinking during the day, he approached a plan of asking his neighbors if they had spotted any unscrupulous characters around his home. If his stalker had been following him to his home for two years, someone had to have seen something.

When he knocked on the Ballards' door, he expected Denise to answer, but her husband Cole was the one who opened it.

"Hi, Mister Ballard."

Cole narrowed his eyes as he scrutinized his visitor. "You're Cory from next door, right?"

"Yes. I had a question."

"All right. Shoot."

"Someone... not welcome... has been coming near our house. I was wondering if you've seen anything unusual."

He pulled the door open further, and Cory saw he was clutching a comically oversized spoon in his hand. "Is someone stalking one of your sisters?"

Cory grinded his teeth, despite how much it ached. "Yeah," he lied, not wanting the door shut in his face. He was humiliated enough.

"Yikes. That's creepy."

"Yeah, tell me about it. So... you haven't seen anything?"

He lifted his shoulders in a three second shrug. "No, I can't say I have, but I work all day. I don't pay much attention to what goes on outside."

Though he expected such an answer, he remained dismayed at not obtaining any clues. "Thanks, Mister Ballard. Tell Denise I said hello."

"Will do. Hope you catch the bastard."

With the weight still on his shoulders, he crossed his driveway to his other neighbor, Shepherd. The untended weeds crunched under his sneakers, and the dying plants begged for just a single drop of water if it could be spared. When Cory rang the doorbell, no one came to the door. He saw Shepherd's car in the driveway, but there was no sign of life within the house, not a single sound or hint of movement. He knocked on the door and rang the bell a second time. Then, he heard those slow, tired footsteps coming down the hall within, and the door drifted open.

William Shepherd's eyes were half-shut, and his nose was slightly runny. In a groggy voice, he croaked, "Cory." He sniffled just before his whole body shook as a chill swept in, his dark hair soaked with sweat, as was the thick black and grey argyle sweater he was wearing. His otherwise young face appeared aged and worn, like he had slept through a year of his life, and lost a hundred pounds in the process. Before Cory could speak to him, he turned his head to cough.

For a moment, Cory forgot his own problems and sought to offer help if he needed it. "Are you okay, Shepherd?"

"Yes, yes. Just caught a seasonal bug, I suppose. How can I help you?"

"I'll make this quick so you can go back inside."

"Don't worry. I'll be fine. Take your time." He coughed again, sniffed, then wiped his nose, pushing his loose glasses back up after they had been shaken by his heaving.

"I wanted to ask if you've seen anyone unusual hanging around our house."

He patted his own thin chest a few times, perhaps to clear gunk from his lungs. "Unusual?"

"Someone's been stalking... my sister. I want to find out who it is so I can get them to stop."

Shepherd cleared his raspy throat, leaning his head against the doorframe. "Stalking your sister, you say."

"She's really freaked out. Have you seen anyone lurking around, mostly really late at night, or driving past the house?"

He wiped his nose again, slower this time. "A lot of people on the block work really late hours, so I see many cars driving down this street at that time. Sometimes blaring rap music. Good lord, I hate that so much."

His comment roused a laugh in him. "Me too. Don't you just want to strangle the asshole that woke you up from a good night's sleep?"

Shepherd had a weak smirk, which faded as he barked out another cough. He spoke with congested breathing. "Yes. Very much so."

"You never saw anyone stop near our house specifically?"

His eyes drifted up to the gray skies with contemplation, and then he shook his stiff head. "I'm sorry, Cory." He sounded sincere, empathetic.

"Eh, it's okay. I'll handle it myself, I guess."

"Would you prefer I notified you if I see anything suspicious? I will, if you'd like me to."

"Actually, yeah. I'd appreciate it. Thanks a lot, Shepherd."

He coughed once more, straining out sounds of pain. "Don't mention it." He jabbed a thumb against his chest. "Good old neighborhood watch dog."

He nodded at him, eased at how much more open and inviting he was this time around, as opposed to the half-dead version of him he had previously spoken to. "Anyway, you should probably go get some rest, man. You look like you're dying."

"I could be, for all I know." The door started to creak shut. "Take care, Cory."

"You too."

Since neither of his neighbors had anything conclusive he could work with, he knew he had to take the time to write up a response to his follower if he was ever going to get them to emerge. The chance was slim that they would otherwise. He started to sneak off to his room, but his mother stopped him before he could reach the staircase.

"What were you talking to *him* for?"

Cory turned to face her, puzzled by her accusatory glare. "Who? Shepherd?"

Just at the sound of his name, she quivered as though snakes writhed through her bloodstream. "Yes."

"I was asking our neighbors if they had seen my stalker."

"You don't need to speak to him, about anything."

His mother was stressed, and he understood that, but he wasn't sure where her sudden reprimanding came from. "And why is that?"

"Cory, just don't, okay?"

"Mom, I'm confused. I know you don't like him, but I'm not sure why. Did he do something to you?"

"No." The word hung for a moment, as if not quite a question, nor exactly a statement.

Exasperated at her ambiguity, he brushed it off. "Look, he seems like a nice guy. I don't know why you hate him so much."

Samantha perched her hands upon her hips, her cheeks tightening. "Even if I told you, you'd just ignore me anyway."

Cory shook his head, annoyed. "I'll be in my room if you need me." She didn't follow up on the topic, and left him alone. Once he was in his own space, he pulled up the chair to his desk and sat in it, looking over the letters once again. Instead of giving them a cursory glance, this time he really read them.

Constructing a reply letter, especially one where he claimed to be interested when he felt he wasn't, was a much more challenging task than he anticipated. When putting the pen to paper, he thought he would be able to jot anything down, make it sound enticing, believable. He didn't want to have the opposite affect on his stalker, and make it obvious that he was lying, repelling them further when he was trying to draw them out. He supposed that the best way to start was by doing so with a shred of honesty.

> *To my admirer,*
> *You've been doing this for a long time. Even I have to think that it's very impressive for you to keep it up. If you've been doing it for as long as you say you have, I must mean a lot to you. You say that I've touched you in some way, that I've done things that give you hope. I admit that it's nice to know I've inspired someone, even if I don't know who they are.*
>
> *I'm sorry that I threw your rose away. I kept the other one you gave me, the one you put on my car. When I started getting your letters, it really came at a bad time, and stressed me out. I haven't exactly been a happy camper lately. I'm sure you know that. You've been watching me.*
>
> *You speak so much of your feelings for me, but you haven't told me anything about yourself. I know why you've chosen not to. You wouldn't write the letters anonymously if you didn't know there'd be consequences if you were found out. But how can we start to get to know each other if I don't know who you are?*

I want to be able to put a face to these nameless notes, but I would also like to stop feeling so lonely. Maybe we could start out as friends? It'd be nice to speak to a real person instead of passing letters. I'm sure you'd like to talk to me as a human being and not a piece of paper, too. It'd mean a lot to me for us to have a conversation.

Hope to hear from you again,
Cory

It could have been better, but it also could have been worse. He assumed it was enough to get a point across, and would possibly identify the guilty party. When finished, he stuck it in an envelope, wrote **For My Watcher** on the front and sealed it, then took it out to the mailbox.

He wouldn't say so aloud, but he looked forward to hearing back. It was a bizarre emotion, a blended mix of aggravated fear and lingering dissatisfied curiosity. At that point, his motivation was no longer locking up his stalker, but simply finding out who they were, to learn who exactly had been following him for so long without saying a word to him. How could he not want to meet such a person, even if just to ask them a multitude of questions?

Without much of anything else to do with the rest of his afternoon, he helped Erica do another perimeter search for Missy, checking under vehicles and in backyards. That evening, she told her brother she loved him, a sentiment that wasn't often expressed in the household. His help really meant a lot to her, especially when no one else seemed to care.

"We'll find her, Erica," he vowed. "I won't give up. I promise."

His sister's smile was enough to remind him that he really was appreciated, even for little things that might not matter as much to him. Someone out there, an anonymous stranger, was in love with him for it. He wondered what kind of person they were, to inform him that he was doing a good job as a person using illegal and eccentric means. Whatever type of person they were, he hoped it wouldn't be long before he knew.

4. Slash

The crisp autumn temperatures plummeted overnight, and there was talk of an early snowfall. Much to Cory's approval, no flurries fell, and the sun once more provided lasting, mild October breezes. Half of the leaves of the Anderson's birch tree had covered the lawn, coloring it orange and yellow, the boney branches shedding their decorative coatings for another cold season ahead.

Cory started his day with a fresh cup of coffee and a bowl of wheat cereal, which was always fully stocked. He was the only one in the house who enjoyed it. After putting his shoes on, he set foot out of the house, but not to go to work— to check the mailbox. After pulling open the plastic door, he saw an envelope sitting inside, not sealed, but with the flap tucked in.

The letter he wrote to his follower was now gone, and replaced with a new note. He removed the thick, folded paper inside of the envelope it came with. The black ink seemed less fluent this time, but hasty and excited.

Sweet, lovely Cory,

I always considered you a wonderful young man, but never thought you'd try to get to know the freak within me. I am smiling painfully wide as I write this. It means so much that you want to give me a chance, even when it's obvious I have many problems.

Believe me. I want to reveal myself to you. It's still a bit too early for me. But since you were kind enough to ask me what kind of person I am, I'll tell you a few things: I am thirty-four years old, exactly ten years and five months older than you. I still can't believe it when I say that. How did I manage to live to this age? It's young for most, but I feel as though I've lived an eternity!

I am an artist. An oil painter, to be exact. I paint many things, from landmarks, to people. I prefer landmarks, personally, especially in nighttime environments. There's a certain essence of beauty in a place at night. It calms me, as well as my own inner darkness.

I also want to be able to have a conversation with you, to discuss your life, to listen to your words. I feel tempted and teased at the concept of confessing what I've done to you, and to have you understand me for what I am. It's so incredibly far-fetched, but it's a nagging craving that won't go away. I want to draw the gap, to close it forever, to seal the wound, and to give myself confidence. To tell you everything you need to know; why this began, why I wanted to be near you.

In time, I may decide to show myself. Until then, I'll be dreaming of you, of us, happy together.

It wasn't a new thought for him to consider that someone in his inner circle was the shadow, but he couldn't think of a single person that matched the description of the letter's author. He wasn't close with anyone over thirty years of age.

Maybe it's not someone I'm close with, he realized, refolding the letter and replacing it in the envelope. *Maybe it's a coworker, or even a friend of a coworker. Whoever it is, they know my birthday.* He carried the letter back into the house, putting it in a desk drawer in his room before brushing his teeth, preparing for another work day.

Once his teeth were clean, he left his bathroom just in time for the doorbell to ring downstairs. It was out of the ordinary for anyone to come to their door so early in the morning, so it came as a surprise to him. He descended the stairs, seeing his mother and Amanda sitting in the kitchen. Samantha was making pancakes, which she did on a rare occasion if her mood suited it.

"I'll get it," he told them, seeing that neither of them had budged at the sound of the tone.

"Thank you, honey," his mother called over the sound of sizzling.

Cory pulled the door open, readying himself to shoo away solicitors, but his voice dropped when he saw who was standing on their front porch. William Shepherd stood before him, shivering, wearing that same black and grey argyle, and seemed to be over whatever sickness had been tormenting him before. He beamed at the sight of Cory, and was holding something in his arms— a writhing, mewing animal.

"Hey, Cory," he said in a smoky breath. "Look who I found." He lifted the dirty, whining feline up, his pale hands clutching it around the stomach.

"Hey, look at that! You found Missy!" He scooped the cat out of his arms before it could fuss any longer.

At the sound of his words, the two women in the kitchen came rushing over to see if it was true. Sure enough, after checking her tags, Cory confirmed that it was Erica's cat.

"It's really her!" Amanda sang, taking Missy from Cory, now that she began to growl and nip him. "Thank you, William. I can't believe you found her. My sister is going to be so happy."

"I think she might be a bit hungry," Shepherd informed her.

"I'll go feed her right now. Thanks again." She jogged to the kitchen to prepare a meal for the starving creature.

Samantha hadn't said anything to Shepherd, and Cory was glad she hadn't, because if looks could kill, hers would many times over.

"How the hell did you find her?" He asked before his mother made any sort of comment.

"She was under my car, sleeping." He took a step back, away from Miss Taccetta. "Probably to keep warm." He adjusted his glasses, which wouldn't stop slipping. "I don't know how long she's been under there, but my guess is a while."

He shared a pleasant smile with him, then reached his hand out for him to shake. He gazed down at it for some time, but after a bit of deliberation, he shook his hand and smiled back, flashing two rows of stained teeth. "Thanks, Shepherd. My sister has been sick with worry ever since she ran off. She's going to be so relieved now. You've really helped her out."

"I'm glad I could help your family. They're..." He glanced once more at Samantha, who turned her head to break the eye contact. "Good people." Without a gracious word to William Shepherd, Samantha walked off with a high chin and twisting shoulders.

Cory snickered, holding a sarcastic grin. "Sometimes." A cold silence followed his odious remark. He caught on to how offensive he might have sounded, and he attempted to alter his tone. "I mean, don't get me wrong, I love them. It's just..."

"I know," Shepherd eased. "No family is perfect, are they?"

"Truer words have never been spoken."

"Listen..." He scratched a patch of skin on his neck, beneath his chin. It looked reddened and blistered. "I'm glad I got a chance to speak with you. I had a question."

"Ask away," Cory told him, stepping outside to get away from the seething glares of his mother.

"You work at Hot Wire, don't you?"

He let out a mild huff. "Unfortunately."

"What do you do there?"

"Sell TVs, mostly. But I also work in repairs. That's kind of my dream job. I love to repair things."

"Really?" His eyebrows peaked. "How much do you normally get paid to repair things?"

He laughed, crossing his arms over his chest to keep warm as a breeze rustled his shirt. "Not much, I can tell you that."

"Do you fix televisions? I have one in my house that doesn't appear to function anymore, it just won't power on. I could pay you for the work."

Cory didn't normally do personal jobs for people, but Shepherd looked so hopeful that turning him down was difficult. "You found my sister's cat. You wouldn't have to pay me. I'll do my best to fix it for you, Shepherd. No charge."

He smiled so wide he thought his face would split in half. "You're a lifesaver. Thank you so much, Cory."

"Don't mention it. I'll stop by after work if you're home, and I'll take a look at it for you."

"Sounds good. I think I might stop by your store later, too. I'd like to buy a new television for my basement. You could help me with that, couldn't you?"

An easy customer, someone he already got along with that wouldn't tell him, the expert, if he was right or wrong about how he did business? "Absolutely."

"Great! I guess I'll see you later then." With that, he waved to him and jogged back to the disheveled sanctuary he called a home. Cory returned the gesture, then stepped into the house, seeing that Erica had come down and was crying and cooing over her beloved returned pet. He called his mother into the living room, away from the teenagers.

"What is it, Cory?" She snapped, her eyes burning.

"Shepherd found Erica's cat. You didn't want to thank him?"

She grumbled, chewing on her bottom lip. "If I want to thank someone or not, it's my business."

"I don't get it. What did he do wrong?"

"Why are you *defending* him?"

"I'm just confused, that's all. And I thought he deserved a thank you. Is that something that's hard for you to do? To thank someone for helping another person?"

She stamped her foot against the carpet, trying to stop her son from saying anything else. "How do I know he wasn't the one who stole her in the first place?"

And I thought I was paranoid, Cory thought, bewildered.

He took a deep breath, preparing for a trivial argument to arise. "Why? Why would he do that?"

"Don't pretend that you never heard what the neighbors said."

"The only one I hear talking about him is you!" He threw his hands in the air to signal his surrender and stormed away, slipping his jacket on before leaving the house to head to work. Now he was annoyed and stressed once again, not just because of his mother, but because of the never-ending mystery of his stalker's identity. He was making progress, and hopefully in their next message, they'd tell him more. In the meantime, he'd have to try to slim down the list, to interview people he knew.

Cory took a good look at each of his coworkers that day, attempting to estimate their ages. Most of them were his age, some of them even younger. When he was finished checking out the employees on the sales floor, he looked over the cashiers. There was Todd, an avid gamer in his early twenties that didn't go a day without putting gel in his hair, but was also polite and easy to relate to. Cory had spoken to him many times, and always in regards to what game console was the most advanced. Then there was Stacy, a timid, mild-mannered blonde, who most definitely had a thing for Todd. Lastly, there was Gina, a gothic girl with red and black-dyed hair and several piercings; the polar opposite of Stacy in every way. She looked somewhat older than the rest of them, and could pass for mid-thirties. Cory had seen her doodling sketches now and then in the break room.

Maybe she paints, too, he calculated.

On his first break of the day, he saw her in the back room, sketching in a book she kept in a knitted handbag.

"Nice artwork," Cory complimented, sitting down at the table with her.

Gina lifted her head, raising one of her pierced eyebrows, and for a moment she was speechless. "You're talking to me."

"Uh… yeah, I am."

"You *never* talk to me." She lowered her pencil. "I'm sorry. I'm just a little stunned."

He folded his arms on the tabletop. "I don't? I thought we've talked before."

There was a tiny clicking sound as she knocked the stud in her tongue against her teeth. "We have, but not much. You've never commented on my artwork, that's for sure."

"I apologize. I guess I thought you hated me."

Her breath caught in a petite laugh. "No. I hate Ross, but not you."

"Who doesn't hate Ross?"

"Did you hear he quit so he could start some garage band with his friends? He invited me to come to some show in the park where they were playing one night, said 'I might like their music.' Let's just say I'm not into electronic rock."

Cory spoke through a chuckle, "No I didn't hear that, but I'm glad I know now. If I ever see him again, I'll never let him live it down." Still smiling, she echoed his laugh. "Do you paint too?"

"Yes. Why, were you thinking of buying something from me? I could use the money."

"I was just wondering." She was silent, so he went on. "What kind of stuff do you paint?"

A sinister smile spread on her dark red lips. "Nothing you'd be interested in, I'm sure."

"I wouldn't? Why do you say that?"

"It's kind of dark stuff. You know, death and blood, that kind of thing. If you're looking to make your room look cooler, I can do neon paint. It'll glow in a black light."

"You don't ever paint landscapes?" He knew right away what the answer was when she blew a rejecting raspberry.

"If you're looking for some, I can tell you where to buy it, but I won't paint it. It's boring."

"Nah, that's okay. I just wanted to know. Thanks, Gina."

"Sure. Whatever." She shook her head at him and went back to what she was doing.

Cory felt that he might have a worse problem on his hands than he thought. *The only other person I think in their thirties that works here is Al, and he sure as hell doesn't paint. Who does that leave? Who else knows me well enough to know my birthday, and yet not be seen by me every day? How is it even possible?*

After returning from his break, the hopeless feeling came back. It soon faded from his mind, however, when he saw William Shepherd browsing the television section, his face containing that same perplexed look people always had when they searched for a new TV. He snuck up to him before a separate customer stole him away with questions and greeted him with his rehearsed "how can I help you" smile he practiced all day.

"Hey, Shepherd. See anything you like?"

"Cory," he answered with a blend of exhaustion and exuberance. "I was wondering when I'd see you."

"Sorry, I was on my break." He walked him along the wall where the televisions hung, all of them playing the same flashy commercials for their store. "What kind of TV were you looking to buy?"

He sighed, matching his pace as they walked side-by-side. "That's the thing. I'm not really sure. It's been years since I've bought one, and technology has changed so much since then."

When Cory glanced at him, he did so with comfort. "That's okay. You're not the only one. I get that a lot here."

"That's a relief. I don't want to look like a *total* fool." He released a loose chuckle, scratching his neck like he was earlier that morning. From the tired expression on his face, Cory was concerned he might collapse at any given moment.

"The first key to buying a television," Cory began, guiding Shepherd around the isles while directing his gaze to the large flat-panels on the wall. "Is to ask yourself how much you want to spend, and what kind of bang you want for your buck. For instance, you could get a very decent forty-six inch for six hundred."

"I don't think I'll need one that big. It's not like I ever have visitors."

He assumed it was best not to ask him to divulge his personal life, and went on, taking him over to the smaller TVs without questioning it. "These here are all pretty cheap, but don't get one too cheap. You want it to last a long time."

Following this suggestion, Shepherd hesitated, presenting a troubled look of infinite discretion. He peered at the many sets on the shelf, but it was obvious that he was not versed on the subject, and had no idea what might suit his needs. "Maybe you could recommend one to me?"

Seeing how uptight he was, he gave him a friendly smile of good workmanship. "Sure, of course I can. You have your LED and your LCD, right? LED is my personal preference, but I'm sort of obsessed with detail. You might want an LCD. It's cheaper and would probably fit you better." He planted his hand against the side of a set that was thirty-two inches in size. "This might be a good model for you. It's not too big or too small, and it has a good warranty."

"If that's what you think is best, Cory. I can admit that I don't really know what I'm doing. I'm glad you could help me." Appreciation painted his grayish eyes a brighter tint. "I'm grateful."

"Hey, don't mention it. It's my job. I do it all the time. I'll go get your TV for you, and I'll check you out at the service desk so you don't have to wait in line, okay?"

Shepherd thanked him again. Cory found the appropriate box containing the item and carried it out to the service desk, waving Shepherd over. While ringing him up, he heard him clear his throat.

"Were you still going to try to fix my TV later?"

"Yeah. Of course." After tapping his finger against the touchpad a few times, he scanned the barcode on the box, then told him his total. Shepherd pulled his wallet out, and passed him cash, which to Cory was unusual, since most people paid with credit cards. He stuffed it in the register before fishing for his change and handing it to him. "Do you want any help taking it out to your car?"

"No, no. I should be able to do it myself." He raised his chest and shoulders to cease his slouching. "Thank you, though. You're very considerate."

After handing the box over to him, he glowed with fondness. "You're very welcome." He saw someone familiar step up behind Shepherd, a frequent visitor to Hot Wire, a man he had seen on several occasions and yet had never before worked with. An impatient scowl glinted off of his glassy, yellowish eyes, his upper lip twitching, his joints fidgeting. The Asshole Customer had made his prodigal return yet again, and Cory's luck had finally run out. It was now his turn to face him. Not wanting to put up with his inevitable bullshit, he stalled.

"So… you said your TV won't power on, huh?" He asked Shepherd, rocking on his heels, trying to appear busy.

"That's right." He nodded, scratching his neck again. "It was working fine recently, but then it just stopped. I'm sure a wiz like you can fix it."

Flattered by his compliment, he shrugged, hiding his bashful face. "It just sounds like a power supply problem. What commonly occurs is that the capacitors in the power supply bulge, and then…" He stopped when the impatient man pushed himself forward, shoving Shepherd aside, making him flinch as if he had just been shot in the arm.

"Excuse me!" The elongated man's face contorted, resembling a deep-dwelling sea creature waiting for unsuspecting prey to float into his descended maw.

Cory suppressed a sound of aggravation that craved to be let out, glancing at Shepherd in desperation, pleading him with facial signals to rescue him from his predicament. "Sir, one moment, I was speaking to a customer."

"Well, now you're speaking to me." The overbearing smirk on his face could not possibly be a friendly one. His visit would undoubtedly result in another one of his screaming fits.

Christ, how embarrassing. My neighbor just had to come in on the day this psycho chose to confront me.

Shepherd stood nearby, watching the spectacle with deep intrigue as the ranting began. Cory had no choice but to wave goodbye to him and tell him he'd speak to him later. Shepherd hobbled to the exit and Cory watched with the same sympathy as a parent would to their bullied child.

"I didn't think the thing would break down after one day! It's ridiculous! I want my money back!"

"You said you didn't have the receipt. I'm pretty sure we don't even sell that brand of television in our store. How can I know for sure that it wasn't stolen or bought somewhere else for much cheaper?"

"Are you calling me a liar?!"

This exact same conversation had been replayed many times over in the Hot Wire store, and over the course of those many times, Cory had witnessed firsthand the man argue to the point of exhaustion. He always knew what his coworkers meant when they spoke of him, but never did he fully understand the process of dealing with him. He would much rather shove a plate of upturned nails directly into his face. The pain would be far less severe.

"Sir... please." He had been arguing with the man for close to thirty minutes. Half of his day had been ruined and wasted by nonsense. "If you'd like me to get the manager..."

"I know the manager, he's a prick! He's not going to help me."

When he left after what seemed like an entire hour, vowing never to return (though he likely would the following day), Cory took a deep breath of fresh air after having choked on nonsensical crap for so long. When he was fully out of the building, he let out the groan he had been holding in since he approached him. That's when he heard Rick's familiar chortle as he slid up to him like a kid on a water ride.

"Now you know," he informed while administering a consoling pat to his shoulder. "You poor, poor sod."

"Can I die in peace now?"

"Not until later, my friend. I have to go help someone put a TV in their car, but until I get back, stay away from the light!"

"The heavenly choir beckons," Cory joked, reaching his hand up to the ceiling's florescent bulbs. "They sing my name. It's time." Rick headed for the sliding front doors, laughing.

His remaining duties now seemed like agonizing chores, but he did them with a smile as he was required to. While shelving and un-boxing items, he heard a commotion coming from the front of the store. He peeked over the shelf he was placing coaxial cables onto, and saw that Mister Scammer had come flailing back into the store, screaming obscenities.

"Do I look like I'm fucking around?! I'm pretty sure I don't!"

Cory walked closer to the fray, the wild-eyed, braying big-mouth shouting at his coworkers and one of the supervisors.

What the hell does that dick want now? He stepped near a cashier station to watch the show.

"Why are you just standing there?!" He screeched to the Hot Wire employees. *"Call the fucking police!"*

He leaned close to Todd and whispered to him out of earshot of the other employees. "What the hell happened?" Todd's mammoth-sized grin managed to grow even larger.

"Looks like the douche bag finally got his comeuppance," he chuckled.

"What, how?"

"Someone slashed his tires in the parking lot." He said each word with an inclining cackle.

His blood ran cold, frost encasing his skin. At first he thought the man was trying to pull a fast one by staging a crime, but he learned that it was true— two of his tires were indeed cut open. He didn't want to believe it, but he knew his stalker was the one to blame. At first, he was terrified that he would be tied to the crime, that perhaps he might lose his job for "possibly knowing" the culprit, and since car vandalism was a felony, there was a threat of prison time. It was ridiculous to fear such a consequence, since there was no evidence tying him to it, but it was something that haunted his mind.

Did my shadow really do this? Dwelled Cory as he stood quietly beside the giggling Todd. *Did they risk going to prison just because someone yelled at me?* As he watched Larry the branch manager calm the screaming lunatic, he felt a smile creeping on his own face. *For the first time, I feel like I want to shake their hand and thank them.*

After the police arrived, Hot Wire was alive with patrons recording the events on their phones to later upload to video websites. Larry and the scammer discussed the matter with police, and they reviewed some security footage together. When Cory learned that they might see his stalker recorded on video, he would have paid any amount of money to be in that security feed room. He later heard that the recording proved inconclusive, that whoever had done it always faced away from the cameras and wore gloves, and they didn't see them driving away from the scene. Mister Scammer would only park his fancy, expensive car on the side of the building away from the other customers to avoid the rare, absurd chance that it might get scratched, and his overprotective nature cost him several witnesses to the crime. They did tell Cory an interesting piece of his own puzzle, however: judging by their physique and height, the criminal was more than likely male.

He had many thoughts throughout the day, but one in particular kept rattling around in his mind: *I thought I'd be shocked to know if the shadow was a man, but I'm actually far from surprised.*

Now confident that he had conclusive evidence, he left work that day with high spirits. When he approached his car, he saw a note tucked under the wiper blades like once before. It flapped in the low, lazy winds, and Cory snatched it up before it could get carried away. He opened it and read the sloppy, rushed handwriting.

> *Who has two flat tires, a big mouth, and doesn't know when to quit?*
>
> *THAT guy.*
>
> *He could have just left you alone and driven home in his fancy car like he always does, but now he'll have to pay for a tow truck. Too bad, so sad. Some matters just need to be taken into our own hands.*

I doubt he'll be coming back to bother you again… that is, if he knows what's good for him.

I hope the rest of your day is a beautiful one. The sun is out, and shining brightly. Soak it up, and enjoy your life.

"Enjoy my life," Cory repeated while clutching the note. At first, he considered bringing the note to the police, who were inside the store questioning the scammer. Then, he changed his mind, not for fear of consequences, but to protect a person he didn't even know the name of. Any number of Hot Wire employees wanted to deck that guy in the face on any other given day, but there was risk of losing their jobs, and of going to jail. He had tormented his coworkers and friends for months, without a single apology or without giving any sign that he would stop. His shadow was indeed a creep, but he did him a favor. He did them all a favor. He had to admit that even Larry looked relieved that the guy might never come back. It was a weird day, but not exactly a bad one.

He drove home with the window open, letting the brisk wind catch his face, a refreshing treat after the annoying afternoon. When he got home, he changed into more casual clothes, grabbed a small bag of tools and went next door to Shepherd's house. He once again had to knock and ring the doorbell a few times before he came to the door, but he did show up, even if it took him a while.

"I'm so sorry," he murmured as he permitted him entry. "Sometimes when I lie down, I just sort of pass out without any warning, then I'm out for hours." He dragged his fingers across his nostrils a few times.

"Not a problem. I wish I could sleep like that." As Cory glanced around Shepherd's living room, he noticed how untidy it was. Dust was coated on almost everything, dirty wine glasses were lined up in rows on the coffee table's wooden surface, which had many old spots and stains. The eroded and damaged couch looked millennia old, and had giant gaping holes revealing the wooden skeleton beneath. When he was done observing the mess, he looked at Shepherd, whose pale face suddenly turned bright pink.

He began scooping up the dirty wine glasses from the coffee table. "Oh, gosh. I'm so embarrassed by this. Please, forgive the mess. I haven't really been in much of a state to clean."

Amused by his abashed stammering, he told him, "It's cool, Shepherd. It's your house. If you like a mess, that's up to you."

"I-I just didn't want you to think I was a slob."

"It's not any of my business how you keep your home. It makes no difference to me." He pointed at the old twenty-four inch plasma television that he guessed was from the mid-nineties, sitting on a lonely shelf with nothing else on it. "Is this the TV?"

"Yes. Yes, that's the one." He vanished into the kitchen to clean up the assorted glassware.

"Any particular reason why you want this television fixed? It looks kind of old." He heard the floorboards creak as Shepherd slowly walked back into the living room, and he shrugged.

"It has some sentimental worth to me." There was a moment's silence as he stared at the set. "It's not exactly mine. It was... left here."

"Ah, I see. I'll take a look." He attempted to lift the awkward object into the air, but it was too unbearably heavy. Thankfully Shepherd rushed over to help him out, taking the opposite end of the set and carrying it with him to the floor. It landed on the wood with a resonating thump and shook the remaining three wine glasses on the coffee table. "Sucker's heavy." An unnecessary comment, but the silence was otherwise too deafening.

"Yes. I know. I should throw it away instead, but I can't seem to part with it."

"Let's open her up." Cory did just that, after setting the screws aside in a safe place. Shepherd sat on his couch, his ankle crossed over his knee, watching him in fascination.

"You will let me know if you need any help," he suggested after fifteen minutes had passed.

Cory chuckled, wiping sweat from his brow. "Trust me. I can handle it." While he checked the motherboard inside, he made some idle chit-chat. "So you live in this big house all by yourself?"

He leaned back in his seat, relaxing. "Not by choice."

Over the sound of his tinkering with the board, he spoke at a somewhat raised volume, albeit with a grunt. "How can you afford to live here alone?"

"To tell you the truth… I can't."

"So why don't you move?"

"There are many reasons. Most of them have to do with my attachment to this home." He drew in a slow and shaky breath. "That and I've really just hit a wall in my life. I can't move forward, and I can't move back. You could say I'm sort of stuck here."

Cory took a pause in his work to look up at him, seeing a sorrowful gloom cast over his face. "You sound like you've been through a lot."

"Yes. Well, I get by." He elevated off of the couch. "Would you like some coffee, Cory?"

"I'd love some, thanks." Shepherd vanished like smoke, dragging his heels into the dining area while Cory checked the power supply. "Yup, looks like you need new capacitors. I don't have any that will fit this particular board, so I'd have to order some online for you."

The lanky man returned with two coffee mugs, one for each of them. He sat down on the couch once more, clutching his warm cup. Cory took a few fresh gulps from his, smacking his lips afterward. "I don't want you to do that," he told Cory once he situated himself back into his spot.

"It's nothing. It doesn't cost much."

"I just don't think I'm comfortable with it. You don't have to go through such trouble for me. I'll just store the thing in the basement." His hands shook, and coffee spilled onto his wrists. He steadied them and wiped them on his pant leg.

Cory attempted to calm his disturbed nerves with a cheerful smile. "It's no trouble. Really. I don't mind."

"If you're sure…" He grinned crookedly, but it fell directly afterward. "Thank you."

"No thanks necessary, Shepherd."

"Will."

He peeked over the top of the television, watching him sit on the couch like a gargoyle on its perch. "Huh?"

"Call me Will. 'Shepherd' is what everyone on the block calls me, usually the people that don't like me. Unless you don't like me, either. Then I suppose 'Shepherd' is good enough."

"No, that's not it. It's not that I don't like you. I wasn't trying to offend you by calling you that. I'm sorry."

He twisted his cup in his hands. His sweaty fingertips squeaked along its rim. "It's okay. I know you meant no harm." He raised his cup-holding hand with the grace of a broken robot, taking a extensive sip and drifting into silence.

Cory ducked back down to the power supply and his kit. "I actually think you're kind of cool."

He thought it was impossible for it to happen, but it did: Will laughed. "You think I'm *cool*? I'm many things, but I'm as far from 'cool' as you could get."

"Come on, don't put yourself down. Take a freaking compliment, man."

"But... why do you think that?"

As he spoke to him, he reassembled the television. "I don't know. You talk to me like you know me really well. Kind of like an actual friend, which I seem to be lacking these days." He noticed a piercing stillness in the room, and he looked up to make sure Will was still awake.

"Do you consider us friends?" He traced his thumb along his steaming mug, and wouldn't look at him.

"Maybe. I'd like to, I guess."

"That's very touching. But you don't have to pretend to like me. No one else around here does."

"Come off it, will you? I think you're interesting, and frankly I don't see why everyone has such a problem with you. I know you're a bit of a shut-in, and you're the only one on the street that doesn't have a family, but that doesn't make you psycho."

Will had fresh tears in his eyes, but blinked them away. "That's a very kind thing to say."

He wished he could think of something to say that would make him feel better, but he was clueless as to how to respond. It was all very bizarre to him. He did, on the other hand, sympathize with him, and figured helping him do things he couldn't perform on his own would mean a lot to him. "Well, I'll order those capacitors for you when I go home. Then I'll get this sucker fixed."

"You didn't have to agree to do any of this, especially for free. I'm very grateful." His thin, but broad jaw line was taught. Will's teeth were grinding too. It was a strange thing for them to have in common.

"Don't mention it, Will."

Satisfied, Will nodded with an uneasy smile of gratitude. "Perhaps I'll see you again soon."

"Of course." He once again shook Will's hand, which was damp and clammy. As he left the Shepherd house, he felt indescribable. He wondered if Will could also feel it— an unexplained connection between them, one that made very little sense, and yet also told so much.

Two more days went by without a note from his stalker. Cory wondered where he was now, if he had given up. Then, one early morning on Saturday afternoon, he received it: the final note to ever be given to him. This time, it was sitting on the doorstep, weighted down by a black rock, which looked to be marble. He opened it as soon as he picked it up.

Cory,

I can't hide from you anymore. The guilt is crushing me from the inside out. I don't want to lie to you, and I don't want to hurt you. I've done enough. I want us to meet. I want you to know who and what I am.

I want you to be comfortable, so I'd like to arrange for us to meet in a public place. The Grayson Mall. I'll be there at around one o'clock, on the bench near David's Jewelry kiosk, behind Elliot's Bookstore.

I didn't tell you in this letter who I was because I felt you deserved more than just a written confession. You deserve to be told to your face. I'm also afraid that if I reveal it here, you won't show up, and I'd really like you to.

Even if you never love me, I want you to know the truth. It's what's fair to you.

He checked his watch. He had some time to kill, and he would do so by spending it with his neighbor.

5. Surface

The shadow had to be closer than Cory imagined before. Who had the time to travel to his house and back several times a day, but then also find time to follow him to work? No one he was close with, and no one he worked with, not unless they owned a time machine. It just wasn't possible. He knew what to do, and what to say. He just had to confirm his beliefs.

After tucking the letter away in his desk drawer where he kept the others, he told his mother where he'd be going, and what he had so far learned. It was a deed he soon regretted.

"You're going where? Doing *what?!*"

He stood before her, stiff and alert with his hands tucked into his shallow pockets. "I don't want you to worry."

"You're asking a hell of a lot from me!"

"Mom, I can handle this. I don't think this is going to end with me in a gutter, but just in case it does, you'll know what happened to me."

"Why aren't you just calling the police?!"

It was a valid question, one he didn't have a resolute answer to. He told her the first thoughts that came to mind. "I don't feel threatened. Not anymore, at least. If my stalker is who I think he is…"

"*He?!*"

"Then I don't think he wants to hurt me. It just sounds like he wants to come clean and have an adult discussion."

"Is this some kind of... *man* thing, or something?"

He flinched at her accusation, put off by her sickened tone. "What's that supposed to mean?"

"Honey, I know the way you are. I know that you probably think that if you call the police, it'll feel as though you didn't take responsibility. That you weren't being 'man' enough, and that you were too weak to deal with it on your own. Is that worth your life?"

"That's *not* what I'm doing." He thought his stern look would make her back off, but it didn't. She continued to stare him down with those glistening, overemotional eyes that frustrated him even to this day. "This has nothing to do with my *manhood*. And honestly, I do feel a little insulted that you don't think I can take care of myself. Aren't I responsible?"

"If you wouldn't make rash, impulsive decisions, I wouldn't think that way, Cory!"

He jabbed his fingers against his temple. "I'm not being impulsive! I've thought this through! I know what I'm doing!"

"You haven't thought about it enough."

He figured it was best to give up. They weren't going to see things the same way. She knew where he was going to be, and that was the important thing. He stomped off, crossing through the house and breezing his way outside before they could get into another one of their useless arguments.

Cory entered Will's yard, his hands shaking from that encounter. He loved his mother, and always would, but she was an overprotective hawk. He was sure that he was the cause of at least half of her stress since she still saw him as the tiny little boy she raised. It was times like this that he wished his father lived closer to him. Though he was furious with him for breaking up their family, he and his father had a warmer kinship. He would have understood what he meant when he told him his situation. He wouldn't insult his manhood either.

William Shepherd's doorbell was so loud, yet he never seemed to hear it right away after he had rung it. Usually he would have to knock a few times, but he heard quick steps rushing to the door, which flew open in one swift blink of an eye.

Will seemed stunned to see him on his front porch, but glad. "Hi, Cory." He smiled in his usual disorganized way.

"Hello, Will. Do you mind if I come in for a second?"

"Yes, of course, come in." He stepped aside, holding the door open for him. Cory followed him in, shutting the door behind him. "Can I get you anything to drink?"

"No, that's okay. I just wanted to ask you something."

"Go right ahead."

He stuffed his hands into his pockets, looking at the blank, dead walls, which were all off-white and completely barren of any photos or posters. It was a grim sight. "I'm going to the mall. I have to meet someone there. Do you want to come with me?" The term "jaw-dropping" was an expression he had heard, but he had never seen anyone literally drop their jaw the way Will did.

He folded one arm over the other across his chest, shifting his stance back and forth like a rickety scarecrow blowing in the wind. "W-why?"

"You looked like you needed to get out of the house the last time I saw you. When was the last time you went anywhere for fun?"

Wheels creaked in Will's head, and he hunched his shoulders. "I can't remember." He sucked on his lip.

"Exactly. So come with me."

"Who did you say you were meeting there?"

"Just a friend."

"What kind of friend?"

Cory couldn't help but look at the various stains on the walls. Some of them were dark and splattered. He shuddered and turned away from them. "I don't know yet. I'll have to see when I meet him."

Color flushed from Will's face. "H-him?"

"Yeah. Meeting a guy, I know, it's weird. So, you in, or out?"

He didn't expect Will to give in, but he surprised him. "All right. Let's go together."

It was strange that he worded it in that way, but at the same time, it made perfect sense. "I was really hoping you'd say yes."

Will trudged out the door like walking down death row. Cory followed him out, but gestured for him to follow to his car, instead of getting into Will's.

Cory hadn't been acquainted with Will for long, and wasn't familiarized with many of the details of his life, but he had never seen him so fearful. He trembled like a wet dog caught in a torrential downpour, and looked outside the passenger window with desperate longing, like it was the last time he would ever see the sun.

"We are really going to the mall…" Even his dark, breathy voice quivered. "Aren't we?"

He glanced at Will for a moment as he switched lanes on the expressway. "Where else would we be going?"

"I… I don't know."

"Are you sure? You sound doubtful."

"I'm sorry." He wouldn't take his eyes off of the passing trees. Not once since they got in the car did he look at Cory.

When it went silent for some time, he softened his voice, altering it to sound conciliatory. "You seem afraid."

"I am afraid. I'm terrified."

"What's scaring you so badly?"

"You're acting very different, like you suspect me of something. It's making me uneasy."

He let up on the accelerator, which he noticed he was pressing a bit too hard. "Now what would I *possibly* suspect you of?"

Will sighed, resting his palm against his forehead and eyes, rocking back and forth slightly. "Let's wait until we get to the mall. I'm uncomfortable in vehicles."

"Oh, poor you," Cory sneered. "Does this make you uncomfortable? Does this make you feel trapped, like you have no means of escape? Gee, I can't imagine what that's like!"

"Please, Cory." His voice broke off into a whimper. "Please. Don't be angry with me."

"How could you possibly ask me not to be?!"

"I'm going to be sick." From the way he was panting and choking, Cory knew that he meant it. "If you don't want me to puke in your car, I suggest you pull over right now."

He pulled over to the side of the road when he had the chance, and Will immediately jumped out and collapsed to the ground, heaving acidic bile to the grass. He spent a minute or two like that, hunched over and puking, and Cory was forced to shut off his car and step out of it to make sure he wasn't dying, even as flustered as he was now.

Once he was finished upchucking, he sat back on his knees, his head hanging. It was such a feeble sight that Cory thought of bending over to pat him on the back. "I know how it looks. It's true no matter how you say it, and I know it is."

Cory crossed his arms, grimacing at the sad sack of man crumpled up at his feet as he pressed his back against the side of his car, but he softened his tone when he next spoke. "I have one question, one that's been on my mind for as long as I could sense you hanging around: why did you do this to me?"

"My letters to you didn't make it clear enough? I thought I was very eloquent in my emotions."

"You knew I was afraid."

"No. That's not true." He spit onto the grass. "Not that it excuses my behavior, but it wasn't until fairly recently that you seemed so scared. Chasing you away would have been a bit counter-productive. I wanted to hold onto you, not make you disappear."

"But you still knew it was wrong! What you were doing to me was wrong! Jesus Christ, two years! Do you know how absolutely fucked up that is?!"

Will slowly staggered to his feet, stumbling weakly, fixing his black rectangular glasses. "Yes, Cory. I do. And..." His shameful eyes locked with Cory's infuriated ones. "I'm so terribly sorry."

"Your apology is two years late. I don't even know if you really mean it when you say you're sorry. Someone who was truly apologetic wouldn't stalk someone for so long."

"I know I hurt you. When we actually had conversations together, I saw how well we got along. What I should have done in the beginning was try to get to know you by more conventional means, not follow you around. I just thought that you'd turn me away in disgust. Then over time, I saw how good and sweet you were. I was wrong. You wouldn't do that, to anyone."

"How much of my personal life have you watched?" Cory was now the one that was beginning to feel ill, but he also felt a surge of invigoration when the weight was lifted from his chest. "What have you seen me do?"

He sympathetically answered, "Not as much you think. Please don't assume that I'd camp out in my house with binoculars or something. It wasn't like that, I promise. Once you were in your house, I never tried to watch you. I guess you could say I thought that would be going too far, ironic as that sounds. Even I have morals."

"Oh yeah, it really sounds like it."

"Believe me, Cory, I know I'm not the sanest man. Everything I said to you in my letters is still true. You make my life better when you're in it."

"But I'm *not* in it. You tried as hard as you could to force yourself into mine, but I sure as hell wasn't in yours." With a quick stride, he circumvented the conversation by climbing into his car, jamming his keys into the ignition and bringing the engine to life as drizzling rain began to fall against the windows. He looked outside at Will, who stood in the sudden downpour, unmoving and waiting for approval to join him in the car.

Is he waiting for me to just drive off? Maybe I should. I should drive away and leave him here, with no way home. He'd have to ask a total stranger for a ride, and wouldn't that be a scary thing? He'd know then not to screw with me.

His conscience reminded him, however, that he wasn't the type of person to do such a thing. William Shepherd had issues, but he also helped Erica, and got rid of that customer everyone hated. He chose to reveal himself to Cory, despite the risk of possibly going to jail, and apologized. There was a chance that there was some good in him, and that he wasn't all bad.

Cory popped the passenger door open and waited for Will to climb in. Once he was inside, he shivered from the cold. "I wouldn't have blamed you if you left me here."

Neither of them spoke for many seconds as Cory thought of what to say. He listened to the rhythmic dragging of the wiper blades, and watched the rain pick up and begin pouring down in thick, heavy droplets. "You're lucky that I'm as kind as you say. If I had been a crueler man, I would have. Fortunately for you, I don't think you're a bad person. I think you're *delusional*, but you did things for me, and my sister. On some level, I know there's more to this than you obsessing over me, or wanting to get into my pants."

Will dried the lenses of his glasses off with the tail of his shirt. "Sexual contact was never my motivation. I told you I fell in love with you by accident. I started following you for a completely different reason than you think I did."

Cory pulled back onto the highway and continued on his journey toward the nearest exit so he could turn back the way he came. "And what reason could that be?"

"I don't know if I want to tell you. You think I'm crazy now?" He shook his head with the corner of his lips cocked.

"Try me. If I haven't left you on the side of the road by now, I think I can handle it."

"I know you could. I just don't think I'm ready to talk about it, not just because of how personal it is, but because it's extremely difficult to explain."

"Fine." His hands creaked when he tightened his grip on the leathery steering wheel. "Then let's discuss what you did at Hot Wire a few days ago." When he looked at him, there was a faint burn of reminiscence in his face. His memory seemed to be tracing back to the event.

"I permanently erased a problem. That guy had been coming in there ranting and raving for too long. I already hated the prick, but once he started yelling at you..." He breathed deeply through his nostrils, which were a bit stuffy at that point. "My blood boiled. He got what was coming to him, so I don't see what the issue is. Are you angry at me for it?"

Though he was inhaling and exhaling at slow, tense speeds, he was still and passive. "Actually, no, but it does make me think that you're a violent person."

"I'm not. Not to *you*."

"But others?"

"If they're going to hurt you like that, yes."

His teeth were mincing again. He could feel some of the enamel crumbling. "He wasn't hurting me. He was just trying to scam me."

"Well, I didn't hurt him either, did I? Just his car. He'll be fine."

Incredulous that he was even having this surreal conversation, he felt it might be best to let it go, drop Will off, and move on with his life, but the more he spoke to him, the more he wanted to know. "It's not that I don't appreciate you doing that for us, I guess. Frankly, I'm glad it happened, and that he'll stay away. But you have to know that doing it was pretty crazy. Most people don't go around slashing tires when someone pisses them off."

"Maybe they should. You ever think of that?" He turned in his seat to face him, restrained by his seat belt, and Cory peered at him through his peripherals, sweat collecting on his brow. "How many times do we see assholes every day of our lives, people who only care about themselves, and wish with all of our might that we could make them pay for their atrocities? I'm sure everyone at Hot Wire really wished they could have done what I did to that guy without risk. I'm practically invisible to everyone else, because no one pays mind to what I'm doing."

"Well, you're wrong, because I kind of do," he jeered.

"I'm your next-door neighbor and you sure as hell never noticed me. That's how little I matter to the world, and to you."

"I met you *once* before I came to you about my sister's cat. How was I supposed to have recognized you? Do you know how many strangers I meet and talk to every single day?"

Will had an eerie laugh, one that combined darkness with a slight hint of mania. "That's kind of my point, Cory. Maybe deep down, all this time, you knew it was me. Maybe you did see me, on many occasions while I was behind you, trailing after you. I could have sworn on more than one occasion that our eyes met, that we brushed against each other when passing one another. Our skin might have collided on occasion. You've smiled at me before. The way you looked at me, the way you reacted... it was like you knew, almost like you were comforted by my presence. Then you put it out of your mind, and you chose to ignore me."

Pin pricks moved along his spine and veins, and his muscles tensed. Did he really do those things? He couldn't remember. It had been going on for so long that he thought most of it was the result of an overactive imagination. He worried that Will might have been right. "Oh, please," he whispered, now on edge. "Cut the sob story. I'm the one who's a victim here, Shepherd, not you."

"I'm not giving you a sob story. I'm spelling something out for you. In all of two years, why *didn't* you pursue the matter? You said you knew you were being followed all that time. You could have easily discovered it was me. I tried from time to time to step out of the shadows, draw your attention. Sometimes I even left you clues, because subconsciously, I wanted you to find out. Why did you wait to actually hear from me in letters to follow the hints, to find out the truth?"

Everything that Will said to him made too much sense, and his questions were a bit too tough to find answers to, not to mention mentally invasive. "I was afraid, god damn it."

"Afraid of how it made you feel, possibly. You felt wanted, desired, that someone out there might actually give a damn. You told me in your letter that you were lonely. You weren't decorating your words for me. It was true. You didn't call the police when you knew it was me, because you didn't want them to take me away. You wanted to keep me around. Maybe you never outwardly or even inwardly expressed that you liked the attention, but I believe part of you really did. I think, in all honesty, something in you wanted this. Call me delusional and needy if you want to, but I'm not the only one in this car who is."

Blinded by his own confusion, Cory pulled into the nearest gas station, screeching into a parking spot and jamming the gear into park. "Listen to me. Do you think I'm angry at you for this because I just like to be pissed off? I'm not an idiot, so don't take me for one. I wanted to seek you out on my own because I thought involving the police was unnecessary. I wanted to prove that I could handle this. I was ashamed of being stalked, it felt pathetic."

"If that's all true, then why do you even feel the need to explain yourself to me? You're defending yourself an awful lot for someone who isn't guilty of something. Maybe your anger is originating from your disappointment that this is now going to end. You'll be all alone again, without even a stalker to talk to you."

His words bruised his emotions, causing tears in the already perforated seams in his heart, but he shielded it with contempt. "You are really desperate, man, and reaching, at that. You want to believe that all along I wanted to be with you so that *you* don't feel guilty. You really want it to be true that I desire to be with you in some way, so you're making up these excuses." Will's head bowed in apologetic humility. "I'm calling the police when I get home. Don't ever come near me again. Don't give me letters. Don't give me roses. Don't follow me to work. Don't follow me home. Just stay away. Stay. Away."

Will forced a nod, his skull bouncing on his stiffened neck. "I suppose I'll find out soon if you're true to your word." He opened the passenger door and climbed out of the vehicle, bending over to look inside at Cory. "I'll walk from here. Home isn't far. Thank you for giving me the chance to be honest with you. It's really helped me, either way this turns out. I hated keeping it from you for so long. I can't deny, though... I wish it had turned out differently for us."

"Yeah. Whatever. Just go, okay?" When Will shut the door and stepped away from his car, he peeled out of the drive and sped home in a frenzy, but not before glancing at the pale, soaking man in his rear view mirror, standing in torrential rainwater, watching him as he departed while the puddle beneath his feet swallowed the soles of his shoes.

Why did I think that could have gone well?

He pulled into the driveway of his home, running inside before he could get pelted on by rain. As soon as he stepped in, his worrisome mother rushed to his side, barring him from going up the stairs.

She began her flurry of questions. "What happened? Did they hurt you? Who was it?"

He hesitated in telling her that Will was the stalker, knowing that she would lose her mind, and maybe cause more trouble than it was worth. After wondering why he bothered to protect Will at all, he changed his tone. "It was Shepherd."

"What?! Call the police, right now!"

"I'm working on that, mom. Can I go up to my room, please?"

She resigned her post, stepping aside, but hollered at him as he ascended the flight. "Tell them he lives right next door!"

Toning her out, he slipped into his room to find a phone book he kept in his desk drawer, and dialed the number for the police station.

Two officers, both male and in their forties, arrived not long after Cory made the call. When he greeted them at the door, his mother's desperation to speak with them was so palpable that Cory wanted to lock her out of the room before she could figuratively castrate him before their eyes. She watched the scene from a short distance, readying herself for exposure if her foolish son left out any details.

"I don't think you'd be surprised to know that this isn't the first time we've gotten a call in regards to William Shepherd," said one officer, a fair-skinned man with graying hair.

"Really?" Cory waved his mother back when he saw her starting to creep up to them. "What else has he done?"

"He used to get into some pretty bad domestic disputes with his boyfriend. Screaming and smashing, scaring the neighbors. When we'd show up, they'd act like nothing was going on. It was strange.

Shepherd was upset, but he never pressed charges, even with bruises." He gave his head a downhearted shake as he recalled the tragic memory. "He'd try to convince us he injured himself. I'll never know why he protected that scum bag. Maybe he really liked getting beaten. Who knows?"

"He had an abusive boyfriend?"

"Calling him 'abusive' would be putting it lightly, kid. Not that Shepherd was always right in the head. Whenever I'd try to ask him what happened, he'd give me this thousand-yard stare, kind of like saying there was nothing I could do for him. It screwed with me, I'll tell you that. It was haunting. I swore I'd put his boyfriend away someday. Then the guy died. I guess there is a God after all."

"How'd he die? What happened?"

The second officer, a man with dyed hair, stepped forward. "Drunk driving accident. Not a big surprise, for us anyway. I've never met a bigger lush in all of my days on the force, and I see a lot of drunks. I swear Shepherd stole booze for him. Could never prove it of course, but I'm convinced he did." There was a brief pause as he studied Cory's face, lingering on it for some time. "Come to think of it, you kind of look like the guy."

The first officer got to the point, and interrupted the sudden nausea settling in Cory's stomach. "You said he was stalking you?"

"Yeah. Yeah, he was. I spoke to one of the officers at the station about it. The letters he gave me had no fingerprints, so I guess there's not any solid evidence except my word."

Evidence was apparently something they didn't need. "What would you like to do? Do you want to press charges against him today?"

He knew that ultimatum would disembark, and before they had arrived to the house, he would have definitely said yes, with no remorse or regrets. Now, he was having second thoughts. He didn't quite understand Will's reasoning, or if he was truly going to quit, but if he would, he could forgive him for his mistakes. "Isn't there something you can do without pressing charges? Just warn him not to bother me. I don't think I want to send the guy to jail."

"No," Samantha chimed in, moving in beside Cory, who groaned. "He wants to press charges."

The confused officers exchanged puzzled looks, and the one with the dyed hair said, "Which is it? We don't really have all day."

Cory turned to his mother with steadily increasing aggravation, but with a soft hint of patience. "Mom, let me handle this, please."

"Honey, he's dangerous! Don't be an idiot!"

His molars grinded again. "I wasn't asking. Go help Erica with her homework, or something. This is my business, my problem, and I'll deal with it the way I want to." She backed off, like he hoped she would, but not without fearful looks. He tried to think of a time when his mother wasn't crazy with worry over something, and he just couldn't. If such a time existed, it was well before he was born. He faced the officers once again. "Just give him a warning."

"If that's what you want. We'll be back in a moment." They walked out the front door, their heavy, authoritative footsteps resounding loud and clear from a distance, and Cory ran to the window to watch them in action and to see how the situation unfolded. The first officer, the one with grey hair, pounded on Will's door, then rang his doorbell in what seemed like ten times.

The door slowly opened. Cory couldn't see inside, but what he did see, and hear, was the two officers talking sternly with him. Judging by their impatient, elevated arguing, he assumed Will was trying to explain what was going on to them with a dramatic performance. After several long minutes of them getting in Will's face, demanding him to stop harassing Cory, they came back to Cory's house.

"He said he won't be pestering you anymore," the officer with dyed hair reassured Cory. "But he's pretty emotionally disturbed, and delusional. If he keeps bothering you, call us immediately."

"I will," Cory vowed.

"He told us you wrote him a letter, responding to his."

"I… I just… wanted to lure him out, find out who he was. I didn't know at the time."

"He showed it to us. It sounded like you wanted to meet him for companionship. Why would you do that?" He fell silent when Cory made provoked, agitated sounds.

"I call you here because a guy is stalking me, and you're pointing fingers at me? What the hell is this? An officer told me to write him back in the first place! I didn't know it was a crime to try to find a man who was stalking me!" As soon as he blurted out his defense, it bothered him, because it caused him to question why he did it, and why he was so sensitive in regards to the matter.

The grey-haired officer waved at his partner to ease him back, and he didn't bring it up further. The older officer said, "It's all right, Cory. I'm sure you didn't actually want this. I can't imagine who would. None of it is your fault."

"Yes. I know." As much as he wanted to, he repressed the need to stab them with caustic glowers. They wished him luck and bid him farewell, then vacated the premises. Once they were gone, and Cory was alone in the room, he took a good look at Will's house. He was sure he meant what he said about leaving him alone. He seemed humble when they discussed it in his car, but the whole thing just didn't feel right.

For the first time, he really wanted a drink.

6. Guard

Over a week went by of total silence from William Shepherd, and Cory was once again able to relax. Though Will lived next door to him, he had almost ceased to exist. He never saw the man leave his house, and for some time, actually presumed him dead, until he saw him roaming around past the windows.

One evening before going to bed, he took the trash to the curb, a task that for some strange reason was assigned to him and him only, and saw the reflections of dim light seeping from the windows of Will's house. As he walked up and down the driveway, he peeked through the small slit between the curtains draped over the window and saw Will sitting on his couch in the living room. From the way he was holding his face, hunched over and trembling, Cory knew he was sobbing. He might have imagined it, but he could even distinctly make out the faint sound of his cries.

Don't feel guilty. It was imprecise why he made this demand, but it seemed necessary. *It's not my fault that he's like this. He should have known better.*

He and Will never had a real relationship, but he was convinced that Will had an imaginary one, a fantasy romance in his head. It was all shattered when the police pounded on his door to wake him up from his dreams and bring him back to reality. Reality was something William Shepherd had trouble coping with.

Sometimes life gives you lemons, Cory wanted to say to him. *And usually when it does, the last thing you ever want to drink is lemonade.*

He figured it was best to ignore Will. If he gave him attention, he might see it as affection and mistake it for Cory desiring him. He didn't want to give him the wrong idea, especially when he was in the phase of dealing with the heartbreak of the incident.

To lift his spirits from the gloomy ordeal, Cory visited Angie, who was more than happy to have him come by. When he asked her if it would be a problem for Derrick, she told him he wouldn't mind. He found that pretty tough to believe, but he trusted her to tell him the truth.

It was during their time together at her place that he explained his situation with Will and his stalking him. To say she was aghast would be a mild interpretation. "Why didn't you tell me any of this while it was going on?!" She asked the first chance she got.

"I tried. You were always laughing and teasing me. I didn't bother."

"That was before I knew you had proof! I thought you were just being paranoid! I didn't think it was true!"

"Well, now you know. Can we eat dinner now?"

She leaned close, eyes sparkling with electric intensity, titillated by Cory's dramatic news. "No, wait a second. What happened to him? Is he in jail?"

"No. I didn't press charges. He seems pretty broken up, as to be expected, but he's at home." He didn't acknowledge her when she scooted closer to him, not even with a quick glance.

"Why the hell didn't you press charges?"

He didn't want to discuss it with her any longer. His motives made sense to him, but he knew he'd sound very foolish to his friend. "I have my reasons. Really, I just want to drop it. I'm hungry. Are you still going to make something for us, or are we going out?"

Giving up the fight, she got up off the couch, disappointed. "Yeah, I suppose I'll cook for you. You like spaghetti, don't you?"

"Right now, I'll eat anything."

Over dinner, which was overcooked and somewhat bland, Angie discussed her ongoing relationship and how well (or rather, how poorly) it was going. He tried to offer pieces of advice, but she ignored them. Eventually, he didn't remark on it at all.

In time, he changed the subject to something that had been stirring around in his mind for some time. "Angie, why don't you ever call me?"

A wet slurping sound came from her mouth as one of the noodles she was eating disappeared into it. "What?"

"The last time you actually called me in roughly three months was to ask me to take you to a bar so you could get drunk."

Her chewing stopped, even if just for a brief moment, and she sat back in her chair, dazed. "Where is this coming from?"

While picking at his food with his fork, he shrugged. "I just wish you would make as much of an effort to be my friend as I do to be yours. If we spend time with each other, it's because I call you or text you and ask you. I think you hang out with me because you feel sorry for me."

"That's bullshit, Cory! Don't even say stuff like that. I just have my job and Derrick…"

"And what else? Hanging out with potheads that you're better friends with? Sitting at home networking with your buddies, telling all of your friends how much hotter they look from the last one hundred pictures they posted, but can't take the time to say anything to me? When was the last time we actually had a deep, meaningful conversation, about *anything* significant?"

The temperature in the room heightened, and Angie's frustration had reached critical mass. Her short fuse was about to blow. "Hold on! First of all, I had no idea you felt this way. This is coming totally out of the blue. Second, if I'm such a pain in the ass to hang out with, why do you bother?"

"Because *no one else* does, Angie! No one! You're the only friend I have, and it hurts that you don't seem to put as much effort into it as I do! I admit it, okay? I hate living under the same roof as my harebrained mother and sisters, but I don't want to abandon them when they need me, even if we don't really get along. I just want to be happy for fuck's sake, but I'm not, and I never will be." Angie's heartbroken stare was tough for him to bear, and he felt sorry for saying such things to her, but after doing so, he felt some of his stress melt away. "I love you and all, I just wish things were… better between us."

"So…" She continued after the smoke had cleared. "You're calling me all the time to hang out with me because you're desperate for someone to pay attention to you?"

"I'm sorry, Angie. I know I'm being sort of a dick here, but you're the only one who gives me the time of day. People like to call themselves my friends, but they're as much my friend as my own reflection is."

She stood, her chair screeching along the tiled floor. "I can't believe you. You have no idea how wrong you are." Although he wasn't finished eating (and didn't want to continue eating, anyway), she grabbed his plate regardless as a trivial punishment and took their dishes into the kitchen.

"Thanks for dinner, and all that," he muttered. She didn't respond. "Where's Derrick? Isn't he supposed to be home by now?"

Dishes clanged against the sink as she washed them. "He was supposed to be home an hour ago. He's late sometimes. I don't know what he's doing. Shouldn't you be heading home? You have work in the morning."

"Are you pissed at me now?"

She sighed, and there was a pause in her chores. "I'm done talking about this. Just go home."

"Fine." He left his seat, walking to the door. "I'll wait to hear from *you* this time." He took her dismissive huff as his cue to leave. She might contact him for the weekend, and she might not. What mattered was that either way, he wouldn't get too worked up. He said to her what he needed to say, and it felt good to let it out. It had been building up for months.

Wild winds swept over Lansing that evening, but Cory enjoyed the cold. He drove home with his window cracked open, letting frosty gusts seep into his car. He spent his quiet ride home dwelling on his future, which looked infinitely bleak. How long would he live with his mother? How long until she moved into a new house, found somewhere cheaper, found a new boyfriend and allowed him to leave so that he could have his life back? Would he ever meet a girl that was actually interested in him? Did he even want a girl? None of it seemed possible. Returning to the family house in Lansing proved to be like a death sentence for him, due to the fact that since his living there, he was surrounded by melodrama. He was sure it couldn't possibly be his location of residence, but the company he kept.

Something must be wrong with me if I'm naturally attracting and drawn to these types of people, he weighed, beginning to feel melancholy. *When I wrote Will that responding letter, I told him the truth. The policeman at the station told me to do it to lure him, but that wasn't the only reason why I did it. Will was right. I wanted someone to notice me for once. It's crazy to think how alike we might be, frightening even. I avoid relationships like they're deadly diseases, and yet I crave them so badly it hurts. Just the thought of someone in love with me is not only shocking, but makes me happy. How can I call Will delusional? I really did like the attention. I liked thinking there was actually someone out there that wanted to be around me. I think I owe him an apology.*

As he stared out his front window at the oily black streets and full moon, he pondered, *But would he forgive me?*

When he pulled in to his driveway and parked, he fixed his attention on Will's house. Something deep within him— an overpowering desire to speak to him man-to-man, to sit with him and address their situation like adults without perceiving too much or too little without getting overemotional— was consuming him from the bottom up. This powerful yearning came to him at a surprise. Only a week ago did he emotionally castrate the man, warn him never to speak to him or come near him again, and now he wanted to reconcile. It was possible that he had wanted reconciliation all along and that he truly did wish to befriend Will, seeing as how they got along before he unmasked him as his shadow.

Will was far from wrong when he told him that he had to have known his stalker's identity all that time. Something had drawn him to Will when they spoke to each other, something he would never have contemplated before the letters started coming to his mailbox. When they started speaking face-to-face, he felt like he already knew him, and understood that there had to be a reason for that. They had met many times before, but he truly had ignored him, just as Will had enunciated. His proclamation had been one of dread, but of fervor. He knew exactly what he was pinpointing, and that there was an element of truth to it, though it wasn't the best time to do so. Had Cory not been so angry, he might have been more open-minded to his affirmation at the time.

He stepped out of his silver car, shutting the door with a gentle shove so that his mother wouldn't know he was home, and then ambled into Will's unattended yard. He knocked on the door three times, then rang the bell twice. No one answered, and he worried that he might be hurt. Strange, he thought, for him to be concerned for his health after all they had been through. Perhaps, in a way, he truly was maturing to some degree.

"Will, are you home?" He called, peering in a window. Lights were on all throughout the house and his car was in the driveway, so he had to be there. He rang the bell once again. No answer.

He might think that cops are knocking on the door again, or that I'm trying to trick him, he perceived, pacing the porch in ambivalence. That's when he noticed a car pull into his mother's driveway, a vehicle he didn't recognize. Fearing that they might try to break into his mother's house, he rushed over to it as it sat quietly in the driveway.

"Who's there?" He yelled at the dark, tinted windows.

The driver's side door popped open, and out stepped Derrick Holden, wearing a crooked smirk, his yellow T-shirt matching the color of his tobacco-tinted teeth. "Cory," he called with a threatening grunt.

"Derrick?" He looked in the car for Angie, but didn't see her. Derrick came to his house alone, and from his aggressive stance, it didn't look like he came to talk civilly. "What are you doing here? And how did you find out where I live?"

"I didn't want any trouble with you, but you just keep asking for it."

"What the hell are you talking about?"

"Angie keeps telling me you're 'just friends,' but I'm not an idiot, okay? You're at our place *a lot.* I know you're there late at night sometimes, too. You're fucking her." He turned the angry dial up a few notches when Cory rolled his eyes at him. "Yeah, go ahead and deny it! The more time she spends with you, the more distant she's getting from me. I can *feel* us drifting apart."

"Derrick, I barely know you, so I know you probably don't understand the kind of person I am, but I wouldn't do that. Angie is my friend. That's it. Believe me. I have *zero* interest in sleeping with her."

"I don't believe you."

"Look, it's not my fault that you're too stupid to ask *her* what's going on." He knew as soon as he spat out these assaulting words that they wouldn't go unpunished. He prepared for the worst.

Derrick took a swing at him, decking him square in the eye, and it threw him off his feet. When he stumbled back into the grass, he placed a hand over his face to calm the sudden swelling. When he staggered back to his feet, Derrick laid another punch on him, this time in the jaw. He then shoved him to the ground with a blow to the stomach.

"You want to rethink being a smart-ass now?" Derrick challenged, his voice ripe with menace.

Cory spat a wad of blood on his white shoe. "Fucking asshole," he groaned while clutching his aching stomach.

These words only stoked the flames, and he kicked Cory while he was down. He curled up in a ball to protect his genitals from the flailing feet. If he could get through the beating without injury to his testicles, he might make it out okay, though he had no plans of reproducing in the near or distant future.

A light beaconed nearby. He first thought it was a guiding beam from Heaven, but after his blurry vision cleared, he saw it was Will's porch light. Derrick had stopped wailing on him, and was also startled by the sudden appearance of an uninvited third party. He edged closer to his car, but wouldn't leave Cory's crumpled form unattended. Cory watched Will's silhouette sprint across the wet grass, and he took the chance to climb onto his feet like a drunk leaving a bar at closing hours.

Time seemed to slow, even as the events occurred quicker than Cory could comprehend them. Will had punched Derrick, thrice times in the face before shoving him to the ground, straddling his chest and pinning his arms, putting his hands around the young man's neck. Derrick coughed, struggling beneath him, fresh crimson blood spraying from his nostrils and drizzling onto his mouth.

"Apologize to him!" Will screeched. "Apologize to him *now!*"

"Oh fuck!" Derrick cried in desperation and fright, gasping for air. "Let me go, please!"

"Do it, or *I will break your fucking neck!*"

Though he felt a flourish of victory for once, and he felt like laughing at how Derrick's arrogance had turned against him, he worried that if Will held onto his neck any longer, Derrick might actually die. His face was turning purple and his lips light blue, but Will never let up, and didn't look like he planned to any time soon.

"Will, let go, you're going to kill him." His own voice alarmed him, not because he said it unwillingly, but for the emotional emptiness in his statement.

Like a lapdog obeying its master, Will released Derrick's neck on command. Derrick gasped and heaved, sucking in as much oxygen as his body would allow. Though Will had relinquished Derrick's throat, he continued to sit upon his chest, holding him down.

"Let me go," Derrick pleaded, crying in both shame and defeat.

Will spoke to him as though he was spitting a million tiny frozen needles into Derrick's face. "You haven't told Cory that you're sorry."

"I'm not apologizing to him." When Will's hands dove for his neck a second time, he gasped: "Okay! Okay, okay, I'm sorry! I'm sorry."

Cory didn't answer, only shook his head at the pathetic sight.

"That's a good boy." After applying a condescending pat to Derrick's swollen cheek, he let him up. Both Will and Cory watched him run to his car and dive into it. He tore into the street, leaving behind fresh tire marks.

Will and Cory were left alone, standing side-by-side in contemplation like two war veterans that each had the same traumatic flashback. When Cory's balance began to break, Will caught him before he could fall.

"How badly are you hurt?" He ensured with fondness, letting him balance on his upper torso. "Do you need to go the…" His voice grew distant for some unexplained reason when saying the following word: "Hospital?"

"No. I just need some ice for my face. I'll be fine." It wasn't the first time he had lost a fight, and he was sure it wouldn't be the last. Relying only on packs of ice or bags of frozen vegetables was something he was used to. He didn't recoil from Will's touch, but instead leaned against him for support.

"Would you like to come inside? I'll get some for you."

"Sure." He added a nod, in case Will didn't hear him. He limped into his neighbor's house with his help, and sat down on the couch where he guided him. His bones twitched and ached, even as he lowered himself into the creaking seat. Will disappeared into the kitchen, digging ice out of his freezer, then he stepped into another room, which Cory assumed was a bathroom. When he returned to Cory's side, it was with a bottle of extra-strength aspirin, a glass of water, and ice wrapped in a towel. He passed two pills to him, along with the cup, and Cory took them without question of what they were. Will then pressed the cold compress against Cory's bruised eye, tenderly with devoted affection, and for some time, they shared a comfortable silence that was vacant of their previous tension.

"Will…" Cory whispered after a few minutes passed. Will was all ears, waiting for him to speak. "Thank you."

"You don't have to thank me." He dabbed his face with the ice, chilling the swollen skin tissue.

"Yes I do."

"No, you don't. I didn't do it for your gratitude. I did it to protect you."

"I know, and that's why I have to thank you. After the things I said…"

"You had every right to say them to me. It was what I needed to hear."

"And I called the police on you…"

"I would have done the same in your position." He moved the ice pack to the other side of his face now, tending to his injured nose. "Besides, you didn't have me arrested. I would have understood if you chose to, but you didn't. Why do you feel you have to be sorry for protecting yourself and your family? You did what you had to do, and I don't blame you for any of it."

He sighed, closing his throbbing eyes, hoping the pills would kick in soon. "It's not that. I actually meant to talk to you, before that rabid gorilla jumped me."

Beside himself, Will chuckled at his joke. "Talk to me? What else is there to say to each other?"

"I wanted to tell you that, what you said to me…" He winced at the sharp pain in his ribs as he drew in a breath. Will gently placed a nurturing hand on him when he saw his expression. He was warmed and soothed by it, though he wouldn't say so. "You were right."

"I was?" Will grabbed a nearby box of tissues from a table and placed one underneath his nose, which he hadn't noticed was bleeding until he started wiping it. "What exactly was I right about?"

He swallowed, which proved to be difficult with a dry mouth. "About me liking the attention. Your attention. You were right. I did."

"That must be a very difficult thing for you to admit. Especially to me."

He breathed out a soft laugh, though he didn't say anything amusing. "It is. But not because it was you who stalked me." At the word "stalked," Will bowed his head. "It's because I didn't want to be crazy. I didn't want to look like one of those people classified with some psychiatric problem, with all of my traits written down in some doctor's little notebook. You know what I mean, don't you?"

Will nodded, wiping blood from Cory's nostrils and lips. "I do understand, but I don't think you're crazy, Cory. And I didn't mean to imply that when we last spoke. It was wrong of me to accuse you of being like me. Everything I did to you was wrong, and you shouldn't ever feel responsible for the things I do."

"I don't. I'm just taking responsibility for the things I think. Saying that you're fucked in the head would be a bit hypocritical of me, wouldn't it?"

A thoughtful smile grew on his lips, and he held the ice to his face once more. "I appreciate you trying to level with me. You're very understanding, and that's what I love about you."

The swelling in his eyes had diminished, and a lot of the pain had dwindled. He had to admit, Will had a healing touch. "I wanted to ask you something else."

"You can ask me anything."

"Your last boyfriend, the one you lived here with. Did he die?"

Will removed the ice pack from Cory's face after a protracted pause. "Yes. Who told you?"

"The police. I'm actually shocked my mother hadn't mentioned it to me. I swear she thinks you're the Devil."

His surprising smirk told him he was tickled by that observation, but nonetheless, he regretted bringing his mother into the conversation. "She never liked me, ever since I moved in here with my partner. Always glared at me. Honestly, very few people actually do like me. I keep to myself a lot."

"I don't wonder how I got so screwed up. She spent most of my childhood obsessing over what my father was doing, whether or not he was cheating on her that she really didn't find the time for me or my sisters. Now she really has no choice but to coddle us like we're all three years old." Cory took Will's hand, the one holding the compress, and brought it back to his cheek, reapplying the cooling sensation to his wounds. Will took the hint and continued healing him.

"Your parents… they're divorced, aren't they?"

"Yes. My mother's even more… stressed than she used to be. As for my dad, I love him, but he's made some stupid decisions. He left my mom for someone younger, more attractive. It crushed my mom's self-esteem. I suppose that's why she relies so much on me."

"That's awful," Will empathized while wiping the dampness from Cory's cheek as the ice in the towel started to melt. "I know how horrible that feels."

"I didn't want her doing anything drastic, so I moved back in with her." He sighed, somehow relaxed in Will's presence. "It's starting to feel a little better now."

"That's good. The aspirin must be helping. You can take more if the pain starts up again."

He beamed at his graciousness with malleable gratitude. "It's not just the aspirin." Touched by his saccharine approval, Will produced a cheerful grin. "The police told me something else about your relationship with your late partner. I mean, we can drop it if it makes you uncomfortable, but I was curious."

"No, it's okay. I don't mind. I owe you some explanation anyhow."

"They told me he was abusive. He was an alcoholic and beat you after drinking."

Will's eyes shifted downward. His fingers trembled. "They told you that, huh?"

"I'm sorry. I probably shouldn't have brought it up."

Will rose up from the couch like climbing out of a grave. "I'm going to get some more ice and some wine. Then I'll tell you everything."

"All right. If you're up for it." When Will came back with the items, he saw just how large the glass of wine was and wondered if he was going to drink it by himself. Judging by the collection of empty wine glasses cluttering the rest of the room, it wouldn't surprise him. He went on to place the towel of ice against Cory's cheeks again, saving the wine for when he was done with the task.

"At one time, Ian and I were more than just lovers," he explicated while tending his injuries once more. "We had a lovely, prosperous life together, and were practically married. He worked at a bank, which was a job he was really fond of, and I sold many of my paintings. We were happy. We relied on one another, leaned on each

74

other. We were both a couple of cynical assholes, but it brought us closer together. It was relatable to me. His realism made him seem more human— more authentic. Not once did I ever believe that his attitude would worsen, or his anger.

"Ian wasn't close with his family. They didn't get along. Both of his parents drank, his father gambled, and was always calling us asking for money. But he did get along with his grandmother. They were very close, closer than he was with his own parents. She always supported us and our relationship, supported Ian for being gay, which his father disapproved of. She loved Ian like he was her own son, and he loved her like a mother. She was a very strong woman, incredibly wise, and Ian related to that. It was as though they made up for the fact that her son and his father was a deadbeat. Then she died, and Ian fell apart."

"That must have been hard for him," Cory empathized.

"It was very hard for him. So hard, in fact, that I noticed him picking up his father's habits. He started drinking profusely. He changed from this youthfully skeptical man to this monster I didn't recognize anymore. Any signs of lighthearted humanity in him had disappeared, however faint those signs were. That's when the screaming and the hitting started. He said awful things to me— like that he hated me and wished me dead. And I took it. I took it all, because I loved who he used to be." He was holding back tears, but Cory could tell how close he was to crying. He didn't know what to do or say to comfort him.

Will went on after a quick break. "I thought if I tried with him, really tried to help him and remind him how much I loved him that he might stop. It was too late. The Ian I loved was long gone, buried deep underneath this vile, putrid blackness that he had become. Maybe that version of Ian was the one I really fell in love with in the beginning, unintentionally, but I didn't realize it until it was over. Maybe it was the real him, and he had been holding it in all those years, keeping it from me. I didn't want to believe that, though."

Will removed the compress from Cory's face so that he could chug down the wine he had poured for himself. The red liquid retreated down his gullet before Cory even realized he was drinking it. "I'm so sorry," he told him when he saw Will turning his head to wipe his eyes, hiding his sadness from him. "I've never had such a thing happen to me, but I guess I can understand why you stuck with it."

"It's actually very comforting to hear you say that. After he died, I've despised myself ever since. I've always been one to hate myself, but when I met Ian, when we were happy, I didn't have to hate myself anymore. That changed when he started drinking, and got worse when he died. I look back on my life, the way it used to be, like it happened to someone else entirely. It didn't happen to me. It couldn't have. How could I do such things? How could I allow them?"

Cory had heard his mother speak in that exact way about his father, blaming her actions and saying she was ugly and old, telling him it was her that drove him away. "It's not your fault." He always told her this, and now Will had taken her place. "You shouldn't blame yourself for what he did to you."

"It's in my nature, Cory. I'm afraid I can't help it."

He didn't argue with him, feeling it wasn't his business. "The police said he got into a car accident."

Will nodded, closing his eyes. "He got behind the wheel while intoxicated. He crashed into someone else, then flipped into a ditch. Thankfully, no one else was fatally wounded. He wanted to go out for more drinks that night, after having one too many already, and I made the mistake of telling him he couldn't drive, and withheld his keys. He beat them out of me, knocked me out cold." He took a deep breath and exhaled a morose sigh. "The last time I spoke to the man I planned to spend my life with was in the hospital— where he drew his final breath." His quiet tears ceased when Cory placed a consoling hand on his shoulder. "After the unforgivable things I've done to you, you still show me kindness. You don't have to do that."

"I forgave you because I wanted to, not because it was an obligation. Your stalking me was strange, but I'm willing to move on from that. I really think we get along."

"If only you were gay," Will noted with grim, but laughed at his own pitiful luck.

His hand slipped from Will's shoulder and he grinded it against his other palm. "Yeah. If only." He wanted to drop that subject. It was an area he refused to tread, a concept he secured behind a brick wall and left there for further construction. Him? Gay? Even bisexual? What an absurd thought, though his two closest friends were homosexual, and now he was working on a third. On second deliberation, it would make all too much sense if he were accused of it by someone who didn't know him well enough. He'd keep silent on the short, transitory imaginings that sometimes preyed on his insecurity: the wonder and curiosity of what it would be like to pleasure another man, both sexually and romantically. It was meant for his brain and his only, despite how accepting, and even excited his companions would be at such enthralling news. They might scream with joy, or even say they knew all along. Even then, it was something he couldn't consider lightly. If he was uncomfortable with the notion alone, his voice might never reveal what his mind so frequently conjured during his most loneliest of moments. He locked up that box of fantasies and threw away the key, then altered the conversation's path. "There's something else the officers told me that I wanted to bring up to you."

Will went back to taking care of his visitor, wiping the remaining blood from his nose. "What's that?"

"One of them said I looked like Ian. Is that true?"

There was no reverie required for Will to give him a direct response. "It's true. You look almost exactly like him."

"Are you serious?" He nodded. "Is that why you started following me?"

"For a long time after Ian's death, I denied that he was gone. I didn't want to believe that he had really left me forever, and I felt guilty for letting bad things happen to him. I didn't want the abusive Ian back, but I wanted the old one, the one who loved me. When I met you, it was like I was meeting him for the first time all over again. Trust me. I know how crazy it sounds."

"It makes sense to me."

"It does?"

"Yeah. Just how alike did we look?"

"You could be his long, lost twin brother. Here, let me find a picture of him so you can see." He stuffed his hand into his back pocket and removed his leather wallet from it. It creaked as it opened, the creases and stitching worn with age and use. He passed a wallet-sized photograph to Cory, who was struck with a dreamlike sense of familiarity once he laid eyes on it.

Ian's hair wasn't the same length as his, but its hue was also auburn-brunette. Each of his facial features, down to his ridiculous pointed chin, was an almost identical match to what he saw in the mirror every day. The only notable difference was the short, prickly hair on Ian's jaw and chin, and their age difference.

"I would have sworn this was a picture of me if you hadn't told me it was of Ian. The likeness is creepy." Cory hadn't before believed in parallel universes, but he pondered if whether or not he stepped into one. Coincidences like these didn't just happen, not to his knowledge.

"Now you understand a little better why I felt the need to be around you all the time." He tucked the photo back into his wallet, a safe slip in the back behind his license that would go undisturbed, settling back into the couch cushions beside Cory. "At first it was because you looked like Ian. Then I saw how much nicer you were than him. A couple of years ago, when I began to..." He made exaggerated gestures with his hands, then pointed to Cory, who although bewildered, understood he was conveying his stalking with subtly. "It was during the winter, and the roads were icy. I ended up swerving right into a ditch. I guess you could say I had it coming to me. I saw your car stop right after that."

"Wait," Cory interrupted, rubbing his bruised chin. "I remember that day. I came to your window asking if you were all right. You said you didn't have a cell phone, so I called a tow truck for you."

"Ian would have never done that for someone else, at least not for a total stranger. You didn't recognize me. You didn't know I was your neighbor. You didn't know me, but you helped me anyway. I knew then that you weren't Ian's ghost. You were someone else. You were someone better. Even just a simple act of selflessness made me want to get even closer to you, to see the kind of life you lived, and if you were happy or not. If you truly were the nicer man I never really knew."

"You know that you could have just come over and knocked on the door if you really wanted to get to know me. It worked when you asked me to fix your TV."

"I know that now. I was just afraid. That and I didn't think I deserved any respect, even when I became hopelessly obsessed with the concept of being with you— with starting over."

"You said you've seen me do other things. Nice things."

"You're a very giving person. I learned that right away. You like to offer help to others."

"How do you know I'm doing it to be nice, and not to have more control in my life?"

Will frowned, disheartened by such a suggestion. "I don't know. But if that's true, then it doesn't matter either way. Even if you're helping people for your own reasons, those people still have someone that reaches out to them when they need it. It may affect your life in the way you want it, but it affects theirs too. It makes them happy to have someone listen."

"What if I'm not as good as you think? What if I'm selfish? I feel pleased when people let me help them, but I get really upset when they don't. Maybe I'm not the altruist you think I am."

Will tilted his head. "What are you trying to tell me, Cory?"

He looked Will in his sorrowful face with solemnity. "I don't want to hurt you."

Touched at his words, Will leaned closer to him, close enough where Cory could feel the warmth of his wine-scented breath. It gave his neck an unpredictable tingle. "Then you won't. If you're as selfish as you believe, then I don't think you'd really give a damn."

If Will was any closer to him, he might have leaned away, but for now, he didn't mind it. "I'm going to break your heart. I sort of already have." He expected Will to become emotional, but he didn't.

"My heart is hardly in one piece anymore. I doubt you could do it any more harm. I know well enough that you will probably never reach intimacy with me. If not, that's okay. I'm happy to know you, even if just as a friend. I can't promise I won't be in love with you, but I can promise that I won't harass you."

Cory didn't need his promise, but he accepted it anyway. "Fair enough."

Fidgeting, fixing his crooked, black glasses, Will stood up and cracked his neck. "I love speaking to you, Cory, but it's getting a bit late." The clock read ten forty. He might have had an earlier bedtime than Cory did, but he still found it weird. Everything about Will was weird.

"All right. I have to work in the morning anyhow." When he stood, he took one last look at Will, who twitched and jittered. "Thanks again for... you know."

"I would do it again in a heartbeat. Feel free to come over any time you want to talk."

"Yeah, absolutely. The same goes for you, too."

"Your mother…"

"Forget her. I don't need her approval. I choose who I'm friends with, not her."

"What if she has a right to fear me?"

"Does she?"

He rolled his head around on his neck, closing his eyes. "No. I would never hurt you, but you can't argue that I have problems. Your mother is mindful of that. She's met Ian. She knows what our relationship was like."

"We both have our own vices, Will, but I'm not afraid of you."

"I hope that doesn't change." When his whole body shook, he walked his companion to the door before Cory had time to ask what was wrong with him. "Have a good night, Cory. Sweet dreams."

"Yeah, you too." He gifted Will with a smile, but he shut the door before he could smile back. Baffled by his sudden desire to be alone, he wondered what might be happening beyond closed doors in William Shepherd's house. It was clearly something he didn't want Cory to see.

I want to help him, he decided as he walked back to his house. *And if I can help him, maybe I can help myself, too.*

Earlier, his future looked bleak. Now, it had a bit more meaning. It had a purpose.

7. Admittance

Cory found himself in a basement of some kind, one he had never seen before, one with stained, rustic walls and dripping water, with bottomless, yawning darkness and the strong scent of earth and dust. Unlike most basements, this one was empty, other than the enormous piles of dirt on which he clambered to reach the floor above. Whatever route he managed to take, it would only lead to a dead end, or he would fall back to the ground. A sinister voice whispered to him, one that sounded very much like his own, saying that if he didn't get out, and soon, something awful was going to happen to him. Horrors laid in wait beyond the darkness, atrocities worse than his imagining.

Then, the musty basement room was bathed in golden light, and his terror faded as he followed its call. It wasn't long before he realized the light was not coming from a fixture. It was warm, endlessly flickering, and as he inched closer to it, he could smell burning ash, and black smog stung his eyes. In the blink of an eye, he was no longer in the basement struggling to escape, but a rain-soaked street. In the distance, he saw a pillar of flame and the roadside ablaze. He heard the screams of a familiar voice, and he followed them, closing in on the horrible accident that lay before him.

When he got close enough, he learned that the previously incoherent screams were actually yelling his name.

"Coooorrrrry! Oh God! *Cory*!"

He picked up his pace, and ran to the site of what was a burning car alight with orange flames. When reaching it, he saw a charred body in the driver's seat, smoldering and crackling. Sirens wailed in the distance, fire trucks and police cars arriving on the scene, but he didn't pay attention to them. Instead, he searched for the screaming voice, the one belonging to his friend.

He saw him, William Shepherd, kneeling upon the pavement weeping in agony. "Please, God, no!" He bellowed. "Cory!"

"Will," Cory meant to shout, but only silence transpired. He waved to him to let him know he was safe. "I'm here," he mouthed, flagging him down.

No one else seemed to hear him calling, but Will had. He lifted his tear-stained eyes to his friend, then pointed to the car. When Cory looked at it a second time, the rustic flavor of blood filled his mouth when he realized it was his car that was on fire, and it was his body inside of it.

No. Not his. Ian's.

Although Ian's corpse was the one aflame in the vehicle, Will had been crying Cory's name. In slow motion, he slumped toward him, arms out, reaching for Cory in order to suck him in against his chest. He pulled him close, his arms clasping him like barbed wire, squeezing like tentacles. He remained still, startled and confused, frightened at what he was seeing.

"I tried," Will sobbed. "I tried to save him. I couldn't do it."

Tried to save him, Cory echoed in his mind as if he had been saying it to himself. *Tried to save him.*

Will released him, now emotionless and stoic. His tears had vanished, and he strolled to the burning car. A red can of gasoline rested on the curb, which he lifted in his forefingers, showing it to Cory, who was unable to stray from where he stood, his shoes glued to the ground.

"Know your limitations," he warned him. "Run."

Running wasn't an option. No matter how hard he tried, he couldn't move his legs. He was stuck, forced to watch as Will dumped the can of gas over his own head. "*Stop!*" Cory shouted, but he wasn't heard. The gas was like no normal gas, but a kind that spread at rapid speeds, first over Will, and then ran in rivers along the ground until it snaked up Cory's pant legs like stretching vines, covering them up to his knees. The fire burning throughout the car caught on Will's sleeve, and soon he too was engulfed in flames. Neon blue and red fire followed the gas trail on the ground up to Cory's ankles, and he felt the scathing hotness searing his flesh, coursing up his body.

He was ripped awake by his own sudden gasp for air. He clutched his chest, searching his body to see if life was still within it, and sighed with relief when he realized he was in bed, safe and sound and not on fire.

As he lied there, still and silent, he reviewed the bothersome nightmare in his mind a few times before his cell phone rang. He rolled his aching body over onto his side, pulling a muscle in his bicep when reaching for his vibrating phone resting on the bedside table. With his eyes still partially closed, he put the phone to his ear after answering the call.

"What did you do to my boyfriend?" Angie, who almost never called him, had finally phoned him to have that "meaningful" conversation, but it wasn't the kind he was hoping for.

"What did I do to *him?*" His sarcastic laughter wasn't enough of a clue for her, so she interjected.

"He told me he came over there to talk to you, and you started beating him up, then you had a friend help you. Cory, please tell me you didn't do that."

Although he didn't blame Angie for taking Derrick's side on the issue, he had to wonder if she still thought him the violent type, the same kid that once started fights on the playground, who was always in detention. Could she also then recall how he lost most of those battles and ended up in the nurse's office? "You believed him?"

"Of course I did. Why would he lie to me?"

"He came here to fight with me, not to talk. My friend was just protecting me."

"Who was it? Your stalker neighbor?"

Her remark put him into defensive mode, though he wasn't very close with Will. "Yeah, but compared to your boyfriend, he doesn't seem so bad, does he?" She made that little clicking noise she did with her mouth whenever she was disappointed in him. "Why are you suddenly acting like I'm your enemy?"

"I'm not. I just believe Derrick. I can see him wanting to talk to you, and I can see you starting a fight. It's who you are, Cory. You like to 'control the situation.'"

He tried not to let her words get to him. Despite all that had happened, he still cared for her, and it took a lot to push him away. They have had childish arguments on many occasions, most of which resulting from misunderstandings. On the other hand, hearing her defend Derrick after he assaulted him was a bit too much for him to bear. "All right, Angie. I can't force you to agree with me or believe me. I thought we were friends, but if you can't trust my word, I don't know where that leaves us."

"I thought we were friends too, until you started acting like you were more important than me, claiming I should always be calling and paying attention to the great and wonderful you."

"It's better than the alternative!" He screamed into the receiver, then hung up on her, turning off his phone before tossing it aside. No one else was going to call him anyway. As soon as he had done it, he wished he hadn't. He was always one to exaggerate, to make things worse than they were on the surface. Angie had every right and reason to believe her boyfriend. If you can't trust your own significant other, who can you trust?

It was a cold and wet Saturday afternoon, and on any other day he would spend it indoors, sleeping or modifying his PC case, or crafting a new one by hand, which he enjoyed doing in spare time. If he did, he'd have to go to the garage with some power tools, and it was too cold for that.

What could I do with my day off? He considered while looking at all of the spare electrical equipment in his bedroom. *I could put some neon fixtures around my desk... or I could visit someone. Will might enjoy it if I stopped by.*

He rolled out of bed and promptly got dressed, combed his hair and shaved. When he came downstairs, he could smell breakfast cooking and could hear his sisters chattering with his mother. He planned to sneak by them and leave the house undetected, but his mother could always hear him, just as she could when he was nine and tried to sneak cookies from the jar.

"Where are you going?"

Why did she have to treat him like a child? He was old enough to go where he wanted without her permission. He wasn't stealing cookies anymore. He could take one if he truly wanted one. "What difference does it make?"

When he told her of his incident with Derrick and Will the other day, she seemed even more paranoid of their neighbor, if that was at all conceivable. Will defended him when someone else hurt him, and she wasn't grateful to him, but was instead convinced that Will had some form of underhanded scheme to achieving success in his endeavors. It was out of the question to tell her how asinine that was.

"You don't want any breakfast?"

She tried to fence him in, but he would hardly be so easily contained. "That's where I'm going right now."

"I'm cooking. You don't have to spend money. Just eat here."

"I don't want pancakes. I'm fine with spending money." He left the house before she could argue with him any further. Even when he was outside, he could still feel her eyes following him. She could probably see that he was going next door, but he didn't care.

Will's yard was even tougher to walk through when it was soaked with fresh rainwater, and he was relieved to reach the front porch without getting his pants soaked. He rang, knocked, then rang again, as he usually had to. When Will came to the door, he looked groggy, exhausted and pale, but he smiled nonetheless.

"Cory," he sang. "Good morning."

"Did I wake you?"

"Yes, but it's okay. It was about time I woke up, anyway. How are you?"

"Hungry. I wanted to ask if you'd like to have breakfast with me."

He ducked backward as though a hidden net were waiting to ensnare him when he stepped out of the house. "Like... go out?"

"That's the idea, yeah." Seeing how nervous he was, he smiled at him to let him know there wasn't a catch.

"Well..." A deep sigh left his nostrils. "It sounds wonderful, Cory, and I appreciate you asking me. I just don't think I'd be eating very much."

"What's the matter? Are you sick?"

"Sort of. But I would still really love to go with you. If you give me a few minutes, I'll get ready."

"Sure. Take your time. I can wait." Will allowed him into his house, and Cory sat on the couch.

"Help yourself to anything you'd like. I'll just be a second." He slipped into the bathroom, where he shut and locked the door.

While sitting alone in the living room, he looked at the framed paintings on the walls, which looked recently hung. They were gorgeous works done in oil paint, mostly of rivers running through forests. There was one in particular that caught his eye when he got a glimpse of it: a city skyline at dusk. Homesickness enveloped his heart when he laid eyes on the view of the busy city, and he wished that he could be there with three clicks of the heels, but he knew that things were not that simple. He missed his friends, missed the club, even missed the nights where his inebriated pals would try to coax him into threesomes. It was his home, and it always would be. He had friends, a job he liked, and he met each day with a smile on his face. How his soul ached for a return there, even for just a day, to say hello to Scott and Alex, wish them well and hug them. To escape his prison was merely a dream, a dream best left unlived. His mother drove him toward the brink of insanity, but he still worried for her, and he had to do what he felt was right.

When Will returned from his trip to the bathroom, Cory pointed at the painting.

"Did you paint that?" He asked.

"I did. I just finished it a couple of days ago. Do you like it?" His need for assurance was somewhat endearing to Cory. He felt that his opinion mattered a great deal to him.

"I actually love it. Can I buy it from you?"

"*Buy* it? You're more than welcome to have it."

"Come on, I don't want to take it from you without paying for it. This is your job."

Without answering in words, he pulled a chair up to the wall and stepped onto it with his wobbling, trembling skinny legs. He hauled it off the wall and passed it down to Cory, who hesitated taking it from him. "Take it home with you later."

"I don't know if I'm comfortable taking it from you."

"I insist."

Retrieving the framed artwork from his hands, he placed it gently upon the floor against the center shelf. "Thank you, Will. I'll take good care of it."

"I know you will. I trust it with you."

Annie's, the local diner complete with salad and breakfast bar, was overcrowded, and Will showed his immediate discomfort in being amongst the public. He suggested going out for a coffee instead, but when Cory asked what was wrong, he changed his mind and spoke no more on it. Once seated, Cory ordered steak and eggs, while Will only asked for coffee.

"You're not going to eat anything at all?" Pried Cory, who snuck glances at the surrounding tables and the patrons sitting at them. They all seemed far cheerier than his companion.

Staring at the surface of their table, which was recently wiped with a damp cloth, he responded in a hushed, raspy tone. "I don't have much of an appetite these days. However, it was polite of you to invite me. I never would have imagined that you'd..." He trailed off, his concentration veering off-road.

Sarah, their waitress, brought Will his steaming cup of black coffee with two percent milk, then asked if he needed anything else. When he grunted "no," she walked away to tend to other people. In deep fascination, Cory watched Will like observing a lab rat in a cage, seeing firsthand the way he interacted with the world. The first thing he did since ordering his coffee was search the table for specific contents, and he apparently couldn't find them, because his dissatisfaction grew imminent.

"There's no sugar at this table." The awe-struck and panicked look on his face tickled Cory's funny bone. "I can't believe this! There's no sugar!"

"It's okay, Will." Laughter began to seep from his vocal cords, which he restrained as best as he could manage.

Suddenly, dead seriousness shadowed Will's already darkened eye sockets. "No, it is not okay."

Baffled by his overwrought behavior, his laughter and smile died like a fading light. "Why not?"

"If I don't have *sugar*, I can't drink my *coffee*. If I don't get my *coffee*, my whole day is out of balance, and the routine has fallen out of place. It's like taking a step backward when you want to go forward."

"Will, seriously, it's fine. I'll just ask the waitress to bring us some. It's not like they ran out of sugar. You'll get to drink your coffee. Relax."

Though he didn't relax as soon as he was asked to, he did eventually calm down, but not without pulling at individual strands of his dark hair. "Forgive me," he offered, his temper simmering.

"It's okay."

"It's been so long since I've gone out just for entertainment or social interaction. I forget what it's like to be with people, or to share things with them. By now, the concept is so foreign to me. I lose myself."

"It's all right. That's why I wanted to take you somewhere."

"You make a very decent and loyal companion, Cory. Your little girlfriend thinks so too, I gather."

Will's perked eyebrows suggested that he wanted to know Cory's relationship status, and despite himself, Cory wanted to inform him. "Angie's not my girlfriend."

"She would like to be, though."

"What makes you think so?"

For no apparent reason, Will unfolded a napkin in his lap though he expected no food. To Cory, it seemed so compulsive. There was a lot about Will he had yet to understand. "I've seen her with you. She clings to you. Hangs on your arm, touches your hair, your face. It's enough to make a man like myself fiery with jealousy. If she's not in love with you, she certainly loves touching you and drawing your attention."

He was hardly in the mood for discussing Angie on an empty stomach, but he figured it would be the best for the both of them if he got it out in the open as soon as possible. "If Angie loves me, it's because of how much attention I give her. She likes having someone around that will make her feel special. I don't want to be that person. We're not compatible."

"You sound like someone who was let down."

"Well, her boyfriend attacked me, and she defended him and implied I was the psycho. How's that for friendship? Oh well. Water under the bridge as they say, right?"

"You've been friends a long time, haven't you? That's a very important thing to throw away."

He knew that he was trying to make a point, but Will didn't understand who Angie was, or their history. Still, he paid mind to what he was trying to say. "Yeah. I know. We've fought and forgiven each other before. I'm sure we'll talk it over."

Sarah the waitress came back to the table with Cory's food and orange juice, and Will stammered at her to bring him some sugar. She followed up with his request and brought him what he asked, and he opened the tiny packets so ravenously that he spilled some of the white powder upon the table. He scooped tiny granules off the wooden surface in his fingertips and placed them in his cup with Cory's eyes fixed on him in bewilderment.

He really likes sugar, he mused.

After taking long, hearty sips of the dark beverage, his slow sigh was almost orgasmic. He licked his upper lip, then rested his cup gently on the small dish it came with. "Now that relationships are the topic of discussion," he continued in a borderline erotic voice. "Do you actually want one?"

Hiding from the answer he truly wanted to give, he replied, "I don't know."

"It's a tough question to answer, isn't it? Romance requires a lot of responsibility, a mutual understanding of undertaking great challenges. Many of us miss out on them just to avoid what people refer to as 'drama.'" He brought the cup back to his lips, and Cory expected another moan, but he contained himself. He was grateful for this, because he enjoyed the sound of it a little more than he would like to admit.

"Interestingly enough, it's not the drama that scares me. I'd rather have drama than be alone."

Though he dropped the moans and sighs, he did smack his lips. "Then what is it that frightens you?"

Never having been asked this question before, he wasn't sure what to say at first. Why did he space himself so generously from romance? At the start, it might have been that he didn't find it nearly as important to be in love as everyone made it seem, but he could disagree with that now. He did wish to be in love. What he said then, after his thoughts bubbled, was an admission he never would have made to anyone else. "That one day, after being in love with someone for a long time, they'll suddenly realize I'm not so great after all. I want a relationship, but I don't at the same time, because as much as I want to be close with someone, I know how obnoxious I am. I want to believe that 'the one' is out there, but… what would I do if I met them? I'd be so scared of pushing them away that I *would* push them away. I couldn't bear that."

"The immeasurable fear of abandonment," Will clarified. "It's where you and I are alike." They swapped identical smiles. "You'd think two people who feared it would do well together."

"I'm also way too much of a hothead to be in a relationship. I'm definitely not shy when it comes to my opinions. I'm too honest, sometimes to a disgusting degree."

"In certain situations, that can prove to be useful."

Cory prodded at his remaining breakfast with the prongs of his fork. The toast was too dry and slightly burnt, and he had no interest in eating it. "What do you see in me, Will?"

"I've already told you that."

"It can't just be because I look like Ian and I'm 'nice.' There must be a lot more to it."

Another few gulps and his coffee had diminished. "I can't explain how I feel. It's like defining a habit. It's there because it's a part of me. I'm afraid I don't know what else to say."

"I guess what I mean to ask is: what is your goal? What do you want?"

He twisted his cup upon its dish slowly. It turned like a broken down carousel, vacant of cheerful riders. "Whenever I create a new painting, I always love the halfway point— when all of the colors blend seamlessly together. It always reminds me of when I was happier, when everything was falling into its right place. I recall the blossom of mine and Ian's relationship, how ecstatic we were to be around each other, and one thought never ceased to repeat itself in my mind: it can't get much better than this. When a love is new, so many other mundane and pointless things in your life just don't matter anymore. I miss that feeling so much, Cory. To be close to someone, to be truly *addicted* to them, to feel that without them, nothing else is of importance. It's been so long— too long— since I've felt it, that I've convinced myself I'm hardly human anymore."

A permeable silence struck them, though the rest of the diner was noisy with simultaneous conversations. "I've felt that way. Once. Only it was one-sided. The feeling wasn't mutual."

He went back to drinking his coffee, drawn in to Cory's confiding. "I'm sorry. Tell me."

Cory didn't let on that it was Angie he had such a dramatic past with, not wanting to give Will the impression that he might still feel the same way after so many years, because he definitely didn't. "We had a sexual friendship. I wanted something more, but she didn't. I think she had a crush on someone else. It doesn't matter much now. I'm over it, and it happened a long time ago."

"When she let you know she didn't feel the same way about you as you felt for her, how long did it take you to accept it?"

He clasped his hands together, his fingers interlocking. "Too long. I was still crazy for her even after I graduated high school. I had to move away to New York to forget her and this place and hopefully make some changes and some new friends, which I did. I was closer with them than I was with anyone here… and I left it all to help my mother."

Will took a moment to finish what was left in his cup. "She's lucky to have you, even if she drives you crazy."

"Yeah. I suppose so."

Their conversation came to a halt when the waitress returned to their table to ask if Will would like any more coffee. When he declined, she gave them their bill, and Cory paid for it in full. As they left the diner and walked to Cory's car, Will thanked him for taking him out and that he loved getting to know him.

"I felt like I was the center of attention the whole time," he apologized. "I took you out intending to get to know *you*."

"There will be plenty of chances for that. I just enjoy hearing you talk."

"I'm glad someone does. It's quite a switch from what I'm accustomed to. I don't like the sound of my own voice."

"Few people do."

When Cory pulled and parked into Will's driveway, neither of them left the vehicle, the engine remaining idle. "I don't want to go home yet," he explained with his hand on his keys. "Maybe I could come inside and we could chat some more."

Will's sarcastic leer was disconcerting. "You're actually interested in that?"

"Seeing as how I didn't learn much when sharing breakfast with you… yeah, I'm interested in that."

"Why?"

Cory was caught a bit off-guard. Why *did* he want to get to know Will so much? The reasons hadn't made themselves as clear to Cory as the desire to do it. "Do I need a reason?" When he glanced at Will, he was scratching his neck again.

"If you wouldn't mind giving one," he uttered, his fingers dragging up and down.

"I don't know, Will. Maybe I think you're interesting? Maybe I'd like us to be friends?"

"Are you so desperate for friendship that you would bother pitying a fool like me?"

"What? What do you mean? I'm not spending time with you because I *pity* you."

"You must feel some level of sympathy for me. You wouldn't be here now if you didn't."

When Cory turned to face him, he looked away. "Sympathy and pity are a little different. I'm trying to understand you, not be condescending."

Hunching forward in his seat to scratch the back of his neck now, he grunted at him. "It's all the same to me. I'm not a charity case, so don't treat me like one."

Cory unlocked the car doors, tapping his thumbs on the steering wheel. "I'll see you again some other time, then."

"Wait," Will eased. "I didn't mean it the way it sounded."

"You think I want to be friends with just anybody who gives me the opportunity, don't you? I know we got to this point under some pretty strange circumstances, but I like talking to you. That might make me weird, but weird, I can live with." He bit onto his tongue after lashing out the way he had, and hoped that in doing so, Will wasn't offended.

"I-I'm sorry, Cory. I didn't know your feelings were genuine. I assumed you felt sorry for me."

"I do, but not in the way that you think. You seem like a nice guy that's been through a lot, but that's not why I consider you my friend. You're my friend because you're intelligent, you're easy to talk to, and you're interesting. I think in a lot of ways, we're alike, but I haven't seen it until now. You have this way about you... you're humble and soft-spoken, and I like that. I want to be around someone I can relate to. And I can relate to you."

Hope brightened Will's face, a look that was uncharacteristic for him. "Can you, really?"

"Yes. At least, I think I do."

"There's a lot you don't know yet."

The wall that Will built around himself was virtually impenetrable, but Cory didn't give up trying to knock it down. "So give me the chance to learn."

"I know you once said you didn't want to hurt me, and I believe that you don't." Will took a moment to stare into space, outside the front windshield. He seemed fixed on his decaying front door, as if picturing someone walking out of his house. His head oscillated as his focus traveled down the foliage-covered path that lead into the drive, then into the street. Cory had to wonder just what he was looking at, and what he was waiting for, but thought it too rude to press the matter. "Okay. You can come in for a little while." He was the first to vacate the car before Cory shut it off, and Cory followed him out as soon as he killed the engine. "Don't misunderstand me," Will continued once they were inside the house. He flipped through a fresh stack of mail. "I'm delighted that you want to spend time with me." He huffed at the sight of overdue bills. "I'm just nervous, that's all. I don't want to lose you before…" His voice faded as he headed toward the kitchen, opening his creaky cupboards and fridge, pouring something into a glass. "Can I get you a drink?"

He slipped his jacket off and draped it over a chair. "What have you got?" It was a stupid question, as he realized when spotting the dirty glassware around the room.

"Wine," he told him matter-of-factly, as if it should be obvious.

"Guess I'll have that." He sat on the couch, and Will entered the room with two full glasses of red liquid. As soon as he sat beside him, he dragged his nails across his reddened neck. "Will, I'm sorry, but I have to ask. What's up with your skin? You're always scratching it."

Lowering his hand, an anxious quiver ran up his arm. "It's a side effect of some medication I've been taking."

"Medication? Is it safe to be drinking all of this wine with it?"

"Probably not." His glass was empty as soon as he began pouring the wine down his throat. "But I don't have much to live for, do I?"

Will's gloominess eliminated any good feelings Cory had. It was one thing about Will he didn't enjoy. It was as though someone switched off a light and bathed him in darkness when he needed to see what he was working on. "I need to ask you something."

"I assure you that my teeth are stained because of how much coffee I drink."

"The condition of your teeth doesn't matter to me," he answered with a bemused laugh. Will seemed surprised, however pleasantly. It may have been a declaration that rarely struck his ears. "When you slashed that guy's tires, it was like you've done it before. None of your fingerprints were on the letters you gave me. You seem like an experienced criminal."

Will pursed his lips, sucking the wine off of them. "Do I?"

"What else have you done? And don't lie to me. I'll know."

Will leaned over his coffee table, running his finger along the rim of the empty wine glass. It might have been half a minute before either of them spoke again. "All right. I guess there's no point in hiding it from you." He sucked in a heavy breath in preparation. "I've stolen."

Stealing wasn't as big of an offense to Cory as Will might have thought. When he was a kid, he stole baseball cards from the local convenience store. Not once did an employee ask why he was in there so often, or why he left without buying anything. "What did you steal?"

"Whatever I could. Sometimes I shoplifted, usually from corner stores with little security, but I've gone as far as to breaking into cars."

Cory whispered, dubious: "*Why?*"

"I'm afraid you might judge me." He lifted his shoulders, like blocking an oncoming punch.

"You just admitted to me that you steal and I'm still here. I wanted to learn more about you and that's what I'm doing."

Will's anxiety never let up, but he put his faith in him, and trusted him to take the truth. "Why do most people steal? Money. It was to help support Ian's habit. He was not only draining every liquor bottle he got his hands on, but he was also draining me of all of my funds. After a while I couldn't afford to buy him alcohol anymore."

"He wouldn't go to rehab? Or try other ways of quitting?"

He twitched with fake, sympathetic chuckles as one would at a child's obvious and overused joke. "One of the many signs of an addiction is denial. He didn't think anything was wrong with it. If I suggested that he should seek help, I'd get hit for it. So many times I braved the storm, confronted him on our issues, until he raised a hand to me. He knew that I'd succumb to it."

"You said you endured it all because you loved the way he used to be. You couldn't accept that he wasn't going to change back to the old him?"

"Of course I couldn't accept it. We had once vowed to find a way to marry each other, and we were that close for years. The change was so sudden that I was convinced the real Ian was trapped inside of him somewhere, hanging on for dear life, begging me to release him. I thought he would come back to me. This monster, this alcoholic, whoever he was— it wasn't the man I fell in love with. I swore that I'd do anything to help him, and I couldn't help him if I abandoned him."

Incredulous at his reasoning, he searched for deeper answers. "But stealing for him and feeding him alcohol wasn't helping him, either. What did you think would happen?"

"I thought he would change for me if I showed him I still loved him. That I'd always be there for him."

"If he loved you, he *would* have changed." Cory didn't think saying this would break him, but he crumpled forward and clasped his face. He didn't intend to push him over the edge, make him fall apart to pieces before him, and wished he could take back the harm he caused him. "I'm sorry, Will. I shouldn't have said it like that. I'm sure he loved you in his own way."

"No," he sobbed. "You're right. He was too busy getting drunk to even notice me anymore. I was his ticket to free booze, and nothing else." On this note, he wept, leaning away from him as he removed his glasses.

Cory decided that of all of the options he had to choose from, it would mean the most to Will if he comforted him. He closed the gap between them, scooting nearer to his shaking torso, and placed his palm on his back. Once he gave it a few gentle strokes, Will gave him a perplexed stare. Then, his confusion turned to glee. Cory had touched much more than just his boney back.

"Why couldn't it have been you instead?" Will begged the answer from a mysterious, nonexistent force, but nothing other than silence followed.

After drinking a generous plethora of wine, Will dove into an intoxicated state over the course of the afternoon. Cory told him to take it easy, and asked him to stop, taking his wine glass away from his unrelenting iron grip. It didn't take him long to pass out on his couch, exhausted from alcohol consumption and spinning tales of a once quasi-happier time with Ian, like a dreary old man weaving stories of how "times were like back in the day." Cory didn't necessarily want to leave him alone, but he knew his mother was probably concerned for him, since he had been gone all day. It would be best to put her mind as ease, and he would visit Will again the following day, just to check on him. He took the painting that Will offered him after setting a twenty dollar bill on the shelf where it was resting, sneaking it up to his room before he was attacked by the question machine that was his mother.

After sharing dinner with his family, and applying lights to the inside of his computer case, he went to sleep that night with heavy thoughts. He knew it wasn't his job to play as Will's therapist, but he was drawn to it like a magnet. Unable to bear that someone out there could be hurting as much as he was, and that no one else was going to help him, he had convinced himself it was his duty to do so, regardless of the intense burden he might take on. If he could focus his emotions and thoughts on Will and his problems, he could forget his own troubles for a little while, and keep things in order.

It was a little after three in the morning when the crash woke Cory. In some ways he was grateful for the nocturnal interruption. His nightmares were worsening lately, and the one he had been stuck in that night was no better. When he first heard the sound, he assumed it came from his subconscious, a part of his mind begging him to wake up, but when he heard his family fretting on the floor below, he knew it was no dream. He leapt out of bed and into his clothes as lightning speed, bursting out of his room and tumbling down the stairs to his mother and oldest sister standing at the base of them.

"What was that?" He asked them, shaken and still trying to wake up.

"It didn't come from our house," Amanda clued him in.

"Will," he gasped. He shoved his shoes onto his feet and threw his jacket on, dashing out the front door before the women had time to understand what he was talking about.

8. Friendship

Brisk autumn winds nipped Cory's cheeks as he ran next door into Will's yard where the solemn man was standing, facing the front of his house and staring at the hole where his window once was with a shadowed face pulled into a soulless glare. Leaping over wads of wet plants, Cory rushed beside him, and Will's silhouette turned.

"What happened?" Cory asked as soon as he noticed his presence. "Are you okay?"

"I'm fine." He sounded a bit too casual. In fact, his tone was more of a concern to Cory than his broken window. "My window, on the other hand..."

Swiveling his head in all directions, Cory searched for the offending party. "Did you see who did it?"

"No. I was sleeping on the couch." He groaned and slowly palmed his throbbing forehead. "Or rather, I was passed out on it."

"You seem awfully detached over the whole thing."

"I never liked that window."

He was trying to be funny, perhaps to keep calm and to prevent Cory from worrying, but in his opinion, someone had to. "I think I might know who did this to you."

"Anyone could have. I'd even give you a whole list of names of kids on this block who would do it in an instant, and that's without being betted or double-dared."

"The kids around here are assholes, yeah, but they aren't vandals. Remember that guy who got into a fight with me the other night?" As he and Will discussed this, more of their neighbors switched their lights on, and some of them even stepped out to have a look. Most of them went back inside after a few seconds without offering any help.

Smirking, Will briefly shut his eyes. "The one with the squeezable neck?"

The unsettling eroticism in his voice had him stepping away a foot or two. "Yeah. Him. He's my friend's boyfriend. He sees me as some kind of threat to his relationship. I'm sure it really killed his pride when you kicked his ass."

"As it would anyone's, I'm sure." He hid his hands in his pockets, leaning closer to Cory when he saw the widening space between them. "But is he really stupid enough to come back here looking for more?"

"Did he seem at all intelligent to you?"

"Let's say it really is him that did it." He rubbed his hands together, blowing warm air into his palms. "What are you planning to do?"

"I think I might just pay Angie a visit later. I hope he'll be with her."

Will planted a hand on his shoulder and gripped it in his worn, dried fingertips. "Don't go getting yourself into trouble for my sake. It might be better for the both of us if you left it alone."

"I'll be fine, don't worry. I wasn't planning on starting a fight, as much as I'd love to."

"Even so." He was uncompromising, resolute, as firm as his grip to his shoulder. "It's not worth it."

"I'll be the judge of that. Just let me handle it, all right?"

"Don't get hurt," he beseeched, his clasping hand loosening and releasing him. "That's all I ask. You're too important to me."

Cory found the sentiment captivating, despite the situation. "I'll be all right, Will. I'm perfectly capable of taking care of myself."

"If you say so. Go back inside before you catch your death out here. I'll talk to you later on. I need to go to bed before my head explodes."

After bidding him good night, he parted ways with Will and rejoined his family in his own house. When telling his mother of what happened to their neighbor, she implied that it was a deed he most assuredly deserved, and had no right to grievances. Ignoring her pettiness, he returned to bed to get some rest.

Angela "Angie" Finley's apartment door had a fresh crack and chipped pain near the hinges. Contemplating the scratches on the door's lock, Cory knew they must have been made recently, and he only had one guess as to who had done it. He rapped on the wooden pane, and Angie opened her door quicker than Will usually did his. A bit of a refreshing switch, he had to admit.

A restless, "Hey, Cory" snuck out her lips, and she stepped aside so that he could enter. "What are you doing here?"

"I wanted to talk." As soon as he stepped over the threshold, he saw the mountain of wadded tissues on the glass coffee table, untidy, ruffled blankets crammed in a ball on the couch where Angie had been camping out. Dirty dishes were piled up in the kitchen sink, and the trash can in the corner between the dining room and kitchen area was overflowing, muffin wrappers sticking out on all sides. He turned to Angie when he heard her shut the door, baffled by the strange sight, his jaw loosely hanging. "Did something happen?"

In the midst of stumbling toward her destination— her nest on the couch— she mumbled something incoherent to him about Derrick.

"Did you have a fight with him?"

"We broke up," she nasally announced, pulling blankets around her chest for comfort.

He decided that now wasn't a good time to get into an argument, and instead tended to her emotional wounds. "Do you have any tea? I'll make you some."

"In the cupboard above the sink."

As he prepared some hot water, placing a tea bag in one of her mugs that had a cartoon smiling cat on it, he leaned against the wall while folding his arms. In spite of their recent feud, Cory didn't enjoy seeing his friend in pain. "Is he moving out?"

"I don't want him to." A honk emitted from her nose as she blew it into a tissue.

"Where is he now?" He switched his posture to something more casual when she shot a suspicious eye at him. He supposed he did ask the question a bit more urgently than he intended.

Shaking her head, she wiped her nostrils. "I don't know. Probably trying to pick up some girl hotter than me."

"Why do you say that? Was he cheating on you?"

"My best friend saw him at a bar, talking to women, buying them drinks. I thought we were working out our problems. I thought we were doing better."

"What happened to your door? Did he do that?"

"He kicked it when I locked him out. He even cried to me, begging me to let him back in and forgive him. I'll give him some time to prove he's worth the aggravation. He's on the lease, so it's not like I can throw him out right now." The pile of tissues grew even bulkier when she added to its numbers. "Is that tea ready?"

He ducked back into the kitchen, pouring the steaming water into the mug. "When did this happen? Last night?" She told him it occurred late the night before. "I think he vandalized my neighbor's house. Smashed his window pretty good. You must have put Derrick in a pretty bad mood." He brought her the freshly steeped tea after adding honey and milk, a way he knew she liked it, and received sorrowful gratitude.

"The stalker?" Her query wasn't in amusement or even revulsion as it was earlier, much to Cory's surprise.

"Yes. His name is Will. Will Shepherd."

"You call him by name now?"

"He's not so bad."

She gently sipped her tea while mystified. "He stalked you and he's not so bad? We must think very differently."

"Hear me out a second. I got to know him a little bit. Yeah, he does have some issues, but he seems really nice. I think it helps him feel better when we talk to one another."

Angie tapped her long fingernails against her cup. The clinging hurt Cory's ears. "Why do you feel like you have to help him at all?"

She didn't have much insight on how Cory felt, and it was his fault for that, but he still felt it necessary to defend himself and Will. "I don't understand what's wrong with it. He fought Derrick off when he was beating on me. I think that's enough of a redemption, don't you? I forgave him for what he did, and I get along with him."

"Cory, I love you, and I'm sorry for... you know," she indicated to their fight over the phone, then followed up with unshakeable fortitude. "But I can tell you right away what's wrong with that. I can't convince you of something if you're already in a certain mindset, but this guy seems kind of dangerous to me. I saw what he did to Derrick... his neck. He really hurt him. What if he hurts you too?"

"You have sympathy for him after that? Can you not see the bruises on *me*?"

"Don't ignore what I'm trying to tell you. I know you believe it just as much as I do that the guy... whatever he is to you now... needs a mental hospital a lot more than he needs you."

Cory spaced out, repeating the words "mental hospital" in his mind enough times to where it sounded silly. Would Will really be better off in one of those places, living amongst the screaming psychotics and incessant rambling? Sure, he had his moments, but he wasn't like them. "I don't think Will would hurt me."

Taking the time to finish her tea, she went on after setting her cup down on the table. "You don't *think* he'd hurt you?"

"I *know* he wouldn't. It sounds completely insane, but I just don't think he's capable of doing that to me. You should see how he is when I'm around him. It's like he's walking on glass and eggshells trying not to force me away. I trust in my perception. Will's a lot of things, but he's not a bad person, and that's something I just sense."

She nodded when their discussion reached its pivotal "don't go there" status. "Is he attractive?"

Cory's lips parted, but words failed him for a moment. "I... I don't know. Why are you asking me that?"

"I just wanted to know what you thought." A hint of a sly smirk was hidden on her lips, which she then blocked with the rim of her cup, though it was already empty.

"Why would I find a guy attractive?"

"You tell me."

Whatever game she was playing, Cory didn't enjoy being a piece in it. Her words aroused wiry tingles under his skin and tinged his face crimson. "I should go," he told her while making an escape toward the door, before any more implications could come forward.

"Don't be mad. I'm cheering myself up. I'm sorry if I insulted you."

"That's just it. You didn't." He zipped his jacket up to the collar, preparing for the near-freezing fresh rain outdoors. "I'm not the least bit offended."

"I was just teasing you," she justified, despite his denial.

"It doesn't even matter." The heavy apartment door dragged roughly against the thick carpet when he pulled it open, and he took one last look at Angie before leaving. "I'm sorry you and Derrick broke up, but it's for the best. He was an asshole, and I'm glad you're free of him."

"I'll talk to him about the window," she promised. "I'm sure he'd tell me."

He left after thanking her, telling her he hoped she'd be all right. Upon returning home, he saw Will outside, which was already strange enough, but he was actually doing yard work, raking the scattered, dead leaves into an organized pile. Where he was going to put that pile, however, was left a mystery. Cory didn't bother going into his own house, but instead strolled to his neighbor, smiling as soon as they noticed one another. Will's look was not only that of adoration, but of relief.

"I'm glad you're back." He dropped his rake onto the grass, which swallowed it in its long, gangly strands. "I was tired of raking."

"How long have you been doing that for?" Cory pointed to the tan-colored mass he had gathered.

"Since I woke up and saw you leave. Would you like to come in?"

It didn't take long for him to agree to his offer, and followed his lead into the house. A garbage bag was sitting up against the wall where the window was smashed in, and plastic was taped over the gaping hole. When shaking the edges of the bag, Cory heard it clink and rattle as glass shook on the bottom.

"Drink?" He was already filling a glass with wine.

He starts early, Cory worried, hoping he wouldn't spend another afternoon dealing with an inebriated man slurring tales of his depressing past.

"No, I shouldn't. Maybe you shouldn't, either."

"I know I shouldn't, but unfortunately, it's a bit of a comforting habit." He dissolved into the dim hallway while slurping from his glass, opening a battered wooden door. "Come with me, Cory. I'd like to show you something."

Cory had never felt positive at being invited into a basement. He didn't like basements; never did. The musty smell, the wet walls, the peeling floors— not a single aspect of it was appealing. However, he got the sense that Will had something important he wished to share with him, and even if it meant visiting a section of house that Cory did his best to avoid, he would do it for him. Will descended the flight of stairs into a pit of blackness, and it wasn't until he turned on the light that Cory followed. Down below on the lowest level of the house, it was much cleaner than it was upstairs, and, in an interesting twist, smelled less of mildew than the upper level did. In the middle of the room, a large metal easel stood before a tall, black stool, and each sat beside a large desk, which was flecked and stained with dabs of paint. On all four of the walls hung paintings of all kinds, some of them unfinished, left for another time. Against the north wall was a full sized bed beneath two large windows, covered in dark, thick blankets, which were messily tossed.

On the west wall was the television Will recently bought at Hot Wire sitting on a tall table, a burgundy sofa and small coffee table facing it. It looked as though it hadn't been used much since the day he bought it, if it had been used at all. The spacey basement room was barely lit by a dimming bulb that Will apparently deemed too unimportant to change, which shrouded the area in a gloomy half-glow. When Cory took a good look around, he faced Will, who was downing his glass of wine with increased thirst.

"So this is your room, essentially," Cory verified.

"Yes," he mumbled after swallowing. "I guess you could call it my home within my home."

Narrowly avoiding a foot full of paint, Cory edged around Will's art desk. "Why don't you sleep in the bedroom?" Will brushed past him, but not without touching the skin of his arm. He crept to the couch, which was in the darkest part of the room, flopping onto it hard enough for dust to rise from its cushions. Cory took a seat on the armrest, keeping a mindful eye on him.

"There are memories throughout the rest of this house. Everything upstairs belonged to Ian. Contrarily, I can't part with any of his belongings. It will only be a matter of time before my appliances get shut off, and then it'll just be a cold storage shed for Ian's things."

"You don't have anywhere else to go if that happens?"

Once he had finished off his glass of wine, adding it to the line-up of other stained glassware sitting on the table, he slouched and sank into the couch. "I suppose my parents would let me stay with them, but I've burdened them enough already with my..." His words trickled, fading into nothing, but Cory could have sworn he heard him say "bad habits."

Offending Will with a forward question wasn't something Cory wished to do, but if he planned to help him, he had to first understand him. "So you're just giving up, is that it?"

Will eyed his wine glass with a forlorn frown, disappointed that it had been empty. "Ever since Ian started drinking, I felt that my life was hopeless. I was lost, because in my eyes, he was already gone, long before he actually died. There is nothing for me here, in this home, or in life... except you, perhaps." His lips twitched, but he hid it from him.

Cory inched closer to him, the proximity enticing Will, a pulled smirk on his otherwise pale and lifeless face. "I appreciate you holding me so high," he began. "But there's a limit to how much I can do for you."

"Don't misunderstand me, Cory. I appreciate your friendship because you help me forget how much pain I'm in. I'm so glad I have someone... anyone... to talk to. You've already given me so much that I could never bear to ask anything of you."

Cory was familiar with feeling like the only man on the planet. Even in the company of others, the sensation would creep up on him. When near Will, on the other hand, it would keep its distance. "I like talking to you, Will."

"Do you really?"

"You give me someone to chat with, too, and you're serious about it. That means a lot."

Will had such a heartwarming smile that Cory couldn't help but mimic it. No words needed to be uttered when he smiled like that, because the room lit up with him. During the pause in their conversation, Will reached for his empty wine glass, intending to fill it. When stretching out his arm, the sleeve of his argyle slipped up toward his inner elbow, revealing a large, white patch that was taped onto his skin.

Will did his best to hide it by yanking down his sleeve. It was too late. Cory had noticed it. "What's that on your arm?" He was no longer carefree, but strict, almost parental in nature.

"What's what?" He pretended not to understand his question, and his eyes shifted back and forth.

"There's a bandage on your arm. What happened?"

"Nothing."

"If it's nothing, why can't you tell me?"

Will drifted toward the staircase with his empty glass. "Honestly, Cory! You sound like my father!"

"Your father is familiar with you needing bandages? It sounds pretty serious, then."

"With all due respect," Will answered with mixed fear and disturbance, his head twitching. "It's not any of your business. There are things I'd like to keep from people because they are humiliating to me. This is just one of those things, and I'd like you to honor my privacy." The word "privacy" was choked on, and barely made it past his teeth.

Cory left his seat and strolled toward him. He backed up a few steps, signs of fear materializing on his face. "All right, Will. I'm sorry. I didn't mean to be invasive, I was just concerned."

Will relaxed as soon as he saw that a smack or punch wasn't about to punish him for his defiance. "It's very touching to think that you care. That at least *someone* cares."

"I wouldn't be speaking to you so much if I didn't." Once rosy tint bled onto his cheeks, Will vanished up the staircase, and Cory followed. "So if bad habits are keeping you from living a happy lifestyle, why don't you just...?"

"Change my habits?" Will finished, refilling his cup. "Do you think I don't want to?"

"Well, I'm sure you do, but I don't know how much you've already tried." He turned up his palm to deny a silent offer of booze. "You need to be able to live."

"Do I, though? Some days I'm not sure I even want to continue living. There are a few things that keep me going, but they've become pointless now, just white noise in what could be everlasting peace." A few gulps diminished the red wine from his glass as Cory stared him down in disbelief. A fresh sheen of sweat was developing on his brow, and he wiped it off with the back of his hand. The tip of his nose was slightly wet. He was shaking, and couldn't stop. "However, I'm still a human being, and our strongest instinct is that of survival, of living a full life, no matter how mundane and repetitive and useless it may be. Like most people, I fear death, even though I've looked straight into its eyes on more than one occasion. I guess you could say I'm waiting— waiting for something to show me that it's all been worth it."

Cory leaned his back against the counter, Will standing before him, pining as he looked over his youthful body and licking his lips in romantic thirst. "So you think that trying to live is a waste of time. Is that accurate?"

"The world doesn't have room for people like me in it." He paused when there was an unconvinced shake of Cory's head. "But it's not *entirely* accurate. I don't *want* to be this way. I don't want to be afraid. I don't want to wake up from nightmares anymore. I want to be happy. I'd do anything to be happy, to forget the way I am now, or eliminate it completely."

"Does it make you happy when we see each other?"

"Yes. It makes me very happy, simply because you take the time to listen to me. It's more helpful than you can imagine."

"I'm happy, too. To have you as a friend, I mean."

Without warning, Will took a gentle hold of the back of his neck and pulled him into a hug. "I'm sorry," he apologized immediately, though Cory was unsure of what he was sorry for, and even slipped his arms around his neck to return the embrace, which appeared to surprise him. "I'm just glad you said that."

"You don't have to be sorry."

"Am I being creepy?"

It was tough— not only because of what he said, but how he said it— to keep from laughing. "Not to me."

"That's good." After releasing Cory, he fixed his glasses, which were slanted from his slight impact against him. "I'm still not sure whether or not it's a good idea you're so kind to me. I can't tell if it's doing more harm than good."

"How could it do any harm?"

"Because you're not... like me."

"Haven't you ever heard the term 'opposites attract?'" He winked after asking him. It was involuntary, and he didn't understand where it came from.

"You know what I mean, Cory." The faucet that Will turned on hissed as he rinsed out his glass. "You're not attracted to men, and though I won't beg you for romance, I don't take rejection easily, especially if I'm being teased beforehand."

He threw his palms into the air. "Hey, I'm not teasing you, at least not on purpose. I'm not trying to lead you on. When I say I like you... I mean it. Maybe not in the way that you want, but I do mean it."

Will sighed, hunching over his sink, leaning on his forearms. Cory backed away, thinking he was going to vomit when he swallowed several times. "You're right, you haven't. I wasn't implying that you..." He suddenly clutched his mouth, ducking around Cory and ran out of the kitchen into his bathroom, where he slammed the door.

Startled by the abruptness of Will's departure, as well as his inexplicable onset of illness, he approached the bathroom door and placed his ear against it, hearing heaving sounds from within. "Will, are you okay?"

"Yes," he answered with weak spitting sounds. "It happens all the time."

"Isn't that *more* of a cause for alarm?"

Continuous puking sounds resonated from within. They died down somewhat before he spoke again. "I'm fine." He didn't elaborate. Will's extroversion on some subjects and introversion on others was a riddle Cory found all too vexatious to solve. "Maybe you should go."

"I'm not going if you need help."

"I *don't*. I just want you to go. Please, just go."

He didn't want to get hurt, and he didn't want to hurt Will, but when he felt for once the possibility that he may care for him far stronger than he did for anyone else in his life, he questioned why it was so vital for him to hide it. If Will was important to him, why on earth was it so difficult to admit it? It couldn't be as simple as the fact that he was male. He wouldn't leave just because Will asked him, not without checking on him. "If something is wrong..."

A stint of coughing, spilling, and spitting followed, then he croaked, "I just need to take something." He didn't specify what. "Thank you for being so thoughtful, but I need to be alone."

Giving in, he took a step away from the bathroom door. "All right. If that's what you want, then I'll go. Just come and get me if you need me for something, even if you just want to talk."

He responded with something incoherent, but very similar to "I love you." When Cory left, thoughts of Will lingered in his mind, even for many hours after seeing him. He never stopped by to speak to him, even in the evening after dinner time. Worried that he might be in some kind of danger or perhaps too sick to call for help, he crept outside while not under the protective gaze of his mother and wandered next door with a hammering heart. He rang the doorbell several times, and eventually Will appeared, who seemed far better than he was earlier.

"I came to check on you," Cory announced like a king's dutiful messenger.

The warm surprise of his visit tugged his mouth into a smile. "You're very sweet. I'm okay."

"What happened?"

"If I go too long without taking my medication it makes me… violently ill."

"What kind of medication does that?"

"A bad kind." He left it at that, and Cory dropped it after seeing his dark, ominous countenance.

"Listen, I wanted to ask if you'd like to go out for lunch with me tomorrow."

"Why, Cory! That sounds like you're asking me on a date!" His exclamation was one of hope and adoration.

"Yeah, it kind of does, doesn't it?" He gritted his teeth and twisted his foot back and forth on the ground.

"But I'll understand if it isn't. I'd be willing to have lunch with you either as friends or… whatever."

"I just don't like being at home with my family, and I honestly have no other friends that would go with me, and I like to have someone to eat with, you know what I mean?"

"You don't have to explain yourself. I'm happy to come along. Tomorrow, I'll be waiting."

9. Heart

Cory had just finished eating a bowl of cereal before Angie called him that morning. He didn't mention it to Angie when they spoke, but since waking up, he carried with him a light, positive air, and everything, even mundane chores, felt delightful. The night before, he got plenty of sleep for the first time in a week, his breakfast tasted sweeter, and not even his pestering little sister nagging him about leaving shaved hair in the sink bothered him. He wasn't a very talented whistler, but he did it anyway, because his mood told him to.

Angie didn't share his alacrity, and the day didn't appear as bright to her as it did to him. At great length, she complained about her ex, and Cory endured it, hoping she would answer the question he posed half an hour ago. Then, she got to the point. "He confessed to smashing your neighbor's window."

"How'd you manage to get it out of him?" He asked with a mouthful of fresh and crispy, however dry toast. It still tasted amazing with jelly on it.

"I convinced him I'd see him next weekend if he told me the truth. He sounded pretty desperate to have just a day with me, so I guess he thought it was a fair bargain. I'm sure he doesn't know I'm snitching on him to you, and I feel a little bad about that, but honestly, he deserves worse for trying to cheat on me." She finished with a woebegone sigh.

"You're not *really* going to see him, are you?" Despite having just finished a whole glass of juice, he craved more of its sweetness. He dug his hand into the back of the fridge and knocked back the gallons of milk like a cat pawing at a rodent inside a hole it escaped into. "I mean, it doesn't matter what he says or does. He's still scum." He found a carton of orange juice, popped the cap off, and chugged it down fast enough to be practically drowned in it.

"Well, he seems like he's going really crazy without me, so I might. I'm not going to lie, I miss him. He keeps apologizing over and over, telling me he wasn't thinking, he was drunk, the usual excuses. I've been there, we all have. I can forgive him if he shows me I have a reason to."

He yanked the phone away from his mouth so that he could let forth a thick belch of epic proportions. He could see Angie cringe even over the phone. Regardless, the release of pressure in his chest was satisfying. "He just didn't know what he had until he lost it. He also probably thinks you dumped him to be with me. Beware the man with low self-esteem."

"You should talk," she mumbled, indicating that it wasn't meant for him to hear.

He heard her anyway. "What's that supposed to mean?"

"Nothing."

"No, really, I want to know. What did you mean by that?"

"Forget it, Cory!" They both snorted in disapproval, but neither of them hung up. "What are you going to do now that you know Derrick broke the window?"

"I'm sure you know what should be done."

"Don't try to start a fight with him, for fuck's sake."

"No, no. At least, not a *physical* fight. We're going to take him to civil court, and you're going to be our witness."

There was an exaggerated cough from her end. She might have been drinking something when her friend reported this plan to her. "I don't know if I can do that."

"Come on, Angie. You're my friend, aren't you? I can count on you."

"It's going to be very awkward for me. Are you really going to put me in that position?"

"You don't have to go. Just write me an affidavit if you want. I know it'd be weird seeing Derrick there."

Silence, just for a moment. Then, "No. No, I'll go. Maybe it'll wake Derrick up a little to see me side with you on this. But I'm doing it for *you*, not your stalker."

Cory grumbled, "He has a name. He's my friend, okay?"

"*I'm* your friend. I've never followed you to work and watched you from the bushes."

"Okay. We'll talk later, Angie."

Angie wasn't ready to let it go, Cory could tell that much, but she agreed to disengage for the time being. "Fine. Let me know if he files a lawsuit." They said their goodbyes and hung up.

Cory knew that Will wouldn't be awake, so he fashioned himself a new fiberglass window for his computer's case while the extra long hours ticked by toward lunch time. He preferred to see and speak to Will, but it would have to wait. Waiting, on the other hand, took some strength.

The diner wasn't as crowded as their previous visit, but Will still hauled around the bag of tension he brought with him everywhere he went. Being in the presence of strangers was more than just an everyday task for him, but a challenge, and he couldn't manage it without shifty-eyed glances and hunched shoulders. He loosened up as soon as they sat, but couldn't sit still, scratching and wiping his skin. His fidgeting began to drive Cory up the wall, so he decided to say something.

"We could sit further in the corner if you'd like."

"No, this is fine," Will exhaled, then lowered to a softer whisper as though someone was listening in on their conversation. "I can see the door."

"Why do you need to see the door?"

"In case I need to escape out of it."

Cory was fascinated with what scenario he might be coming up with in his mind that required fleeing. A robbery, perhaps, or a hostile takeover by a foreign government. Whatever it might have been, Cory didn't ask, because it made little difference. If Will was comfortable, then he was comfortable. After that, he went straight to business. He told him what he and Angie discussed over the phone, and proposed the same thing he had to her earlier, that they sue Derrick.

"I've never gone to court before," he told Cory, twisting his hands together. The surfaces of them were pinkish.

"I'd help you through the whole process."

"Cory, are you sure it's even worth it? I don't even know the value of that window he broke. I can't say I even care that much. I can't afford court costs. I can't even afford gas money." A waitress served them, and once again Will ordered nothing but coffee while Cory ordered a turkey sandwich.

"That's why I want you to do this," he continued when she left. "You need the money, don't you? I'll pay the court costs, and I'll drive you to the courthouse. Come on, Will, you can't have plastic over that shattered window all winter, you'll freeze to death."

"I'm going to anyway. You do realize that, don't you?"

Cory wouldn't allow Will to give up so easily, though it was his dilemma and not his own. "I think it would be good for you to do this. Trust me."

"I… I do. I'm just overwhelmed, is all."

They shared their lunch with one another, and Cory now felt comfortable under Will's watchful eyes, as opposed to the apprehension he felt before. There was so much he wanted to say to his friend, so many questions he had left to ask, but Will seemed perfectly happy sitting there in silence with him. He almost didn't want to wreck the moment by digging up painful history and memories. On the other hand, he knew there was much more to Will than what he had already told him. When he felt Will was comfortable enough, he asked, "Why did you endure so much abuse?"

Slurping on his coffee, he glanced up at Cory over the stained, white rim of porcelain. "I told you, didn't I?"

"You let him beat you because you loved him? Is that the truth?"

Will stared into the dark liquid within his cup. "I don't think you want to hear what's true."

"On the contrary, I really want to know. Why would anyone allow that to go on? Why would anyone lie to the police to save the ass of someone who beat him, knowing that it's only going to happen time and again?"

"I wasn't doing my job as his caretaker, and I was punished for it. That's the balance of all things, Cory. You do what you're asked, without putting up a fight, and you do it devotedly whether you want to or not. If you don't, you need to be punished for that."

It wasn't feasible to Cory that someone would say such a thing with a straight face. "What? Come on, man, you're not serious, are you?"

Will raised his head, looking pained at his mirth. "Of course I am. Society asks you to do things without putting up a fight, to do as you're told, or you get punished for it. Isn't that so?"

Cory frowned when he realized that Will was not, in fact, joking. "Not everyone obeys laws because they fear jail time. Most people are amicable because they're genuinely good people." Will lowered his head once more. "Will, you didn't *deserve* to get beaten up just because you didn't obey Ian. No one *deserves* that."

"What if you ask for it? What if you get some kind of solace out of it? What if you want it because it's familiar to you?" He wiped his mouth after quickly sipping more of his coffee, giving his now-empty mug a glare of disgrace. "What if you think it's the best you'll ever do because you're not worth something greater?"

Sighing, Cory leaned over the table, nearing Will's face. "I'm not saying it's your fault that you feel this way, but clearly, something needs to change. What happens if the next guy you end up with does the same thing? Do you really want to end up in that position a second time?"

"I wasn't betting on anyone desiring me, so it wasn't a concern."

"Well, it should be! You can't let people hurt you like that because you think you deserve punishment." Cory felt Will's clammy palm touch his forearm. He could only glimpse at it, feeling too awkward to return the gesture. His grip was cold, but flexing, a silent form of residual comfort. "Ian's not the first one to do that to you, is he?"

Feeling Cory's arm muscles tense, he slipped his hand away. "It doesn't matter, does it? What difference does it make?"

"It makes a lot of difference, because you'll find someone else to do it."

"Why does this affect you so much?"

He leaned back in the booth, no longer interested in his sandwich. There were so many ways to answer him, and so many directions the conversation could go in, and he knew he had to choose his words carefully, or he could destroy everything. "Because… I don't want to see that happen to you."

"Why?"

A stalwart grunt left Cory's nostrils. Why couldn't he accept that he cared and leave it at that? Did he have to make him say it all? "It's not fair to you. I don't want to think of you getting hurt."

Will was touched, and it showed not only in his smile, but his voice. "So you're saying you care about me."

"Yeah. Yeah I guess that's what I'm saying."

"Was that so hard to say?"

Turning in his seat so that his back was against the wall, Cory stuck his thumbnail in his mouth and chewed on it. "Sort of."

"It's okay, Cory. I care a lot about you, too."

The two men returned home, and Will thanked him for taking him out, despite how cold the whether was getting. Cory said he'd be happy to spend more time with him whenever he wanted to, and even supplied him with his cell phone number. Will was ecstatic at this exchange, regardless of how differently they saw it.

Over the course of the next few weeks, Cory's friendship with Will grew into something more meaningful. He managed to get him to reveal his many likes and dislikes, and for once Cory felt that he wasn't all sadness and brooding, but that there was a man inside of that pale, hollow shell, full of anecdotes and whimsies, of laughter and playfulness. Cory then learned something about his friendship with Will he hadn't considered before: they had a lot in common. Will had liked movies that Cory thought no one else in the world had even heard of. They shared the same taste in music, in television, and in preferred flavored beverages. Will became much more open with him, and told him of the schools he had gone to, his parents, his many romances, and his ephemeral friendships.

One evening, after their kinship had grown into the final days of its third week, Will confessed something to him. "I'm not biologically related to my parents. They adopted me when I was seven."

"Do you remember your biological parents?"

The scent of fresh wine wafted from Will's mouth as he exposed it for a moment. In their silence, a train honked in the distance, and it was thunderous even through the thick stone walls of the basement. "I wish I didn't, but I do."

"Why? What did they do?"

He shook his head, his upper lip tight. "I don't want to talk about it. I don't even want to remember it. You understand, don't you?"

"Of course," Cory answered, now more curious than ever, but respected his privacy. "You don't have to tell me anything you don't want to."

"If I ever do wish to talk, I'm sure you'd be the first one I'd come to."

Cory checked his watch, which was off by two minutes, according to the clock on the wall. It was ten minutes after eleven o'clock, and though he was beginning to yawn, he turned to Will to ask him another question.

"Would you mind if I took you somewhere?"

Will was just finishing up a glass of wine before he answered. "Where would you like to go?"

"It's a place I'd visit all the time while I was growing up. I wanted to show it to you."

"I would love that." He followed him upstairs and outside after they dressed in jackets. He walked alongside Cory obediently as they followed the street's curb, every once in a while guiding him away from cars, though Cory didn't need his aid. "Is it far, this place?"

"Not at all. It's the bridge on Warner Road. You've been there, haven't you?"

"I think so, yes, but…" When Cory broke their linear path to dive off-road, Will followed him into the brush. "Cory! Wait, where are we going?!"

Cory didn't race too far ahead of him, allowing him to catch up. He knew as soon as they entered the clear pathway into the woods that his friend wasn't accustomed to exploring forests. "Just down this path. Follow me, it's all right."

"You're sure we won't get lost?" He knocked some pine needles out of his face as he came up behind him.

"I know my way. I told you I'd come here all the time when I was a kid." Even in the blackness, he could see how uncomfortable Will was. He could even see his hands shaking as he blew warmth into them. They continued to tremble even when shoved into his pockets. His most outstanding feature was the look of dread on his face. "What's wrong?" Cory asked once they came to a small clearing.

Droplets of new rain fell onto his glasses from the crying branches of overhead trees, but the spots now covering his lenses didn't seem to concern him. "You're taking me out to the middle of the woods at night? I'd be lying if I said I wasn't a bit nervous."

He had to laugh. It was too much for him. "You think I want to hurt you?"

"I think everyone wants to hurt me."

"That's not why I brought you here. It's actually quite the opposite." The fear had fallen from his face, only to be replaced by puzzlement. He couldn't blame him for being confused. Unbeknownst to Will, Cory had been planning to bring him to his secret spot under the bridge for a few days now, but never found an appropriate time or way to ask him to come along. Their recent bond had him craving the opportunity to get much more personal with him.

The bridge on Warner Road, or "The Bridge" as he and his childhood friends called it, was a place of sacred gathering visited by him and his buddies throughout his many years of school, an area where they would sneak to in order to engage in careless behavior. He remembered passing a stolen cigarette between each of his peers, drinking liquor that was taken from the cabinet of his friend Patrick's house (which he was subsequently punished for by his parents), and as he grew up, he brought each of his girlfriends under the bridge. The first girl he ever kissed was beside the flowing stream beneath the overpass, and though she ended up being less than impressive as far as girlfriends go, it was a fond memory.

He didn't let on immediately that he had more than one reason for bringing Will there that night. The more he spoke with him, the closer he became with him, and the more he liked him. He was certain that Will wouldn't have a problem with that, so he didn't fear his rejection, but had a lot more trouble admitting it to his own self. Will was most definitely a good friend, but even beneath the denial and inner conflict Cory had been managing lately, he couldn't help but feel that he wanted something else; perhaps even something more.

Never before would he have said that Will was attractive, nor would have even considered thinking it, but now when seeing him smile, he was far more open to the lightheaded sensation sweeping his weary body, as well as the adoration he was beginning to feel.

There was no longer a doubt in his mind that Will made him happy, especially when he could make him laugh. It reminded him of whenever Angie would giggle at his jokes when they were younger, and how charmed he was at her laugh, even when it seemed faked. Will's laugh was not only much warmer, but real. Whenever he could help him forget his troubles, when he'd see him smile, he could forget all that ailed him.

After cutting through long strands of tall grass, dead leaves crunching softly under each of their steady tracks, they came upon a babbling stream underneath a cement bridge. Large stones layered the walls of dirt on either side of the water, each as big as Cory's supple frame. When Cory motioned for him to follow, Will hesitated and muttered, "Are we going to be climbing on all of these rocks?"

"Yeah," Cory told him, matter-of-factly. "It's fun."

"You're not worried about falling into the water?"

"It's just water, Will, it's not lava. If we fall in, so what?"

"I don't like to get wet. A-and it's cold."

Seeing that Will was not going to cooperate, he approached him with his head high. "Let me do the worrying, please." He slipped his hand into Will's open palm and clasped it. After receiving the motivation he needed to follow Cory anywhere, even if it was to death, he eased up, gripping his hand and following him to the set of stones lined diagonally along the stream. After several minutes of climbing and grappling the rough edges of rock, they found a smooth surface where they could sit.

Will placed his rump upon the bumpy stone, but Cory lied on his back and looked up at the stars, folding his hands behind his head. Neither of them said anything for quite some time, spending a quiet moment together. When the timing felt right, Will lied beside Cory, who turned his head toward him, the scratchy points of the rock rubbing on his scalp.

"I'm not even thirty yet," whispered Cory as soon as Will was next to him. "And I already feel like I'm too old."

"How do you think I feel?" Will joked.

"I'd do this kind of thing all the time when I was a kid— climb rocks and trees and shit like that. At a certain age, we just stop, because we have other things, more important things to worry over. Then when you're older, it's suddenly a hell of a lot tougher to climb the same tree that was so easy to climb years ago." When their eyes met, Cory felt an involuntary smile find its way onto his face. "I was such an awkward teenager, the way I flirted with girls all of the time. I thought I was charming. They thought I was an asshole." Will chortled. "I don't blame them. I *was* an asshole. I just didn't realize how much of one I was until it was too late. I found a girl that liked me back, though, when I was fourteen. I brought her here on our first date. She wasn't as into it as I was, and she didn't really appreciate what it meant to me. But I can see that you do."

He fixed his glasses so that his vision was clear enough to see his companion. "Of course I do. It's a part of you, isn't it?"

"You tried so hard, from the moment we first met to get to know me— the whole me. Sure, you did it in an unorthodox way, but you wanted to know who I was, who I really was. I know you said you did it at first because you missed Ian, but Ian eventually didn't influence you. Is he still on your mind, even right now?"

His head made a few serious shakes. "No. I told you, you're nothing like him."

"But I think you wanted it, Will. You wanted to be hurt."

His friend glanced away from him, looking back up at the night sky, which was now covered in hanging clouds. "I didn't *want* Ian to hurt me, but all the same, I didn't fight back, because it felt right. I needed to be controlled." The silence that followed was swift and lingering, and sweat formed on Will's forehead. "I used to be in therapy. It didn't work out for me. I really hope you don't think I'm..." He drew in a shaky, nervous breath. "Screwed up."

"I don't. I appreciate your honesty. I just want you to know that I don't care how much you want it. I'm not going to hurt you like that."

Though it was difficult to move due to the bumps on the granite, Will turned on his side to face him. "What are you saying?"

"I... I don't know." He wouldn't look at him.

"Yes you do."

He propped up into a sitting position, crossing his thin legs. He lowered his head, which dangled towards his chest while he plucked petulantly at small strands of grass sticking up between the layers of rock. "I don't want to say it," he whispered.

"You don't have to. I don't need to hear it." Will sat up as well, their shoulders touching, attached to him like a conjoined twin.

He ripped strands of weeds out of the ground. "I screw up every relationship I get into. I don't know if I'm ready to screw your life up, too. I can't help it, though. I... I want this. Even when it's hard to say, I know I want this." He pressed his head against Will's shoulder, and Will wrapped an arm around him, pulling him close. "You've become a really good friend to me." He felt the tender squeeze of Will's bicep as he clasped him tighter.

"You're my friend too, Cory."

"I want your life to improve. I want you to be happy. I want to make you happy."

"You already do."

"You know what I mean. Don't you?" Will was staring into the middle distance at the hundreds of pine trees when he looked at him, but his cradling arms remained powerful. When he did lower his eyes to him, it happened: his heart pumped, raced at a speed he thought impossible, and he awaited Will's response with bated breath.

"Cory..." He said after a brief hesitation, one which he used to construct his next question. "Are you attracted to me?"

He winced at the painful query that was so easy to answer, and yet was the most pressing one ever asked of him. Honesty would go a long way, he realized that, and it would do no good to continue living in denial. He had to face it at once, and not only tell Will the truth, but also himself.

"Yes," he answered, now with a newfound confidence.

"Would it make you happy if we were together?"

A deep breath filled his lungs, and the air was fresh and clean, not just because of the water, but the atmosphere. "Yes," he said in an alleviating exhale. Once it was out, he discovered just how simple it all was to liberate.

"This isn't a joke, is it?"

A joke? Whenever Cory confessed his attraction to another, he never joked about it, and Will was no exception. He understood that Will was being cautious, and it was a wariness well justified. Not long ago, Cory swore he was heterosexual, that falling for another man was ridiculous in conjecture, let alone in practice. He couldn't blame Will for his bewilderment, because he too was confused by it all, and his voice of reason only now began to shout with full force. It was his proximity to Will, both physical and emotional, that brought this influential feeling forward, and he had to give in to it, or he'd regret it. Cory was not one to live in regret.

Now strengthened with the full awareness of what he favored, he replied, "No. It's not a joke."

Will searched him for deception with looks of skepticism, which Cory had to admit was a mood-killer. They hadn't been friends for years, but he still thought Will could sense his honesty when he presented it. When Cory smiled, showing him his utmost sincerity, he was engulfed by two boney limbs and tugged against Will's thin, frail chest plate. Cory unleashed his inhibitions, as well as his arms, and clung to him with invigorated fervor. "I'll take such good care of you, I promise," Will vowed.

"I know you will. I just want to do the same for you."

"Oh, I'm so happy!" Cory giggled at his repetitive kisses to his head and cheeks. He grabbed Cory's palm and placed it against his chest. "Feel my heart. It's pounding."

Will's heart was indeed thundering rapidly, just as his had been. Their speeds were well timed. "I'm happy too, Will. I think this is the happiest I've ever been."

Before either of them said anything else, Will took his face into his chilled palms, moving hair out of his eyes. Cory didn't fight it any longer— he kissed Will on the mouth, and every second their lips were locked, he grew to enjoy it more. When Will pressed his lips even harder onto Cory's, his enthusiasm invited him to relish in the overpowering enticement, urging him to donate more passion to it. He couldn't remember the last time he kissed someone. He especially couldn't remember the last time he loved it this much.

They made out with each other for a good portion of the night, working their jaws until the tongue wrestling became too exhausting. Eventually Cory climbed into Will's lap, daring him to push to a further base, but he resisted, though he seemed torn. When he distanced himself from his body, as well as his puckered lips, Cory's desperation grew vibrant. Now that he had experienced how wonderful it felt to kiss Will, he wanted to keep doing it until the sun came up. He thought Will might have wanted the same, but when he saw that he was struck with inexplicable regret, he eased him by placing his palms upon his shoulders.

"What's wrong?" He cooed at him, pulling at the fibers of his shirt and stroking the skin of his neck.

"It's a lot to take in, I guess," he voiced, barely audible above the sound of the flowing water. "I still think I'm just dreaming. I don't want to wake up and see that you're gone, that I had... imagined all of this."

He brought his thumb and forefinger to his cheek. "Would you like me to pinch you?"

He gasped, withdrawing, holding his shoulders up to block his face. "No! I-I just mean that now that I have you, I'm afraid to lose you. I know the way that I am. I'll find a way to drive you away."

"Don't talk like that. I wouldn't do this if I wasn't absolutely sure." Cory started kissing Will's neck, but he felt him slip back. When he studied his face, he looked away, staring into the darkness.

"Forgive me," he begged for Cory's patience. "Affection is sort of alien to me. Don't get me wrong, I enjoy what we're doing. It's just been too long since I've done it without..." He paused and sighed, closing his eyes.

"Without what?"

"I imagine you're tired of hearing my sob stories. Besides, it'll ruin the mood. I should be happy that you want me, and I am. It's not that it isn't exciting, either. They're pretty blue right now." He nodded toward his lap and snickered.

Cory echoed his laughter. "Mine too."

"It's getting a bit cold, though, so maybe we should head back."

If it was cold, Cory sure hadn't noticed. His whole body was on fire. "Yeah, you're right. We should."

Once they stood, they brushed dust and stray dirt off of their clothes and climbed their way back to the forest path Cory had led them down, their hands and fingers linked as they headed back to Hunter Street. Will bubbled with excitement the whole way back, and they each had a new spring in their steps. When they arrived to their home street, Will invited Cory to stay with him that night. Anticipating a fun-filled evening, Cory agreed to it, but Will let him down by explaining he didn't want to have sex.

"I just really wanted you to sleep with me," he elucidated.

"I'd like that," Cory said, and followed him into his house. They both went straight down to the basement, and Will turned down the blankets on his bed. He paused when Cory slipped his shirt off and propositioned him with an alluring smirk. "I can't sleep with a shirt on. Hope that's not a problem."

"No. N-not a problem." His fingers clawed at the back of his neck as he rubbed sweat off of it. "Not a problem at all." Cory draped his arms around his neck, but he held his waist at bay with his tight hands. "Don't tempt me," he warned.

"I'm not trying to. I just can't seem to stop touching you. I knew I might like it, but I didn't know I'd like it this much."

"I'm happy you're so excited. I am, too. I just need some time."

"It's okay, I understand. Let's just get some sleep." He was the first to climb into the bed, which was far more comfortable than his own, and he gently sank into its downy softness as he snuggled his head into one of the fluffed pillows. Will hadn't joined him, but instead stood near the side of the bed and stared down at him with dark eyes, almost like he was waiting for something. He didn't speak, didn't move— only his eyes twitched. His look was frightening enough to unnerve Cory, who scooted toward the wall. "Will? What's the matter?"

Will's statuesque form mumbled: "If we're going to be together, and if you're serious about this— about us— I should be completely open and honest with you, right?"

Hairs stood up on his arms. "Yeah. Relationships are based on trust, aren't they?"

"Yes. That's absolutely right. They are."

"Are you okay?"

"I want you to know what you're getting into before you've invested too much time into this."

Fearing that Will might confess to him that he was a murderer or obtained pleasure from torture, his mouth ran dry. "What's going on?"

The argyle sweater Will always wore came up over his head. Right away, Cory saw that the Caucasian color of his skin was hardly visible beneath so many long stripes of pink, white and red covering the surface of his chest, stomach, and arms. Cory jumped out of bed at the first sight of it.

"Jesus!" He exclaimed, having never seen anything like it before. The many patterns of scrapes and scratches covered almost every inch of him, similar to swollen crimson and solid white tattoos. "Did you do this to yourself?!"

Before he gave him an answer, he rolled his wrists around to look at the scars of his forearms. "Yes."

"How long has it been going on?"

"I've been doing it since my parents adopted me. It goes so far back that I can't remember how many times I've done it."

Cory planted his palms on Will's chest and traced his many scars with his fingertips, sensing the stinging pain of every single one. "Why? Why the hell would you do this? Do you like it?"

"I wouldn't go so far as to say I 'like' it. I *need* it." A hiss escaped his lips as he sucked in a deep breath, and his sunken eyes finally met Cory's, which were bulged. He sat on the edge of the bed and Cory sat beside him, unable to look away from the gashes. "My parents found out and did everything in their power to stop it. They put locks on the drawers where they kept knives and they hid all of the razors. They really tried to help me. I know they love me, but they knew as well as I did that just because they hid them didn't mean I was going to stop."

Cory figured something of this magnitude was occurring under his nose, but he had to take it into special consideration now that he swore himself in as Will's boyfriend. He not only wanted, but *needed* to know as much as he could about it. "How often do you do cut yourself like this?"

"Just about every day."

"If you keep cutting, there's going to be nothing left of you."

"I know. That should be enough motivation to quit, but it just isn't. I don't actually want to die, not anymore. It's just that I'm so used to it that I can't bring myself to stop. It comforts me. It keeps me sane. It keeps my head clear. Whenever I'm upset, really upset, it keeps me from losing it completely." He and Cory exchanged heartfelt, though disturbed glances. "I understand if you've changed your mind. This isn't something to be taken lightly."

"Shit," Cory sighed, dropping his face into his open palms with hopelessness. It wasn't a fact that would alter his opinion of Will, but it was a heavy burden to accept. "No," he said after some thought. "No, I haven't changed my mind."

"Don't obligate me," Will advised. "I can make it on my own if you decide to walk out. This is up to you."

"Damn it, Will, stop it. I still have feelings for you. These scars don't change anything. I still think you're beautiful." He leaned against him for comfort, kissing his pale shoulder. "But I don't want to see you hurt yourself. I want to help you."

"What if you can't?"

"Well, I'm going to try."

Will leaned into Cory, nuzzling him like a wounded puppy. "Maybe you're too good for me."

"No. I'm perfect for you."

It was with these words that they both swapped a silent agreement: that Cory was going to stay as long as Will welcomed his assistance, and that he swore that he would do it for as long as he possibly could. He'd stick with it, and him, through thick and thin, through the best and worst, and through the scars that took too long to heal.

10. Expose

On the day that Cory and Will went to the courthouse, flurries of soft snowflakes were falling outside, the sun now in hiding for the upcoming gray season. Cory didn't mind it as much as Will seemed to, who was bundled up in a long-sleeved shirt, sweater, and elongated black coat, his teeth chattering the whole ride there. Cory thought of remarking that his body temperature might be low because of how little food he ate, but he knew it was just another matter that needed addressing lightly as far as Will's habits went.

Angie was waiting inside for them, dressed in a fancy violet top and extended skirt, and she greeted Cory with a powerful hug in the court's winding hallway. "I haven't seen Derrick yet," she verified. Once she got a glimpse of Will for the first time by looking over her friend's shoulder, catching his simple, crooked smile of greeting before he turned his head to hide it, she whispered: "Is that your boyfriend?"

Cory had called Angie the day after his and Will's relationship was official to tell her. To say she was shocked was a gross understatement, and to say she wasn't somewhat repulsed would be a fabrication. She had yet to give him a lecture, but Cory knew that it was coming any day now. "Yeah, Angie, this is Will." He formally introduced them to one another, but when he saw Will retract his hand when Angie reached out to shake it, he winced at the impending outcome of that awkward moment.

"Charming," she scoffed at Cory in disapproval.

"I'm sorry," Will recanted when Cory cocked a brow at him. "I'm pleased to meet you. It's just that my hands are really sweaty and gross, and I didn't want you to feel that."

"What a winner," she said strictly to her friend, but made sure it was in earshot of his significant other.

Cory stepped between them when he saw the sinister glare glinting behind Will's eyeglasses, a look of bitterness he hadn't yet seen Will give in any situation. "Angie, could you at least pretend to be nice to him? If you have a problem with my choices, take it up with me, not with Will."

She turned to him with her lips in a curl, her nose upturned. "I haven't forgotten what he's done to you, or how scared he made you. Neither should you."

He didn't have a reason or explanation for her regarding the way he felt for Will, but even if he had, he knew Angie wouldn't understand it. The shield she had now placed around him was unnecessary, but he appreciated it nonetheless, even if it was the most he had ever seen her care for him. "I'm fine, Angie. I'm not in any danger. Will's more likely to hurt himself than anyone else."

"We'll see."

Before he could retort, she stepped into the courtroom, and he and Will followed her in to the plaintiff podium, guided by the bailiff. Before long, Derrick entered the courtroom as well, scowling at Cory in particular. Had he been a lion, he would have surely ripped out his jugular without a second's thought. It wasn't only primal aggression he saw in Derrick, but utter sadness and rejection when he saw that his ex-girlfriend was standing beside him, opposing him from the other side of the room.

It's his fault this is happening, Cory told his conscience. *He has only himself to blame.*

When the judge emerged, she verified that Derrick was counter-suing Will for the medical bills he incurred to have his neck and ribs checked out. This worried Will from the beginning, but Cory calmed him by stroking his shoulder. When the civil case began, Will couldn't testify without stammering, and the judge had to ask him if he needed some water. When he declined, she asked him to stand up straight and speak more clearly. Will obeyed her the best he could. He told her his story, and Cory confidently spoke as a witness on his behalf. Angie, on the other hand, wasn't as self-assured, but she still spoke out for him as promised to Cory.

Derrick defended his actions by claiming that he wouldn't have done it if Will hadn't brutally beaten him up. When questioned, Will admitted to doing it, but did so to defend Cory. When asked why he didn't file a police report, he said it was because he didn't also want to be arrested along with him.

Unfortunately for Derrick, Angie provided the evidence of his phone call regarding the broken window, so he was forced to pay Will seven hundred dollars for a replacement. Affronted by the verdict, Derrick asked why Will didn't have to pay for his medical bills, only to be told that he shouldn't have asked for trouble.

Outraged, Derrick stormed out of the courtroom, hurt and insulted by the whole ordeal. Angie wouldn't say so out loud, but Cory could tell she felt guilty, even after what Derrick had put her through.

"I'll meet you guys outside at the car," she told the two men, then wisped away.

Stumbling and wiping sweat from his brow, Will turned to his lover and said, "I'm really thirsty."

"I saw a drinking fountain in the hall." He guided him out into the corridor, showing him where the silver spout was located, only to see Derrick in the distance, sitting on a bench which his chin sagging down toward his chest. While Will slurped at the water, he left his side to walk toward Derrick. The scruffy young man didn't speak when Cory came into view, only scowled wolfishly.

He didn't think he'd get many future opportunities to speak with him, and wanted to be absolutely certain of one thing: "Can I rest assured that this bullshit is over now?"

"There isn't much left that you can take from me," he moaned.

"I didn't *take* anything from you." Derrick's eyes welled up with tears, and he was stunned silent by the sight.

"She liked you this whole time, I know she did. She didn't love me anymore. I just wasn't you, and I could never be you. Ever since you moved back here, it's been 'Cory this' and 'Cory that.' She told me you were fuck buddies in high school. Yeah, that's right, I know. How you were in love with her, and she wasn't ready. When you came back, she started seeing you all the time. I'm not stupid. I know what was going on. I tried to find other girls, but all they did was remind me of her. I couldn't do it. Now you convinced her to team up against me. She's with you, isn't she? She left me to be with you. Please, just tell me the truth. Please."

This was a conversation he didn't think he was going to have with Derrick, assuming he was much too immature for it. Although he got his facts incorrect, he was still trying to level with Cory, to talk it out with him. He figured it might have been the only chance he would get to implant the truth into his foolish head. "Derrick, I'm sorry you're having problems with Angie, but I swear I wasn't sleeping with her. I was in love with her a long time ago, but I'm not like that anymore. I did some moving on of my own."

"Don't fucking lie to me," he growled.

"I'm not. I can prove to you that she and I aren't interested in each other."

"And how's that?"

"I have a boyfriend."

Derrick's long, creased frown lifted, and his eyes popped and nearly ejected out of his skull. "What?"

Will was watching from afar now that he had finished quenching his thirst, and spied Cory as he gestured for him to come near. When he obediently came to his side, they swapped a brief kiss on the mouth. Cory saw the locked expression of fear on Derrick's face when William Shepherd gazed down at him, and he hadn't quite seen the contemptuous, lifeless stare Will was giving him. It might have sent a chill up his spine if he had.

"I had nothing to do with your break-up, and I still want nothing to do with it. Can you please just leave me... leave *us*... alone?"

"So you're trying to tell me that Angie was just trying to punish me?" Dubiously, he fixed his never-ending glare back onto his opponent.

"You could put it that way, yeah."

Derrick sneered. "You're so full of it. I don't care if you're queer. That doesn't mean she didn't feel something for you. Maybe when she left me, she didn't know you were a fag."

Placing a hand on Will's shoulder, he held him back when he saw how stiff his stance had become. "Then maybe you should be angry with her, not with me."

"Don't tell me what to do." Derrick suddenly rocketed to his feet with spit flying from his raving mouth as he tossed fierce words from it. "Things changed when *you* came around. *You're* the one who came between us."

"Listen to you," Cory countered, now flustered. "You can't seriously be this stupid, can you? No one can possibly be."

As soon as Derrick lifted his fist, ready to drive it into the surface of Cory's face in hopes to crush his nose to smithereens, Will stepped between them and pulled Cory aside. "That's enough, kid," he interjected, his thin chest raised.

Cory was grateful to see Derrick back away from the brawl, though Will wasn't in much shape to fight. He shrugged and held up both palms in a defensive manner. "Get the hell out of my face." He sat back down on the bench, ceasing his argument.

They both left Derrick alone to stew over his tribulations, joining Angie outside by the car. On the way back home, Cory peered at Angie in the rearview mirror multiple times, until she noticed him looking.

"What," She sighed. "What is it?"

He didn't want to press her, especially in front of Will, who was already uncomfortable enough around her, but he wanted to get to the root of the mystery. "Were you interested in dating me while you were with Derrick?"

Appalled by his accusation, she answered with a soft but exaggerated gasp. "No!"

"Well, he's pretty convinced that you were."

"He's a moron." She rolled her eyes, then unzipped her purse and began to dig into it until she found a pack of cigarettes.

"Since when do you smoke?"

She stuck one of the wrapped sticks of tobacco between her lips and exhaled whirling, white smog after lighting it. "Since now."

Will coughed, and wasn't subtle about it. The winds outdoors had reached near-winter temperatures, but he rolled down his window regardless, bundling up in his shirts and coat. The moment Cory gave him a conciliatory glance, he cleared his throat. "I hate cigarette smoke."

Cory was fully aware that his friend wouldn't like it, but it was his car and his oxygen, as well as Will's. "Angie, can you wait until we get home to do that?"

The smoke cleared from her face, and her nose scrunched up as she squinted at him. "You're kidding, right?"

"No, I'm not."

A long moment's hesitation followed, and then with a jilted huff, she violently mashed her cigarette into backseat's ashtray, muttering something along the lines of "sure, yeah, whatever."

Cory dropped her off at home, thanking her for her help, but she only answered him by slamming the car door and strutting into her apartment. Cory groaned before driving away, looking at Will, who was unsettled by the social disturbance. The loud sounds made him flinch.

"I'm sorry Angie is so... hostile," he soothed. "She just needs some time to get used to you."

"It's not that," he whispered after taking a few steady breaths. "I'm accustomed to being disliked."

"Then what's the matter?"

"Are you certain you've abandoned your passions for her?"

"Are you asking if I'm still in love with her?"

Turning his head toward the window, staring outside at the fresh snow-covered grass, he sighed through his nostrils, steaming the glass. "I might be."

Checking his side and rearview mirrors, he pulled over to the side of the road and shut the car off. Will unbuckled his seatbelt, though Cory didn't understand why. He might have thought that he was going to throw him out of the vehicle. "Let's clear this up right now: Angie is focused on her own feelings, not mine, and I'm focused on you now. Angie and I had our thing when we were younger. It's over with, and I'm not looking to revisit it."

"She was lying, you know." Unsure of what he meant, Cory only gave him a puzzled look, so Will elucidated. "About wanting to date you when she was with Derrick. She might even still want you."

"And how do you know that?"

"She couldn't take her eyes off of you in that courtroom. She smiles when around you, laughs even when it's unnecessary. She's jealous of me, that much I can sense. I think, in all honesty, she was happy that Derrick left so she could try getting with you. Now you're with me. I imagine that stings her quite a bit."

Cory couldn't help but smirk at that, which put Will off. He frowned immediately after. "It doesn't matter. She had her chance with me in high school and passed it up. I just think she hates seeing that I'm happy with you."

"Are you happy?"

Smiling with passionate affection, Cory reached over to the back of Will's skull and softly stroked the short follicles of his hair. "Yeah, I am."

"Even if I'm dragging you down?"

"You're not dragging me down."

Will licked his dried, cracked lips. "Are you sure? Be honest."

"What the hell makes you think that?"

"I know how much more difficult I've already made your life."

Cory simply laughed that comment off. "Shut up, no you haven't. You've improved it."

Will swallowed. He seemed hopeful, but wasn't convinced. "I have?"

"Yes." Leaning across the seats, he pulled Will close to him and kissed him. Will's face glowed and grew warm at his loving touch, and they each smiled.

By the time they reached Hunter Street, a massive downpour thundered overhead. After parking in Will's driveway, they ran into his house so that they wouldn't get soaked, but it didn't help much. Cory shook the water from his long hair as he entered the dry home, and they each stripped their jackets off. Cory meant to ask Will how he wished to spend the afternoon, but he slipped into the bathroom before he could say anything. If it was one thing Cory was used to seeing Will do, it was hide in the restroom. Now that they had been together for over a week, and he was well-informed on Will's self-abusive habits, he worried what he might be doing in there. Most of the time, he never heard a toilet flush while he was in there, and rarely heard the tinkling sound of urination. He didn't want to impose on him, but he also didn't want him carving himself like a Thanksgiving turkey, either.

"Are you okay?" He called from the couch where he was now sitting, having been waiting half an hour.

When Will answered with a resound, "Yeah, I'm fine," it sounded a lot more like, "Mind your own damn business."

"You're not cutting yourself in there, are you?"

"No." He then softly coughed and sniffed.

"You've been in there a long time."

"Damn it, Cory," he grumbled. "I'm fine. I'll be out in a minute."

Cory hadn't yet heard him snap at him like that, and to him, it was very revealing. Did he really want to know what else Will had tucked under his sleeves? As Will finally stepped out, there was again a lack of toilet flush, and his concern grew to unthinkable heights. "You're not sick or anything," he proposed, hoping that Will would take the chance to converse with him and reveal some of the more private things he kept concealed.

"Sick? No." He killed the bright light inside the room, then sat on the couch beside Cory and cuddled up to him, sneaking out a tired yawn, burying his head into his neck. "Do you want to come to bed with me?"

He did, very much so, but not to sleep. He was growing fonder of Will each day that passed, and he was anticipating making love to him. He had never had sex with a man before, and he was excited to experience it for the first time.

"That depends," he whispered in an attempt to be seductive, kissing him.

"On?" Will answered between smooching.

"What we'll be doing in it."

In a dry, nearly emotionless voice, Will confirmed what Cory had wanted to know. "I'd like to have sex with you."

"I thought you weren't into it."

"I never said *that*." It was true that he hadn't, but Cory wasn't sure what other conclusion he could come to when Will avoided it so much. "It's just not something I usually instigate. I don't normally have the freedom." Cory said nothing, only raised a curious eyebrow, but Will eagerly took his hand and pulled him to his feet as he climbed off the couch. He followed Will into the basement and to the bed, standing with locked knees and shuffling feet as he watched Will undress in a mechanical and ritualistic manner. It lacked the passion Cory had been hoping for, and he felt more like Will's medical examiner than his lover when he presented his nude body to him. He studied his many scars once more, and he could see several new ones that Will was very astute at hiding from him, but could also see the outline of every one of his ribs. He looked badly starved of any nutrition, and like he hadn't had a decent meal in years. His hip bones protruded outward beneath his skin like spikes. Every vertebra was outlined along his spine. Will looked unwell in more ways than one, and when Cory laid eyes on the tragedy that was his physical form, he didn't feel turned on, but sad, especially when he had a very weak and shy grin on his face as if to say, "It's not much, but this is me. I hope you like it."

It was clear that Will was already very embarrassed at the state of his own body, so Cory didn't remark on it, though he wanted to drag him to a hospital the second he saw it. "A-aren't you going to get undressed too?" He asked with a embarrassed whisper, cupping his hands over his genitals, which he was also apparently ashamed of exposing.

"Yeah, of course." He pulled his shirt off and tossed it into the same pile Will's clothes were in. Once he was down to his boxers, which was a colorful silk pair with decal patterns of stars, Will climbed into the bed and lied on his back, spread eagle, a position that Cory's loins grew warm at witnessing, but also seemed a bit too systematic to him. Will had taken it automatically without cordial agreement, or imposing anything otherwise. He was used to doing it without argument, and without question, whether he liked it or not. Cory had never seen a woman do this, let alone another man, and it made him curious where it all started, what brought him to behaving in such a manner. Will's methodical treatment to sexual endeavors was a red flag to him that perhaps a lot of the sex Will had in the past might have been against his wish, a "lie back, stay quiet, and it'll be over soon" approach that Cory found disturbing in any case.

With that now in mind, Cory wondered if Will thought their sex should start the same way, if that was what he considered romantic. He, on the other hand, had to disagree if it had been the case. It was the opposite of romantic. It was wrong.

"Are you sure you want to do this, Will?" He tested with fondness when he saw Will's uneasy preparation.

"Yes, Cory. Of course."

"You seem like you don't want to."

"I do." He didn't sound encouraging, but remained firm. "You're okay with being a top, aren't you?" He scratched at various patches of his skin while waiting.

Cory really had no idea. He hadn't done this before. "I guess so, but, are *you* okay with that?"

"I've never known anything else. I've always been… underneath them."

"I know I've wanted to do this with you, and maybe I've been too needy. I'm sorry I've been acting that way. You don't have to do this just for me."

"I want to be intimate with you," he secured. "I want to share this with you. It's important to me. Please."

He figured that this would be the best assurance he would get out of him. If Will truly didn't want to have sex, he might not confess it to him, but he didn't know how to coax that information out of him. He would remain withdrawn, hiding beneath his scars. When Cory finally removed the final article of clothing from his body, he saw Will's legs instinctively close as if barring intruders. His hands were clutching his privates, shaking.

"You're beautiful," Will sighed lovingly as he beckoned him to lie atop his body, though his eyes were begging Cory to let no harm come to him.

He smiled and slipped into bed with him, pressing his chest and stomach against Will's, and his legs opened just enough so that he could slip his hips between them. "So are you," he whispered while sweetly kissing his face.

Will let out a chuckle, though it was wrought with discomfort. "No I'm not. But I appreciate you saying so." He released his crotch, becoming more comfortable at Cory's tenderness.

Initiating the foreplay he longed for with Will, Cory proceeded to deeply kiss him while their entwined, rose-tinted skin collided and writhed with one another's, until they were each so warm, so excited, that there was only one direction to go in. Cory, having been a novice in any kind of gay sex, made great use of Will's guidance, which was oddly formal considering the act they were engaging in. When his knees propped up and his legs opened, Cory was mystified by his decided desire to continue to the actual act of sex. He knew for a fact that the foreplay was exciting for him— the evidence was in his erection— but he seemed to try to move on to the part that he wanted to get over with, as if it was a chore that he didn't want to complete, but would feel better once it was over.

"You want me to just... go in dry?" When Will nodded to confirm, he was perplexed. "Is that going to hurt you?"

His dark, sunken eyes lowered to Cory's worried frown. "I'll be all right." It wasn't really the answer Cory was looking for. It was hardly an answer at all.

Unsure of what else to do, or say for that matter, he slowly and gently eased himself inside of him, instantly feeling a clench as soon as he entered. He did his best to relax him by kissing his neck and face, but Will's eyes never ceased their tight squeezing. He didn't push or thrust, but only tried to comfort him with various forms of warm fondness, only until Will shoved his hips downward like impaling himself on a spike. "Rougher," he begged, though his voice broke into a pained squeak.

Cory froze. He wanted to move harder, but Will looked so sore with the whole ordeal that he felt he was causing him physical injury just by loving on him. "I don't know if I can."

"It's okay, really. I like it rougher."

"I won't hurt you?"

"No," said his lips, but, "Of course it'll hurt, that's the idea," was what his heart conveyed.

He didn't need to ask to know he was fibbing, but Will did admit to him once that sometimes pain and pleasure were one in the same for him. He might not have anything to feel guilty for if Will wanted it. Appeasing his lover's needs, he did as he asked and began thrusting his hips more powerfully. Will approved with lustful, erotic moaning, encouraging the stabbing, heavy jabs further, and it was glorious, heavenly music to Cory's ears. After many long minutes filled with grinding and grunting, Will groaned two little words that altered the course of action, and brought Cory to pause in incredulity.

"Hit me."

At first, he didn't think he heard him right. Maybe he said something else and he misinterpreted it, but he couldn't imagine what else he could have said. "Huh?"

"*Hit me*," Will accentuated now that Cory had stopped hammering his hips. "Hard."

Cory gathered that surprise shouldn't have been his first reaction, but he couldn't wrap his head around this request, no matter how well he thought he knew Will. "No. Why are you asking me to do that?"

"I like it. Please. You won't hurt me, I swear."

With a forlorn sigh, Cory fell against Will's bare, sweaty chest and rested there for a moment, panting from the physical exertion. "I can't."

His lips now curled back, he spoke between his gnashed teeth. "Please!"

Not only puzzled by his anger, but flustered at his lack of options, he snapped, "Will, I can't do that! I don't *want* to do that!"

Will threw his head back against his pillow and shut his eyes, giving up the fight, but was now disillusioned. No longer in the mood to finish their act after such an awkward and unexpected interruption, Cory collapsed atop Will, dismayed at how passionless it all was. Soon after, he could hear Will faintly whimpering, and he didn't know what else to do but cradle him, nudging their cheeks together, feeling the dampness of his tears merge with the sweat on his skin. Will seemed touched by his comfort, and he pulled his weak arms around Cory's neck, holding him tightly.

"I'm so sorry," he said, hushed. "I ruined it. I knew that I would."

"It's okay," Cory mitigated while giving his cheek a tender stroke. "It wasn't ruined."

"You're a terrible liar, Cory Anderson."

He was right, however he did hear in his voice that he was calmed by him showing how little it all bothered him on the outside. "I'm sorry that I couldn't do what you wanted me to."

"I don't blame you for it."

Dragging his palm over his damp cheeks, drying his wet eyes, he planted kisses on his face and jaw line. "I love you."

He pressed his face against his palm sorrowfully, though he looked grateful for his empathy and devotion. "I can't imagine why."

"I love to make you happy."

"You do?" Cory nodded, and Will squeezed him tighter. "I love you too, Cory. More than I thought possible."

"We'll try again some other time. Why don't we just relax for a while and try to enjoy the rest of the afternoon, maybe watch some TV?"

Will agreed to the proposal, and they went straight to the couch together without bothering to put their clothes back on. Instead, Cory pulled a blanket around them to keep warm, which calmed Will so much that he fell asleep against his chest within a short ten minutes. Cory didn't mind his passing out, but rather found it endearing, and he made sure that for the duration of his cozy nap, he didn't release him.

Because Will had little to no food in his home, Cory needed to eat breakfast at his own house before work, and every day his mother saw him, she grew more and more uncomfortable at the hidden truths that neither she nor Cory wanted to bring into a discussion. Perhaps, Cory felt, it was better to leave his frequent absence unspoken of, because an argument would only stress the both of them out, and he didn't exactly want her pounding Will's door down to threaten him, either.

Unfortunately, she couldn't hold it in any longer, and chased her son out of the house one snowy morning while he left to go to work. "Can we save this for later?" He eluded as he unlocked his car doors.

Shivering and hugging her chest to protect from the blistering cold, teeth chattering, she sustained prying information out of him. "Something is going on with you and him, I already know it. It's not going to hurt you to explain it to me."

"I don't see why I have to. What does it matter?" He slipped one leg into the car, intending to get in before she could corner him.

"Honey, you don't know everything about him."

She wasn't just going to let him leave that day without giving him a lecture, and as annoyed he was, he assumed she only wanted his reassurance that he wouldn't become a victim of a domestic crime. "And you do? Really, how well do you know him? How many times have you spoken to him? You just believe a bunch of rumors before you even talk to him or get to know him. He's a good guy, and he treats me really well."

"I don't have to speak to him, Cory. I know him for what he is."

Giving his wristwatch and exaggerative stare, he heaved a sigh. "I'm going to be late for work."

Giving up the fruitless debate, she nodded and turned on her heel to retreat into the house. Now that he had the chance, he vacated the premises and headed to Hot Wire to start another grueling day of convincing people to buy televisions.

Rick, his friend and coworker, had been informed many days ago of Cory's unexplained switch in his concealed sexuality, and seemed happy for him when hearing how pleased he was at the change in his life.

"If it's a man that makes you happy, it makes no difference to me," Rick told him with assurance. "As long as you're content in your relationship."

Cory nodded and grinned from ear to ear. "I think I'm pretty happy. We haven't been together that long, but he already means a lot to me. It's been a long time since I felt that… floating feeling, you know?" Rick agreed with a nod.

"As long as I've known you, you've never been in a relationship. I'd say it's about time."

The sliding entry doors of the electronics store buzzed open, and William Shepherd came bounding in with sentry eyes and exaggerated head twists. He was looking for him, and frantically. Cory saw him approach a couple of his peers, and he assumed he might have been asking where he was.

"Hey, there he is," Cory mentioned to Rick, bewildered. "That's my boyfriend. What's he doing here?" He jogged over to Will as soon as he noticed him, Rick following, and Will's panic-stricken face lit up when his beloved came into view.

"There you are," he sighed with confounded relief before swinging his arms around his neck. Cory nervously eyed his coworkers who gawked at the odd display, some of them snickering. His face glowed. "How's work going?"

"Uh… fine." He cleared his throat and drifted his head back, not only to see into his eyes, but to sever their awkward PDA. "Is everything okay?"

"Not exactly. Do you have a second? I wouldn't want to humiliate you." He faked a half-smile, gazing at their ogling onlookers, and Cory instantly felt a twinge of shame for his embarrassment regarding their obvious romance.

"Yeah, I'm on my break. Let's go outside." As they headed for the employee exit near the back of the store, Cory tried his best not to look at any other member of the Hot Wire staff. He didn't want to feel shy of publicizing his relationship, but he also didn't want to be fired from his job by his homophobic boss. "What's the matter?" He asked once they were alone, standing under a blanket of snowflakes.

"They're coming to shut my electricity off today. I don't have any money. After that, they're probably going to shut off my gas. I don't know what to do, Cory, I'm scared. I could barely afford to drive here."

His first thought was to calm him and stop him from shaking, and he put a hand to his face and stroked it. It seemed to do the trick, and his trembling slowed. "What do you need? Do you need money?"

"I couldn't possibly ask you to give me anything. I just wanted to be near you so that I could relax."

"Well I can't let you starve and freeze, can I? What else do you want me to do?"

"Just hold me for a while." He rested his head upon his chest, and Cory's arms encompassed his waist.

"I love to hold you, Will, but this isn't going to get your electricity turned back on. I have to do something to help you." Will only made a humming, cooing sound as Cory's hand traced his back. "How much do you owe?"

"Maybe a thousand dollars?"

"What?! How the hell do you owe so much?!"

"I haven't been able to pay it in a long time, and they charge late fees and interest. It happens, I suppose."

"I'm going to help you pay for it, okay?"

"Cory, no." He took a step back and shook his head at him. "You really shouldn't."

Speechless for a moment at his avoidance, he asked, "What is with you? I just want to help."

"It's my fault that I'm like this, not yours. I'm not your responsibility."

"What?! Of course you are! We're in this together, Will." Will dipped his head, mumbling something incoherent. "How much will it take them to not shut it off?"

"I have to pay it in full. I know you don't have that kind of money."

"I love you, Will, but for fuck's sake, I wish you hadn't come here. If I send you away without giving you cash, I'm going to feel like shit for it! If you knew I don't have the money to give you, why'd you show up here? To make me feel bad? To make me feel helpless? What am I supposed to do now, just let you rot in that house all alone, with nowhere else to go?"

Now on the verge of tears from Cory's harshness, he fidgeted, shrugging his shoulders and stuffing his hands into his coat pockets. "I'm sorry. I just wanted to see you so I could stop panicking. You always make me feel better. I thought you'd be able to do the same in this case. I guess I was wrong."

He kicked a ball of ice across the lot, letting forth a grunt. "Now I feel even worse. Thanks." Will said nothing, only stood with his feet inches deep in snow, his lower lip twitching. Grumbling to himself, he fished his wallet out of his pocket and thumbed around for several dollar bills. "Don't argue with me, and don't reject this, just take it." He held out a wad of cash, a collective sum of fifty dollars. When Will opened his mouth to decline, he cut him off. "If you don't take this, you're hurting me."

Now understanding where he was coming from, Will took the cash from him. "I wish I could explain to you why this is a bad idea, but I don't want to hurt you any more than I already have."

"What the hell is that supposed to mean?"

"I've told you before. You're too good for me. I can't make that clear enough."

"I'm supposed to treat you well. Besides, isn't that what you wanted? My 'goodness'? That's why you wanted to be with me, isn't it?" Will didn't answer except with an indolent nod. Despite his earlier angry outburst, he lovingly kissed Will's face and mouth, but it only seemed to sadden him as opposed to cheer him up like he hoped. "I don't want to see you go under and think I could have done more to be there for you. Buy yourself something to eat, honey, okay? You're getting skinnier every day I see you."

Will made no comment, nor did he confirm what he would use the money for. Instead, he returned one of Cory's many kisses. "I'll see you tonight. Thank you for being... you."

"Being me is what I do best." He smirked, though he saw something was definitely wrong. "I love you."

"I love you, too." Will sauntered around the building to his car, vanishing into the blanket of white flakes, the tails of his coat swaying and dragging like a tattered curtain.

Now plagued with bad thoughts, not only of Will, but his position with him, the rest of his work day was tougher than usual. He didn't want to believe that Will intentionally weaseled money out of him, but if he had, he knew just how to do it. He was sure he had used that same tactic with people in the past to squeeze dough from their already loose pockets. He was once a thief, after all. He might even still be one, for all Cory knew.

It's possible that he has moved on from that chapter in his life, Cory weighed forlornly. *But it's also possible that he hasn't. If he's not eating food, and not paying his bills, where does the money go? When he sold two of his paintings the other week, the money he earned from it vanished so quickly that I wasn't sure he even received it. What is he spending it on?*

He banished the thought from his mind that Will was deceitful, possibly even manipulative. He didn't want to believe he could fall in love so easily with someone like that, because it would also mean that there was something wrong with his personality. He wasn't that foolish, was he?

His heart remained heavy until he arrived home. He had thought about it all day until it was time to clock out, even considered that his mother had been right all this time. Perhaps he was just being paranoid, but he decided to hear her out on the topic for once. His mother was still at work when he came in, so he waited patiently for an hour or so, sitting at the dining table while sifting through junk mail addressed to him over a quick bowl of cereal.

When Samantha entered the house, she was surprised to see her son there, and even more stunned when he approached her with concern. "Mom," he uttered while she hung up her thick winter coat. "I want you to be honest with me and tell me why you hate Will so much."

"Can't I relax for a while before we have this discussion?" She offered while striding into the kitchen.

"You've wanted to have it with me all this time, haven't you? Now's your chance to explain."

"I don't know, Cory. He's…" She paused as she opened the refrigerator door, shoving her arm inside. Objects rattled around on the wire shelves. "I've heard things. People… talk."

He sat down at the table. "What did you hear?"

"He and that boyfriend of his fought almost every day. I know he got beaten, and I feel bad for him regarding that whole issue. When his partner died, a rumor went around that he killed him."

I guess I should have expected this, Cory pondered. *Mom would believe crop circles were done by aliens if someone told her so. Dad used to tease her and tell her that those fake horror documentaries were real. It kept her awake for days. Guess he regretted it after that.*

"Ian died in a drunk-driving accident," Cory clarified. "Even the police told me that, and that he was a total lush."

"He was. He was always drinking, all the time, then screamed and yelled at Mister Shepherd. I called the police more than once on them, because the shouting and crying got so bad. Every time the cops came, Mister Shepherd would send them away. I didn't understand why he would do such a thing, and I came to wonder what kind of man he was. I didn't understand him." Samantha took the ground coffee and filters out of the cupboard and began prepping the pot on the counter. "When I met him, I felt so chilled. There was no life in his eyes, just sadness."

"And you resented him for that?"

"No, honey, I didn't. But after I while, I started to think something was very off. He'd sleep during the day and pace around his house at night. He didn't speak to anyone. He let the lawn go. Then his boyfriend died. The whole block started rumors, suspected him of murder. He became even more of a recluse after that. I don't know, maybe it's our fault he behaves that way now. I don't know how kindly I would take to being called a murderer." She shook her head as she poured fresh coffee into a clean mug. Cory was surprised at her empathetic view on it. He didn't expect it. "All the same, I could tell that you liked him when you started speaking to him. I wasn't trying to control you. I was trying to protect you. I didn't want you to end up dead if the rumors were actually true. Now I don't even know if I believe them."

She knew? She knew he liked Will? How could she have known such a thing? Even he had no idea. Was it really so obvious that he was attracted to him, even when there were no visible signs of homosexuality in him? Perhaps, he thought, there always were signs, ones he couldn't identify. Just like many things about his personality, his mother could pinpoint them without him even realizing it. "How could you tell?"

"Your mannerisms change when you like someone," Samantha told him. "Determined. Stubborn. You get it from your father. He was the same way with me when we first met." Her voice lowered as she relived the memory to her oldest child. Her frown was deep and heavy. "My parents didn't like him, either." She laughed at the touch of irony. "I'm sorry, Cory, but when you found out Mister Shepherd was stalking you, I was terrified, because I remembered what everyone said. But I see how happy you are now that you're with him, and I don't want to get in the way of that because I'm paranoid. Please tell me he hasn't given you any thought that he might hurt you. If you do, I want you to call the police right away."

Once he had the opportunity to speak again, he had forgotten how. He didn't know that it was so obvious he was attracted to Will from the start, but his mother knew him better than he knew himself. "No. No, no, of course not. Will's not like that, mom. He's actually really sweet."

"I guess I'll have to believe you." Her voice shook with uncertainty.

"Really. He's not going to hurt me. Maybe it's just the high of being in love, but I trust him."

If I love him, I should trust him. Shouldn't I?

"Even so," his mother went on forcefully. "I want you to be careful. I don't want to lose my only son."

"I'll be fine, mom. You should talk to Will. You might even like him once you get to know him."

"I'll think it over." She only took one sip from her mug before Cory got out of his chair. "Are you going over there now?"

"Yeah. I have to see how he's doing. He's going to lose his electricity."

"I'll see you in the morning then, honey." She followed this with a sigh.

Cory said his goodbyes to his mother, as well as his oldest sister when she came down the stairs, and jogged to the house next door, slipping occasionally on icy patches. The first thing he noticed was that Will's door was unlocked, so he didn't bother knocking. He instead slipped inside, calling his name when seeing the living room was vacant. The first room he checked was the bathroom. Upon inspection, even with the door closed he could see it was occupied with the light on, but it was completely silent inside. He rapped twice on the chipped and scratched wooden frame, putting his ear against the panel. "Will?" There was no answer, or any other indication that he was inside. He twisted the handle, which was curiously unlocked, and slowly pushed the creaking door.

Sitting slouched on the filthy bathroom floor, William Shepherd was wedged between the toilet and the tub, a distant, spaced-out look in his eye, even as he turned his head toward the doorway where Cory now stood. Though he didn't seem to have the energy to stand, he had enough to give Cory a look of alarm. Other than a pair of torn briefs, he was nude, and his legs were outstretched with his feet pressed against the stained wall, a stream of fresh, crimson blood snaking down his left forearm. Clutched in his fingertips was a small, thin straw, dark blue in color, dented and worn from frequent use. Resting on the floor beside him was a handheld mirror stained off-white from a powdery substance.

Will's wide eyes never blinked, but his lower lip quivered. It took Cory more than a few seconds to understand what he had just walked in on, that Will was not expecting him to do so, and that he may have just come to a crossroads, one where his choice in direction would be a very dire decision either way.

Just how important to him was Will? He cared enough for him to be very disturbed by what he was looking at, thinking only to race to his side without thoughts of consequence or even any deposition. He meant what he said when he told him he wanted to help him, to be good for him, and he wouldn't go back on that promise, but he had never dealt with— or fallen in love with, for that matter— a drug addict.

Will didn't move, and perhaps he was unable to. Cory had no clue what it was he had just snorted. His pupils were pinned, nearly microscopic black dots in his grayish-blue irises, and his breathing was slowed. The blood on his arm was from a fresh, somewhat deep cut he had inflicted on his forearm, one that looked non-fatal from Cory's view, but still pretty nasty. His opposite hand, the one crumpled on the floor against the tub hidden from view, was the one holding the razor he had utilized for the job. By looking at the scene, he could surmise that Will used the razor first to chop up whatever drug he was snorting, used the straw to suck it in, then proceeded to engage in his other harmful addiction.

Now kneeling before his wounded boyfriend, who had by now shut his eyes to avoid looking at him, and maybe keep from seeing his disappointed face, he checked the open wound on his arm. From what it looked like, he had cut over two to three existing scars, overlapping them by creating new ones. After quickly unraveling almost a couple of feet worth of toilet paper from the roll, he applied it to the fresh cut with pressure. He hadn't yet addressed Will's drug use, but he didn't plan to pretend he never saw it. Will didn't resist his aid, but he was much too mortified to speak to him. If he hadn't been slowly oscillating his head, Cory would have thought him dead.

With the toilet paper pressed onto the cut, Cory ravaged the medicine cabinet for antiseptics. Once he found a small bottle of peroxide, he kneeled back down to Will, and at last, his limp, lifeless hands twitched.

"I wouldn't worry, sweetheart." It was the first thing he said to him since Cory caught him, and his voice was so thick with remorse that it even caused Cory pain. "It's not infected. My razors are clean. I'm not going to die."

"Did you even see how deep this cut is?" Cory snapped.

"I've cut a lot deeper than that before. Trust me, it'll be fine."

He ripped the toilet paper off of the new scar. "You call this *fine*?!" Will winced at his shouting, inching further against the tub, expecting to get slapped. It dawned on Cory that if he had hit Will for doing what he did, it wouldn't be the first time he was struck down for it. "You're sitting in the bathroom in your underwear cutting up your arms and snorting God knows what! You can't possibly tell me that you don't see anything wrong with this!"

"I'm sorry. I've been doing it for so long that it's all second nature to me."

"What did you take?" Demanded Cory as he applied antiseptic to his cut, regardless of what Will told him. "What have you been snorting?"

"Are you going to hit me?" It was unclear whether he was fearful or hopeful, but it sounded like a mixture of both.

"No," he grunted as he pressed the tissues back onto his arm. "You know I wouldn't. Just tell me what you've been taking."

"Oxycodone, usually. Not to get high, though, not anymore. I can barely afford the pills anymore, so I have to essentially use them to avoid withdrawal symptoms whenever I'm able to get my hands on them. I've been snorting them for years, so if I go through withdrawals... let's just say that coming down with the worst virus in the world would be a walk in the park compared to it." Cory was hesitant in replying, so he went on. "You came home a lot earlier than I expected you. I wouldn't have allowed you to see me like this if I knew you were getting off work so soon."

After dabbing the tissues onto his skin a few more times, the bleeding seemed to slow down, and he searched the cabinet once more for bandages. "How long were you planning to keep this hidden from me?"

Resting his head against the cold porcelain tub, Will made an achy sound of sleepiness. "Until a moment like this, I suppose."

"You were never going to tell me?"

"Honestly, Cory. If you were addicted to a drug, would you inform me? I'm afraid enough as it is of losing you. Even my parents don't know. It's not exactly something you go around telling people."

"But you're supposed to trust me, Will. I'm supposed to trust you, too, but I can't if you don't act like a trustworthy person." Cory ripped open the paper packaging of a bandage and removed it, which he then placed over the large cut.

Will watched him as he mended his injury, wriggling his fingers. "You're so good natured that I assumed you'd hate that part of me, and that you might leave. I didn't want you to."

This new revelation wasn't all too surprising, but it was overwhelming. Every time he turned around, something else was wrong with Will; he had another problem that required aid, another situation that needed attention, and he was the only one around to do anything about it. "I want us to work out." He meant to say this to himself rather than his partner.

"I do too."

"If we're going to be serious about each other, we have to tell each other the truth. We can't keep secrets anymore. Okay?"

The Adam's apple in Will's throat twitched as he swallowed, warming up under Cory's firm, serious stare. "The pills… I bought them with the money you gave me today."

Cory groaned, "I told you to buy food with it, Will! Why did you do this?"

"I told you earlier that you didn't understand what you had done. You're supporting a bad side of me, Cory. I'm sorry."

In response, Cory merely planted his face drably into the palms of his hands. He felt compelled to finish their relationship and walk out, but if Will really was in this much pain, he needed him more than ever. There was an absolute challenge in helping Will to reclaim a healthy lifestyle, but he would not allow him to face it alone.

11. Supplicate

In the following couple of weeks into his relationship with Will, Cory remained ever vigilant to his addictive behaviors. It bothered him that he didn't seem to be eating. No matter how hard he tried to convince him to put any kind of food into his mouth, he wouldn't bother. In time, it frustrated him more than it should have. Did he have to beg him? Get down on his knees and plead that he eat something, just one measly piece of toast or even an apple? Surely he could do that for him just to make him happy.

Will didn't like it, but Cory began to pressure him into going to a rehabilitation center. He told him, with exasperation, how he hated hospitals, but never made clear his reasoning. He explained that he would take the horrible sickness of withdrawals over a hospital any day, and Cory was forced to believe him on that point. Though it was a little more than maddening, he tried to steer him off of a path of habitual pill-snorting, but Will made it evident that it wasn't exactly fun for him. It was a requirement.

"I won't deny that I miss the euphoric feeling, though," he said to Cory one day just after inhaling a line of ground medicine, doing so by the light of the sun streaming in through the window now that all electricity had been shut off. "It's not as good anymore. I wish I could afford something stronger."

Cory, sitting beside him on the couch, was bundled in his jacket now that the temperatures were dropping. "I'm glad you can't. It's bad enough that you're doing oxy."

"If I was brave enough, I'd deal with the withdrawals, but I'm not. There are some forms of pain I just can't tolerate."

After another few days of Cory worrying over and taking care of him, Will tried to repay his generosity by initiating sex with him, this time showing actual interest in it. When Will had actually put the effort into it, he was alluring and seductive, and Cory's sustained and growing attraction to him only strengthened when seeing and feeling him come on to him. This time around, there were no sudden requests for violence, and Cory was allowed to move at a chosen pace, making for a much more comfortable scenario that the both of them enjoyed. Will's satisfaction meant the world to him, and if he could make him happy in every way possible, he was doing his job correctly.

During the passionate tumble, Will still seemed rather distracted, lost in his own world, but Cory didn't hold it against him. He expected some degree of physical distance.

Following their intimate moment, Cory talked Will into eating something, even if it was something as small as grapes. He downed it as a child would do penicillin, but didn't complain. It wasn't much, but Cory considered it a form of progress, and saw it as a sign that Will was willing to listen to him.

During a relaxing weekend, one in which Will was much peppier and upbeat than usual, Cory got a call from Angie. He hadn't heard his phone ringing the first couple of times during a shower he and Will were taking together, but he noticed the blinking light on his cell phone indicating a voicemail as soon as he entered the basement studio-bedroom. He put the phone to his ear to hear the message, hushing Will with a waving hand gesture to stifle his whistling for a moment. The affronted "don't shush me" expression on his face was too adorable for him not to smile at.

"Hey it's me," his distressed friend sighed. "Just call me or come over when you get a chance. I need someone to talk to."

When he shut his phone off, Will appeared to notice his apprehension. "Is everything okay?" He asked.

"That was Angie. She sounded really upset." He stripped off the towel he was holding around his waist and started getting dressed. "Maybe we should pay her a visit today."

"We?" He chuckled at his suggestion, and Cory fell silent as he pulled his navy jeans up to his hips. "I don't think she likes me very much. It would probably be better for you to go alone."

"What if Derrick is there? I apparently can't outmatch him in a fight, so if he wanted to kick my ass, he could."

"He's weaker than he looks." This rigid statement caused Cory to frown. "Besides, I doubt he's going to mess with you again after everything that's happened."

"I don't know. He's not a very rational thinker. You heard him at the courthouse." After a short nod from his partner, he continued. "Angie's going to have to get used to you whether she likes it or not, if we're going to remain friends."

Will only shrugged, accepting his conditions. They left the house as soon as they had clothes on, enclosed in coats for the breeze outdoors. During the drive to her apartment, Cory phoned her back to let her know they were coming.

Angie hugged Cory as soon as she opened the door for them, her whole body quaking while in his clutches. He did his best to calm her as she invited them both in, though she was more reluctant to granting Will entrance. While his friend clung tightly to his neck, Cory didn't have to look at Will to sense that he was bothered. He took a step back to stop a fight from erupting, looking Angie in her glazed eyes.

He guided her to the couch, letting her sit while he rested in a chair close by. "What happened?"

"Take a guess."

"Derrick? What'd he do?"

"You won't believe what I found in my room." Until she had reached for it, Cory hadn't noticed the small digital camera sitting on the coffee table. "He left this here when I threw him out. You know what I found on it? Videos of us having sex. I didn't even know he was recording us."

"What did he do with the videos?"

"I asked him. He wouldn't tell me." She slapped the camera back onto the table, one that came across as a few hundred dollars in value. "I tried to get him to 'fess up, but I know he probably collects them. Maybe he still watches them, I don't know."

"I'm sorry, Angie. I'm sure he's not showing them to anybody and he's just keeping them to look back on good times." Angie snorted, silencing him.

"He knows to ask my permission when he wants to do things like that." As Will sat down on the floor beside Cory, taking his hand for a visual emphasis on his link with him, Angie turned away her upturned lip. "That's not all. I think he has a copy of the key to my apartment. I told him to give me his key when he moved out and back in with his parents, but I think he made a new one first. He's been in here while I was at work, I know he has. I never told him he could come in here at all, unless we set dates to meet up."

"Have you called the police? Because if not, you should."

"His name is on the lease. I'm not legally allowed to throw him out the way I did. He could actually end up taking *me* to court this time. With his name on the lease and with me not formally evicting him, I can't even go to the cops." She shrugged and lit up a cigarette. "I don't want to call the cops on him anyway. It's not like he's hurting me." She puffed, then exhaled. "Maybe if I ask him nicely, he'll bring the copied key back."

"It sounds like you want to keep the little pest in your life," Will added his two cents. "Why? It's asinine."

"I'm sorry," Angie retorted. "Are you speaking to me like you know me? I'm pretty sure you don't. Do you really think it was *asinine* of me to toss him on the street after what he did to Cory?"

"Don't pretend like you care for Cory."

"What the hell do you mean by that?!"

"Will, it's okay." Even as Cory attempted to put a verbal barricade between his lover and friend, he could tell it had a weak impact. "Leave it alone."

"What do you think I mean?" Will went on. "From what I can tell so far of Derrick, he's a self-important misanthrope with no morals, and you seem relatively enamored with that. You threw him on the street only to imply you'd welcome him back if he begged you enough. It's pathetic, if you don't mind me saying so."

Angie stood, directing her insidious gaze onto Will's stained eyewear. "I don't think *you* have any room to call someone pathetic."

"Whoa, whoa," Cory interjected, easing Angie back into a sitting position. "Cool it, all right? Angie, I'm sorry. Will is... direct, sometimes." He ignored Will's disappointed frown and sinking, shamed head. "I do have to wonder, though. Is Derrick worth how upset you're getting?"

"You know how much it sucks being lonely."

Cory had no comment on that particular remark. It might have been harmful to agree, no matter how much he did. "Maybe you should stay with your parents for a few days." Before she could protest, he pressed on. "I know you don't want to do that, but it's for your own safety. Whether or not you want Derrick back in your life, he's a really violent guy. Talk this whole thing out with your landlord, too. Maybe he can help you. I don't want to see you get hurt, Angie."

She wiped her eyes when they began to rain clear tears. "He wouldn't get violent with me. Derrick may have a bit of an anger problem, but the last thing he'd ever do is hit me. He's too protective."

"Protective," Will replayed in a scoff. "Not a word I'd choose to describe such an individual."

Though she didn't get up off of the couch this time, she did tilt her head and roll her eyes. The tension between both her and Will made Cory uncomfortable enough, but it grew thicker each passing second and became almost unbearable. "I know him a little better than you do. Just because you almost broke his neck doesn't mean you know anything about him. He and I have been together for *years*. You know, a real, serious relationship, not some creepy secret crush that turned into a fling."

Cory knew she was hinting at his relationship with Will, but he tried not to let it get to him, despite the itch to protest. "In all of those years, he never took his anger out on you?" He asked, knowing Will had the same question on his mind, but might have asked it a bit more sarcastically.

Turning back to her friend, her posture became more relaxed. "No. Not physically. He's broken things... some of *my* things... but I knew he did because he didn't want to break any of my bones. He's shown me in his own way that he loves me."

Both Angie and Cory jumped, startled, when Will exploded into insane cackles. Cory nervously giggled alongside him, but he would never say out loud that it frightened him. Sometimes his laugh was so bright and jovial, and other times, sadistic.

Will spoke as soon as his crazy fit of giggles ended. "Are you so sure he loves you? Give it time. He'll do something he can't take back."

"No," Angie sighed. "I don't believe that. He would have hit me before now. He never did."

This very declaration seemed to open an exposed wound in him. "If you take him back... he will. He will, and it'll be too late to go back. You'll be sitting in piles of broken glass and your burnt dinner that he threw at you. Broken objects become broken hearts, then broken wrists and broken jaws."

Angie stood her ground. "Not Derrick. Never. Call him whatever you like, and see him any way you want to, but deep down, he's soft, he's sentimental, and he cares. He cares about me."

"But he hurt Cory," Will continued, unable to drop the subject, despite Cory's rebuking glances. "You seem awfully okay with that."

Cory placed a tight hand upon his brow and stroked it while letting out a soft groan. "Guys, please, don't argue. Will, Angie can take care of herself, she never asked for your therapy."

They both ignored him, and Angie threw her hands into the air. "I don't know what you want me to say... *Will*. When Derrick and I got together, I knew he was sort of the violent type. Did I want that in a man?" She shrugged and looked away, outside her window. "Maybe. When I saw how pissed he'd get when another guy flirted with me, I kind of liked it. I liked that he fought for me. I liked that I mattered. That doesn't mean I wanted him to hurt my friend. Cory isn't blameless, either, though. He knows just what to say to set another guy off, and he probably said something just like that to Derrick. He pushed his buttons, I just know it." Will opened his mouth with a tight jaw and clenched teeth, ready to bark out another scandalous insult, but she interrupted him. "I know. That doesn't make it right. As for his cheating on me... he told me he didn't. I believe him."

"Of course you do," Will huffed. "You'll believe it all, just to feel secure."

It was then that Angie became fed up with his observations. "I'm sorry, but what the hell is your problem?"

"Let's just drop it," Cory interjected, wanting to avoid getting between a screaming match. He looked especially at Will as a lion tamer would to an unruly beast.

"He'll come home with a big bouquet of flowers and big fucking smile on his face," Will continued, not taking Cory's advice, or submitting to the whip. "And you won't have any idea. 'Hi, honey,' he'll say with his fingers crossed behind his back. 'I missed you! How was your day? Mind if I stick my dick in someone else from now on, then have you suck it'?!"

"Will, for fuck's sake! Just *stop*! *Drop it!*"

The crack of the whip this time was striking in Will's ears, and he pulled his knees to his chest in defense, tucking his chin between them and hugged them tightly. *I'll shut up, just don't hit me,* was what this pose seemed to chant. Cory cursed under his breath. He never wanted to be the one to snap at Will, to give him any sort of impression that he would react to his ways with violence. On the other hand, it was not the appropriate place or time to get so personal, and Will seemed insistent on dragging his past into every discussion he had with another human being. Cory couldn't help but feel a little frustrated about that, regardless of his love for Will.

There was a long, awkward silence, until Angie sighed. "If Derrick does still have a key to the place, there isn't much I can do. Maybe he and I will discuss it over dinner or something. If he lets me know how much I mean to him, I might test him to see what he's willing to do for me. I'll confront him on the tapes, too. He better not have put them on the Internet or so help me…"

While stroking Will on the head to ease his stress, and to keep threatening tears from falling, Cory said, "It's your life, Angie. I can't tell you how to live it. You just need to be careful. You can't just turn off violence. Even if he promises not to hurt you or anyone else again, can you really trust that? All it takes is for you to say or do one wrong thing…"

"Even then, Cory. Derrick would never hurt me. Not like that."

"I guess even scum need standards," Will whispered, to himself and no one else. He hadn't heard Angie's remark on him not understanding how irony works, which Cory was grateful for. One argument was enough for the day.

Following yet another pregnant pause, Angie turned back to Cory. "Thanks for being here for me. You didn't have to drive out here, but I'm glad you did. I miss the company."

"You don't have to thank me. Keep me posted on the situation. Let me know if I can help you."

"I will." She watched her friend stand up and begin buttoning his coat, Will following suit, and she too got up and blocked the doorway. "You're not leaving already, are you?"

"I think if you and Will spend another second together, you might tear each other's throats out. I want you guys to get along, but I don't see that happening."

"I'm sorry, Cory. He's just..." Seeing her friend lower his head, breaking their hardened stare, she sighed. "Never mind. You seem happier, and I should be glad."

"He's not as bad as he seems. He has flaws, but we all do. I'll talk to him." Angie remained silent. "Please, don't judge him. Don't hate him. Underneath it all... there are things about him. Amazing things."

"You don't have to convince me. I'm not interested in him. What matters is what you think."

Cory nodded, then hugged her. "I'll see you again soon."

"Drive safe. It's dangerous out there."

The road home was now covered in heavy snow, and the falling flakes were massive in size, blinding Cory's view of the road. Even with his wiper blades on a high setting and the guiding lights of the cars in front of him, he drove far under the speed limit to keep from crashing into a ditch. His fellow drivers, especially those behind him, seemed to have fewer worries regarding the weather, and honked at him to indicate he should be going faster.

"Fucking pricks," he grumbled while maintaining a slow speed. "Fine, go faster! Crash for all I care!"

"You seem a little tense," Will noticed, then gently caressed Cory's hand as it gripped the steering wheel. "It's okay. We'll get home."

"I know, I know." He relaxed at Will's soft voice and touch. "Listen... about Angie..."

"I know I should have kept my mouth shut." Cory glanced at him out of the corner of his eye, then looked back at the swirling blizzard encompassing them. "I just remember what she did to you. You told me she hurt you. Sometimes she talks down to you, and I... I overreacted to that."

"She did hurt me. But we're still friends. We grew up." His mouth twisted at the corners. "It's my call how to handle it, not yours."

"I thought you said we were in this together. That we were each other's responsibility. If she chooses to date that guy and he goes on harassing you, that's just as much my business as it is yours. If she continues to love him, after what he did to you, how can you forgive her for that?"

"Because she's my friend, Will. She might not make the best choices all the time, but she's important to me, just as you are." Once Cory put both Will and Angie in the same category, he huffed through his nostrils in disapproval. "Yes, Will. You are *both* important to me. You're my boyfriend, whether or not she loathes the idea, and she's my friend, even if you scoff at it."

"She's a fool. That's all I'm saying. A damn fool."

Cory didn't mean to, but he smirked at his hypocrisy. "Were you never foolish when it came to love? What about Ian? I'd call you foolish for some of that."

"Of course I was! That's exactly my point! I was only trying to help her by speaking from experience. She chose to ignore it. That's all I was doing. Honest."

"Maybe she doesn't want your help. Maybe she doesn't want your advice. She's a grown woman. She can take care of herself." He rode on the breaks over a patch of ice, his heart racing for a moment as he skidded. Will asked if he was okay. He nodded. "I think you wanted to fight with her, challenge her or something. I think... and forgive me if this comes out wrong... that you enjoy fighting. It's like you were waiting for me to slap you."

"No. I don't want that. I don't *think* I do." He sighed, pressing his head against the window. "I'm sorry. I know I'm a fuck-up, okay? As each day goes by, I feel like I barely know myself anymore. Sometimes I don't even feel like me. Does that make sense to you?"

"Who do you feel like if not yourself?"

"I don't know. Someone *else*. I can't explain it well enough. You ever get the sense that you're being...?" He paused, then shrank downward in his seat and hid his face in the folds of his coat. "N-never mind."

Cory *did* never mind. He wanted to discuss "being followed" no more than Will wanted to admit to following him. "How much do you love me?"

"More than anything."

"If I told you I felt that something was wrong, would you try to fix it for me?"

"I would try." Fear caused him to quake, though it could have been the cold. The look in his eyes said it was the former. "W-what do you think is wrong with me?"

"I want you to go to rehab."

Will sighed, aggravated. "I can't do that."

"You don't have to go to a hospital. You could deal with the withdrawals at home. I'd take care of you."

Will's frustration shifted to adoration, and he smiled when he heard this, stroking Cory on the shoulder. "I know you would, but I'd feel guilty if you missed work. Even though you haven't been sleeping much at your own home, your mother still relies on you for that money. If I get sick, it's going to be a long process to get through it."

"They have medications they can give you for that, don't they? You could see a doctor and get some prescribed."

"I'm not exactly rolling in Benjamins."

"I'll pay for it. I'll take care of everything if you just try. The reason why you're in debt in the first place is because of the habit." A black car swerved in front of him and he was forced to slam his breaks, skidding in place for a moment. Angered, he bleated his horn. "Fucking Michigan drivers," he mumbled. Once he was back on his steady path, he sustained his lecture. "If you get rid of the source of the problem, you can work back up again."

"Would you say that I'm the source of *your* problems?"

His lips went taught as he thought how to best answer such a direct query. He dodged it just as Will had snaked around the issue at hand. "I want you to feel better, Will. You make me happy, but you'd make me even happier if you quit drugs."

"I don't know if I'm strong enough, even for your sake. Believe me, I wish it was that easy. Besides, you shouldn't have to pay for me to get better."

"You're right, I shouldn't. You should be trying to help yourself."

Pulling up into the driveway of Will's address, Will left the vehicle before it even came to a complete halt. Cory first thought that he was angry with him, but as soon as he shut the engine off and joined him on his front porch, he saw what was really bothering him. A small note was taped to his door, a pink slip with large, bold text stating the words **FINAL NOTICE**.

"Great," he snarled while wiping snowflakes out of his hair and entering his house. Cory followed him in, and saw him toss the note onto the coffee table, as well as rip his coat off and throw it onto the couch, before walking into the bathroom. He spied the name of a gas company on the note, and read that in less than a week, they were going to shut off the gas in Will's home. He rushed to the bathroom, watching him feverishly open a zipped leather bag.

"Will, slow down a second. What are you doing?"

"Where the hell are all of my new razors?" He barked with a tightened jaw and clenched teeth. The question wasn't intended for anyone in particular. "God damn it!"

"Would you calm down?" He grabbed the tail of the bag and did his best to fight it away from him. Will pulled with unexpected strength, ripping it from Cory's hands, only to send several silver blades scattering all over the stained floor.

Immediately dropping to his knees, he panted like a raving madman as he gathered them up like pulling eggs back into the safety of their nest. "Now look what you've done!" He snapped. "They're all dirty now! They need to be disinfected!"

Cory was speechless, beside himself at his strange, unruly behavior that seemed to come completely out of nowhere. "Relax," he comforted, dropping to his eye level. Will's head only shook from side to side as if it were a heavy stone dangling from a wire, and refused to make eye contact.

"You don't understand." He muttered in long sequences without pause as he collected his sharp objects one by one, chucking them into the sink. "They're dirty. They need to be soaked in alcohol now. They need to be washed, because the floor is filthy, it's utterly filthy, and they need to be washed. I can't cut myself with dirty blades. Do you want me to get infections?" His hand dove into the medicine cabinet, where he grabbed a bottle of rubbing alcohol. He began to fanatically dump the clear liquid onto the blades inside of the sink. He poured so much that the burning smell was overpowering. "Do you think I want to go to that place? That awful place?!" Whatever "place" he was referring to was a mystery to Cory. "I can't, I can't, I have bills I can't afford and I'm almost out of oxy and I have *nothing*. What am I going to do? I need to clean these, I need to cut, I need to, I need-"

"*Will!*" His sudden sharp yell silenced him, and his hysterical sobbing and babbling halted. "Take a deep breath, okay? Just breathe." Bracing himself on the edge of the bathroom counter, his head low, he drew in slow, deep breaths, his back and chest rising and falling. "There. Are you okay now? Are you calm?" His dangling head bobbed up and down. "I know it feels like the end of the world, but it's not. You're going to be fine."

"Look at me, Cory. You know as well as I do that I'm far from fine. I'm the *opposite* of fine. I'm the embodiment of all that is wretched and dismal."

"You're just panicking. Try not to worry. We'll figure something out."

"You're wasting your time on me. You can't help me, and you can't possibly love me."

Though Will had many regrets, as well as an abundance of injuries, both internal and external, he thought of how Will smiled and laughed when they would share stories or discuss movies they both liked, intimate moments they had so far experienced, how close they had become to one another, and he felt that Will's burdens weren't enough to make him regret falling for him. He whispered fondly: "I *do* love you... no matter what you've done."

"I love you too." He forced out these words, which were painted with sorrow.

"Now, come out of the bathroom, and let's talk about what we can do for you."

He turned his cadaverous eyes to him. "I need new razors."

"You know I can't just buy you tools to cut yourself with."

"You can't stop me from hurting myself. I'm going to do it no matter what."

Cory was well informed that he couldn't switch off Will's self-abuse, especially if he couldn't be around him all day, every day, but it was worth a shot trying to reason with him. "Maybe you should practice going a whole day without cutting. Use a pen instead."

Sarcastic laughter left his dry, oxygen-starved lips. "'Use a pen,' he says. You're funny, sweetheart."

Exasperated, he gave up the argument for the time being, stepping out of the bathroom to avoid the suffocating aroma seeping into his lungs. He didn't expect Will to follow him out, but he did, apologetically clinging to him, doing his best to show how sorry he was, how ashamed he was of burdening Cory. He squeezed him, clasping him against his chest, reminding him that he was there for him.

Within the next few days, Will had finished his supply of oxycodone, and didn't have the funds to purchase any more. On the day he snorted his final pills, he gazed upon Cory in the darkness of his cold basement with dread, a pen light still clamped between his lips. The metal scraped his upper row of teeth as he slipped it out. "Well, looks like that's it. I'm probably fucked for the next few days."

Cory didn't want to insult him, but he had to ask: "Is it really that bad?"

Guiding his view with the beam from the pen light, he leaned back on the bed where they were sitting beside each other. His appendages fell limp as he leaned against Cory for relaxation. "Have you ever had a hangover?"

He corrected him. "I barely drink."

"You've at least had the flu."

"Yes. A few times."

"Imagine all of the agony you're in while suffering from it. Now multiply it ten times." Cory thought Will was exaggerating, possibly even being a bit of a whiner, but when he started to shake in near convulsions thinking about the upcoming pain, he took him a bit more seriously.

Cory sighed, draping an arm around him as he curled against his chest and shoulder. His shaking slowed, then ceased. "Are you going to be all right?"

Will pulled blankets around himself, soaking in the warmth of Cory's body heat. "I'm not all right *now*."

"You know what I mean, Will. Is it going to kill you?"

"Kill me? No. I'm a bit on the dramatic side. I'll be f..." He didn't finish, perhaps to avoid telling Cory a lie.

Feeling hopeless, Cory continued to hold him to keep him warm. "What can I do to stop it?"

"Nothing. Unless you want to give me money."

"I'm pretty broke, myself. I had to pay my car insurance, my phone bill, and rent money to my mom. I don't even have anything to give you."

Once again shivering in preparation for the worst while clinging to Cory, he said, "Then I guess it's a risk that I have to take. M-maybe it won't be as bad as the last time I was sick. Maybe I'll be okay." He didn't sound too certain.

Cory could barely see anything but Will's silhouette, but even in the darkness, he could find his lips and kiss them. It was the best comfort he could offer him at the time, but he wished to have the foresight to come up with something better before he wasted away into nothingness. Will eventually passed out against him, and after he crawled under the blankets with him, he couldn't keep his eyes open much longer.

The basement was as an icebox all night, and despite being fully dressed and layered with several blankets while pressed against Will's body for heat, his shivering kept him awake. When the alarm on his cell phone rang, he had never found it more difficult to climb out of a bed. As he started to roll out from underneath the covers, he felt Will yank him back against his body, moaning.

"Don't go," he gasped. "It's so cold."

He wanted to stay. He wished that he could. "I have to go to work."

He beseeched his partner with a desperate, wide-eyed stare. "Please, stay with me. Just today."

Cory had already prepared to slip his shoes on and tie them, but he lingered a bit more before doing so. *I can't, I'm too broke*, was the first thing he thought to say, but then he abandoned it for how dismissive it seemed. He turned, shivering, to look at his bedridden lover, who was trembling in both fear and cold.

"Please," Will begged once more, reaching for Cory's arm, weakly grasping it in his icy fingertips. "I need you."

It was difficult to turn down work when he so desperately needed money, but it was even more difficult to turn away Will, who so urgently clung to his nurturing manner. He released a heavy sigh, then rolled back into the bed, cradling Will's skull against his warm, flat chest. Will's arms draped around his waist, weak and loose, but there was tenderness in his embrace that only a sweetheart could bring.

"Okay," he whispered, calming his shaking body with slow strokes to his back. "I'll stay." Will's trembles melted away.

"You're so warm," he said, delirious. "Without you, I might freeze to death down here."

"I wouldn't let that happen to you."

He didn't need to look at Will to know that he smiled. "Thank you for doing this. You didn't have to."

"It's okay. I want to be here. Someone needs to look out for you." As he said this, it reminded him to feel Will's forehead, which was already drenched with sweat. "Christ, honey, you're burning up." He left Will's grasp, thinking of going upstairs to get some ice. Will yanked him back to their nest.

"Don't. Don't leave me." He sniffled his overflowing nose.

"I'm going to get you some ice and aspirin for your head. I'll be right back, I promise."

Will twitched as though tiny shocks were coursing throughout his nervous system, but he allowed him to go. "O-okay."

Cory climbed out of the warm bed, now exposed to the many pins and needles the frosty air shoved into his skin. Hugging his own chest to prevent his ribcage from freezing over, he hobbled upstairs, hopping across the tiled floor, which felt as though a fresh sheet of ice had covered it. He filled a glass with water using shaking, stiff hands, and snatched the aspirin from the bathroom, rushing the items back down to Will. He hadn't even been upstairs for more than a minute.

As soon as he rejoined him, placing the glass of water on a nearby table, Cory dove back into the large bed and clung to his partner, the two of them shivering in unison. "Ah, your hands!" Will shrieked in surprised pain. Cory removed them from Will's spine. He hadn't noticed just how cold they were until Will brought it to his attention.

"Here, take this, okay?" He moaned with chattering teeth, passing him the glass of water and medicine. Will obediently downed them. He sipped the water, but nearly spat it out.

"Tastes like the inside of a pipe." He stuffed his face into his pillow, grumbling to himself. "And I don't know where that smell is coming from, but it's disgusting. Ugh. It's making me want to puke."

Cory didn't smell anything, but hadn't bothered questioning it. "Try to relax. Get some rest." Cory moved his palm over Will's back once he felt his hands were sufficiently warmed up.

Will whimpered. "Everything hurts. It's not even at its worst yet."

"Try for me, okay?" His soothing words seemed to help, but it didn't prevent Will from making frustrated, exhausted sounds. "I know it'll be tough, but I'll be right here beside you." He continued to wipe stray sweat from his brow. His eyelids were hanging low, his nose running. Either he was about to pass out, or he really wanted to.

"I… luff you…"

Despite the circumstances, Cory was touched by his gratitude and respect. "I love you, too. I'll call in to work."

"What are you… going to… tell them?"

"That I'm sick."

"You're going to… lie for me?"

"You'd do the same for me." Will nodded, then shut his eyes, smoggy breath drifting from his mouth. Cory retrieved his cell phone and called his supervisor, but it was Rick that answered. "Rick? Where's Aaron?" As he spoke into the phone, he kept a watchful eye on Will.

"He's running late. What's up?"

"I'm calling in sick today. I've got the flu or something."

"Oh gosh. I'm sorry to hear that. I'll let him know as soon as he gets in. I hope you feel better, Cory."

"Thanks." Before he said farewell to his co-worker, he thought of something. "Rick, before you go, I had a question. What is the best kind of treatment for someone going through withdrawals?"

There was a pause of serious thought between each of them. Then, Rick asked, "Are you…?"

"No!" He laughed, but not because his speculation was at all humorous. "Not me! Someone… who isn't me." At first, Cory believed he hung up on him, but then he heard his gruff voice answer.

"I see. I think I understand. What is he withdrawing from?"

"Oxycodone?"

"How long has he been addicted?"

Now that Rick might have known they were discussing Will, and that he seemed willing to help, Cory dropped his guard and relaxed. "I don't know. A while, he said. Years, at least."

Rick pondered the predicament with humming. "He won't go to a hospital, or—"

"Believe me, I've made that suggestion. He won't do it." Will's eyes were piercing him just as strongly as they had the years he had watched him from afar. His gaze felt guilty, as it always had.

There was a sound of sandy scratching on Rick's end, which could only mean he was itching at the beard he had been trying to grow. "Has he tried methadone?"

What's methadone? Cory thought to ask, but didn't bother at the risk of sounding foolish. "I don't think so. Let me ask him." He cupped his hand over the phone and turned to Will, whose eyes were misty. He shook his head when he posed the question, but he looked hopeful. He brought his mouth back to the cell phone. "I guess not. Where can he get some?"

"I know there's a clinic nearby. You might be able to find the address online."

As he brushed wet hair out of Will's cloudy eyes: "Are you sure it's going to help him?"

"I'm not positive, but it should. Listen, I have to get back to work, but I hope he... and you feel better."

Cory thanked him before they hung up, and he explained the situation to Will. He looked too exhausted to speak, but he seemed relieved. Giving him a bit more time to rest, Cory headed next door to use his computer and look up the address of the nearest clinic. He quickly wrote down the directions, then jogged back to Will's to try to coax him out of bed.

"I can't move," he wheezed, a rattling groan from his murky throat.

"You're going to have to if you want to feel better."

"A-are you coming with me?"

"Of course I am." He grasped Will's hand in his own, tugging him toward him. "Come on, now. The sooner we get there, the sooner you can stop feeling sick."

Will's clench was weak, but he followed his guidance, shuffling out of his bed. Cory helped him up, but could already tell how much the moving around was bothering him. Will wrapped his arms around his chest, hopping from one foot to the other as his feet touched the floor. "More clothes," he requested in desperation, his teeth clicking. He pointed to the corner where his dresser was, and Cory followed his direction, opening one of the many drawers. He grabbed a clean pair of pants and a clean sweater, and brought them to him. He began to assist him and pull his old, sweaty, raggedy argyle sweater up over his head, but Will smacked his clammy palm around Cory's wrist, prying it from the cloth.

"No," he whispered, holding his hand away. Cory could only stare at him, vacant, surprised. "Not this one. Leave it on."

"Why? It's filthy."

"Please. Just don't. It's important to me."

Lowering his hand, Cory nodded. "All right. If that's what you want." Instead of removing the argyle, Cory pulled the second one onto him over his head, then dressed him in a clean pair of pants while his bones rattled together the entire time. After bringing him his shoes, Will slipped his feet into them.

Cory left the house with Will, who resembled a well-dressed snowman. In fact, his outfit looked so cramped that Cory asked if he could breathe properly. Even when Will nodded, he wasn't convinced. Once they were in his car, Will cranked the heat up, and their dreary journey began. Cory tried not to dwell on how sick Will was, or if the methadone would help him, or if he would find the clinic at all. He didn't want Will to feel even worse than he did.

During that lengthy car ride, Cory allowed Will to tightly grip his hand the whole way until they would reach their destination.

12. Taste

Wᵢₗₗᵢₐₘ Daron Shepherd, a man whose thirty-four years of age showed prominently on his creased face, thought that his only punishment for his many bad deeds (including his constant theft to support Ian Michaels' alcoholism) would be years of quiet isolation. He felt that Ian's death, his separation from the only person in his life willing to speak to him, even if it was in drunken slurs with occasional fist-throwing, was enough. If there was a greater force, a higher power, one that represented the essence of balance, it was laughing at him now, ridiculing him for his horrible choices and pathetic lifestyle. It would anger him if he believed in such a force. He learned long ago that it was a fruitless belief.

Now he had reason to acknowledge that his addictions, his self-abuse, and his ceaseless self-loathing was barely enough of a sentence for him, and apparently a suffering beyond his imagining ought to be included on the list or burdens to bear. Cory wouldn't understand even if he laid it out for him in simple English. He was cursed from the day he was born, and nothing he achieved ever mended that.

It could have been because he was delirious from his severe dehydration and anxiety, but he could almost hear the voices of his disappointed foster parents calling him a "failure." They would never do such a thing in reality. They loved him, and he knew it, but he also knew that he had failed them in the worst ways possible. He should have heeded their warning regarding Ian's temper in the beginning.

They knew he was wrong for him, right from the start, and he didn't pay attention. Perhaps he even wanted his relationship to go poorly. Now he was punishing himself for allowing his partner to die, blaming himself each and every day, just as he felt when he was sent into foster care. Just after the disaster with his biological parents.

He pushed them from his mind. It would only cause a panic attack.. Cory was worried enough, and Cory meant the world to him. He didn't want to make him any more upset than he was.

As he wriggled in his seat, which would not grant him comfort no matter how he positioned himself, he pulled on the collars of his dual sweaters, which were both stifling, and yet not enough warmth. As his fingers twisted around the soft fabric, he glanced down at the repetitive diamond patterns circling his neck, which were nearly blotted out by the V-neck of the sweater on top of it. He remembered the day he first saw that pattern when it was hanging on a rack inside a department store. It wasn't only his eye it caught, but that of the young man whose heart he devoted his life to.

"Hey, just my style," cheered Ian as he approached the display, wearing an overbearing grin. "What do you think, babe?" He held the grey sweater in front of his chest, waiting for his opinion.

Will knew that Ian wanted him to say it looked good on him, and wondered why he bothered asking his opinion at all. He would purchase the damn thing either way, and not without scoffing. "I think it looks ridiculous."

Just as he had suspected, Ian had tossed some of his reddish hair out of his eye and huffed through his nostrils, dismissing his comment. "You would. You wear those damn dress shirts and ties like they're going out of style. Do you really have to dress so formal every time we go out? It embarrasses me! You look like you're going to a funeral."

He didn't reply. There was no need to. It would only result in an argument, and he didn't want to make another scene in public, like they had the week before. "All right. It's handsome."

"Yes, it is!" Ian pinched his cheek, like he always did when proving a point to him, and every time he did it, it became more and more humiliating. It made him feel like a child, and childhood was something he never wished to revisit. Every once in a while, he'd follow the pinch with a light tap, reminding him who was boss.

After Ian's untimely death, he inherited the sweater unwillingly. Strangely, he remembered, picking the item out with him in that store was one of the few good times they had together, and it wasn't even a particularly romantic moment. It reminded him of how sudden changes could arrive, all in the blink of an eye.

He wanted to get to the methadone as soon as possible, but he also wanted to tell Cory to slow down. Every bump in the road the car bounced over, his stomach ran a spin cycle. Despite Cory's protest, he fiddled with the temperature dials, blasting the heat to its full strength, and then lowering it again when he felt nauseous at the burning smell. During any other car ride, the sound of tires against pavement wouldn't annoy him so badly, but now, it was a loud reverberation, a riotous, overpowering hum ringing in both of his ears. He tried to reposition himself in his seat yet again, but his discomfort never ceased. His every bone ached.

"Are w-we almost there?" He murmured to Cory while wiping sweat off of his face. He worried they may never get there, that Cory might be lost. If he was lost, he would have to spend even longer feeling like hell, and then he'd have only worse sickness to look forward to.

"We're close. Hang in there, it'll be okay."

Will thought seriously on Cory's behavior. *I wonder why he's still with me. He knows I'm a hopeless cause. I can see it in his eyes all the time. Does he really love me that much? Or is he attracted to people with problems? I suppose it could be a little bit of both.*

Not that he could help it much, but he thought more of Ian. Would he have also taken time off work (had he not lost his job in the end) to help him feel better? Of course he wouldn't. He was not entirely cold-hearted in the beginning, but there was a glimmer of impatience within him, a deep, welling frustration with the rest of the world that even love couldn't overcome. Ian was, just as Will had been, tainted from the beginning, but he was adept at keeping it hidden from those who held him closest. When his single cherished family member died, a part of him died with her.

When the doctors and nurses rushed into that room to try to get his heart beating again, thought Will as he heaved and panted, trying to stifle the grumbling, twisting motions in his gut as his intestines wrestled each other, *they could see the emptiness in me, that I couldn't cry. I wonder if Cory thinks I'm empty. He must not if he puts all of this energy into our relationship.*

Cory had noticed him whimpering. He felt the gentle caress of his hand on his shoulder, and though he jumped in alarm at the first sign of physical contact, like he usually did when his personal space was intruded, he relaxed afterward.

"We're almost there, just a little longer," Cory coached. "You still with me?"

"Y-yes. I just d-don't want to open my mouth. I'm afraid I'll puke." Sincerity shined in his glossy eyes when he glimpsed at him for a moment. "This is a hassle."

Cory answered with confident adoration. "I'm going to get you some help, no matter what it takes. If this doesn't work, I'm going to try to find another way to help you."

He wanted to tell him not to bother, that he was prone to repeat bad habits, because they were old habits, and old habits die hard. Hurting himself was just something he felt he had to do. There was no simple solution to ending it. Nevertheless, he didn't turn him down if he was so willing to aid him.

When they arrived at the clinic, Will observed right away the number of shady individuals looming around on the sidewalk near the front doors, perhaps hoping to score from a stranger. He grew apprehensive at the surrounding clientele, each of them wearing puffy winter coats that could potentially conceal weapons. It took a reminder that addicts would rather have drugs than prison to relax him, but all the same, the looks they gave the parking car he rode in showed no sign of restraint. He wasn't in the mood to be clung to, to be begged. He had so little worth of his own to offer.

His bicep muscles throbbed as he pushed the car door open, but once he had swung it far enough, he couldn't bring himself to get out of the car. It was cold out there, freezing in fact, and the harsh winds nipped at his pale face. He wanted to be at home in bed where he could sleep off this wretched sickness, but the tiny cup of green liquid was waiting for him inside. Not a cure, but a medicine, one that could stave off the quakes and aches in mere minutes. It was just a matter of walking to it.

Before he even knew where he was or what he was doing, Cory was at his side, helping him out of the car. His jaw vibrated, and his eyes stung at the stabbing sunlight reflecting off of the fresh snow. The dizzying effect caused him to collapse against Cory, who supported him and held him up.

His mouth now pressed near his lover's ear, he breathily whispered, "Kill me."

Cory laughed, not because it was funny, but to keep him composed. "Too late. We're already here."

He hadn't noticed his frown, but he was grateful for that. He didn't wish to explain that he was somewhat serious in his call for sympathy. Hobbling alongside Cory, leaning against his torso, they reached the front glass doors. Will slipped out of Cory's grasp and separated their link. Before he could ask why, he elaborated. "I can do the rest on my own."

"Are you sure?"

"Yes. I hope it won't take too long." He kissed his cheek with chapped lips, but warm breath, avoiding his nose so that he wouldn't smell how rancid it had become. "I'll see you soon."

They parted ways, Cory returning to the vehicle with a worrisome air. Will felt bad for not inviting him along inside, but he didn't want him to sit around in a stuffy waiting room if it came to that. At least in the car he could listen to the radio, assuming he welcomed the inane repetition of holiday tunes.

The clinic smelled ripe of fresh lemon, a cleaning product that made the floors shimmer and reflect the florescence of the above fixtures. A plastic, standing yellow sign warned incomers of the wet tiles. With each step, his snow-caked shoes creaked, even as his weak legs wobbled like cooked noodles. Guarding the hallway were two security officers with metal-detecting wands, which they used to wave over Will's body, asking him to empty his pockets of any metallic contents. They patted him down, doing a quick search, most likely for substances or weapons he might be trying to smuggle in, then allowed him to proceed.

A stream of classic eighties songs played in low volume on overhead speakers, songs that Will remembered being fond of once upon a time. Now they were just a nuisance, annoying ambience that nauseated him beyond the stomach pains he was already enduring. It sounded so much louder than it truly was, and he never realized before when listening to them in the past just how cyclic and irritating they were. He understood the chorus the first time. He didn't need to hear it over and over again.

At the end of the shiny, lemony hallway was a bulletproof window with tiny holes for speaking through, a middle-aged woman with curled, fiery hair standing on the other side, jogging papers together. She hadn't looked at Will when he first approached, or when he cleared his throat. He placed a sweaty palm upon the glass, wheezing out: "I need some methadone." He bundled his long, thick coat around his sickly thin body as cold air snuck into it, tucking his clammy hands under his arms.

The clerk at the window stapled some papers together, and still hadn't given Will a courtesy glance. With a bored sigh, she tossed the papers into a tray, then finally said, "New patient?"

"Yes. This is my first time here."

"You'll need to fill these out." A tray opened, and stapled papers on a clipboard were passed through. Will hesitated in taking the board and chain-hooked pen, but her impatient look spooked him. He snatched it up, clutching it against his chest like he would a stuffed toy during a thunderstorm. "Please be aware that there is a three week waiting list in order to be given methadone."

The clipboard he clung to clacked to the floor, his reddened eyes bulging as wide as saucers. "W-what? Three weeks?! I can't wait three weeks, I need it now!"

"Sir," the clerk answered in monotone, as though accustomed to the hysteria. "Lower your voice. There are other clinics you can go to that can give you methadone right away."

"Where is the closest one?"

"Detroit."

Left with no other option but to panic, Will grabbed clumps of his messy, uncombed hair, pulling at the strands in frustration. It only exacerbated his throbbing headache. "You can't be serious. I can't feel this way any longer, do you get me?! I'm hurting all over, I can't take this!"

"I'm sorry, sir. It's just policy." She waved her delicate, stringy fingers. "Could I have the clipboard back if you don't plan to fill out the forms?"

Will chucked the board back into the tray where he earlier retrieved it, then shoved his way past a few nameless, unfamiliar visitors as he made his way back outside. Once he was reunited with the blowing snow and skin-peeling frostiness, he groaned loudly, his pain and anxiety relentlessly overwhelming. Maybe he could rob a store. He had done it before, without getting caught. He needed something, anything he could sell or trade for drugs, even if it was overrated movies on DVD. Cory wouldn't have to know.

Some of these cars are in poor shape, he thought as he glanced around at the parked vehicles in the lot. *I bet I could break into them without much effort.*

His stomach gurgled, and his knees rattled. In truth, he didn't have the energy to break into any vehicles. Vomit was coming up his throat. He smacked a hand over his mouth, but it hardly contained what wanted to be let out, and he ran to the side of the building. After upchucking burning bile into the snow, which caused the flurries to steam, he dropped to his knees and sobbed, holding his gut to prevent it from going off again.

I'm going to feel this way forever. Not just sick, but "sick." I'm always going to be the bottom feeder, the pathetic wreck, the hopeless and the helpless. What if I did quit opiates? What good would it do? I once took them to forget how much I hated my life. There is no "cure" for me. There is no light at the end of this tunnel. There is no hope.

"Man," called a soft voice, as gentle as the whistling winds around him, angelically masculine. "Hey, man."

Will lifted his blurry eyes, wiping spittle from his mouth and stubbly, unshaven chin. "Huh?" He uttered with his eyes half-open.

"Over here."

His ringing ears pointed him at the sound of his young voice, and he turned his head to see a man standing beside him, leaning against a wall, bundled up in a blue coat. "Yes?" He slobbered when his mouth moved.

"They put you on the waiting list, didn't they?" The man in the blue coat, a man roughly the age of twenty-eight, smiled when their eyes met. When Will nodded, he clicked his tongue in disapproval. "I can tell. You look pretty sick."

"I'm sorry," Will answered in a raspy voice. "Can I help you?"

Mister Blue Coat kneeled down beside the crumpled heap of wounded man, lowering his tone a few notches. "Do you want to get un-sick?"

Confused at his behavior and odd series of questions, Will squinted behind the lenses of his black-rimmed glasses. "What do you think?" He spit in the snow.

The man beamed at these words, clearly hoping he'd answer in just that way. "I can sell you something that'll help you."

"And what is that?"

"Heroin, of course. What are you withdrawing from?"

"Oxy." He spit again, his arms still locked against his stomach. The snow was starting to soak his pant legs, but he could care less.

"Oxy?!" The young man laughed, though Will didn't find any amusement in his condition. "You don't need that hillbilly shit. You need something better."

Rising up to his feet, stumbling part of the way, Will took a deep breath of fresh air, trying to calm the storm in his intestines. "I've never bought heroin before. How much is it?"

"I've got bags for ten a piece, and around here, that is *cheap*. There are others selling them for fifteen to twenty, so you're getting a really good deal here, man. If you get them in a bundle, that's seventy. Again, great deal. So what'll it be?" The young dealer lit up a cigarette after checking to see if he was out of view of the methadone patients filing in and out of the building.

"Seventy dollars..." Will processed while stroking his scratchy jaw. "You only take cash, don't you? Not checks?"

He shrugged, cocking his head to the side. "Wouldn't you?"

Will grinded his sweaty, yet freezing hands together, thinking of his chilled skin, his wrenching stomach, his throbbing head and runny nose, and how badly he wanted it to stop. He wanted to feel high, happy, and motivated again, and knew there was only one way to do it. "Could you wait here? I don't have cash on me, but I might be able to get some."

"I'm not going anywhere, man. I've got product to sell here."

Will dashed off behind the building, slipping in slush, and spotted Cory's car. He launched himself against the driver's side door, knocking loudly on the window. Cory, after leaping out of his own skin, rolled the window down.

"Jesus, Will," he panted, a hand over his heart. "You scared the shit out of me."

He wondered if he should go through with it. He did tell himself before that it wasn't Cory's fault that he was fucked up, and therefore, it wasn't his problem that he wanted to get even more fucked up.

It'll get better. I'll feel better. Cory will be happy with it. Everyone wins, right?

He chewed on his bottom lip, pushing his canine teeth hard against the skin. He winced at the jolting pierce in his flesh, but it was a necessary pain. "I need seventy dollars."

Cory was stunned, and blinked several times before answering him. "For what?"

"The clinic." He bit the inside of his cheek now, pinching skin between his molars, his eyes watering at the sting, which was both welcoming and unbearable. "They want me to pay them for the treatment I'm getting, and I have no cash on me. I told them I don't have any insurance, or a traditional job. They still want my money."

"I don't even carry cash."

"Can you go get me some? I'll find a way to pay you back. I'll sell some of my artwork or I'll donate blood, anything! Please, please!"

"Okay, okay, calm down. I'll go get some out of the bank. Are you sure it's seventy dollars?"

"Yes, it's ridiculous, I know, but what else can I do?" When he felt comfortingly pat his hand that was resting on the edge of the door, he bit himself harder. Why did he have to do that, and at that moment? It almost caused the truth to spill from his mouth.

"It'll be okay, Will. We'll get you fixed up either way."

"Yeah," Will choked.

Cory left the clinic's parking lot while Will waited for him to come back. The winds didn't feel so harsh anymore, nor did his stomach pains. Just the simple thought of reaching a high once more lifted his spirits. He might just be able to go back to feeling normal— to *being* normal.

When Cory came back to the parking lot, he handed Will the cash and told him he'd see him soon. Will disappeared into the blinding snow to the awaiting dealer, who had never moved from his spot. He grinned when he saw him stepping through the foggy air, and greeted him with a friendly wave.

Will counted the cash in his hand and showed it to the young man, who nodded when he saw it, then unzipped his puffy jacket, reaching into one of the inner pockets. He withdrew a bundle of heroin packets, which was wrapped in a rubber band. Each of the bags were stamped with a pink logo labeled "Toxic Love" and individually wrapped with care. Will looked at the stack of tiny packets resting in his hand.

"I've never shot up before," he said in hopes that the dealer would give him hints. "I don't even like needles."

"That'll change quickly," the young man said as he adjusted the zipper of his coat. "You'll see what I mean when you start."

He never took his eyes off of the bundle, already desperately wanting to get a rush, and to stop his sickness. "Where do I get needles from?"

"Around here, some pharmacies will sell rigs to you no problem, but others are *really* strict. Your best bet is any grocery store that has a pharmacy in it. They don't seem to give a fuck."

"Do you have any?"

"I have a bunch of new ones in my car. It's sort of a 'starter package' if you get what I mean. I'll sell you five for five."

Will cursed his dumb luck, his chapped lips getting more parched by the second. A car in the near distance peeled around a corner after slipping on some ice and the tires screeched upon the pavement. He put a hand over his ear to block the irritating sound, regardless of how distant it was. "I gave you the last of my cash, I'm afraid."

The young man in the stuffed blue coat gave Will a look of concentration while twisting his mouth. "Tell you what. I'll give you the rigs on the house. It's not like you won't be back, because you will be."

"Will I?"

"I don't shoot the stuff I sell, but I know it's pretty pure. I highly doubt you'll be disappointed. After all, it's better than that oxy you've been doing. A *lot* better."

He looked once more at the bundle in his palm, then slipped it into his pocket to keep it safe. "In that case... thank you."

"I'll grab those rigs for you, and give you my cell phone number. By the way, the name's Randy." Randy, puffing away at his cigarette and walking with a confident stride, made a lone walk to the parking lot to retrieve the last of Will's product. He graciously presented him five insulin syringes tied together with a rubber band when he came back, as well as a piece of torn paper with his cell phone number on it. "Don't call between midnight and nine a.m. My girlfriend hates it."

"Any advice on how to shoot? This is a bit new to me."

"Everyone does it differently, so it's tough to say." Randy smoked the rest of his cigarette as quickly as he could before anyone could get a glimpse at it. "Your best bet? Look it up online."

"I don't have Internet access. I don't even have a computer."

Randy stared at Will with a raised eyebrow. It was something he probably didn't often hear. "Regardless, it's still your best option. If you know someone with a connection, you should use it. I doubt you really want to look up shooting heroin at a library."

They shook hands, and Will hid the syringes in his coat. "Thanks again. I should get going."

"Enjoy, man. See you soon, and get well. Maybe even better." He saluted him before putting his finished cigarette out on the snow.

Will went through the transaction in his mind when he returned to Cory's car, confronted with the possibility that he might need to tell his partner the truth. How would he even manage? It was hard enough admitting to himself what he had just done.

My eyes itch inside of my head. Is that possible?

"Are you okay?" Cory asked when the busy-minded man entered his car and said absolutely nothing, only stared into the horizon.

"Yeah... I'm okay. Take me home."

Cory's cautious staring unsettled him, but he didn't let on yet that anything was wrong, at least not on the surface. "Did they give you any methadone? You still look pretty sick."

"Y-yeah, they did, but they said it takes a while to kick in or something."

"How long does it take?"

"I... I'm not sure. Thirty minutes or so, I think." He knew that even Cory could smell the stink of dishonesty reeking off of his breath. He wiped his runny nose using his glove, apathetic of the snot now painted on it.

Cory didn't give any sign that he heard him, or that he believed him, but he didn't have to. Will was well aware of how skeptical he was. During the ride home, he tried to hide his remaining withdrawal symptoms, but he couldn't manage. Each one was as loud and powerful as fireworks. While stopped at a red light, Will's constant fidgeting, shivering, and rhythmic rocking seemed to be enough evidence for Cory.

"They didn't give you any methadone, did they?"

Wiping beads of sweat collecting on his eyebrows, Will croaked, "No. They didn't." The light slapped green and the tires squealed as Cory peeled forward, lurching Will backwards against his seat. His stomach tumbled. "Watch it!"

"If you didn't get methadone, what did I just give you seventy dollars for?!"

"I don't want to tell you."

"Tell me, or you're walking home."

As unfair as that exchange sounded, he complied. "Heroin, okay? I bought heroin." He looked Cory in the face, seeing veins bulging in his neck.

"Are you fucking insane?!"

How could he ask him such a thing? It was true that he lived in constant darkness, but he wouldn't exactly call himself "insane." Did he really appear that way to Cory? "It was either that or suffer. They were going to put me on some waiting list just to get the methadone, and it was for weeks."

"Maybe you should have chosen to suffer! You think oxy ruined your life? Heroin's so much worse! What the hell are you thinking?!"

"Ah, you know so much, don't you? Are you even aware of how this feels? You've never been through this. You've never been in this pain before." He grasped his skull in both hands, trying to ease his pulsating headache. "It's more than just a little sickness. The agony never stops. Nothing I take makes it go away. I can't even drink it away. Everything hurts. My own thoughts hurt. Even my *breath* hurts."

The aggressiveness left Cory's voice and he attempted to be soothing, even understanding. "I don't want you to suffer, either, but I know what heroin does to people. It destroys their whole lives. I don't want that for you." During their heated discussion, Will saw the sign for their street whiz by, and Cory hadn't looked at it, only continued onward.

"You passed our street," he said, hoping it was a mistake and he just hadn't noticed.

"We're not going home," Cory answered with a straight face.

"W-where are we going?"

"I don't care if you want it or not. I'm taking you to a hospital." In between Will's gasping, panicking breaths, he elevated his voice to speak over them: "They can give you something for withdrawals, I know they can."

His lungs were collapsing. His stomachache doubled in strength. His limbs, which were already seizing, quaked like crumbling wood. "No. *No!* I'm not going! Please, no!"

"Whatever your problem is with hospitals, I don't know, and I don't care. All I know is that I can't just let you take heroin."

"*Take me home!*" Cory stiffly shook his head at him. "Turn this car around! I want to go home!"

"Listen to you! You're acting like a kid!"

Will saw how inevitable it was. Cory cared a bit *too* much, if such a thing was permissible. He wasn't going to relinquish his position, nor would he give in to his demands. Screaming at the top of his lungs was the only thing he could think to do, and he even made Cory flinch at the volume.

"Will, would you chill the fuck out? I don't know what you have against getting help for yourself, but I don't think I can deal with it much longer. I'm trying to hang on for you, but I'm hanging by a thread. If you won't go to a hospital then I'm just going to take you to a rehab center."

The sweat that so freely poured from Will's feverish head dampened his hair, and it clung tightly to the skin of his face, giving him a sinister, impish look as he stared his lover down like a rabid canine. "You can't make me go." His voice was deep and soft, albeit threatening. "They won't let you, see, they won't let you force me in. I have to do it on my own volition, do you understand? If I don't agree to it, you can't take me."

Growing ever more frustrated by his resistance, Cory didn't give up. "What if I tell you I'll break up with you if you don't?"

"I don't need you."

"That's certainly a lie."

A lie it most certainly was, but Will stood his ground. He wanted to hold on to Cory, but there was no way he was going to a hospital. His esteemed companion didn't quite grasp his fear of them, and it wasn't something explained with ease. He'd have to go into detail regarding memories he'd rather not visit. He was in enough pain as it was. "I don't care what you say, or what you do. I'm not going to a hospital."

"You're not leaving me much choice, are you?"

Furious, hot rage boiled within him, steam leaking from his ears. "If you love me, you'll turn around and take us home, do hear me?"

"*If* I love you? There's no question that I love you. That's why I'm doing this."

"Pull over."

"Forget it, I'm not—" Before he could even finish, Will grabbed both of his hands, yanking the steering wheel in the direction of the curb. Alarmed, Cory had no choice but to lay on the breaks as the car went scuffing into the slushy dirt aside the road. Will leaped out of the vehicle, clasping his coat tightly around himself as he stomped heavily in the direction of Hunter Street. "Will!" He was calling him from the inside of the car, but he didn't look back. Cory didn't get it. He would never get it. "Will, come back!" He pulled his car back onto the street and followed Will, lingering at a slow pace alongside the sulking man. "God damn it, Will," he preached after rolling down his window. "Is this fun for you?! Well, it isn't for me! I want us to be happy, a normal couple with normal lives! We can't have that if you don't start using your fucking head!"

He stopped walking, mostly because the many holes in his shoes were letting cold snow in, soaking his socks. Cory also stopped his car, fog rolling out of his mouth as he exhaled, patiently waiting for him to come to a decision. Will's tear-stained, sunken eyes and pale, lifeless complexion turned to Cory's more colorful, healthy face, and he slowly shook his head. "Why can't you just leave me alone to rot? Just let me die off." Cory didn't answer him. He seemed to be struck with a stunned silence. "You're not going to fix me, Cory. There's nothing you can do for me! Don't you get that yet?! There are some things that are just beyond hope. I'm one of those things."

Assuming he got his point across, he continued walking, even though his feet were turning to ice. Cory pulled his car over to the curb one final time and chased him down on foot after waiting for passing cars. Will tried to gain some distance between them, not wanting him to come near, but Cory raced toward him anyhow. Trying to speed up, he slipped on a thick patch of black ice, collapsing to the ground like a shattering egg to a solid floor. He screamed in pain as white hot needles coursed up his fragile knees and hips, a pain that might not have been as powerful had he not been undergoing withdrawals, and if he actually had meat on his bones. His faithful partner skidded to his side to help him up, but Will shoved him away with a weak toss.

"Cory," he sobbed. "I'm nothing but poison to you."

At first, Cory said nothing, only forcefully pulled him into a loving embrace. Will made no effort to escape, only whimpered. "You're not," he comforted when his crying died down. "I'm pressuring you because I love you and I don't want to see you in this much pain. These addictions of yours... they're eating you up, and I can't stand to watch it happen to you."

"They've been with me long before you ever came into the picture," Will said with staggering breath. "You can't just throw them away. It's not that simple."

"Well I'm not saying good-bye to you, either. I don't want to give up on you."

"Fine. It's your life." Cory didn't answer, not knowing what else to say that would alter his thinking. "I know you don't understand, but I can't go to a hospital."

"What the hell else can I do, then?"

"Find me a guide I can read on how to inject."

"And if I don't?"

"Then I suffer, I guess."

He didn't provide an answer right away, but he stood up and helped Will get to his feet. He didn't think that he would, but after getting in the car with him, Cory turned around and headed home.

"You told me you didn't have any money to give me before," Will brought up when they were entering his house. "Why did you lie?"

"I *didn't*. I just gave you everything I had left. You're lucky I was willing to empty my checking account for you. Don't turn this all on me."

His face burning, as well as his forehead, he shuffled to the couch and collapsed onto it. He curled up on his side, hugging his coat around himself to keep warm. When he glanced at Cory, he saw he was standing over him, his incriminating stare fixed on him.

"Don't look at me like that," Will grumbled, pulling the collar of his coat up.

"I don't think it's a good idea for you to stay in this house anymore. The conditions are unlivable."

"Do you mind telling me where else I'm supposed to go?"

Sitting down on the couch next to him, he said, "What about your parents?"

Will further stuffed his own head into his coat. "No. I can't do that to them."

He sighed while rubbing the throbbing veins in his forehead. "Well you have to go *somewhere*. Maybe if I sweet-talked my mother into letting you stay with me in my room..."

"I wouldn't let you if I was your mother. Think of the sin we'd be living in."

His attempt at being lighthearted didn't invoke the spirit of laughter he aimed at enlivening. Cory only circled his fingertips around the temples of his skull in deep concentration. "Angie might let us stay with her," he mumbled to himself, ignoring Will's tossing, turning, and groaning.

"She hates me," he grunted as he gripped his stomach, which was churning again. The bathroom seemed like it was miles away, but he knew he'd need to get up soon. "Besides, I don't want you to leave your own home just because..." He shot up and rocketed for the bathroom, messily tossing his coat onto the floor on his way there. The sensation of burning in his throat was something he could almost get used to. The smell of unwashed dishes in the kitchen, on the other hand, was far too vile to tolerate. The aroma seemed so overpowering now, and he couldn't ignore it.

"I'll give her a call anyway," Cory continued in an raised voice, speaking over his vomiting. "She's not usually very charitable, but she might stick her neck out for me, even if it involves you." He couldn't answer him back. Speaking was a skill he might have lost along with some of the lining of his stomach. "Will, I don't want to see you like this. I don't want you to do heroin, but there aren't many other options."

At first, Will thought he was implying he might kill him and put him out of his misery, which seemed to him like an incredible relief. *Please do kill me,* thought Will while spitting in the grimy, stained toilet bowl. *End this ridiculous charade. How much longer can it go on, anyway? Certainly not years.*

"I'll go use my computer next door, and I'll find you some instructions."

He wasn't serious. He couldn't have been. After all of the lecturing he had given him, he seemed more inclined to leave him than he was to help him do drugs. Regardless, he believed him, and if he had been telling the truth, he was forever grateful to him, which he would express had he not been puking.

By the time Cory returned, he was out of his bathroom, back on the couch wrapped in several blankets and his coat, shaking like a rattle. He brandished a sheet of printer paper in his right hand, and brought it to his partner sitting in the nest of warmth on the sofa.

While he was next door preparing the directions for him, Will had laid out the syringes and heroin he had purchased earlier in a neat row on the chipped coffee table. It seemed to unease Cory, but he hid it quickly to dictate to his shivering mate what he needed to do.

"It says you need to boil the solution," he emphasized boldly, waving the printed pamphlet like a bible. "We need a sanitized spoon and a lighter. Syringes, which you have, a cotton ball, something to tie off your arm... your belt, I guess... and it recommends that if it's your first time to have an experienced user or a friend help you inject."

"I-I don't know anyone else that uses," he answered reluctantly.

"I know. I'll help."

There was no proper way to reply but with jaw-dropping awe. Just a few moments ago, this man was trying to force him into rehab, and now, he had done a complete one-eighty. There was honesty in his eyes, compassion and understanding, something he would never have expected anyone else to have for him, especially under these circumstances. If he could speak without stuttering and clattering his teeth, he would tell him just how much warmer he felt at those four simple words.

Cory reviewed the directions with intense focus and discretion, retaining the details in his memory, no doubt. When he finished reading, he asked Will if he had a lighter. He informed him that one might be in the kitchen, and Cory made haste there. From the living room, he could hear him poke around in drawers, the sound of silverware scattering and clanking together. The faucet creaked on next as Cory washed something. Whatever he was carrying, he took into the bathroom and applied something to it, possibly the rubbing alcohol he used to put on his razor blades. He returned with a glass of water, a clean spoon, and a pink florescent lighter, sitting back in his spot on the couch. He detached one of the stamp bags from the bundle of packs tied with a rubber band, the "Toxic Love" label rubbing off in the process.

"You're going to have to take your coat off."

Will shivered at the thought of cold air breaching the hull of soft, downy covering. "Do I *have* to?"

"How else do you expect me to inject this?"

There was no other choice. If he wanted to feel better, he had to live through a bit of chilliness, just for a short while. He opened the first layer of blankets, which he already began to regret, and peeled off the remaining layers, then his coat. He quaked, smoke drifting out of his mouth, but he tried to focus on anything but winter in hopes it would help. His mind only returned to images of glaciers and frozen lakes, just as his blood felt like. He groaned. It was the only sound he could manage making.

"I know, honey. I'm going as fast as I can." He didn't sound impatient, but supportive.

Instead of thinking of his freezing veins, he watched Cory as he added water and heroin to the spoon and heated the underside of it with the torch of the small lighter, which he appeared to have trouble holding still due to the shaking of his arm. During the process, Will's apprehension grew like an inflating balloon about to burst.

"I-I'm s-scared," he admitted.

"I won't let anything bad happen to you. You should be able to handle this dose, anyway."

"W-what if I c-can't? W-what if I o-o-overdose?"

"I read what I should do if that happens, and I'll be keeping an eye on you. Don't worry, if it comes to that, I'll be prepared. Just trust me, okay? I'll get you through this."

He did trust him. In fact, he trusted him with his life. Somehow, he was convinced that everything would be okay. He could stop feeling sick. He would get that euphoric feeling back, the wondrous opiate high, and he wouldn't be alone. Cory would be with him, beside him, and he could lean on him if he needed to. Now, he did nothing but look forward to it, and wished Cory would work a little faster, though he appreciated his cautious steps.

While muttering the directions to keep focused, Cory dropped a tiny piece of cotton into the boiled solution. Will watched in fascination as a child might do when watching a parent cook or drive a car, until he finally stuck the needle of a fresh syringe into the solution and filled the tube with cloudy, brown heroin water. He then flicked it with his finger and grinned.

"I always see doctors doing that in the movies," he joked, keeping his partner at ease. Will smiled, despite how nervous he was. Once he set the syringe down on the table, he removed the belt Will was wearing and proceeded to wrap it around his arm tightly. When he winced, his lover soothed and apologized, but said the tightness was necessary. He pulled the strap up to Will's mouth and firmly said,

"Bite." Will clamped his teeth onto the belt strap to hold it in place, feeling nauseous at the rancid taste of old leather. He held in his vomit the best he could.

Shocked with sudden jolts, it took a moment to understand that Cory was smacking his arm in order to raise a vein. He then rubbed his palm over it several times before smacking at it again. "Found one," he sighed with relief. He glanced up into Will's wide, childlike eyes as he scooped up the syringe. "Are you ready?"

"I… I think so." He swallowed a burning wad of spit. The taste of leftover throw-up was absolutely foul.

Without another word, Cory stuck his vein with the needle, pulling the plunger back to check for blood, then pushed it and the solution into Will's arm. He withdrew the needle afterward while pressing a cotton ball on the new wound.

Warmth. That was what Will felt right away. Radiant, glowing warmth running through the veins of his arm, spreading throughout his body like static. Then, it grew and grew; twenty orgasms multiplied ten times over, pulsing rhythmically in his ears, filling his entire body with a sense of peace and joy. Everything was good. No, more than good. *Everything was wonderful.* There was no pain, there were no bad memories, there was nothing but this feeling, this floating, sailing sensation of pure delight. Those tingles had come back, those wondrous tingles, racing up his spine, down his arms, his fingertips, even in his groin, and he welcomed them graciously. He didn't know it then, but he was grinning so wide that his lips were splitting. He had no control over it. His cheeks had a mind of their own. *Smile!* They chanted, and he did, and it felt so right to do so. Everything did. Because everything was so much more than it was, so much better than it had been before. There was no going back.

He would stop at nothing to hang onto this.

"What's it feel like?" Cory asked out of curiosity when seeing his lover smiling like a fool.

"Oh, God." These two words were the only thing Will could muster. His face had lit up like a holiday tree as the orgasmic sensation vibrated in waves within him, and he yanked Cory into his arms in both a symbol of gratitude and of erotic joy as he clutched and stroked his back, moaning blissfully. "Oh, fuck."

"That good, huh?" Cory followed up in wonderment.

"You have no idea." He took a deep breath as he sank into the warmth of Cory's body. His touch had improved somehow. His soothing hands and caressing fingers created waves of chills across his skin. His calves trembled, and he buried his face into his shoulder. "You have... no idea."

Please, if there is any kind of higher power out there, Will pleaded, hearing the sound of his own voice as plainly as he would if he had said it aloud, *don't let this feeling go away. Let it go on forever.*

"And the sickness? Did it go away?"

Will nodded, his eyelids low, his lips still pulled into that wide smile. His cheeks were still cheering at him, telling him to smirk like a fool. He didn't care much how it made him look. "Oooh yes, it went away." He couldn't find the right words during the intensity of that incredible high, but he wished he could. He wanted to tell Cory how much he appreciated his loyalty. Instead, he mumbled, "I love you. It's so good. I love you." Had he said "I love you" twice? He could have sworn he only said it once, but he heard it twice. How strange.

"I love you too," he vowed in earnest, stroking Will's cheek, which was now warm again. Color was seeping back into his skin, and his twitching had stopped. "I'm sorry for what I said. For what I tried to do."

"It's okay. Forget it. Forget all of it. Everything... is just right." That peppy smile never faded, though the hands that he had planted on Cory's back started to feel fifty pounds heavier, and they dropped to his sides. He now rested against his partner in deep relaxation, feeling glorious, at one with himself and with Cory, and his new best friend: the therapeutic hit of pure ecstasy. "I don't... blame you for it."

"I shouldn't have done it. It was wrong of me to try to control you like that." He felt the pressure of a tender, loving squeeze as Cory clung to him, and sleepiness overcame him.

"I can't... thank you enough." With that, he allowed him to get some much-needed rest, and once again wrapped him up in blankets, where he pleasantly snoozed against his chest, the smile never leaving his happy face.

13. Relocate

Will wasn't much for holidays, especially Christmas. Each holiday season, his parents would always ask him to help them decorate the tree, a ritual they deemed important, one that Will found unnecessary. They always told him that it drew them closer as a family, and in a way, he could understand where they were coming from, but he also had no idea what else to feel other than depressed. Once he opened his presents, however, he'd smile again. His father always knew just what to get him: books. Lots and lots of books. Fiction, non-fiction, even textbooks excited him. His mother always bought him underwear. It got so excessive that both he and his father had to tell her to stop, because he soon owned so many pairs that he couldn't fit them in his drawers anymore. Why did she think he needed so many, anyway? He didn't get them *that* dirty.

Cory used his holiday time off work to spend with him, and he even bought him a gift: a collection of new oil paints with hundreds of different shades. When receiving such a thoughtful present, he became tearful. It was just the sort of thing he would buy himself if he had the time, or the money, and it gave him the sense that Cory knew him, not just physically, but was familiar with what lied in his soul. Though heroin had now consumed most of his daily routine, he promised his beloved that the paints would be put to good use, even if he didn't believe he'd ever paint again.

"I should have gotten you something," he said while sniffling, not only because he was crying, but because he had yet to take his "breakfast shot." "I might have to steal it, though." It was only partially a joke. Thankfully, Cory ignored it.

"My mom was nice enough to give me some leftovers from the big dinner she made last night. I heated it up in her microwave, so we can eat it together if you're hungry."

He dragged his dry hand over his wet nose, zipping up a sweater he had slipped on earlier. "She did that for me?"

"Well, for *us*." Cory removed the plastic wrap covering the warm plate, and Will eyed the gravy-covered turkey with contempt as he would an invader on his lawn. "But since you look repulsed, maybe I'll just have a bite."

"That's just it. It looks good, I just don't want it. I'm not even hungry. I can't remember the last time I was."

"Maybe you should eat something, anyway, Will. You look…" He sighed as he stuffed some mashed potatoes into his own mouth with a fork that was tucked under the plastic. "Unhealthy."

"Of course I'm unhealthy. That's no secret." He watched Cory as he chewed, his jaw swirling like a cow's. "I need a hit." Cory set his fork down and licked salt from his lips, then leaned over to the right side of the couch to a small shelf with a drawer. Will ritualistically undid his belt and pulled up his sleeves in order to wrap it around his boney arm while Cory retrieved the stash of heroin, the lighter and a clean syringe. He did his usual trip around the house to get a spoon and cotton, then returned to the couch once he collected each of the necessary items.

After having done it several times, Cory had gotten quite skilled at the job of shooting him up, and even starting adding extra steps to benefit his health. With Cory in control, Will felt that he wouldn't make horrible mistakes that he could possibly end up dying from, and he felt comfortable with him being mindful of how many shots he took in a day. It prevented him from going overboard. Cory had long accepted that there was no stopping his addictions, but he could at least manage them and keep them from hurting the man he loved too terribly. Will understood that his concern was his safety, and as long as he didn't try to force him into anything, he would do it his way, and they made it a compromise.

After the injection, Will was relaxed again, any threat of sickness fading. He was met with the great sense of heaven, the release of all stress, and sleepily leaned against the shoulder of his supportive companion, who was by now snacking hungrily on the leftover dinner.

Will later woke up to the sound of Cory talking on the phone, as well as his own teeth grinding together. Even the blanket that Cory must have draped over him, along with his long-sleeved shirt and argyle sweater, wasn't enough to warm him up. Cory had said once that the conditions in his house were unlivable, and he was right. If he stayed there any longer, his house would become an icy tomb.

"I can't thank you enough for this," Cory was saying into his cell phone, pacing the floor back and forth. "I'll see you in a little bit. Uh-huh. Bye." With a press of a button he hung up, and Will observed his movement, trying to put the pieces together of what might be happening. He drew in a slow breath to begin speaking, but he was stopped by a abrupt, inexplicable ache in his groin. He had experienced morning wood before (or "afternoon wood" in this case), but none like this. The sting was unbearable, and unrelenting, a constant pulsing, aching throb, and not a pleasurable one. He didn't intend to alert Cory to this, but the pain was so great that he couldn't contain the groaning.

"Hey, you're awake," cheered Cory, but approached him with caution, like reaching out to pet a grumpy dog. "Are you okay?"

"I don't know." If he brought up the aching, Cory might want to coddle him, and he wasn't in much of a mood to be touched. "I think I just need another shot."

"But you just had one four hours ago."

Four hours? Had I been out that long?

"Oh. Well, I think they're starting to wear off faster."

"You might just need a bigger dose. Listen, I just got off the phone with Angie. She's agreed to let us stay with her... that is, after I spent a great deal of time talking her into it."

"They're going to declare my house abandoned," Will warned, sitting up, but hunching over with his hands still clamped on his persistent woody. The damn thing just wouldn't go away, and it wouldn't stop hurting. He considered putting ice on it. "I'm behind on my mortgage... my taxes... I don't know what I'm going to do."

"It's okay. We'll find some way to work everything out." When he sat beside him, the couch springs moaning with age, Will leaned away, though he didn't intend to. Cory's tone dipped into rejected disappointment at his disinterest in being physically close. Will knew how he felt, more than words could say. He had been there before. "While staying with Angie I can help you find a new place of your own. You could work on your paintings and try to sell them and at least try to work up some cash to pay your debts."

I don't care about my artwork anymore, Will argued, silently. *Doesn't he know that?*

He didn't say what it was he had been thinking, only, "Yeah. Yeah, maybe."

"I know you feel like you've given up. I don't know, maybe you have, but I've seen how beautiful your paintings are, and how good you are. You shouldn't just forget something like that."

"I haven't forgotten. I just don't see the point, I guess." He picked at an itching blemish that was rising behind his ear. It produced a scab. Just another scar for the *Will's Scrapbook of Injuries.*

"I thought you were going to start motivating yourself," Cory guided. "Don't you want that? I don't want to see you living in misery the rest of your life, wallowing in self-pity. If something is hurting you, I want it to go away."

"I know that, Cory. Maybe I just need some time." Who was he trying to fool? Cory was no idiot. Still, he trusted his word, at least out loud. "Please don't give up on me."

"I wouldn't."

"Are you sure Angie will be okay with me living there? Being an addict, and all…"

Cory prepared the needle and spoon, like always, hesitating on his answer. "I haven't exactly told her that part."

Well, that's wonderful, Cory. What else did you leave out? How we don't have sex anymore? How we're more like a nursemaid and patient than we are lovers? Not that I blame you, darlin'. I'm the farthest thing from attractive these days, not that I ever was.

"Are you *planning* to?"

"My goal is to get you somewhere to stay temporarily. If I tell people that you're a junkie… you're going to end up homeless."

"Technically, I am homeless." He wrapped his belt around his bare bicep. "This isn't much of a *home.* It hasn't been for many years.

Even when Ian was alive." He laid out his arm, palm out and pointing at the ceiling. Cory smacked his inner elbow, avoiding his scars as best he could, not that Will would have minded it. Hell, he might have enjoyed it. "She's going to see my track marks. She'll find out anyway."

"I'll risk it." He finished boiling, stirring, filling the syringe, then stuck him with the rig. "Besides, you wear long sleeves."

"Scars *are* why I wear long sleeves." He winced at the pain of the needle going in. "Need another clean one, again," he casually advised. "This one's starting to sting now."

"I'll get some new ones when I go out in a couple of days. Stores are closed right now."

After his second injection of the day, this time with a larger dose, his eyes drooped once again, and the couch now felt like a lifting cloud, sailing over calming oceans, carried by a gentle breeze. There was a faint sense of being touched— his hair being stroked. He complied in his imagination, but lacked the energy to on the outside. His lips moved to the words "thank you," but his voice had forgotten how to work.

"Don't leave the toilet seat up." Angie amended an already extensive list of demands for the two men standing in her living room, indicating numbers by holding up her fingers. They were each nodding in harmony, their shoulders hunched. "Don't drink all of the coffee, and if you do, make more. If you leave a mess, clean it. And above all, *please* don't fuck on my couch."

"We can do all that, no problem," Cory tiredly said. He hadn't spoken to him much during the drive over to his friend's apartment, and Will saw it as the first dreadful sign of the inevitable "end of relationship" shipwreck. It was a sign he had grown familiar with over many years of broken hopes and dreams, of men wanting something more than him, something likeable. The clarity of the situation had Will concerned, however. He didn't want to lose Cory. What would he do, and where would he go? "We're not total pigs. We'll be okay."

"Are you afraid we'll get homo germs on your sofa?" Will snickered, but he was the only one.

A cast-iron, gritty glare from Angie was aimed right at him. He inched his head down. "You should be grateful I'm doing this for Cory. If he hadn't sounded so desperate, I would have said no."

He *was* grateful, in his own way. He didn't think he would ever like Angie as a person, but he was quick to judge on surface appearances. Regardless of how they treated one another, it was a redeemable favor in Will's eyes. Even if just for Cory, and the sake of being diplomatic, he would tone down his sardonic wit. "My apologies, Angie. I'm just being… quirky."

She rolled her eyes, then turned back to her friend. "What does your mother think, Cory?"

"She knows I'm doing this. I'm still going to be paying her some rent money in addition to the money I'll be giving you. My stuff is still there. She'll be fine."

"She must be worried sick, with you dating…" She pointed her eyebrows at Will.

"Actually, she's cooled down a little. I don't think she *likes* it, but she's given me space on the issue."

"Really," she said with surprise. "Maybe she thinks it's something she's forced to get used to, with him being her neighbor and all."

"You can speak directly to me, you know," said Will.

She didn't. However, she dropped the subject. "I don't want you both in the shower together, either."

Cory fussed quietly to himself. "It's okay. I don't think Will even showers."

He might have been right about that. When thinking about it, he couldn't remember the last time he showered. He sniffed himself. Ugh, how foul. No wonder they didn't have sex anymore. He almost felt an apology was in order.

"I just want to thank you for doing this for us. Will really needed a place to stay until I help him get his life sorted out."

"Honestly, I'm not doing it just for you," she confessed, her hands mounted on her hips. "Derrick technically still lives here and he comes here all the time. It'd be nice to have the extra company in case something goes wrong."

"He's scared of Will," Cory declared with both pride and affection. "If he saw him here, he might hot-foot it."

"I hope you're right. Just in case, I think Cory should sleep in my bed with me."

"I'm sorry, that's completely out of the question," Will instigated before Cory could agree to the terms, which he knew he would if it meant staying there. "I'll consent to all of your other rules, but do you really expect me to let my boyfriend sleep with you? No. Just, no."

"I don't care if you like it or not. This is my house, and those are my rules."

"Isn't it Derrick's house, too? I don't imagine *he'd* like Cory sleeping with you, either, would he?"

His smugness didn't amuse her, but only stoked the already crackling flames. "Don't like it? There's the door. You can forget the whole deal."

"Will, it's okay," Cory pacified. "Nothing's going to happen. I'm not going to cheat on you after all of this troub— *stuff* I'm going through for you."

Don't sugar-coat it, sweetheart. You were going to say I was "trouble." I know it, you know it. You wouldn't be wrong, either.

"Let's just do as she says," he went on when Will said nothing. "It's only temporary."

He remembered the once desperate craving to be with Cory before their initial relationship, how loyal and considerate he seemed, and how he would kill to experience love with him. Cory never changed, and he was as wonderful as he imagined he would be. It was him that was changing, hanging onto his own life as he would dangle from an outcropping by the tips of his weak fingers. He trusted him, but his neurosis would also consume him, and this was something he couldn't alter to how he saw fit. He knew because he lived it, on Cory's end of the relationship. If he wanted to change for the one he loved, he'd have to put more faith in his judgment.

"All right," he grunted. "I trust you." *I don't like it, but I do trust you.*

Once the deal was enacted, Angie told them where they could put their belongings, two stuffed duffel bags filled with spare clothes. She told them she would make them some dinner if they agreed to clean up afterward. They agreed to without dispute.

After dinner, which Will forced down, he and Cory washed dishes together in the sink while Angie sat down to watch television. It wasn't something that he would mention aloud, but the act felt very domesticated, a task for a married couple. Even in their silence, they had excellent teamwork, and could sense what each other wanted and needed without asking. Cory didn't seem to mind it, although he didn't make much conversation with him for quite a while. Nearing the end of their chore, he spoke to him in a lowered voice, drowned out by the sound of sitcom laughter in the living room.

"This weekend, we can go for a drive around town."

"That sounds relaxing." It truly did. Any alone time with Cory would now be something he treasured, thanks to their new living situation.

"I think there's an art gallery nearby that's hiring. Maybe they need someone to cut and frame things."

"I guess I could check it out." He had let Cory down so much already. Even if he thought this employment opportunity would go nowhere, he wanted to make him happy. His partner seemed pleased with his accordance, and invited him to watch television with him. Though he wasn't too interested in being near Angie (or watching any of that trite drivel on TV), he accommodated his wishes, figuring it was best to sit down anyway. Heavy drowsiness was still coursing through his veins after a shot he had earlier.

Their new roommate seemed displeased with their cuddling when she saw Will's arm around Cory. She might have expressed disinterest in loving Cory romantically, but she still envied them their closeness and love, however much of it still remained. Her relationship had been shattered, along with her hopes and dreams, and to simply see a harmonious couple together was enough to drive anyone in that predicament completely insane.

Angie's discomfort became like a foul odor permeating throughout the room until she left the couch, muttering obscenities under her breath, mentioning something along the lines of "bad decisions". With her now out of earshot, Will cracked a dirty smile.

"What do you think she'd do if we started taking our clothes off?"

Cory snickered and playfully hit him in the chest, but it lacked sincerity. The hopelessness Will then felt at Cory's waning affection was reaching intense severity, and there was nothing either of them could do. Whatever fragments of happiness there were in their romance, they were starting to die, and it was entirely his fault. The light was beginning to fade, the cloud beginning to sink, and they were falling from the short-lived heights they had indulged in.

Take a bow, William Shepherd, sang Will in his darkened mind. *The curtain will soon be drawn. Those flames that burned so hot before were merely staged special effects.*

"You're out of heroin," his companion forewarned. "And I'm broke. What are you going to do?"

A panicked sweat formed on Will's brow, as he could already feel the affects of withdrawals destroying him, long before they had time to reach him. "W-why didn't you tell me sooner?"

"I didn't know how to tell you."

"More like you wanted to punish me."

"That's not it! I wouldn't do that!"

"I *will not* get sick again. I refuse. What am I supposed to do, Cory?"

"You could deal with the sickness for now until you get a job. Then you could buy it yourself."

Exaggerated chuckling left Will's tight mouth. "Deal with it? No. I won't. I'd rather fucking kill myself. You would too if you had to face it."

Cory said nothing, only sulked while watching shows he obviously didn't enjoy. It showed on the inside and the outside: he was miserable. There wasn't much Will could do to make it up to him. He wanted to try, but what other options did he have?

He would have to give Randy a call the following day to see if they could come to some kind of deal or trade. There were many skills he could lay out at his disposal, or he could find something to pawn, though Angie didn't seem the type to keep expensive goods, ones that he could steal without being noticed.

The descending night was met with discomfort when Cory's eyes grew too heavy to force open any longer, and they both knew that they would soon have to part. Though he would only be in the very next room, being away from each other was an agony all too consuming. Angie was a night hawk, hovering over them to make sure Cory was going to hold true to his promise of sleeping in her bed. Cory eventually kissed Will good-night, a gesture that seemed strained, but he did remind him of his love for him. Will repressed the desire to ask Cory to sneak back into the living room to sleep on the couch with him, even if Cory would sleep on his chest, and regretted his submissiveness. He would miss his warmth for the entirety of the night.

Will's bedtime came far later, after hours of infomercials for cooking utensils and exercise equipment. The thought of his next shot was prattling incessantly in his mind, and no amount of boring television would silence it. Sleep was out of the question now unless he had a dose of the dragon, as his brain was now trained to submit only to its powers of lulling relaxation and nothing else. The threat of sickness thickened like rising smoke, and sweat had coated his hair in a layer of oil that made him look even filthier than he previously had.

His eyes opened. The room was a blurry mess, much like his paintings while they were in their first stages. Acknowledging that his glasses might have fallen off, his hand dove to the floor and scrambled as it searched like a hunting hound for the object he often labeled as a "crutch." His index finger knocked into the stem of the rim, and he felt the rest of his fingers around its rectangular shape. Had he fallen asleep? He didn't remember passing out or even feeling tired. Was his sleep cycle that out of whack?

Reattaching the glasses to his face, he focused on the flickering light of the television. The commercials had stopped, and an adult "comedy" show seemed to have replaced them. Now fully awake, he slowly rose to an upright position and smacked his dry, cottony lips, swallowing in his scratchy throat. Standing was a challenge, and his knees didn't wish to work properly, or obey his internal commands. Was he really that tired? Why then did he feel so awake? His brain told his legs to go toward the kitchen, but they only wanted to listen half of the time. He desperately searched for a cup in each of the cupboards, licking his lips.

Filling glass after glass of water, and chugging each of them down with the same fierceness as one would returning from a desert hike, he heard the sound of metallic jingling in between gulps. Keys entered the lock of the door as someone in the hallway tried to get in, and Will turned on the kitchen light, protecting himself behind the counter to have a clear view of the doorway, peeking underneath the bottom of the cupboard.

The door creaked open and a shambling figure stumbled into the apartment, slurring broken English nonsense, tripping on his feet. The intoxicated silhouette crossed the living room, and was now staring directly at Will. In a sudden blinding flash, the apartment was filled with stabbing, golden light, which Will blocked with the back of his hand by pressing it above his brow.

All of the drunken silliness seemed to fade from Derrick Holden's face once he laid eyes on the intruder. "What the fuck are you doing here?" He called to him through clenched teeth.

Will lowered his hand, though only slightly, the light still burning his retinas. "Mostly watching television. What are *you* doing here?"

With a curled lip, jagged teeth protruding out, he barked, "I *live* here."

"That's not what Angie tells us."

"Us?" Derrick paced the living room, looking in all directions. "Where's your boyfriend?"

Would he outright tell the truth, or be deliberately vague? He had to admit that seeing Derrick worked up excited him. Would they violently clash into a rolling ball of furious fists? Would they tumble upon the floor, wrestling one another, as he brought his fist across his cheek? His heart raced. What on earth drew him to enjoy such a thought? He certainly didn't enjoy it when Ian would do it to him. "I could tell you, but I don't think you'd like it."

Walking with abrupt effortlessness, Derrick drifted down the hallway in the direction toward the bedroom, the boots on his feet crunching against the carpet. It took Will's brain a few moments to catch on, but when it did, it warned him that Cory might soon be in danger. His provoking nature may have unintentionally worsened the whole situation, and if Cory was about to be hurt, he would have Will to blame. Zipping away from the kitchen, he rushed after the territorial man and grabbed his bicep to pull him back. The likelihood of getting decked in the face was feasible, but he took his chances. Thankfully for his face, and his glasses (which he couldn't afford to replace had they been shattered), Derrick only shoved him backward, stabbing him with eyes aflame.

"Back the fuck off," he portended rather considerately, despite the hatred in his voice. Will wondered where this very awkward predicament could wander to if he contended with Derrick, and whether or not it would stop him from hurting anyone. It was Cory he was trying to protect after all, and Angie's safety meant little to him. If he wanted Angie, he could have her for all he gave a damn. It wasn't his mess to clean up.

"It's going to look entirely different than how it really is," Will advised, moving in front of him to block his passage. "I don't like it any more than you probably do. You think I'd agree to something like this? Cory did what he had to do."

"What the hell are you talking about? Man, get out of my way!" Despite being under the influence, Derrick's shove packed a mean punch, and Will smacked against the wall like an airborne spitball. He would lay the blame on heroin for being so much weaker than before, but it wasn't the only habit he could accuse by this point.

There was no time to stop him or begin constructing a battle, and Derrick burst his way into the bedroom with the force of ten elephants, stomping like a raging dinosaur let loose on a quiet suburban neighborhood. A feminine shriek filled the dark room, then a masculine gasp of incredulous terror from Will's weary lover, who sounded as though he were ripped violently from dream land.

"*What the fuck?!*" Howled Derrick, who was now enraged beyond the point of human comprehension.

"Derrick?!" Angie screamed in what sounded like faked surprise.

Derrick didn't answer her. Instead, he grabbed Cory by his hair and yanked him off of the bed he was once sleeping on. He gasped in shock and jolting pain, especially when Derrick's fists began erratically swinging. Will, who still had his back pasted to the wall and watching the scene, heard his desperate cry for help, and was filled with insurmountable ire, much as he did the first day he met Derrick.

Leaping from the shadows like a camouflaged panther, he wrapped his thin, veined, badly bruised arm around Derrick's neck, holding him in a headlock. Derrick jabbed his elbow repeatedly into Will's ribs, but adrenaline had killed some of the pain. He held onto his neck for dear life, never relenting, and bathed in the sweet, glorious sounds of him gasping and choking for air.

"Let him go! Please!"

The red faded somewhat from his vision when he heard Angie's plea, and it confused him. He glanced from her to his collapsed partner on the floor, who was staring at him with either awe or revulsion. He couldn't really tell, and it didn't matter either way. As he calculated their stares carefully, he continued to listen to the heavenly cacophony of gasps and gags rising from Derrick's throat, and though causing grievous bodily harm to Derrick would have made the evening end happily, he released him as Angie wished him to.

Sobbing like a child, Angie rushed to the aid of her choking ex, cradling him like a newborn baby, looking at Will in horror. Cory wobbled when he stood, disoriented and dazed, speechless. He planted his face against Will's shoulder and moaned, "Aren't you getting tired of rescuing me?" He tried to make a joke, but it only ended up sounding like a serious question.

"I was enjoying myself." He presented this with the same affection as an employee would to his boss when it was time for a raise.

He said nothing else, but when he next looked at his friend sitting on the floor holding the very same psychopath that looked ready to take his head off just minutes before, he cringed in what looked to Will like disgust. He felt his grip on him tighten. *Don't let him hurt me again* his grasp seemed to beg.

Derrick came to, and his eyes fluttered open, his speech returning to that sloppy incoherence as it had been when he first walked in. Angie preened his neck, which was glowing red, both from anger and from being choked. "Thank God," she gasped when she saw Derrick had not been, in fact, dead. Neither Cory nor Will said anything to her.

"I knew you were in love with him," Derrick panted, gulping every few seconds. "I knew... knew you lied..."

"That's not what's going on here," Angie tried to explain, although calmer than one was expected to after experiencing such a thrilling event, but Derrick helped himself to his feet, tripping backward against the frame of the bedroom door. "He's only sleeping in here because there's no room on the couch for him."

Will didn't bother adding his opinion to the argument, knowing it would only cause further problems. After catching the air and finding his balance, Derrick turned to the two men standing in the bedroom that once belonged to him. He jabbed a long, thin index finger at Cory like he was launching a rocket at his forehead.

"This isn't over, asshole," he preached like a zealot up on a stand, staggering. "Don't th-think I'll forget. One of these times your buddy isn't... won't be there."

"You can't be serious," Cory sighed, rubbing his aching scalp. "What the hell did I do?"

"Let's go outside and talk," Angie proposed to her ex-lover. Derrick momentarily forgot Cory and agreed to join her outdoors for this so-called discussion she wanted to have. She walked him out, leaving Cory and Will alone.

Will was the first of the two to sit down on the bed, then Cory dropped beside him. "What the hell is wrong with Angie?" He wondered aloud. "That's the second time her boyfriend almost killed me, and she doesn't seem to care."

He had already come to a conclusion. "She likes that he needs her. She has an element of control over him."

"Do you think that's why she had me sleep with her? So that he would see us?"

"I don't know. It looks that way to me."

"So she used me? She used me in some little game she was playing with him?" His dismay showed in his dropping head, and Will tried to comfort him by leaning into him. "What if Derrick was carrying a weapon? What if he *killed* me?"

"Maybe she was willing to risk that. I don't want to say things about your friend without knowing any facts, but…"

"No. No, you're probably right." Cory hugged Will around his neck. His arms engulfed Cory's waist. "Maybe I should ask my mother if you can live with me."

"You know as well as I do that she'll turn you down. We can stay here. Angie just needs to know that you can take care of yourself, and me, when it comes down to it."

"If I don't agree to her terms, she's going to throw us out anyway, not that I blame her. It is her house. There has to be somewhere else you can stay."

"You told her you'd be paying her for us to stay here. We have some rights."

Cory stood up, shuffling drably into the hallway. The way that he dragged his heels, Will could tell that the energy he was putting into their relationship had reached pitiful lows. He was ready to leave, and he knew it, not just Angie's apartment, but him. There was only so much he could take, and Will could hardly blame him.

He would try to find a way to bandage their relationship another time. For now, he had to plan out how he would obtain heroin the following day.

14. Stray

Randy gave Will a time to stop by, a time that was inconvenient for him because of how long he would have to wait. On the other hand, Cory would be off work by then, and he could borrow his car to make the pick-up trip.

When he asked the dealer if he traded drugs for goods other than money, he said he did all the time, as long as it was of value to him. There just had to be something in Angie's apartment that she wouldn't miss or even notice was gone if he pawned or traded it to Randy. Everyone had items like that in their possession. He just had to find them.

The first place he searched was her bedroom. Her drawers didn't contain many valuable items, only a hundred and one pairs of underwear and twice that many in bras. She didn't keep any jewelry there from what he could tell, so he abandoned the dresser. He hit her closet next, spying shoeboxes on the upper shelf. He brought them down one by one, pulling the lid off of one with colorful flower patterns on it, the brand name of a tennis shoe sprayed in neon ink across the side. Inside revealed many photographs, some of Angie and Derrick, some of her topless wearing questionable bondage gear (one of which involved a collar), and several close-up shots of Derrick's genitalia. Will was thankful Cory wasn't around to see his face turn pink. He was impressed.

He set the photographs aside, getting back to the important matter of finding trade-worthy items before his sickness developed into the later stages. He was already starting to sweat, far more profusely than he ever did when withdrawing from oxycodone. The symptoms would be bad, oh yes, he could sense it, and if he didn't get heroin soon, he'd have to go down that same old road, a road littered with chills, runny noses, bad smells, and vomit, a road he was unwilling to travel under any circumstances.

He found a pendant in the box, likely a gift from her former boyfriend, but under Will's trained eye, it didn't look as though it was made from pure Sterling silver, but rather silver-plated. In other words, it was a cheap piece of crap Derrick might have lied about the worth of. It was the sort of underhanded bull that he would expect from someone like him. Now that he had cleared one box, he moved on to the next. This one looked like it was for men's shoes, so Will assumed that the box once belonged to Derrick. His beliefs were confirmed as soon as he opened the box and found something that stopped his heart.

Inside the box was nothing but a semi-automatic, silver black-gripped pistol, loaded with a full clip.

He dropped the box and shoved it away, pulling the collar of his sweater up over his mouth and nose as if shielding himself. The room seemed to shrink around him as the air thickened, and his lungs seemed to forget how to draw in oxygen. Turning onto his hands and knees, he shuffled backwards away from the weapon as if it would grow consciousness and come after him. He flattened his back against the side of the mattress, hugging his knees against his chest, trembling as his heart reverberated with trepidation, a burning sensation crossing his skin. A panic attack was imminent.

Calm down. It's just a gun. Calm down. It's just a gun.

His rhythmic chant calmed him, and he took slow breaths to quiet his screaming nerves. Working up the courage to crawl back toward the deadly tool, he envisioned it as something harmless. Finally, he worked up the nerve to grab the pistol in his shaking hand. He had seen the horrid things, unfortunately, but he had never held one. He had to admit, despite his deep fear of them, holding one felt powerful. He believed that by just holding a gun, he could accomplish anything he wanted to, and not a single person would dare mess with him. He supposed he didn't blame those who wielded them.

Why would Derrick leave a thing like this behind? He wondered as he turned the object around in his hand, looking at the barrel from all angles. He traced a fingertip around the shiny silver like he would the jaw line of a beautiful man's face. *A man as violent as him could get a lot of use out of it, couldn't he? Then again, he still comes here every day. Maybe not even Angie knows it's here. I wonder if Randy would take it.*

On that thought, he considered keeping it instead of exchanging it. He wasn't the type to use guns— wasn't even the type to think about using guns— but the powerful rush he felt when holding it was addictive. He wouldn't allow anyone to have it now. It belonged to him.

The symbol of struggle, of death and destruction weighed down his palm, and for once, he felt he was the unstoppable force, as opposed to being on the other side of the beating hand of oppression. He tucked the weapon into his pants and smirked at his discovery, pleased with his innate sneakiness. He wouldn't give Randy the gun, but he knew he'd find some other use for it.

Cory came home first, and by that point, Will was resting on the couch, trying to stave off threatening withdrawals. His beloved greeted him wearily, like a tired wife who had come home to a filthy mess after working a ten hour day. Will welcomed him to sit on the couch with him, but Cory was nonchalant. He wandered into the kitchen first to find a bite to eat.

"Randy asked me to stop by at six," he informed Cory apprehensively, already seeing the tenseness in his partner's back. "You don't have to drive me. I could just take your car."

"Good," he grunted, pouring several flavored potato chips in a large bowl. Will didn't think he would, but he did sit on the couch beside him with his snack. He smiled when Will kissed him, but didn't return the gesture. His eyes were heavy and void of rest, purplish underneath.

"How was work today?"

"Oh… you know how that place is. You've been there just as much as I have." His jaw moved up and down in rhythmic motions as he chewed.

"Yes, I suppose I have." Shivers went up his spine. The sickness was going to get worse. It was going to hit him like a crashing semi truck. "I was thinking today... that maybe we should get a place together."

"You'd have to make some kind of income first, Will. Have you seen how expensive apartments are around here?"

"I know. I... I want to try. I really do."

"I believe you do. Even if you sold your artwork again, you'd be doing something productive. It's good for you to use that brain of yours instead of letting it go to waste."

Will had to commend his refusal to acknowledge his addictions, and to encourage him in other ways. It made him love Cory even more. He glanced at the clock on the wall. It was not even five thirty yet, and the cravings were getting tougher to fend off.

"Would you mind if I used your cell phone to make a phone call?"

Cory answered his question by fishing his phone out of his pocket and tossing it at him. Who he was calling, or why, seemed to matter little to him. He only focused on his bowl of chips.

Will had kept this fact to himself, but he had added Randy's number to the contact list on Cory's phone to make for easier calling. Cory almost never called anyone unless it was his mother, and it was usually to return several calls she made to him in regards to him picking up groceries for her after he got off work, and to ask if he was still alive.

He only had to wait a few seconds for Randy to pick up the phone when he pressed the "Talk" button to dial the stored number.

The dealer used the same vigor and cheeriness in his voice as a door-to-door salesman. "You've got Randy," he sang.

"Hi, it's Will."

A thoughtful pause followed. "I know three Wills. Which one are you?"

"I called earlier this morning. I was going to meet you at six."

"Oh, the Will with glasses, from the clinic. Right. What can I do you for?"

Ian's precious argyle sweater was starting to stick to him. His nose was a leaky faucet and his joints began to cramp. It was starting, and fast, poking and prodding at him like a villainous child constantly stabbing him with the tip of a knife, laughing as he tried to swat him away. "I knew you said I should come by at six, but I'm getting sick. I don't think I can wait another thirty minutes."

"Then by all means, come on by. My last customer just left, anyway."

"Oh thank you, you're a lifesaver."

"That's what they tell me!"

"I'll see you shortly." They each hung up, and Will scrambled off the couch like an unwelcome feline swatted by a broom. Cory didn't look at him, only stared at the television like he was watching his own life play by, and it bored the hell out of him. Will glanced at him as he slipped his shoes on, and he saw all of the inner turmoil wreaking havoc on his depressed face. He had never seen him like that in the years he had known and watched him, even when he had his lonely moments of sitting by himself in a diner or working non-stop in the garage on one of his modular projects. He was detached from everything around him. He hoped that he was only just tired from the previous night, and that he wasn't actually feeling as hopeless as he looked.

"How are you going to pay for it?" He interrogated.

"I don't know. I'll think of something."

"Are you going to steal?"

Lying to Cory was something he hated to do, but what he hated even worse was making a promise he couldn't keep. Despite everything, he was always true to his word. If it hadn't been for Cory, he might have frozen in his house by now.

"Do you not want me to?"

At last, his lover and best friend looked upon him with pleading eyes. "Please don't. I don't want you in jail."

Though his hands were cold and clammy, he stepped beside him and placed his palm against his cheek, which he nuzzled. "I won't go to jail, sweetheart."

"Just promise me that you won't try to steal."

Damn it, Cory. Why do you have to make me swear on these things? I'm desperate, you know that.

He sighed, knowing that he meant well, and feared for him when he thought he might not act rationally. Maybe he wouldn't have to steal. Maybe he could keep his oath.

"I promise."

Cory gripped his hand in his own palm, kissing it, rubbing flavored dust on his skin that had coated his lips. "Thank you."

"I love you, Cory."

Cory sighed. "You, too." He went back to his snack, which he didn't seem to be enjoying much. Will winced at this emotionless response, but didn't instigate an argument. It wasn't a good time.

After retrieving the car keys from him, Will bundled up in his long winter coat and set out for his destination, stuffing his new pistol in Cory's glove compartment. For the entire ride there, he thought of robbing each and every store he passed, now that he had a gun to wave around if he wanted something. No, he wasn't that stupid. Even he wasn't that desperate, at least, not yet.

You promised him, he scolded himself.

Randy lived in a townhouse with his girlfriend, Lisa, a woman that Will only met on one occasion, and felt comfortable to be in the presence of due to her outgoing personality. However, it seemed practiced, rehearsed for meetings with the outside world. She made him think back on the days he pretended to smile around family when he'd show up with Ian to events they were invited to, hiding a horrible secret from them that no one needed to know, and didn't want to know. When Randy explained that she buried her face in cocaine and heroin at least a few times a day, Will already knew, but he was willing to bet she had a few other battle scars she kept shielded by clothes, even from doctors that would ask why she had trouble sitting down because of the pain she'd feel from the bruises on her legs and rear. Whether or not Randy was abusing or raping her, he felt it would be crossing the line to ask, but it was a sort of awareness gained from experience that didn't require questioning.

The gutter outside of the house was littered with trash which rolled in the whirling winds, ice covered the steps, which Will had to climb carefully while grasping the rails, and an old, worn Christmas wreath hung on the door knocker, adorned with colorful red ribbons and holly, a large bell in the center. He rang the doorbell in earnest, cravings causing his bones to twitch. His veins pumped and begged for juice. *Feed us,* they cried from the depths of his skin, urgent. *In due time,* Will comforted.

It was Lisa who answered the door, wearing a heavy pink sweater made of wool, her curly blonde hair curved over her shoulders. She smiled when she saw Will, and welcomed him inside cordially. "Good to see you again, Will." Her face was tinted a soft pink. It was tough for Will to tell if it was makeup or if she had been blushing. Either way, he had little experience in dealing with such things from women.

"You as well," he said. When she turned, Will glimpsed at her back, noticing a purple welt the size of a small apple. He said nothing. It was not his place. It was no one else's place when Ian beat him, either. Maybe she was like him and accepted it as her role in the world: the bottom rung, the battered, beaten, and useless. Maybe she didn't know how or when to escape. He could only give her understanding, empathetic glances of serenity. Somehow, he could tell she picked up on them, appreciated them. They shared a secret that had no words, and she seemed okay with that.

"Ah, there you are," called Randy as he descended a flight of stairs, entering the bizarrely tidy living room with palms out. "The H still doing you good?"

"Perhaps a little too good."

"That's what I love to hear!" He cackled, boisterous and proud, and danced down the last few steps. "So, Will With the Glasses, how much do you want today?" He lit up a cigarette after sticking one in his glazed mouth much like a celebrity would while getting his photo taken. Gregarious and charming Randy was, but hardly a Grade-A citizen, at least in Will's opinion.

Before he had stopped by, he came up with all kinds of excuses and methods to trade for heroin, but none of them sounded intelligent enough in his head. Thinking maybe Randy had some kind of clue on how to go about it, he asked, "What kind of stuff do people normally trade you for drugs?"

Eyes pointed at the ceiling, hands interlocked, Randy clicked his tongue a few times. "Well that depends. It ranges from actual goods to... services."

"What kind of services?"

Leaning his head slightly to the side, he peered around Will to see if his girlfriend was in earshot. She was in the kitchen now, assembling a sandwich in timid silence. He leaned forward, closer to Will's earlobe. "Women who can't afford to pay usually pay me in other ways. You get what I'm saying?" It wasn't scandalous news, but Will still cocked an eyebrow at him. He barely knew him or Lisa, but he thought of her, and of his times when Ian would come home late with lies. Randy caught his accusing look. "Hey, I prefer cash, okay?

But sometimes, I have to take what people can give. If I make the customer happy, they're less likely to rat me out when they get in trouble, you understand? If someone is withdrawing and gets caught trying to score from a cop or something, and I turned that person away with no heroin, who do you think he's going to be the most pissed off at? Me! I'm the bad guy that turned them down, do you get me? If I send them away with drugs and I take something that is of great value to me, no matter what it is, they're not going to snitch, and everyone is happy."

Whatever makes you sleep better at night, kid, Will wanted to say, but chose not to, because once the subject had arisen, the thought had crossed his mind to ask if he had ever received these "services" from men. Will had little confidence in most of his abilities, but he knew for damn sure he was a great cocksucker. Even Ian, a coldhearted bastard, had the generosity to compliment him at what he was good at, even though his acknowledgments were ways of convincing him to do it when he was already unwilling.

"What are you looking at?" Randy had grown uncomfortable at Will's eyes tracing his body.

"How much heroin do you normally give for one of these services?"

Sucking in a great cloud of nicotine, Randy exhaled smoke through his nostrils. "I've given up to a gram for it. It depends on how good they are." His eyes narrowed in suspicion. "Why?"

Will snuck a glance behind him at the kitchen, where Lisa was now sitting at a table and eating. "Maybe we should talk upstairs."

"What for?"

He scratched his head when he felt it twitch. "What if I offered to perform oral sex on you?"

Randy shrugged. "I don't know, man. I'm not queer. And... it's cool if you are, really, it is. It's just not my bag."

"Queer" was a word that Will thought matched an odd person like Randy perfectly. That, however, was for a different discussion entirely. "You don't have to be." When he shrugged again, making a sound of uncertainty, he continued. "Look, I'm not interested in you. I don't want to be your boyfriend. I don't want to take you on a date, and I'm not even remotely attracted to you." He frowned in spite of his congeniality on the matter. Apparently, such news was not common for him, and he took silent offense. "I'm not asking you for a commitment, I'm just asking for an exchange. I just want to make a trade, that's all. You can watch porn the whole time I'm doing it for all I care."

Puffing on his cigarette a few more times, his lips twisting left and right, he leaned against the banister of the staircase. "How good are you?"

"I'm better than any woman that's done it to you." He didn't think Randy would be amused by this, but he laughed. "I'm not kidding."

"I believe you, Will. You just sound… confident. I've been with a lot of women."

"I'm experienced. Why don't we test my confidence, and you'll find out?"

Replaying that same hearty chuckle he had just used, he dragged his fingers along the bottom of his chin. "Well, since you're so eager… follow me."

They both went upstairs to a bedroom decorated in posters for sci-fi movies and television shows. The environment was hardly erotic, but he could care less. He wasn't there to have any fun. He just didn't want to be sick. If he could provide a skill he was talented at in exchange for drugs, why not utilize it?

It was obvious to Will that Randy had no idea how to proceed into the act of getting sucked off by a man, not quite understanding that he had gone through the identical process with women. The only difference was his gender. It was as though he expected a half-time light show with club music to go along with it, or parade dancers to shimmy their way into the room during orgasm, and didn't really know how to feel. Will reminded him that he could just pretend he was female and didn't even need to look at him or think about it. "Are you kidding me?" He asked. "How could I *not* think about it when it's a dude between my legs?" Will asked him to relax much like a nurse would before giving an injection that the patient thought would be more painful than it really was. Despite how awkward Randy made the whole ordeal, Will found his bashfulness entertaining.

Randy had taken Will's suggestion and started playing a video on his computer across the room, one of a twenty-something woman howling fake screams of joy while getting nailed by an older man. Will had a neutral opinion of videos like that, whether they were gay or straight. He didn't love them or hate them— he just never found one that he thought was any good, and his sex drive was far below that of an infertile old woman's. Sex, to Will, was something he did to please others, not to share passionately with a partner or even enjoy by himself. Sucking Randy's dick would be an interesting assignment, but only because he liked to prove his skills, not because he would be getting any thrills from it.

Sex with Cory felt different, he recalled. He watched as Randy undid his jeans while lying on the surface of his queen-sized bed. *It wasn't "fucking," not like sex with Ian was when we started out. He made love to me. I think it was the first time I actually liked having sex. I could feel, just by the way he moved, that he loved me. I wish I was doing that right now instead of… this.*

He put it out of his mind, knowing it would affect his performance. Randy had removed his member from his pants as casually as he would order a meal at a restaurant, and motioned for Will to get to work. It was a commanding hand gesture Will was not only fully familiar with, but comfortable. It almost turned him on to see it. Almost.

The drowning sounds of porn in the distance weren't enough to stifle Randy's noises of approval and surprised satisfaction as his customer went down on him, but Will merely wanted to get it over with, and quickly, even if Randy was enjoying himself. He moaned an encouraging "yeah" here and there, though it could have been due to poor impulse control, which wouldn't surprise him. After many long, long minutes of tiring his jaw out, Randy's exclamations graduated to rapid moans in a tightening, squeezing voice. It was a theme Will related to ejaculation, and he didn't need any other warning signs. He removed his mouth and finished him with his hand, which he knew might get him fewer drugs, but he wasn't interested in swallowing the spunk of a man he wasn't committed to. It was a strange rule to follow, but it had moral significance to him.

Randy was nice enough to thank him, and acknowledged that Will was justified in his earlier self-assurance. Will went into the bathroom and washed his mouth out to rinse away any evidence that Cory might see, or rather smell on his breath. He scrubbed the shame off of his lips and cactus needles growing on his strong, but skeletal jaw. By the time he returned to the bedroom, Randy had filled a small bag with a gram of heroin and tied it off with a bread tie, as well as a decorative holiday tag that was a bit belated. Will thought he might not have known Christmas had already come and gone. He presented it to Will with a wide smile, one of charm and gratitude. He looked the way Will felt after he had received a hit.

Maybe he hasn't had any kind of sex in a while, Will measured with care. *I guess in that case, we helped each other.*

"I should get going," Will told him as he tucked the bag into his coat pocket.

"Of course." He lit up a cigarette, but didn't look his customer in the eye. Will thought he saw blush on his cheeks. "See you again soon, I hope. Uh, for *heroin*, I mean. Yeah. Heroin."

"I knew what you meant." He was tired. He wanted to go back to the apartment, take his shot, and go to sleep. Randy was lingering like a drunken one-night stand, and he didn't have the patience for it.

"Right." He threw a half-assed wave at him, still avoiding any eye contact. Will was tickled by his shyness. If he had the energy or mood to laugh, he would. Just as he stepped out of the bedroom, Randy cleared his throat, indicating a desire to discuss a private issue. Will turned, stopping halfway between the room and the hallway. "Don't tell anyone... okay?"

Baffled, Will shook his head. "Who the hell would I be telling?"

"I know you and my girlfriend kind of get along. You spoke a bit last time you were here."

"I'm not going to tell your damn girlfriend, Randy."

"And if you see any of my other customers..."

Will didn't have it in him to argue with a straight man and his silly insecurities, and he was running out of time before the sickness would settle in. "Don't be so ashamed of getting a quality blowjob."

"I'm... not." His eyes twitched from side to side.

"You're fine. It's not like you're dying. You enjoyed yourself." Randy's face went redder. "I'll see you again sometime." He ended the conversation there before it got any weirder, and he descended the stairs. Randy had vacated the bedroom and was now peering over the railing at him, possibly to verify whether or not he'd hold true to his word on not telling Lisa, but there was an intense longing to his watchful gaze. He thought for sure he was going to call to him, tell him to come back and do it to him again. He was far from interested. He did want to tell something to Lisa, unrelated to him stuffing his mouth with her boyfriend's genitals. *Find someone better, someone who will treat you right.* He then thought of someone saying the exact same words to Cory. He changed his mind, and bid Lisa farewell before leaving.

During the drive home, Will repeatedly checked the inside of his mouth to make sure there were no signs a penis had been in it. It looked just as filthy and yellow as it normally did, and he was repulsed by his own reflection. It was a mystery to him how Cory could ever kiss someone with such a hideous maw.

"I should just tell him," he argued with himself. "I should tell him the truth."

Yes, William. Tell him you chose heroin over fidelity. He'll love that.

"It's better that he knows. Something just like this will come up again in the future. If Randy wanted to keep giving me smack for blowjobs, I'd keep doing it."

Yes. You really would, wouldn't you?

Not a single minute during that drive back to the apartment was Will relaxed, and he knew that even if he wasn't honest with Cory that night, he would have to be eventually. Cory would be shattered, heartbroken, and he might even have to end things if it meant doing the right thing for him for once. If he wasn't true to Cory, he had gone against everything he believed in. He owed it to his partner to give him the choice of staying with someone like him or moving on with his life. It was unfair to torment him any longer.

Will meandered into the apartment with a shadowy heart, a storm cloud hanging over his head. Cory was still watching the TV like a lifeless zombie with eyes slanted, blinking slowly. Will said hello to him, but his only answer was a slight twist of the hand. He looked fed-up, vacant of emotion. Will knew then that he had to release Cory's shackles. He needed to set him free.

Only Will didn't particularly want to leave Cory. In his mind, their relationship was far more harmonious than it was in reality, and he had been lying to himself for a while at how well it was all going. All the same, he loved him, and he didn't want to put him through any more pain.

Cory eventually looked his way as he stood near the door, rocking back and forth on his heels. "What's wrong?" He asked, sounding fearful.

"Cory…" It was the right thing to do to tell him, but he just couldn't bring himself to let him down even further. He seemed so depressed and crushed and tired, that he didn't have a true friend in the world. When his eyes bulged with the growing fright of oncoming bad news, it killed any desire inside of him to confess what he had done. "I... need my shot."

Hope, as well as panic faded from Cory's face, and he slowly shuffled off of the couch, found a spoon and grabbed his other tools, like the cotton and rigs, and motioned for his boyfriend to follow him to the bathroom. It was possible, in Will's opinion, that Cory already knew something was off, and just wanted to get the pain over with. He deserved that much. He knew he did. It was tougher than he had surmised to be the one to administer such agony to the one he loved.

Cory was gentle with his arm when he injected him, even kissed his many track marks. That act of affection stung worse than any dull needle that pierced his flesh. "I love you so much," Will whispered. He meant every word.

Cory could only smile at him. It was dreary, worrisome, but sincere.

The stress and concern of his disloyalty faded from his mind when the luscious serum took affect, and he soon forgot its grave importance. Now that he had just what he needed to steady his nerves and silence his brain, he could relax and get some rest. He couldn't help but smile at the choir of angels singing a lulling chorus, telling him to surrender to the nectar's incredible flow of time, of certainty, and of unity.

Something tapped him on the cheek. "Will," called a distant, familiar voice. It increased in volume, but a deep ocean had masked it with shifting waves. "Will!"

"I'm here," he thought he said, but only his lips answered. His voice had disappeared, run off somewhere. He thought he heard it singing a song he and Ian once loved.

A few more jolting cracks landed on his face, like an irritating wasp that thought one sting was not enough to get its point across. "Will, answer me, damn it!" The familiar voice begged. It was full of fear. "You passed out! Please, answer me. Come on honey, say something!"

Were his eyes closed? He wasn't sure. They sure felt like they were open. Something fleshy lifted his upper eyelid, and he gasped for air like rising from deep waters. He swatted the salty hand away, rubbing the pain out of his eyes, then turned over on his side.

You're lying down. Do you remember lying down?

No, he honestly didn't. Cory had given him his shot... that was the last thing he could recall. The surface he was resting on was hard and cold, and smelled funny. It was definitely no bed or couch, where he thought he was located. Where he was, he had no idea. All he could comprehend was the power of sleep, of worry-free rest.

He was being shaken by something. It roused him once again, though he was hardly fully conscious.

"Will, please let me know you're okay!"

He got a single glimpse of a toilet. Wasn't he sitting on it a second ago? "Mm-err..." He moaned, intending to say Cory's name. Life entered his outstretched hand, and he flexed it in a begging motion.

Take it, he wanted to say. *Help me.*

Cory took it and gripped it, squeezing. He was suddenly weightless, being scooped up off of his comfy nap area, and he growled. Cory ignored his noises of frustration and dragged him across the floor, and Will felt the fibers of carpet burn his skin until it met the downy softness of cushions.

"What the hell is wrong with *him?*" Was that Angie? She sounded even more pissed than usual. No, "pissed" was not exactly right. She was more astounded than anything.

"He's not feeling well."

He was covered with a warm blanket, one made of wool. He snuggled it and smiled, cooing like a child. If only the voices would stop. Then he could truly enjoy his high.

"Why is he grinning like an idiot, then?"

"He's... got a fever. He's delirious."

You're a terrible liar, Cory Anderson. The tickling, itchy sensations on his neck were swelling, and he couldn't even find the energy to lift his hand to scratch it.

"What's really going on here, Cory?" It was silent for many seconds more. "Oh, God... he's a junkie, isn't he? Please, tell me that isn't true."

Both Cory and Will dropped into a lapse of silence. Angie had caught on quicker than either of them had thought she would. It could only go downhill from there. Will could picture her face now. It might have been contorted into a look of puerile abhorrence.

"Angie..." Cory sounded like he would pass out from exhaustion any minute, one thing after another needing his attention, never ceasing. It was too much for him. "Please, try to understand—"

"I don't want to hear it, Cory!" Clomping footsteps paced the room. "I can't believe you. You actually brought a *junkie* into my house! What's the matter with you?! Is this how you treat your friends?! You *lie* to them so they do favors for your drug-addled boyfriend?!"

"Angie... I-I'm sorry!"

"He might have stolen something while we were at work! Probably pawned it for drugs!" There was a slight pause, and Cory was silent, likely hanging his head as he often did when ashamed. "What are you thinking, Cory?! What made you think I'd want *junkie scum* in my home?!"

"He's more than just a junkie to me, Angie. He's... he's everything to me. I know it doesn't mean much to you when I say that, but that's how it is. I realize that I probably hurt you. I didn't mean to."

Angie toned down her fury. "Cory, I thought you had more sense than this. Why can't you see what he's doing to you? I can't watch you destroy your life for him. You're worth more than this, and I can't take stand seeing you breaking your back for someone who takes advantage of you. I'm sorry, sweetie, but while you're with him, you can't stay here." A creaking sound filled the room as a door of some sort opened. Will tried as hard as he could to open his eyes, but it was as difficult as lifting a car would be.

"I'm sorry I didn't tell you. I thought if you knew... you wouldn't let us stay with you. I didn't mean for it to affect our friendship..." There was a sniffle from Cory, and rustling sounds as Angie fished objects out of a closet. "Forgive me."

"Cory," Will managed to mumble, though he thought he dreamed it. "It'll be okay." He knew it probably wouldn't be, but it was something he needed to hear at the moment.

"*You*," Angie snorted, though it took him a moment to realize it was directed at him. The soft covers were ripped off of him, and he used whatever energy he had to throw his arms over his head for protection from flying fists. "Get the hell out of my house." Will's eyes opened now that his heart was pumping proper amounts of blood through him, and he looked at Angie with a mixture of fear and regret. "I knew you were scum the moment I met you, but a junkie? I didn't think Cory's standards were so pathetically low."

"We'll leave if that's what you want," he told her with his hands up as he slipped off of the couch. "Just please, don't blame Cory. This is my fault."

"I don't want to see your worthless ass around here again, do you hear me?"

He looked from her angry face to Cory's, which was covered by a shameful hand. "All right. We'll go." As he rose into a sitting position, he stared at her for a while as she glared down at him. "I didn't mean for this. My habits aren't your responsibility. I'm sorry."

Angie's eyes softened. She turned her head away. "I won't call the police or anything. Just stay away from here." When Will climbed off the couch, she whispered to him, "Think about what you're doing to my friend. He doesn't deserve this. And you don't deserve *him*." He didn't bother telling her that he already had considered that.

Grunting, Will staggered over to his stressed and crying partner, putting an arm around him. He didn't return the gesture, only gathered their belongings off of the floor like picking up pieces of glass after a messy fight. Heroin fought off many things, but it couldn't shut off the guilt. He had never seen Cory so torn up or so broken, like a smashed toy that was discarded in a gutter. When they left the apartment, Cory said farewell to his friend, but the exchange seemed as though he expected it to be the last time they spoke.

Will followed him outside into the cold, and Cory drove them back to Hunter Street. Will took a moment to think seriously on his position. He knew that he didn't want Cory putting himself through hell, forcing himself to live in terrible conditions just for his sake. He didn't want him skipping meals just because he did, or missing work to take care of him when he was sick from withdrawals. He didn't want him to cry because of a friendship he ruined. He didn't want to be the one to destroy the very life he hoped to enchant once upon a time.

"We have to talk." He hated saying those words. It never meant anything good was going to follow. They were precursors to the worst news you could ever hear out of the mouth of someone you loved and trusted.

"We do?" Cory was in denial, and had been since the beginning, but Will saw it in his eyes. He knew what was happening, and didn't like it. "About what?" His Adam's apple flexed when he swallowed.

Will delayed the inevitable. He didn't want to go through with it, no matter how badly it needed to be done. He was just as terrified as Cory looked. "About... you and me."

Cory's watering eyes dribbled and he blinked away the welling drops so that he could see the road. They streamed down his cheeks like rain on a window. "Don't," he pleaded.

"I have to."

"Not now. Please, not now."

It was hard to keep his cool when seeing him fall apart, but he knew too well that the pain was necessary. "When you told me you wanted to be with me, it was the greatest high I had felt in a long time. Then I started doing heroin, and it felt ten times better than that. I thought you were all I needed..."

"Stop it, please," he sobbed. "Will, don't fucking do this to me."

Will paused. He almost didn't go on. Hearing Cory cry was too much for him. No one that sweet should ever have to cry so hard over him. "I've ruined everything, Cory. You were right when you said I should have just dealt with that sickness. I would have gotten over it, and I would still have you. Now I..." He couldn't finish that sentence, because it was a lie. There was no way he could say "I don't even want you." He did want Cory, but Cory didn't need him. "I have something better. I look forward to my shot every day instead of being with you. I was meant to live alone, to *be* alone, with just me and my problems. I'm so sorry I dragged you into this."

The car skidded, and Will grabbed the door handle for support, his heart nearly bursting from his chest. Cory jerked the car over to the side of the road and pulled over, slamming it into park. His head collapsed forward on the rim of the steering wheel, and he cried buckets of heartbroken tears. Will wanted to stroke his back, to do anything to comfort him, but knew it was best not to.

"I know we're going through a tough time," choked Cory, taking uneven breaths. "But I know we can make it."

"You know that's not true." Saying so was like ingesting a mouthful of cinnamon powder— bitter and dry— but it had to be said. "We don't have sex. We barely even spend quality time together.

You shoot me up and I'm out for hours, then I want more. Do you really want to live the rest of our lives like that?"

"But, I... I can help you... I can help you..." This prayer seemed so ritualistic that Will assumed he had told it to himself every day, and it had lost all of its meaning by now.

"You can't, and you never will." Cory began to break down even further. "You shouldn't have to force yourself to take care of me, to try to change me. This is me, who I am, and I'm doing you harm whether you think I am or not, and I can't handle it anymore." He forced himself to look away when Cory's tear-stained eyes peered directly into his.

"I don't want to give up on you."

"Sometimes giving up is the only thing you can do."

"Will, I won't. I promised myself that I'd stick by you, that I'd find a way for us to live—" He cut himself off.

Now looking out the window, he stared up at the sky, where the stars were unusually dim. "Normally?" Cory didn't answer, only sniffled. "If you're not happy with me, why are you doing this?"

"I love you."

"I have to wonder what love means to you. Is it being a martyr? Sacrificing your own happiness for the sake of others'? That's no way to live, Cory. I might be stoned half of the time, but I have the intelligence to grasp that love needs to be mutual... and I think I love heroin more than you."

He realized all too late what he had done, and what he had said. Cory cried harder than he had ever heard anyone do. His heart had split down the center right before his eyes, and he knew that pain, felt it on many occasions, but in time, it would always fade. Telling this to Cory would make no difference, and a wound this deep would take more than just a few weeks of soup and television to heal. His hand ached to touch him, to comfort him, to let him know everything would be okay, but it wouldn't be, not for either of them.

A half hour went by of the both of them releasing their grief, preparing for the moment for their final goodbyes, knowing it might be the last moments they'd spend together. When Cory drove them back home, which Will thought would end in a suicidal car wreck that he might have deemed appropriate and a fitting way to end his life given the past and current circumstances, he parked in Will's driveway first.

Before another word was spoken, Cory hugged Will around his neck and clung to it. Will didn't fight off the urge to hug him back, squeezing just as tight. From the way Cory attached himself to him, he thought that there might be a chance Cory was willing to suffer for him, to be miserable just to stay with him. Maybe misery *was* his happiness. That was an unrealistic view, though. He didn't have room in his life for both Mister H and Mister Anderson, and he had chosen the former. In a way, he told Cory that he wasn't worth all of the trouble he had gone through to be with him, and if he had been Cory, he would have been incredibly insulted. Still, there he was, holding him and whimpering, their wet cheeks mashed against one another's.

"I can't do it, Will," Cory gasped, gripping and scratching the back of Will's neck.

He was really making it more difficult than he needed to be, and Will had no choice but to end things by admitting worse crimes. "I sucked my drug dealer's cock for heroin." He quickly shut his eyes, expecting the familiar sensation of a palm cracking over his face. But the smack didn't come. Instead, Cory's hands loosened, and he slowly released his neck. It was haunting how quiet he had become, how still he was. He stared into the middle distance, reflecting on the words that had just been uttered to him. Will wished he had chosen to hit him instead. At least that he was used to.

Cory killed the car's idle engine and climbed out of the vehicle with austere grim, choking on his own tears while striding toward his mother's house. He didn't even bother to lock the car doors. Will stepped out after grabbing his gun from the glove compartment, once again hiding it behind his belt line, and walked toward his own front door with his duffel bag of belongings. He stopped when he reached the porch and looked one last time at Cory Anderson, the man he spent two whole years following around Lansing because of how badly he was addicted to him, who he traded in for something better. Cory vanished into his house, slamming the door behind him. That's how he knew for sure— he hurt him, and there was no taking it back.

Will needed a shot, and soon. He would have to learn to inject himself on his own, which was something he hadn't considered until now. He saw several notices taped to his door, but he didn't pay them any mind. They didn't matter. He pried his way into his home (minding the patches of ice), and set his many tools on the table that Cory would always use, and found a spoon in the kitchen. He went to work, heating up the heroin and water in the bowl of the spoon, both of his hands trembling as he shivered, his vision foggy from his stained glasses and angry tears. He was disgusted with himself, and everything he represented. How could he let things get this bad? How could he let the one man who actually tolerated him walk away?

His shaking hand lowered the spoon to the table, but only ended up dropping it onto the floor, water and heroin spilling on the rug. "FUCK!" He screamed and dove for the solution, but by then it was too late. The carpet had soaked it up. "Son of a bitch! Can't fucking believe this!" He rushed to the kitchen to wash and sanitize the spoon a second time, but in a fit of rage, he chucked it across the room, hearing it ring as it bounced onto the floor.

Cory wasn't going to be the type to beat some sense in to you. That was Ian's job. You kept him drinking, but he kept you in line. You're on your own now. No one, not even Cory, is around to monitor or control you.

That wasn't true, however. He knew where else he could go. It was just a question of whether or not he was willing to let his parents know that their son was a junkie. They were always there for him when he was cutting himself during his teenage years, but this was different. He had given up everything to have heroin, even his chance at a better future.

He removed his glasses to wipe his flooding eyes, lowering to a sitting position on the freezing cold floor. Cory didn't want to give up on him, and he betrayed him and pushed him out of his life. He would make things right again. He would fix it. He would try to change.

He just hoped it wasn't too late.

15. Mend

Will had finished off every last bit of heroin by the end of the week, and when the final shot of solution entered his veins, he couldn't even enjoy it. Not only was he terrible at making the shot compared to how skilled Cory was at it, he couldn't stop dwelling on the decay of his only existing friendship, and the only good romance he ever had, in spite of its briefness. The pressure of finding a method for obtaining more heroin was also a dire condition, especially when he had no phone to call anyone, and had limited gas in his car's tank. He had to make a decision: either use the last of the gas in his tank to drive to Randy's place in hopes that he was willing to accept fellatio a second time, or drive to his parents' home, which he hadn't visited in close to a year.

If anyone could help him with a habit, it was them. They would be disheartened with him, perhaps even angry, but it was the kind of tough love he needed right now. Cory loved him, but he was too soft on him for something like this, and as much as he appreciated his gentle nature, he needed an authority figure to straighten him out. If they didn't send him to a hospital or rehabilitation center, which he figured they wouldn't, anything they did would prove a valuable technique.

Feeling much too cold to stay in his house another day, or even another hour for that matter, he left for East Lansing, where his parents resided. They had a quaint, one-story home covered in blue paint in a cheery, all-American neighborhood on a road called Oakvale, a place Will often thought was picturesque enough to belong in one of his many paintings. Happy families of all kinds nested there, none of which would allow their children to play with "that creepy Shepherd kid" as he was growing up, and if they did, they'd advise them to stay away. He didn't so much mind being the outcast of the neighborhood, and he supposed they had many justified reasons for behaving the way that they did, but it got him inured to being lonely, a trait that killed the final glimmers of friendliness that might have been leftover inside him after his adoption. With no friends, he relied on authority, and learned to like it that way, even if the authority was a bit too powerful.

The silver door of the garage was rusty, though it looked recently painted, and the driveway was freshly plowed. The motion-detecting porch light illuminated his car as he pulled in, and from the flickering beams of light flashing in the window, he assumed one or both parents was awake and watching television.

Judging by the movement of silhouettes passing back and forth beyond the window, his unexpected arrival stirred the owners. He vacated his car and wobbled to the front door, apprehensive of the outcome of visiting so out of the blue, and unannounced. The brown front door swayed open and an older woman stepped out in a cardigan, sweat pants, and slippers, her jaw descending.

"William?!" She cried to her foster son, who she immediately clung to.

"Hi, mom," he whispered, returning the hug, though his was much weaker.

"Where the hell have you been?" Will's mother, Maria Shepherd, fixed her golden-hazel eyes onto his, and he looked away. "Did something happen?"

"I'll explain everything." He walked her back into the house, glancing at the vacant, super-sized sofa and television, which was showing a scientific program on African wildlife. It would intrigue him if he had been visiting under less grim circumstances.

"Anthony! Your son is here!"

Anthony Shepherd seemed to rush into the living room as quickly as his hips would allow, though his creaking steps seemed to increase in volume as he rocked on older feet. He looked upon his son with equal parts remorse and happiness, and his arms hooked around him like tentacles. "Will," he crowed through his raspy smoker's throat. "How are you, son? We haven't seen you in a long time."

"I know, dad. I'm sorry. There's been a lot on my mind."

"We've missed you so much." He patted his son's shoulders in a fatherly manner, a symbol of both his respectable aggression and love. When he took a good look at Will's face, his own crumbled. "Good God, boy, what happened to you? You're wasting away."

"I guess that's because I haven't been eating." He shrugged.

"Why the hell not? What's wrong with you?"

"Dad... I'm... not well."

Anthony had heard this kind of news many times before, and in practice, he had gotten used to Will coming to him for painful personal issues. He knew just how to look at him, how to speak to him, and how to handle it, due to the amounts of experience he had dealing with Will's dark life. "What's going on?"

When it came down to it, Will just couldn't say out loud that he had a heroin addiction. It was all too much for him to confess to the people who had sheltered him and loved him for so long. Letting them down, telling them that he had failed in life, that he wasn't as smart as they thought he was, was a lot harder than he expected.

He began to fold back the sleeves of his sweater. Each inch they came up, the slower he went, and his hands shook with anxiety. His parents were already in shock from the sight of many self-inflicted scars dating back many years, but the moment they laid eyes on his track marks and injection wounds, they looked faint. Maria might have gasped, but he was too focused to hear her, or maybe he didn't want to. By the time his sleeves had reached his biceps, the looks of horror on each of the faces of his parents were too much for him to lay eyes on.

"Will..." Anthony stammered, his eyes glazing over. "What have you done to yourself?"

Will could only manage to say two words to his father: "Help me." He couldn't finish this request without bursting into desperate tears, but didn't quite realize it until Anthony pulled him hard against his sturdy chest, where he sobbed even harder. He stroked his back, like he had many times before when Will cried, and clung to him.

"Why, William? Why are you doing drugs?"

"I liked them. B-but I don't want to do them anymore. I'm going to lose my home. All of my utilities were shut off. I know I'm usually too proud to beg—" He was cut off by a wave of his father's hand, and he fell silent in an instant.

"You don't have to ask us for anything, Will. This has always been your home, and it will continue to be."

That was just what he needed to hear, and now that he heard it, he could relax. After sucking in a deep breath, his crying died down as he dried his eyes and wiped off his glasses. "Thank you, dad."

"You can stay with us for a little while. Your room is exactly the way you left it the last time you were staying with us… just a little cleaner."

"I'm going to be really sick, you know." He glanced at his mother after he said this, knowing she probably already had a plan in mind to lock him in his room and never let him out. The way she was looking at him made him think she was imagining him trolling the streets, looking for someone to sell him dope, sleeping in gutters. He supposed it wasn't too far from the truth.

Anthony, always comforting but always assertive, gently patted his back. "We'll take care of you. You know that."

"I might get really angry with you, maybe beg you to let me out to buy the stuff. You do know that don't you?" Anthony nodded. "You can't let me do it, dad. You can't let me go out there."

"We'll figure it all out, don't you worry." There were a couple more pats from his hand. Will found it soothing.

"I might try to…" He twisted his palms together, wringing them like wet rags, then continued, "Steal from you."

"No you won't." With that mean, wrinkled cocked eyebrow and deep, aged creases around his serious mouth, Will actually believed him. Just hearing him say so was enough to convince him. "You're going to get better. I'll see to it." Anthony glanced at his wife, who was close to passing out. "Honey, make the boy some soup, would you?"

"I'm not hung—"

"You're eating some soup."

He had to admit— his father's stern dominance was refreshing, and just what he needed to get himself back to normal, or at least somewhat. "O-okay." He nodded in case he didn't hear him. His mother disappeared into the kitchen, and Will already knew she would be cooking up a bowl of clam chowder, his favorite when he was a kid. Anthony guided his son to sit with him on the couch and

Will started to blurt out what had been going on in his life the past year or so. He told him about Cory, that he had left him because of drugs, and that they were neighbors. He assumed it would be best to leave out the fact that he stalked him.

"You sound like you love this kid a lot," Anthony observed.

"I do. Dad, I completely fucked up."

"We all make mistakes, Will. That's a lesson you never truly learned. You considered your mistakes as things you deserved to be punished for. I can see…" he pulled up one of Will's sleeves to look at his scars. "You still do."

Will rolled his sleeve back down. He hoped his father would never know that he still cut himself, but not there was no going back. Regardless, he felt ashamed. He took off his glasses to rub his eyes, which burned from the cigarette smog. "You should have seen his face, dad. I told him I loved heroin more than him. I crushed him, and I feel so fucking terrible." Anthony nodded at him to show he was listening, a fresh cigarette in his mouth now. "I destroy everything I touch, even the ones I love."

"You know that isn't true."

"It is, though. Ian is dead because of me."

"It's not like you put the bottle and the keys in his hand. You didn't kill Ian. Even if you had, I wouldn't have blamed you one bit, son. He was no good for you. He was a terrible person, all throughout, and you didn't need him."

"He wasn't always bad," Will grunted, hunching forward. "There were moments I really loved to be around him. We butt heads a lot, and he got carried away with his anger. It's just when he drank—"

"Which was all the damn time. You called me up at ten in the morning crying once because he drank a whole six pack for breakfast and was already calling you names. I could hear that piece of… hear *him* screaming in the background, saying you were worthless and a loser. Why do you make excuses for him, even now? He's gone, and the world is a better place."

"Denial, I guess." He said it with such vagueness that Anthony had to look at him to see if his eyes were lying to him.

"No, that's not it. It sounds more like *guilt*. I always get the feeling you're keeping something from me when we talk about him."

Will's lips pulled down into a frown. There was no getting past Anthony the Fast. He didn't need to explain how dependent he was on controlling, manipulative personalities, how he attracted those types like an insect to a Venus fly trap. It was troubling that he often fell in love with men like that, but he wasn't made of stone. There was a limit to how much he could take, and Ian pushed his limits to the edge several times. There was no lying that his drunk-driving accident alleviated him. Despite his dependency, he was glad that he would no longer be under the gun. With Cory, he wanted a change, to see the better side of humanity, feeling tired of the sickness and darkness he had been around for so long. He didn't think he would be the one to taint that with his negativity.

It sounded so much clearer in his mind than it would aloud. Anthony wouldn't understand even if he did explain it. How could he tell his own father that he allowed Ian to hit him on many occasions just to have a haphazard sense of security? There were many things he just "got," but his emotional shield wasn't one of them. Cory understood it, though he'd never consent to controlling him in that way. That was one of the many things he already began to miss. He gave the right amount of love.

Maria eventually returned with a steaming bowl of soup, which she set down on the coffee table in front of Will. He leaned over the freshly-cooked goop as he flashed back to times when his parents cared for him when he was sick. He swore he'd never be a burden on them again, but it wasn't that simple. Since birth, he was a mistake, an accident, and was reminded of that every time he botched an attempt at anything. *What's done is done,* Anthony would always tell him after he accidentally broke a dish or spilled something and was ready to start digging knives into his own arm. *You can't help that.* If only he could take his advice.

After staring at the soup for some time, his father's hand clapped upon his spine. "Eat," he commanded. He picked up the thick spoon and started scooping the stuff into his mouth. It might have been his faulty memory, but it tasted so much better in his youth. Now, eating it was just a chore. Still, he did as his father wanted, because soon, he would have to endure something far worse than eating.

He could hear the television through the walls. No matter how hard he stuffed his pillow over his ears, he could hear everything going on in the next room, from the daytime TV, to the sound of his mother crossing the floor over and over again. Why couldn't she just turn the damn thing off and take a nap? It was driving him insane.

She denied his multitude of requests to crank the heat up, and instead tried to bring him food. "I don't want it," he'd mutter with clenched teeth. Food was not going to make his rock hard bed any softer, and it wasn't going to stop the shakes. If anything, the simple smell of food made him want to throw up, especially runny foods like the stuff she made for him.

"You have to eat, William," she lectured, carrying a breakfast tray.

"No," he groaned, pulling the layers of blankets over his head. "I've gone a while without eating meals. I think I'll be fine for the next day or two. Just turn the fucking TV down."

"Don't speak to your mother that way." She said this so calmly that Will thought she was joking. Knowing her, she probably wasn't.

"I need a hit," he moaned, not intending to out loud. "Mom, please, let me borrow some money and let me go. Dad wouldn't have to know."

"You told us not to let you, honey. You can beat this. You're strong enough."

He appreciated her encouragement, but she was wrong. He wasn't strong enough, not for anything. He wasn't strong enough to hold down a job for more than a few weeks. He wasn't strong enough to cope with Ian's death. He wasn't strong enough to hold onto Cory, and he especially wasn't strong enough to rid himself of all addictive habits. If strength was what it took to overcome sickness, he was doomed from the very beginning. His body trembled, not just because he was cold, but because he was beginning to panic and succumb to depression. When his mother heard him crying, she set the tray of food down on a desk in the room's corner and sat beside him on his old, creaking mattress, stroking sweaty hair out of his face.

"I've seen you fight tougher things," she told him as though she had read his mind.

"I know you and dad are really disappointed in me."

"Not disappointed. Afraid. We don't want to bury our own son."

"I don't want to be like this. I want to be normal, mom."

She didn't bother arguing that he was perfect in her eyes, because in essence, he wasn't. "We're not going to let you fall back down. We're going to help you through this. Are you going to be all right when I go back to work tomorrow?"

"I'll be fine." He tightened the blankets around himself, shuddering in disgust at the lingering smell of the cooked noodles sitting on the desk. His pounding head swirled, and all he could think of was smashing it in and knocking himself out. Maria left him alone, and he tried like hell to fall asleep despite the lack of comfort. It was the only way he could tone out that obnoxious television.

A few days of suffering passed, ones of tossing, turning, and dashing to the bathroom, and Will began to feel better. By the end of that agonizing week, color had returned to his skin and some of his bruises faded. He began to eat regular meals, and started moving toward a healthier, non-sickly weight. Once his energy had returned, his father sat down with him one evening to discuss his future.

"What do you plan to do with your house?" Anthony asked while speaking over a cigarette parked between his lips, the silver smoke matching the color of his aging, receding hair.

"I don't know." He pulled a comb through his own dark, wet locks, which his mother took the time to cut a bit shorter, giving him a cleaner appearance. He also shaved until his chin and jaw practically sparkled, and looked entirely different from how he did when he first came by. "What do you think I should do?"

"You should sell it."

"And then what?"

"You're welcome to stay here for a while until you try to earn some income. Then I suggest you find a place of your own. I could probably find you a nice apartment with cheap rent if I look hard enough." He inhaled and exhaled smoke. "Get your life back together, son. Ian died three years ago. He's not worth all of this grieving."

"It wasn't just because of him, you know."

"Could have fooled me." He didn't acknowledge Will's glower, or his ensuing dismissive huff. "I have a suggestion for you." Will didn't comment, but listened carefully. "Start painting again and I can help you sell it online. I could also get your stuff into an exhibition. I saw in the local newspaper that there's a big art show coming to town in a couple of weeks. You could paint something for it. It's a good opportunity for you."

"I don't know how I'm supposed to find the time to paint between moving out of my house and selling it."

"I'll help you with it. You just worry about getting back on your feet."

"And Cory? I... I want to fix things between us, but..."

Anthony flicked the end of his cigarette with his thumb, dropping ash into a plastic tray. "The road to recovery is never an easy one."

It wasn't exactly the type of advice he was looking for, though he was right, as usual. What he wanted to know was if it would be wise to try to win him back. He still couldn't tell when staying away was a better choice than determination. In truth, he wanted Cory back, and badly, but he knew just how horribly he screwed things up for the both of them. Cory might not even forgive him for it. He wouldn't if he were Cory.

He didn't tell his father, but he planned to speak with him when they went back to his house to pack up his things. He at least deserved some kind of explanation why he was suddenly moving away. It was a good enough excuse just to see him.

During the past week he had been enduring sickness, but the pain was thrice the customary quantity in Cory's absence. His now ex-lover was just as much of an addictive substance as any other drug, and it wasn't just heroin he had been withdrawing from. Their separation seemed easy at the time, but it hurt worse the longer they were apart, unlike how much better he felt the longer he was away from toxic substances. The only obstacle was his guilt, and seeing the fresh heartache in Cory's eyes, hearing the pain in his voice. He never thought that waking up next to him, or kissing him before he left for work was something he would crave just as powerfully as an opiate shot, if not more so. Even if he did "get back on his feet" as his father said, none of it would matter if Cory wasn't beside him to share the joy and revitalization with.

There was a slight chance that he might forgive him. He would just have to find the courage to confront him.

In the following two weeks, Will settled matters with the bank regarding his missed mortgage and utility payments, an ordeal that Anthony was helpful with. Unfortunately, he owed more than what the house was worth and wouldn't earn the house's full value, but it would be better than having no money at all, which was his position beforehand. Anthony provided a moving truck for Will for the upcoming weekend and said he would help him pack up during the week.

On the road to his house, sweat clung to Will's hair and forehead as he anticipated seeing Cory for the first time in weeks. No matter how hard he tried, he couldn't stop jittering and fidgeting. Anthony saw his discomfort and tried to calm him with stories that no one on earth would find interesting. Halfway through one in particular concerning a gas station attendant that Anthony didn't particularly like (a young woman that shorted him change when he bought cigarettes), he figured he was just trying to bore him to sleep, or to death, whichever came first.

"There's my street," Will announced, interrupting his father midway through a discussion on stocks. His gut twisted into knots as they neared his neighbor's house, which he immediately checked the driveway of. Cory's car was parked there, so he knew that he was home. Anthony parked his pickup in Will's messy, snowy driveway, and Will almost leapt out of the vehicle before it could come to a complete stop. "He's home, he's home from work. I have to see him, dad. I have to say hello to him."

"Will, relax. Let's get some of your stuff packed first." The driver's side door made a rusty creak as Anthony opened it, and he stepped out to collect several empty boxes from the bed of the truck.

"Dad, I'm going insane here. I miss him so fucking much."

"I know you do. Pace yourself a little. You have to learn to control yourself a bit more, you know? Here, take some boxes."

His swelling, hammering heart now withering like a deflated balloon, Will obeyed his father, and carried boxes into the house. With Anthony's help, he started packing away dishes and utensils (after thoroughly washing them), thinking of Cory during his every task.

Did he see us pull in, I wonder? He absentmindedly scrubbed a plate as images of Cory drifted through his mind. *Does he know I'm here, right now? Does he miss me as much as I miss him? Does it hurt him to be away from me? Does he want to be near me like I want to be near him?*

"Will. You okay, son?"

Will paused his washing to give his full attention to Anthony. "Yeah. I'm fine, why?"

"You've been washing that same plate forever. We need to get cracking here, boy. You have a lot of stuff to go through."

"I'm sorry, dad. I just can't stop thinking about..." He sighed.

"You'll get to see him, don't worry. Try to focus on this right now. Clear your head."

He was right. If it was one thing he needed to train himself to do, it was focus on things he wasn't addicted to. Putting Cory out of his mind was easier said than done, but with his father's help, he addressed the matter of packing his belongings, and stayed on that path without many distractions.

In only one trip around the house, both of them were able to pack as much as his dishes, clothes, art supplies and bedding. By the time they finished, most of the important things were ready to haul back to the Shepherd family home, and Anthony boasted proudly how skilled they were at their job. Will didn't really care either way. Cory kept creeping back into his mind like a family of buzzing fruit flies that were impossible to kill. No matter how hard he pushed and shoved him out of his neurotic brain, he still managed to link thoughts of him to anything and everything he did.

"Please, dad, I *need* to see Cory," Will pleaded desperately, unable to take the anxious tingling in his toes any longer.

"All right, William," Anthony calmed when he took a cigarette break. "Go on. I'll be waiting."

Will didn't wait around for any other words of guidance, any pearls of wisdom or to share a cigarette like he probably should have. Instead, he rushed out of the house, tripping many times on his overgrown lawn shrubbery. His palms burned in the cold air, his wet pant legs chilling and chafing his skin, but it was a pain that meant nothing to him compared to a starvation of love. He dove onto the porch of Cory's home, mashing his thumb against the doorbell, adjusting his hair and glasses.

Amanda was the one to open the door, and Will was greeted with a wide-eyed stare and a soft, "Oh boy."

"Amanda, right?" Will babbled, his tongue tempted to curl up into a ball.

"William," she answered with a slow nod.

"Is Cory home?"

"Yeah, he's here... but..."

"Can I speak to him?" He rubbed his sweaty palms together, bouncing on his heels.

"I don't think he'll want to."

His throat closed up, and swallowing was suddenly a challenging feat. "Why not? Is he mad at me?"

"Mad? Well..." Her eyes darted from side to side.

"Please, Amanda. It's really important that I speak to him. I have a lot to atone for. I'm sure you probably know, judging by the look you're giving me."

Amanda's shoulders slumped and she let out a steaming sigh through her nose. "I don't want you hurt my brother anymore."

"I won't! I mean, I know I did before, but I feel bad, and I want to talk it out with him."

There was an uncomfortable pregnant pause as she thought it through. "Okay. I'll go get him. Wait here." She closed the door, but he didn't hear it click. He peeked through the crack where light was streaming through. Amanda had jogged up the staircase, and he could hear voices, one he recognized as Cory's, and they each grew steadily louder. In spite of the bitter chill, his hair was soaked with sweat as he watched through the gap between the door and the frame, until he finally saw feet coming down the stairs.

The door flew open, and beyond it stood Cory, a glare sculpted onto his young face. His eyes were red, sleep-deprived, and slanted into furious creases. "What do you want?" He sighed.

The skill of speech had been momentarily stripped from Will's brain, and he completely forgot what he was going to say, or why he planned to say it. He had never before seen Cory so angry, so tiredly depressed, that he felt trapped, standing on the porch in dusty snow which soaked his socks. "C-Cory," he yammered.

"We both know who I am, Will. But thanks for coming over here to remind me."

"Are you okay?" Why did he ask? Of course he wasn't okay. The kid was miserable, downtrodden, and it showed.

"Oh yeah, I'm great. Thanks for asking." Just in case Will didn't catch his sarcasm, his glare never let up.

What was the use in trying? Nothing he ever said would make up for what went on between them. A simple apology was not going to recompense the drugs, the lies, and the drama. Nothing would. Cory may have already made his decision to hate him, perhaps forever, and that stone-cold look was enough evidence to prove it.

"Well?" Cory pressed, shifting from one side to the other. "What is it? Do you need money or something? I don't have any."

"I quit heroin," he blurted. He didn't think it would make any kind of impact, but he still assumed he'd like to know.

Much to Will's surprise, Cory's hate-filled expression diminished, as did his strong voice. "Really."

He threw his head up and down in an enthusiastic nod. "I did, I really did. I kicked all drugs. I'm not even snorting anything. Look, I'll prove it." He rolled up each of his sleeves and presented his bare arms to him. "See? No fresh track marks."

Cory took hold of his forearms and brought them closer to his eyes as he checked them with scrutiny. When he discovered that Will was telling him the truth, he looked upon his face with a hint of pride. "That's good."

"I've been keeping at it, too. I've been clean for three weeks straight. Give me a drug test if you like. I don't even have caffeine in my system."

"You do look healthier. You shaved... and your hair is shorter."

"My mother cut it for me. I don't look so much like a slob anymore, do I?" His exaggerated smile had started to hurt. He was so happy to see him, even if he thought the moment wouldn't last.

"No, you don't." Cory crossed his arms and leaned against the frame of the door, waiting.

Will knew what he had to say, and do. "Cory, I'm so sorry."

He averted his eyes, scratching the back of his neck. "I'm guessing you're here because you want me back."

"No. Well, I won't lie, that would be pleasant. But it's not why I came." He closed his coat to protect from a sweeping gust of wind. "I came because I wanted to tell you what an idiot I am."

Cory laughed, his eyes glazed over. Will couldn't tell if his eyes were watering from the breeze or if he really was about to cry. Either way, it was tough to witness. "I'm already well aware."

"I don't love heroin more than you. I should never have said that. It was an awful thing to say."

"You really hurt me, you know."

He did know. He knew more than Cory thought he did. However, hearing him tell him, hearing him say it with such disappointment was all too much to bear. "I wish I could take it all back. I wished it every day since we've been apart. I know there isn't a whole lot I can do, but I wanted to let you know that you've inspired me to change. You made me want to be a better person."

231

Cory shrugged. It was the sort of indifference that Will wouldn't expect from him. "This is really hard for me. I know you've been through a lot in life, so I'm sure you know the kind of shit I've been going through since you left, but none of it gives you a right to do it."

"I know. It shouldn't have been me of all people to do this to you."

Still hiding his wet eyes, Cory started to turn away. Will thought he was about to go back into the house, but it was evidently to avoid looking at him. "You sucked off some other guy, Will."

Until he brought it up, he had almost forgotten that had happened, because in his mind, nothing had. "I-I know. I don't suppose it would help much if I told you that it was just business, that I wasn't even attracted to him. It wasn't even sex to me, it was just a service."

"Yeah, well, just because you don't see it as sex doesn't automatically give you some kind of immunity from being guilty of it. I frankly don't give a shit what you thought it was. You still did it." He shook his head in that same form of disparagement he used before. "To be honest, it wasn't even the fact you sucked him off that bothered me, because I knew you didn't want to be with him. It was the fact that we were supposed to be boyfriends, and not once did you ever give *me* a blow job. You'd rather just go down on some drug dealer to get something better than spend intimate time with me. I bet you still would, too."

"No! I wouldn't! I never, ever meant to hurt you like that. Now that I have a bit of a sober perspective I can see how incredibly selfish it was. I can't apologize enough for it."

"You're right, I don't think you can."

Their conversation was not going the way Will had hoped, but it was closure he was looking for, a resolution. If he had to say goodbye, he at least could do it saying he at least tried to ask for forgiveness. "I wanted to let you know that I'm moving away."

Cory had been upset, perhaps even furious, but he started to fall apart at this sullen news. "Where are you going?"

"I'm going to sell my house and stay with my parents for a little while in East Lansing until I get my own place. I'm going to start painting again and selling my work. I think this time it'll really work out for me. I feel much more in control than I did before."

"Good for you." Although his heart was injured, his praise sounded authentic.

"I have to be honest, though. Doing it all without you… it's not going to seem as great."

"Don't guilt trip me, Will. It's pathetic. Have a little respect for me."

"I do respect you, and I'm not laying a guilt trip on you. That's just the facts. I miss you. That's not something I can deny."

Laying his face into his hand, he choked, "I miss you, too. Even after everything."

"Please don't cry."

He dragged his nose against the back of his hand, then used his palm to wipe his face. "Why, Will? Why are you doing this? Why did you have to fuck up so hard? I know I could have helped you, could have made things better, and you showed me you didn't care about me. Do you have any idea how hard it is to just accept that and move on? And here you are, trying to get back into my life just so you can ruin it again."

"That's not what I'm—"

"I know what you're doing. We weren't together very long, but I felt like I knew you my whole life, and just this afternoon I was wishing you never wrote me those letters." They each stood in the cold, shivering, the winds howling among the distant trees. Its braying call was just as powerful as the song of sadness their hearts harmoniously sang. "Just go away, Will. I can't deal with this."

"Wait!" He smacked his palm onto the surface of the door before Cory could shut it on him. Cory hesitated, waiting for him to continue. "Cory, I still love you. I never stopped. I love you more than anything, and yes, even more than drugs. I want to prove to you that I'm better now, that I've changed. I want to show you that you're worth more to me than anything else in my life. You've done so much for me while we were together, and I owe it to you to return the favor."

Cory eased the door open a bit more. "Go on."

"You're right. I do want you back, and I'm willing to beg. There's no point hiding it. You've been on my mind every single day for the past few weeks. You were with me the whole time I was sick, every minute of every day, and you were my motivation for trying harder. You kept me going, you kept me from giving up. If you never want to see me again, I'll try like hell to accept it, but it'll be harder than enduring withdrawals."

Will was hopeful to see him take a serious moment to consider what he was saying. He stepped outside and shut the door behind him, joining Will in the falling snow without a jacket, or even socks or shoes. "What happens if we get into arguments? Are you going to cut yourself up or go running off to find heroin again?" Will shook his head. "Are you sure?" He nodded. "Because I can't see that happen to you again. I can't watch you fall apart. I can't take it."

"I'm okay. Really, I am. I'm much better now." He brought his hand up to Cory's cheek and stroked it. Though his palm must have been freezing, he closed his eyes and pressed his face against it, breathing him in. "You're what makes me happiest. Nothing else matters without you. Give me another chance. Please."

Light enveloped Cory's red eyes as rays of hope touched his face. "I want to believe you mean it. I want to trust that you're ready for this now."

"I am. I've never been more ready for anything."

Another long pause, then, "Okay. I'll give you *one* chance to prove it to me." Will beamed, overjoyed. "But I'll be less nice if you start up your old habits." He didn't get a chance to say much more because Will had clutched him in his arms and squeezed him.

"We can get our own place, just like we wanted," he sang. "I can sell my art, make some good money from it again like I used to. I can set up my own gallery, and you wouldn't have to quit your job, because we wouldn't be living very far away. It's going to be okay. No, more than okay. It's going to be fantastic!"

"Easy, Will. Let's just take it a little slow, okay?"

"I know, I know, I'm sorry. I just feel so good. It's going to work out this time, I can feel it."

"We'll see," Cory said under his breath. Will didn't remark on it. He felt lucky enough that Cory was giving him the opportunity. "Whose truck is that in your driveway?" He was hopping back and forth on each of his feet, now that they were getting nipped by the cold.

"It's my father's. He's helping me move my things." He glanced down at Cory's bare feet. "Put some shoes on!" When Cory didn't listen, he opened the door himself and shooed him inside. He rolled his eyes, but did as he was told, and slipped a coat on as well.

"You said your father was here?" He asked when he stepped back outside.

"Yes. He's inside my house right now."

"Can I meet him? I should, after all."

Will could already see how this might backfire. Cory's physical likeness to Ian would give his father a heart attack, and if that didn't do him in, he might bash his head in, asking him why he lied about Ian's death. He wouldn't have a verifiable answer for him if such a thing occurred. The situation would be all too horrifying. When Cory gave him a light nudge, he gulped. "I don't see why not." He held his hand out for taking, and Cory peered at it like a shark ready to bite him. After some silent deliberation, he took his hand and held it, walking with him to the house next door.

Will breezed into the house with fruitful exuberance. "Dad! Come and meet Cory!"

"Wow, Will," Cory whispered as he looked around the empty walls and shelves. "It looks even more barren in here than before."

"It's time to say goodbye to this place. I can't say I'll miss it much. I think starting over is just what I need."

"*Jumping Jesus Christ!*"

Both Will and Cory leapt so high that they might have nearly hit their heads on the ceiling, spinning around to look at the individual that snuck up on them. "Dad, what the hell?" Will asked while gripping his chest, but it didn't silence the thumping in his ears.

Anthony Shepherd was standing in the archway between the kitchen and living room, clutching a screwdriver for some reason or other, which he consequently dropped and scooped back up. Will inched in front of Cory, assuming his father was brandishing it as a weapon. "I-I mean, nice to meet you, Cory." Anthony reached forward for a handshake, but his fingers trembled.

"N-nice to meet you, too," Cory returned, shaking his hand.

"I'm sorry I spooked you, but you gave me a bit of a scare, yourself. You look a lot like someone Will used to know."

"Ian?"

"So you know about him." An exchange of wary glances passed between Will and his father. Will nodded at him, but so did Cory. "I'm sorry, it's just a bit creepy, that's all. I mean, you look a *lot* like him. I would have thought Will might have mentioned that." Will scratched the back of his neck, his lip twitching.

I suppose this could have gone a lot worse, he realized.

"I assure you that it's just a coincidence," Cory explained, though it wasn't necessary. "I'm not related to him or anything. I've never even met the guy."

"Weird, that." Anthony couldn't take his eyes off of Cory. He also couldn't let go of that screwdriver he found.

"Anyway!" Will interjected, which Cory seemed grateful for. If he allowed another beat of baffled silence, his father might have made their introduction even creepier. "Cory, I didn't tell you yet about the art show I was going to participate in." As he spoke to him, he lifted one of the many filled boxes to carry outside. "You'll come, won't you?"

"I'd be happy to."

"Great!" As he hauled the box out the door, Cory came to his side to help him carry it, peeking around the corners and smiling at him. Will grinned back, weightless once again at the sight of his beautiful face, at how cheerful he looked now. That's when he thought he heard Cory say something to him, something impatient and bitter. Displeased, he frowned at his snide tone. "What? What's wrong?"

Puzzled, Cory peered around the box corner once again. "Huh?"

"You said something. You sound angry."

"I didn't say anything, Will." His arms shook at the weight of the box, lacking the stamina necessary to go on holding it for long.

"Yes you did. I heard you. What did you say?"

Cory then grunted out a nervous laugh. "No. I didn't. Are you okay?"

He did say something, didn't he? I'm not crazy.

No, not crazy at all. Not like he was. Not now. Give it time. It will happen.

Will tossed his head back and forth, forcing the sinister voice from his mind. "Yeah. Sorry. I thought you did. Let's get this thing in the truck." Fearful now of his mental state, he wondered if it was possible any of his several self-harming habits had induced brain abnormalities, but he knew that was stretching it a bit. He had felt paranoid before. He had heard bumps in the night, the whispering of his name, the sound of shots in the middle of the night, and none of which actually happened. It was possible that he could have just been hearing things again.

Yes. That must have been it. But there was also the possibility that Cory had lied.

Why would he lie? That's not like Cory.

It was a question repeated for a while, until they slipped the box into the bed of the truck together, and Cory once again smiled at him. The weighing thought left his mind as quickly as a feather took to the wind. Cory was happy again. That's what mattered.

They carried several more boxes to the truck until they ran out of space to fit any more of them. That's when they knew they had to part ways for the evening. "Are you going to be back tomorrow?"

"Yes. Probably after five."

"I could help you pack some more. I have nothing planned."

"That sounds good. Thank you." Cory leaned forward and kissed his face, and they embraced one another. Will wished he didn't have to let him go, that he could hold him like that forever, but he knew forever was too long of a time. A deep breath of peace filled his chest, fresh air cleansing his lungs and blood, which had until then been tainted by regret and guilt. Cory had forgiven him, and not only that, but had reaccepted a relationship. It was worth celebrating, even if just internally.

"I'll see you tomorrow, then." While he walked back into his house, stumbling from exhaustion, Will thought his tread familiar. The way he shuffled, his head low, his hands in his pockets; something bothered him, something he wouldn't let him in on. His earlier smile seemed so genuine. Could it have been feigned just for his pleasure? He didn't want Cory to go through that a second time. He wanted nothing more than for him to be happy.

He just needs time. We both do. He'll see I'm not fooling around— I'm serious, more than I ever was.

"I love you, Cory."

He paused while halfway up the porch steps, and he picked his head up to look behind him, their eyes locking. His grayish eye sockets were more prominent underneath the dim porch light. "I love you, too." It was said with uncertainty, and yet with a sense of devotion. His voice and eyes seemed to tell him, *falling out of love with you is inconceivable to me.*

"Come hell or high water," Will preached in a low hush. "We'll make this work."

16. Provoke

The art gallery hosting the show was crowded full of both artists and browsers alike, the halls filled with the hum of mumbling chatter. A young couple, mid-twenties, had been hovering around Will's paintings for the past fifteen minutes, each of them admiring what they saw. Will paced the room watching the many college-age attendants, but kept his eye on those looking at his work. He was hopeful that they might want to make a purchase offer. He had sold many pieces in the past in the very same manner, and he knew a buyer when he saw one.

It wasn't mandatory, but Will dressed up for the occasion— in a raspberry-colored dress shirt and black tie with black slacks, clothes he never got to wear much when Ian was around because of how often he nagged at him for it. His hair was combed, his face clean, and he had even taken the time to adjust the tightness of his frequently slipping glasses, which were now snug on the bridge of his nose. Today mattered to him, and he wanted to show it.

For the eighteenth time that afternoon, he checked his silver wristwatch. Cory said he would be there around noon, but thirty minutes had passed and there was no sign of him. It was times such as these that he wished he owned a cell phone, or even understood how to operate one. He promised himself he wouldn't get nervous if Cory was late, but it was in his nature to worry.

After approximately ten more minutes, he spotted Cory Anderson strolling into the gallery, looking at the walls in astonishment. He appeared to have also dressed formally, perhaps for Will's sake. Will jogged to his side, grinning. "There you are!" He cheered before they hugged and kissed.

"I'm sorry I'm late." Cory hadn't yet looked him in the eye, but it didn't appear to be out of resentment. Something was wrong, and he could see it on his face.

"Is everything okay?" He tried to get him to look at him, but he refused.

"Yeah. Everything's fine." Will knew his smile wasn't real, but he didn't want to upset him further. "Show me your stuff."

Will didn't wish to let the matter go, but if he wanted to see his paintings, perhaps it was a good distraction from whatever ailed him. He guided him over to his work hanging on the east wall. There were three in total: a house at night with two silhouettes sitting on a porch swing, a garden of roses, and an abstract piece with colliding colors and shapes of needles. Cory's fake smile developed into one of pure prideful adoration.

"They're beautiful, Will," he chimed, breathless. He couldn't take his eyes off of one of them in particular. "I'm proud of you." His pleased voice couldn't hide his distress, and it seeped to the surface, even with him trying to bury it.

"Sweetheart…" Will eased Cory away from the crowd. "What's wrong? Please, tell me."

"I'm just having a bad day. I don't want to ruin your show. I'll be okay, I promise." He gave him a stern look to show it wasn't a good time, or place.

"You will explain later, won't you?"

Cory nodded, then regained his composure. "Let's just enjoy the artwork, okay?"

If Cory felt that it was the best course of action, Will would adhere to it without complaint. He felt Cory's hand grip his own, and he gestured for him to walk him around the gallery like a refined prince asking for a tour. Will did just that, and eventually Cory calmed down, elated to simply be in his presence.

"You look really handsome today," he praised at the end of Will's tour of the gallery. "You can really pull off a suit look pretty well.

You should wear them more often." His eyes grew lustful. "I had forgotten how sexy you are."

Will turned his bashful, reddened face to the side. "You know, since I've kicked oxy and heroin, my sex drive has been mountainous, and that's understating."

Cory giggled like a school girl, tickled by Will's flirtatious implications. "Is that so?"

"Oh yeah. It's more than so. It's been a long time since I've actually *wanted* sex, I mean really wanted it. Forgive me, but, have you gotten hotter since I last saw you? You have, haven't you?" Sneaking his hand around Cory's waist, he gave his ass a secretive squeeze. Cory gasped, but grinned, affable, mischievous laughter escaping his mouth.

"I'll be looking forward to it." As he strolled away, he gave his rear a teasing shake.

Oh, me too, he thought, salivating.

By the end of the afternoon, Will sold all three of his paintings for grand prices, and he walked away from the show roughly a thousand dollars richer. Cory left the gallery with him and joined him in the parking lot, congratulating him on his success. "It's a great start to help me get a new place to live," Will expressed with relief.

"I meant to ask— who were those two people sitting on the swing, in your painting of the house?"

"Us, after we had grown old together. I pictured us in a house like that."

They swapped identical smiles, and their foreheads collided while Will nuzzled him. "You really want to spend the rest of your life with me?" Cory asked just above a whisper.

"Absolutely. I've made up my mind. There's no going back now, kid."

"I think I'm pretty sure of what I want."

"And what is that? Lunch? That's certainly what I want."

"That actually sounds great."

"My treat this time."

Their meal was shared at a steakhouse, where Cory asked for a burger and Will ordered lamb chops. As soon as he received his dish, he gobbled into it as though it would be the final good meal he would ever eat. His slurping and crunching turned Cory's stomach, and sucked the color from his face.

"You look a bit flushed," Will said, amused.

"I didn't know you liked lamb that much."

"I've never had it. They just sounded so delicious to me for some reason. And what do you know? They really are delicious!"

Cory nodded along with his explanation as Will dabbed his mouth with a napkin. "My mother got into an argument with me today. She fought with me about seeing you again. I guess she's back to her old self— hating you and all that."

Will took a break from his gnawing. "Is that why you were so upset today?"

"That and other things. My mom and I have argued before over you, so it's not enough to bother me this much, she just did it at the absolute worst time. Angie and I have... well, we've been drifting apart. While you were away these past weeks, I guess she heard Derrick was at some club with one of her female friends. Why she got so jealous, I'll never know, but I guess she's as screwed up as he is."

"More screwed up than a self-harmer with a heroin addiction?"

"Yes. It's like he lives to be pissed off. It's his motivation for everything." He slouched, leaning back in his seat. "Anyway, Angie didn't like that he was seeing her girlfriends, so she told him she was sleeping with me to make him jealous."

"He didn't come back to your house or anything, right? Didn't hurt you, did he?"

"No. Not yet, anyway. Will, I know you wouldn't laugh at me." His deadpan serious face silenced Will in a heartbeat. "I'm not the kind of guy to admit that I'm a giant pussy. Sometimes I really hate crying around you because I'm afraid you'll see me as pathetic."

"You know I would never think that."

They both went silent for a second, then Cory continued. "I know you wouldn't, but that's just how I am. It's really hard to say this, almost as hard as it was admitting that I was bisexual, but I feel like I should tell someone, and it might as well be you. We've had some ups and downs, but you were always there to protect me." His voice trailed off and his head dipped, and Will was patient and quiet, even as the waiter came by to refill their drinks. "I think for the first time in my life I can admit that I'm... scared."

"Scared of what, exactly? What happened?"

"It's not so much what happened, but what I'm afraid is *going* to happen. Call me paranoid if you want to, I know it seems that way, but I think I have a right to feel it." Cory set his hands on the table. Will saw that his nails had been chewed on. "I found out Angie did this through Derrick himself. I saw him at a bar I went to one night. It's some dive bar on Michigan Avenue, The Clover. Derrick was supposedly a regular there, if you can believe those odds. I can't imagine anyone going there on their own unless they wanted to die. The place was depressing, though it was probably just my mood. There are tons of other bars on that street. He couldn't have picked a better one to frequent?"

"When did you go there?"

"Does it matter?"

"Tell me you didn't drink."

Cory understood Will's apprehension on the issue, but he wished that he wouldn't look at him so incriminatingly. "No. I mean, not a lot. I had a few, but that was it. I didn't go overboard or anything."

Will carved a piece of meat off and popped it into his mouth, studying Cory. "Good. I don't want you drinking."

"Anyway," Cory sighed. "He approached me while I was sitting at the bar, asked me what the hell I was doing there, and said that I didn't have a right to be there as if he owned the place. Then he told me what Angie said to him, only he didn't give me a chance to clarify anything. He got thrown out for getting belligerent, but he was sitting in the parking lot waiting for me when I left. He didn't start a fight, but I could tell that he wanted to. Christ, Will, the look on his face… if looks could kill, his would. I swear, I thought he was going to kill me, but I drove out of there before he could even come up to me. I've been stressed out ever since. It's like… I can feel him watching me." He cocked a sardonic eyebrow, but grimaced. "Déjà vu, huh?"

"I won't let him hurt you." He stood by this vow as if it were already written in stone.

"You can't always be there. You know that. We both do."

After folding his napkin, he tossed it upon the tabletop and leaned forward over his plate and glass of wine. "What about a protective order?"

"That's not going to stop him! The guy's insane!"

When hearing those words spoken in such a panic, he wondered if Cory said them in the exact same tone to a police officer when he reported his stalking. He frowned in shame and embarrassment at such a thought. "What did Angie have to say?"

"Well, she wasn't very apologetic, if that's what you're asking. She explained the whole thing as if I was supposed to accept it. Then she told me to consider it 'payback,' of sorts, for keeping a 'druggie' in her house. Can you believe that?"

"Honestly, from her, yes." Will sank back into the cushion of the booth, considering Cory's tale in his mind a few times before speaking on it. "Does he still live with Angie?"

"I assume so. I don't know for sure, though."

Grabbing a butter knife and spreading a packet of butter onto a piece of wheat bread that came with his meal, Will systematically said, "Clearly beating him up solves nothing. I've kicked his ass a couple of times, and he still antagonizes you. He needs to be persuaded in other manners."

"*What* manners?"

"You let me worry about that. Enjoy your burger before it gets cold." He lifted his eyes to give him a look of serenity, to let him know things would be okay. He indicated to his half-eaten burger with his pinky, and Cory picked it up and continued eating it, putting his faith in his word.

Later, Will and Cory packed more of his belongings until late evening rolled around, and to settle into a more lax mood after the work was finished, he started pecking Cory on the face and neck. Cory, still having much on his mind, was reluctant at first, but Will's kissing excited him, and they eventually proceeded to make out for extended periods of time. The empty room was silent aside from the sounds of their wet smacks and blissful noises, which carried in echoes down the vacant halls.

"Do you want to get in my bed?" He suggested with a raised brow. "It's more comfortable than the floor."

"William Shepherd." Cory smirked. "Are you coming on to me, sir?"

"I might be. You'll have to find out."

Cory was the first to rise, and he helped Will up next, and headed for the basement door, but Will stopped him. "Your bed isn't downstairs?"

"Let's go in the bedroom." Will took the lead, pulling Cory along, and opened a door he knew Cory had never seen opened before. Inside, dust coated every surface, including many boxes stacked in one corner of the room, each of them sealed with several long strips of masking tape. They were unlabeled, so he knew Cory had to be curious about them. They each contained many of Ian's private things, things he decided to keep after he parted from the world of the living, but he didn't want to discuss them. To him, they were hardly even there. They were dead, just as his late partner had been.

The dust-covered bedspread, which was neatly made and tucked on all corners of the mattress, was tough to pull down, but with a little tugging, it relented. The sheets were far cleaner, having been protected by the blanket for so many years. Will jumped onto the creaking bed, which sank under his weight (which still hadn't gone beyond one hundred and twenty), motioning for Cory to join him.

"When was the last time you came in here?" Cory queried while he scooted into bed beside him, getting smothered by snaking arms and stroking hands.

"Three years." Hoping Cory would put it all out of his mind, he started kissing him to lead his thoughts more toward sex and away from remnants of Ian.

"No wonder there's dust all over everything." Cory said only this and nothing more regarding the mysterious storage room. He focused on pleasing Will, and the pleasure he received from him.

They hadn't before assimilated just how sexually compatible they were, but now they each grasped how much more alight and enlivened their relationship would be this time around, knowing how wonderful their sex was. Things certainly had changed, much to Cory's surprise, and for the better. Will seemed relaxed, eager, and satisfied. He no longer wore a mask of pure guilt when they shared a loving moment. Things might have finally started to look up.

Basking in afterglow together, holding each other as much as their energy would allow, Will now took the opportunity to concentrate on how he would deal with Derrick as Cory fell asleep in his arms. Perhaps he would be civil enough to have an adult conversation with him. He'd think of something. For now, he focused on keeping them warm for the night, and wrapped sheets and blankets around their torsos, until no heat could leak out. Then, he set his glasses on the bedside table and he too went to sleep. It was a very restful sleep indeed.

The burning, humming neon sign of The Clover flickered as the letter L showed signs of dying. It was only a matter of time before the bar would be named The Cover, because no one ever fixed their broken signs, especially owners of unsuccessful dives. When Will stepped inside, it was quiet, an atmosphere he would have deemed more appropriate for a museum than a bar. The only sound was the bartender mixing drinks in silver shakers and the radio playing newfangled pop songs that Will would never listen to by choice. The bar stools were mostly filled with the asses of older men, likely regulars, and whatever women came in sat as far away from them as possible.

When taking careful glances around the lonesome ambiance, he didn't see Derrick anywhere, but it was still early yet. He took the time to order a drink, a Bloody Mary, then found a seat in the corner where he could watch the door. If Derrick didn't show up that night, he would come back tomorrow and the next day until he finally did. If he thought Derrick was guaranteed to be there, he'd just go straight to Angie's house, but he didn't particularly get along with Angie. She might also call the police on him, and he didn't feel like dealing with Lansing's finest that night.

Taking his time on his cocktail with calculated sips, he checked the clock at five minute intervals. Several regular customers came in, shuffled over to the bar, greeted fellow frequenters and ordered beers, but Derrick had yet to show up. Will was patient. He could wait forever if he had to. He was used to it.

When the clock struck seven thirty-two, Derrick Holden strolled in, going straight for the bar like a dog to a food bowl, ordering a draft. Will watched him with impeccable stillness. He was a shadow on the wall, blended into his surroundings, and Derrick hadn't noticed or recognized him. He allowed Derrick to down a few beers, enough to where he'd be conversational, but not violent, then snuck up to a bar stool beside him and took a seat, still nursing his cocktail.

"Come here often?" He asked as he would a man he'd make a pass at.

Derrick turned his head, glanced at him with scorn, at first dismissing his comment as a pick-up line. Then he did a double-take, the sneer now gone from his previously curled lip. "What the fuck?" Hostility was not present in his voice. In fact, he had his tail between his legs.

Will clapped a rough hand onto his shoulder and leaned in to whisper, "Relax. I just want to have a little chat."

"Yeah, right." Still, he didn't leave his bar stool, or start an argument. He ran his palm over his tossed, curly hair.

"Really, I do! I didn't come here to fight, unless that's what you want."

"No." Wincing, his hand lowered from his head and clutched the base of his throat, showing he remembered the pain that Will put him through. "Is this about Anderson?"

"What do *you* think, Derrick?"

"Look, I was drunk, okay? I thought he followed me here to fuck with me."

Will neatly folded his hands on the bar top. "Do you spend a lot of your time... intoxicated?"

Derrick didn't seem to understand his question, or he was too nervous to think straight. "I-I don't know."

"It's not a tough question. Do you drink a lot?"

"What's it to you? If I want to drink, isn't that my business?"

"It's just that it's become a great concern to me, Derrick. Or rather, it's a concern to my boyfriend, because drunk people do stupid things. They do, don't they?"

A squeaking sound stemmed from Derrick's stool, which he quickly silenced by jamming his foot against one of the metal legs, intimidated by Will's unblinking glower. "Yeah."

"And if you spend most of your time drunk, the chances of you doing something stupid skyrocket, do they not?"

"Look, man, I don't even know your name. The only thing I know is that you're *supposedly* Cory's boyfriend and you enjoy trying to kill me. So if this is going somewhere, I'd like to know, right now. If not, I'd like you to just go away."

Sliding his hands off of the bar, he planted one palm on Derrick's leg and patted it, not as a seductive gesture, but in more of an authoritative nature. He retracted his knee in both dread and disgust. "Cory and I are boyfriends, that much is true. I wouldn't be here if I didn't love him. One thing that does seem invariably dishonest is your ex-girlfriend. Now, maybe I'm wrong, and she's a fine woman, and we've just seen the most awful aspects of one another at terrible times, but she and Cory are not sleeping together. That is a fact."

The frightened man's wide eyes softened a bit once he realized he might not be in immediate danger, though Will could see his biceps flex in natural defense. "How do *you* know it's a fact?"

"Because one of the reasons I fell in love with Cory was his loyalty to his fellow man. If he's practiced infidelity, then I'd be a much bigger fool than I've surmised, and I don't really take myself to be a fool, Derrick, I never have. I make horrible decisions, it's true, but a fool, I am not." He once again cupped his hands around his chilled beverage, taking gradual sips from it. Derrick remained silent. "You, on the other hand, are very foolish. I'll associate that with your youth. Men, and women alike, are still immature at your age, so you get at least a small percentage of forgiveness on that factor. Unfortunately, you also make terrible choices, one of those involving the endless torment of my partner. That's why I'm here tonight. Hopefully I can change your state of mind, irrevocably."

"I told you, I was drunk," Derrick bargained in desperation.

"And thus we get to my point, young man. You can't drink yourself into oblivion, get into a car and crash it, and blame it on the alcohol. It doesn't work that way." In one gulp, he finished off the bottom of his cocktail and passed the bartender his empty glass. Now smiling, baring two rows of tomato juice-stained teeth, a stain that did, in effect, look "bloody," Will extended his hand to Derrick. "My name is Will, by the way."

Derrick took his hand, though loosely, and let go as soon as he could. "Good to know," he uttered.

"Derrick, why don't you tell me what your problem is? I don't just mean with your relationship, but your problem of being you."

"Fuck you," he whispered, but hunched his shoulders when Will responded with creasing, fiery eyes. "Look, I don't know what you want me to say. Anderson... your boyfriend... he came back into Angie's life, they were all buddy-buddy, and suddenly she doesn't want me anymore. I try to move on, but I can't, I miss her too much. She dumps me, and it kills me. You must know what love is like. You protect Cory, he means a lot to you. Angie is like that to me. I can't live without her." When he paused, Will ordered him a beer. "Don't do that, man. Please."

"Too late. Now continue."

He did as he was asked after forcing out a sigh. "Angie was the first girl I've ever really loved. She and I were always a lot alike. I'm sure you can see that."

He's right. I can. He grinned.

"We just fit, like puzzle pieces. We were like that for a while. Then fucking Cory comes around and she's suddenly obsessed with being his friend and hanging out with him. Then Cory gets her to turn on me in court. I can't be mad at Angie for doing it to me— I love her too much to get angry with her." He drank the beer Will bought for him as if it was mixed with nitrogen, that is, after sniffing it.

"So you take it out on someone *I* love? Is that really fair?"

Will saw the veins in his head bulge as he fought with himself over this question, the gears in his brain clicking away. "No, but, you have to understand... they both told me nothing was going on, and then I catch him in bed with her, in *my* house! Then Angie tells me nothing is going on between the two of them, that she still loves me, she needs time, shit like that. Then out of the blue, she calls me and says, 'oh by the way, Cory and I are having sex.' You expect me to be okay with this?"

Will slapped his palm onto the bar. Derrick jumped as he would at the sound of a gun going off. "But they *aren't*. She's *lying* to you to make you jealous. I know you don't know Cory well enough to understand, but he wouldn't have sex with her. They don't even get along that well."

"Oh, I'm supposed to just ignore what my girlfriend tells me?" Will didn't correct him that they weren't in a relationship anymore, at least to his knowledge. "Why would she even say that to me?" He took several swigs of his beer, taking a time out from the debate. He hissed as soon as he lowered the bottle. "You know what? I think Cory told you to come here to chill me out so I wouldn't kick his ass. You probably know they're fucking, too. Maybe you're just as mad as I am."

Incredulous at Derrick's reasoning, or his lack thereof, Will shook his head in frustration. "It's implausible that Angie would lie to you? Everyone is a liar until proven innocent, Derrick. Angie is no different."

"You're the liar, buddy." A couple more chugs of beer went down his throat. "She still loves me. She told me she did. She just needs persuasion."

"And you think this while also under the assumption that she's sleeping with my boyfriend." Derrick didn't answer him. "I'm not going to deny that she might have been attracted to Cory. She hated me from the very beginning, and it seemed to be her mission to split us up. I admit that it had me shaken at first, but I trust Cory. This is between you and Angie, and Cory has nothing to do with it. This is an opportunity, Derrick, the last one I'll give you. You can either take it, or go on like this until something bad happens." He pushed his face closer to Derrick's, who inched away. "Stay away from him. If you don't, it will *not* end well for you."

Derrick cackled, but it was broken and rustic, like a squeaking pipe. "Ooh, real scary, pal. Thanks for the beer, okay?" He turned his stool away and motioned for the bartender, but was yanked back in Will's direction by the fabric of his shirt, and he gasped.

"You think I'm fucking around?" Though he was still as skinny as a twig, he didn't hold back on ruthlessness, or the power of pure bloodlust. He cast enflamed eyes into Derrick's, his nostrils flared, his dirty teeth clenched. "I assure you, I'm not."

Terrorized by Will's confrontational deportment, Derrick pulled his silk shirt back to release it from Will's fist, only to cause a slight tear down a seam. "Dude, calm down! Let me go!"

"Give me some sign you understand these terms. Then I'll leave, and you won't ever see me again."

That's when the bartender came over to investigate the commotion. "Hey, Derrick," he called, gaining the attention of his customer. "Everything all right?"

Derrick looked first at the bartender, then at Will, his face turning a shade of ruby. "Yeah, Brett, it's cool."

Brett the bartender nodded, but had his eyes fixed on Will. "Just let me know if you need anything."

"I will." Derrick calmed himself when Brett walked away, and when Will released his shirt. "I'll stay away from Cory if he stays away from Angie. If I see him with her again, or hear they're spending time together, it won't end well for him, either."

"I'm not the kind of man you want to impose threats upon, young man," Will warned with a rabid snarl. "The last guy that antagonized me is dead now."

Derrick went quiet, and even over the chattering customers, Will could hear his heartbeat. "W-what's that supposed to mean?"

"What do you think it means?" Derrick's skin turned a light shade of green. "I have a story for you. My last boyfriend liked to beat me. At first we got along great, though he was a bit of a hateful, snide bastard, but you know what? I liked it, because we had something in common. Then he got depressed, started drinking, and it was no longer the rest of the world he hated so much, but *me*. I was the source of all of his problems, his woes, and his heartache, and suddenly he was beating on me, all the time." Derrick's face was still pale, but he didn't say anything. "I didn't have a very happy childhood, Derrick. I was used to getting beaten, so it was the norm to me. It was my role in the world to be the abused." As soon as he flashed his large teeth, Derrick turned away, staring at the bar top. "Then the idiot got behind the wheel of a car after drinking three fifths. I didn't feel anything when I got the phone call, when they told me he crashed it. I wasn't even afraid for him. That's when I knew I was stronger than I thought. I didn't have to take it. It didn't have to go on like that anymore. That's when I knew I wanted him to die."

Derrick chuckled, but it wasn't genuine laughter. He fidgeted his fingers. "Am I supposed to believe you killed him? Give me a break."

"No. You don't have to believe it." He leaned on the bar, his voice still pitched deep and soft. "That doesn't mean it didn't happen. I went to see him at the hospital, to see if maybe he had a change of heart after he almost got himself killed. He blamed me for 'letting' him get in the car, blamed me for 'allowing' him to take the keys, which he smacked me down and knocked me out to retrieve. His insurance didn't cover the accident, and he blamed me for that, too. I was hoping he'd die from his wounds, but miraculously he survived. How wonderful my luck must have been." He lowered his voice down to a hushed lull, and Derrick's attentiveness to his tale was tight and unaltered. "I stayed with him for some time until night fell, even held his hand as a final goodbye. Then I unplugged the machines that he depended on to live."

Not only was it a relief to get all of this off of his chest for once, he had managed to scare the hell out of Derrick, whose foot was bouncing up and down at a rapid rate. After a few moments of silence, and seeing that Derrick wasn't willing to commentary his story with rude remarks, he went on. "I watched him struggle to breathe. He died so slowly. It was very hard for me to witness, especially when he looked at me with those pleading eyes, croaking my name, telling me not to do it. Leaving him wasn't an option, you see, because underneath it all, I still loved him, loved the man he used to be. I couldn't have him thrown in jail. It wasn't just payback for how badly he hurt me. It was doing him a favor. I didn't want to kill the man I loved. I wanted to kill the monster, because that's all he was."

Will took a moment to look Derrick over, seeing he was trembling, even as he poured booze into his mouth. After a shocked silence had thickened the air around them, he breathed out, "I take it no one caught you."

"Of course not. He was declared dead by internal injuries from the accident. I fell apart after I did it, started doing drugs. But I'm better now. I feel stronger than ever. I would do it all over again if I had the opportunity." He slapped Derrick on the back, and he jumped, his jaw taught, his lips pulled down into a frown. "Well, I'll let you get back to your alcohol. I trust you grasp the seriousness of your situation, and have at least a small bit of common sense to comprehend what might happen to you if you hurt Cory again. I'll be frank with you, Derrick— I don't *want* to kill you, but I will if it solves the problem." Derrick nodded with a twitching upper lip. "Then I shall bid you farewell, and let's hope we never run into each other again." He stood up and headed for the exit, juggling his keys from hand to hand and whistling.

On the way back to his house, he picked up some Chinese take-out for him and Cory, and shared it over candlelight, using a packed box as a table and chopsticks that came with the meal. Will couldn't stop yammering about how long it had been since he had Kung Pao chicken and how much he had missed it, which Cory seemed amused by as he watched him wolf it down. It tasted so much better than it had years ago. It, like everything, was enhanced beyond what his senses could interpret, and he was able to enjoy the simple things in life.

"This is ludicrously romantic," Cory reveled. "Eating Chinese on the floor of your freezing, dirty house… candles… leftover wine…"

"Hey, it's all I've got right now," Will protested in assumption that it was a grievance, reaching into his near-empty box of food, prodding around with his chopsticks for more chicken. "I'll have an apartment soon, I promise."

"I'm serious! I like it. It's nice. Cozy, almost."

"You wouldn't rather we sat at an actual table?" Cheering with happiness, he found one final large piece of chicken breast at the bottom of the box and doused it in soy, though it was already secreted in the stuff.

Cory slurped a noodle into his mouth. "A table would put too much distance between us. We wouldn't get to sit so close like we are now."

"Good point!" Though his breath was tainted with the scent of garlic, he kissed Cory's mouth. He recoiled at the smell, but laughed. "I only wish I could see you better."

"You know what I look like. Use your imagination."

"I don't think I have your body well enough memorized though." He knew Cory couldn't see it, but he gave him a lewd, spicy look.

"There's plenty of time for that." The amusement in his voice convinced him that they'd be having sex that night anyway. "Let's go out tomorrow. See a movie or something."

"Sure! Whatever you'd like."

They finished their meal and discussed with each other the events of the day, until Will could no longer keep his hands off of Cory. The night was finalized with each of their stomachs full, their spirits high and carnal appetites well-fed.

The following day was productive. With his father's help, Will moved the remainder of his things out of his house, and started looking for an apartment while working on his paintings in the basement, where he was comfortable. He narrowed his list of options down to a few, all with affordable prices for an artist to live. After some time, he managed to sell several works of art, and made a fair sum of money to use toward moving expenses. When Cory's shift ended at work, he'd pick him up and spend time with him for a while, and Cory got to know his parents better. They even cooked him several hefty meals.

A couple of weeks passed before Will began preparing to sign a lease for his new apartment. After a busy day of shipping paintings to buyers and checking auctions, he wanted to stop by Cory's to tell him the good news. He was beside himself with excitement as he drove back to Hunter Street, thinking of the happy look Cory would have, hopeful that he might even want to move in with him at some point. The thought of them having their own place together titillated him, and though he knew Cory might not want to right away, he would eventually.

When he parked, this time in Cory's driveway instead of his old one, he jogged to the front door, ringing the doorbell. He expected Cory to answer like he usually did, but who he got instead was Samantha, whose putrid glare revoked any welcome he originally felt.

"Is Cory home?" He asked when he didn't receive a greeting of any kind.

"I thought he was with you." She now looked bothered, and not just by Will standing on her porch.

"No, I haven't seen him today. He might still be at work. Sometimes he stays later when they ask him to."

"He already came home from work. He left hours ago. I thought he was going to see you."

For once, both Will and Samantha saw eye-to-eye on something. To both of their knowledge, Cory was missing, and neither of them had any indication of where he might be or where he was going. "Would you mind if I came inside and called him?"

Samantha swallowed her pride, as well as her abhorrence, and allowed Will into her house for the first time ever. As soon as Will set foot inside, he was awed by how much cleaner it was than his own. It was no wonder she was always ranting that the state of his yard and home was ruining the values of the houses around him. He lived nothing like her or anyone else in the neighborhood.

Will patiently stood near the doorway, wiping his dirty shoes on the doormat. Even that seemed to irritate Samantha, but she might have been too worried about her son to make demands. She retrieved the cordless phone from the den and brought it to him, standing idly by and watching him as though he might steal something. He didn't mind so much being under her accusatory, steely gaze as he did her assumptions of his mischievousness.

Quickly dialing Cory's cell phone number, ignoring Samantha's venomous eyes, he pressed the phone against his ear, and right away, he heard the familiar message, "You've reached Cory Anderson.

Leave a message." He tried calling several more times, but not once did it ring.

"His battery might be dead. It's going straight to voicemail." His nerves began to weaken as tingles spread up and down his arms and fingers. Oh, God, he would do anything for a shot right now, just to stop the noise inside his brain.

"He *always* has his battery charged," Samantha added, but that was something Will already knew. Cory was habitual regarding leaving his phone plugged in, because, as he said to him once, *you never know what could happen.* It seemed like that mysterious "happening" might have occurred out of the blue without them knowing. "Where do you think he is, Mister Shepherd?"

Will dismissed for now the fact that she still referred to her son's boyfriend by his last name. It wasn't important at the moment. "I don't know. Cory usually visits any of three given places: work, home, and my parents' house, but I just came from my house. He would have called beforehand if he planned to come over." She didn't have to say anything, because he felt it, too. They were both worried. "Did he say anything at all to you about where he was going?"

She was panicking, but couldn't contain it, not as well as Will could. "No. He wasn't here long after he got off of work. He had a little bit to eat, then he just vanished. I thought it was strange, because usually he'll tell me he's going to your house." Samantha would normally never touch Will with a ten foot pole, but she was now standing closer to him than she ever wanted to be. "Please tell me you think he's okay."

"I don't know, Samantha. This is unusual for him." He tried to calm his speedy heart, knowing that if he started panicking, it would only make things worse for the both of them. He didn't need the additional task of calming someone from a nervous breakdown while also fighting the distress of where his missing boyfriend was. "But I'm sure he'll come up. We just have to think of where he might have gone."

"Maybe he went to Angela's?"

It took him a moment to understand that "Angela" and "Angie" was the same person, and that Samantha might have preferred formal name usage. "Do you know her number?"

"Yes, yes, I do. Would you like me to give it to you?"

He thought of the reaction he might get if he was the one to phone Angie. "I think maybe you should call. She kind of, sort of hates me."

There was no debate. She took the cordless phone, or rather *tore* it from him, and dialed Angie's number with fleeting fingers. She stood there chewing on a thumbnail while it rang. Then, Will could hear the sound of a muffled electronic voice on the other end of the earpiece. "Hello, Angela? It's Cory's mom. I was wondering if you've seen him." The wrinkles in her concerned face toughened and squeezed as her expression grew more and more tepid. Will begged, though only in his mind, to know what Angie was saying to her. "No, he never told me about that. Do you think he...?" Another pause, and she was now biting on her lip. Will couldn't help mimicking the action. "No, we haven't seen him for hours. Yes, he's here with me, did you want to speak to him?"

Please don't put me on the phone with that woman, Will pleaded, but Samantha passed the phone to him. He sighed and mashed the hunk of plastic and buttons against his cheek.

"Yes, Angie," he grunted into the mouthpiece.

"Cory was here today. He hasn't come home?"

A lava pit boiled in his gut. "What was he doing over there?"

"To tell you the truth, I still don't know. To fight with me, I guess. He mentioned Derrick following him, and we argued." She sounded stressed, so Will cut her a bit of slack. "He was only here for like, twenty minutes, I swear. Then Derrick came home. He saw him here, so Cory left. Derrick and I had an argument, and he left, too. I'm... I'm worried he might have followed Cory."

"Followed him why?! For what?!"

"I don't know! Derrick didn't say where he'd be going, or why, he just stormed out like he always does!"

"If Cory is hurt, and you know something, I swear to Christ—"

"I don't know! I didn't even know Cory was going to stop by! He just showed up!"

"You'd better be telling me the truth." Will hung up without saying anything else, then passed the phone back to the stunned silent Samantha.

She spoke up in a gentle voice, like she was speaking to a child throwing a tantrum. "Mister Shepherd..." Will looked at her. "What do you honestly think happened to my son?"

"I don't like to speculate."

"I think you know what's going on."

She was right. He did have an idea of what was happening. Derrick might not have been as threatened by his warning after all, and instead took it as a challenge. It was possible that Derrick did something horrible to Cory, and there was no way for him to know, because he couldn't contact him. No matter how he drew the lines and connections, it always ended with Cory getting beaten, killed, or buried alive, and this type of thinking had him pacing the floor so much that he practically burned the rug.

"I'm not sure." It was a lie, but the truth was far worse at the moment. "But I'm certain he's probably safe."

"No. I can see it in your eyes. Something's wrong."

"Would you like me to call some hospitals?"

This offer was debatable to her, and even in the event of her son going missing, she still had to take a moment to ponder whether or not she wanted Will in her house. "Yes. That would probably be best."

Will asked her for a phone book, and she brought him one, then stepped away from him like he was contagious. He called several of the nearest hospitals in the area, none of which turned up any signs of having Cory as a patient. Then, he made one final call to the one he hoped he wouldn't ever have to dial the number for: the very same one Ian died in.

Perhaps it was fate, a message that was meant only for Will, but the receptionist he spoke to told him that a Cory Anderson was admitted earlier. Will pulled at a hangnail with his teeth as they transferred his call to Cory's room.

"Will?" Croaked a young voice in pain. "Is that you?"

"Cory?" He gasped, cradling the phone as if it were Cory's face. "Are you okay?"

"Will…" He could hear that familiar sound, that God awful sound of heart monitors beeping and nurses walking and chattering. The sound he associated with death— of murder. "Are you coming? Please say you are."

"Yes, I'm coming, right now, sweetheart. Okay?"

"Where are you?"

"I'm at your mother's." He glanced up at Samantha, who was clutching her own chest. "Tell me what happened."

"Not on the phone. I want you here with me. Please." The last word was said tearfully.

"I'm going to leave right now. You'll see me soon. I love you."

The phone died.

He chucked it onto a table, then bundled up his coat. Before he could ask Samantha if she would like to ride with him to the hospital, she blurted, "What happened to him?!"

"He wouldn't tell me. He just told me to come to the hospital."

"Why didn't he tell you?"

He didn't have to question her to understand that she felt something insidious was going on between them. "I don't know for sure. He sounded hurt. I just want to get there as soon as possible. Ride with me if you like, but I have to go now."

"I... I think I'll just follow you in my car. I have to get his sisters."

For now, he'd have to get past her begrudging him. He just wanted to see Cory as quickly as he could, even if he had to run over a few people to get to him.

17. Confess

The smell of rubbing alcohol and cleaning solvents were two aromas Will could never get used to. That lingering scent of disinfectant was a painful reminder of decay and loss. Every time he passed an exam room, he saw the familiar setups of the very room Ian died in: the bed masked by a large curtain to hide the shame, chairs placed near it and around it so visitors could sit down while putting up with you, a television (and an old one at that) mounted on the wall so that you could take your mind off of the awful position you were in, and how expensive the whole procedure was going to be. He saw his deceased partner in every one of the rooms he peeked in, reaching for him with a dying hand, gasping for life, calling his name. It was now that he felt grateful Samantha traveled separately from him.

He paced his steps, telling himself he'd only have to be there long enough to see Cory, to check on him, to be there for him and reassure him. Then he could get the hell out of there and never come back, never *look* back, not unless there was absolutely no choice, such as a moment similar to the current. If he had chopped his own finger off, the hell with it— he could wrap it up in several towels and pour peroxide all over it, but he would not come back to this place. He promised himself he wouldn't. Unfortunately, the chaotic inevitable surprised him, and if it meant being there for someone who relied on him, he would force himself to inhale those awful smells, listen to those terrible crying and gasping sounds, watch those nurses push carts loaded up with medication.

Donning a visitor tag on his coat, one showing off a very old driver's license photo, his wet shoes creaked along the hallway, breathing deep when he'd start to feel dizzy and trapped. Breathing became difficult. S17 was the exam room number they told him Cory was in, and when it came into view, he slowed his pace. Preparing himself, he paused midway through the corridor, staring at the bold letter and numbers staring him in the face.

It's Cory in there, Will. Not Ian. Cory is hurt, and he needs you. He held his breath and crept silently into the room across the checkerboard-tiled floor.

On the hospital bed, attached to wires and machines of all kinds, was Cory, his hair matted, coated with blood, bandages around his head. There were oxygen tubes in his nose, which was also specked with bloodstains. One of his eyes was dark purple in color, badly bruised, the other red. His right arm was in a thick cast, and his bare leg sticking out of his hospital gown had new stitches in it. The worst sight of all for Will, however, was the metallic blue neck brace holding his chin up, which creaked as he turned his whole upper body to look at his tear-stricken visitor.

Despite the hoses, wires, bandages, and IV, Cory smiled at the sight of him. His teeth were stained bright crimson. "Will," he said in a slight cheer. When Will froze in place in the doorway with shaking knees and twitching hands, his smile fell, and he beckoned him forth by holding his hand out to him, calling him a second time.

He thought he could take it, but it was too much for him. He slipped away from the doorway and Cory's injuries, pressing his back against the wall outside of the room, sweat collecting on his forehead. Dropping his face into his clammy palms, he began to sob in both anger and sympathy. Cory had always looked like that man he killed three years ago, but none ever so much as in that moment, when he reached for him in the same way, begging for him in that exact manner, his eyes screaming for him to save his life. It was all so overwhelming, and in his moment of reflection, he not only hoped Cory would be okay, but at last mourned that which he had already lost. The circumstances were ill-timed, but it felt so good to do it. It was the ultimate release, to finally say his goodbyes, to get it over with once and for all.

"Ian," he whimpered, and then, as soon as the name left him, so did his demons. It was finally time to let him go.

"Will!" Called Cory from inside the room. "Will, don't leave!" He trailed off in a dry whimper.

He's in worse pain than I am right now, he understood, strengthening his reserves. *I have to do to this for him. It's not just about me anymore.*

Gathering his repose, drying his face and wiping off his glasses, he forced himself to enter the room and came quickly to Cory's aid. Neither of them spoke at first. Will only grabbed his hand and held it in his own, stroking each of his knuckles with precise care. He planted a kiss on his forehead, and even though he did so gently, he winced.

"Please, Cory. Tell me what happened."

There was something he wanted to know first. "What's going on with you? I thought you were going to leave."

"I wanted to." He took a slow breath. "I changed my mind."

"W-why? Why did you want to leave?"

Brushing strands of sticky hair out of Cory's eyes, a gesture he smiled at, he sighed and took a seat in a chair next to Cory's bed, scooting it as close as he could. "I was afraid."

"Of what?"

"It doesn't matter now. I'm not afraid anymore. I'll be right here."

"Is it the hospital? I know you said you don't like them."

"Something like that. But I can handle it."

Cory seemed troubled, but Will's presence calmed him. "I've never feared for my life so much."

"It was Derrick, wasn't it?"

"Yes." The heart monitor beeped a bit quicker. "I went to see Angie. I went to tell her once and for all that I didn't want to be her friend anymore, that she really hurt me. I told her off for what she did." He took a deep breath, the oxygen tubes hissing. Will continued to stroke various parts of his body, their gripping hands never loosening. "We got into a yelling match. She didn't think what she did was as bad as I was making it out to be. That got me angrier. I've yelled at her before, but not like this. She kept saying that Derrick was the one to blame, that he took things too seriously. That's supposed to make me feel better?" He scoffed.

"Derrick has issues letting things go," Will advised. "I know, he told me."

The neck brace on Cory creaked again as he turned his whole collar toward him. "When did you talk to him?"

"I went to that bar you told me you saw him in. He showed up, and I threatened him a little. Unfortunately that didn't seem to have an affect on his mind, however feeble it seemed."

"A threat isn't going to do much to someone whose main reaction to everything is anger."

"An unfortunate mistake." One he planned to rectify.

A wheeze came out of his nose when he sighed. "I told her Derrick was following me around now because of what she said. She didn't seem to care. I know now the whole thing was a huge oversight, and I never should have bothered. I should have just blocked all contact from her and never spoke to her again, but I thought after years of friendship, she deserved my severance in person. While the two of us fought, Derrick happened to stroll in. He probably followed me there, honestly. I think he was standing out in the hallway the entire time, waiting for a good chance." He took a couple of staggered breaths, his heart rate speeding up again. "I was frustrated, and a little scared, so I left. He didn't appear to be following me. I started driving back home, and I saw a car behind me. I didn't think anything of it, until he started hitting my rear bumper trying to run me off the road, until I lost control and skidded into a field. I wanted to call the police, but my cell phone was gone. I must have left it at home." He uttered a curse under his breath. "He got out, chased me down, and started hitting me. When traffic came down the road, he got in his car and sped off. I got back into my own and drove myself here. I knew the way. I had been here before, when I had pneumonia."

"You *drove*?! In that condition?!"

"It hurt, but I made it." He winced and clutched at his ribs, then pulled a blanket over himself when a shiver ran up his spine. "Can't believe it…"

"What is it?"

"It's just really humiliating, all of this. I let this happen. How am I this pathetic?"

"Stop that." He didn't intend to sound so harsh, but his only thought was crushing Derrick's skull under his shoe and it was making him come unglued. "When someone beats you down, the last thing you should ever do is start acting like it's your fault."

"I couldn't even defend myself. I tried... I tried to fight him off, and I just failed. You don't seem to have much of a problem bringing him down. Why am I so weak?"

Will stroked his head, feeling his clenched muscles loosen. "Derrick isn't afraid of you because he knows you don't really want to hurt anyone. It makes you the wonderful man you are. It's a far more observable setback than any physical shortcoming. He fears me because he sees me for what I really am: a heartless piece of shit."

Cory didn't, perhaps even couldn't answer him. He was too emotionally bruised.

"You don't know how hard it is to see you like this. I should have been there, Cory. I'm so fucking angry at myself."

"What? How is *any* of this your fault?"

In truth, he supposed he was at least somewhat responsible. Derrick was just as unhinged as he was, if not more so, he just didn't see as deeply into Derrick as he did into him. Just as there had been something dark inside of him, something just as noxious dwelled within Derrick, and he had let it slip through his fingers, allowed it to wreak havoc, perhaps even set something loose.

But that wasn't the only reason he felt guilty. From day one, he had occupied a role of a watcher, to make absolutely certain no harm came to Cory. Cory never asked him or depended on him to protect him, but he took this job without negotiation or recourse, because it was in his nature to shield that which he loved, after having lost so much. If Cory had died in the fight, or ended up losing one or more appendages, he would never be able to forgive himself for allowing it to happen, whether or not he was involved. After all he had put Cory through and after all of the pain he had suffered for his happiness, it wasn't fair that he had to be stricken down.

Derrick had brutally beaten Cory, and he had gotten away. He would see the light of another day, maybe hide out somewhere for a while, avoid police. Perhaps he even assumed Cory dead when he ran away from the scene. He would track him down like a hound to a fox. Derrick's common stomping grounds were a scent he already had memorized and could pinpoint easily.

"Ow... Will... my hand."

Will hadn't noticed he was squeezing Cory's palm so tightly, and he slackened his seize. "I'm sorry. I'm just a little upset."

"What matters is that I'm alive, right?" He didn't sound too thrilled at this concept. "Not that I will want to live after I see how much the bill is. You think my health insurance will cover 'merciless assault by jealous boyfriend'?"

Although inside, he was filled with rage, he was grateful to Cory for trying to have a sense of humor. He couldn't find the will to laugh, however. "There's a chance."

Samantha had finally arrived, and with Cory's two sisters, who each ran to him with fearful expressions and whimpers. Cory got the same emotional treatment from his family as he did from Will, only his family encouraged him to call the police. There was a reason Will didn't persuade him of this, and he wasn't about to reveal it to Cory. *Sometimes matters need to be taken into our own hands,* he once wrote in one of his many anonymous scribbles to Cory, and that was something he still believed in. He would deal with Derrick in his own way, and that way didn't involve handcuffs or Miranda rights.

He didn't get to spend a lot of time with him once the family came in and cooed over him. Even the lighthearted scene of Cory with his mother and sisters, cracking jokes with them to comfort them about the situation, couldn't bring a smile to Will's face. He wanted to laugh, even wanted to force one out for Cory's sake, but he couldn't even manage that.

Attempting to be a gentleman, Will vacated his chair for Samantha to sit in to be with her son. Instead, she stood beside him with crossed arms and a look of scorn. It seemed that what she really wanted was for him to leave the room, but wouldn't demand it, knowing Cory would argue. As livid as he was, he could see why she didn't care for him. He hadn't influenced her son to do bad or questionable deeds, but he had still caused him grief.

"I'm going to get some coffee, sweetheart," Will spoke up, and Samantha seemed pleasantly surprised at his perceptiveness. "Do you want anything?"

"Oh yes, please, get me some water."

The moment he walked out, he thought of Cory's mother starting a game of twenty questions: *Did Mister Shepherd do this to you? Did he tell someone to do it? You know you can tell me, honey. I know what a horrible man he is.*

Ordering coffee was more of a stressful trial than it needed to be. The line was long, the customers indecisive, and the personnel inattentive. When he finally reached the counter to order his hot beverage, they informed him that they were out of two percent milk, which he couldn't drink coffee without. A screaming, high pitched whistle reverberated in his ears, one that didn't want to be contained. It begged him to let it out, to release the pressure, the sound of cracking embers vociferous. It was something so simple, something that on any other day he would have shrugged off, but now, he wanted to grab the head of the service attendant behind the counter, slam it into surface of it repeatedly until he no longer had a recognizable face. He wanted to let it all out, once and for all.

He went with cream instead, but refused to be satisfied with this discrepancy.

When he passed by a nurse on the way back to Cory's room, he asked her if she could take a cup of water to Cory. She told him she would, and Will made his way back to the exam room he was in. Outside the room waited Samantha, who was leaning against the wall with an assertive posture, at least until Will showed up. At first, he didn't say anything to her, only began to walk into the room, but she stopped him.

"Mister Shepherd," she whispered. "I need to speak with you."

He was exasperated, but he honored her request. "Yes?" He sighed.

"Cory won't tell me who did this to him. Why not?"

He had to admit, it confused him just as much. Why wouldn't Cory tell his mother? "I... I don't know."

"I think I do." She pushed herself away from the wall she was standing against and stepped slowly up to him until they were inches away. "I think he's protecting someone."

"Who?" He already knew, but if there was a chance the two of them could settle a score, now would have been a good time to do so.

"Well, to be frank, Mister Shepherd... you."

"You think *I* did this to Cory?"

"I know the kind of sneaky bastard you are." Her ability to repel vomit at the sight of him seemed to wane, though just enough to take a minute to question him. Even in such short time, Will wished she would go back to coddling Cory. "I know what you've done." She interrupted him before he could reply. "Don't! Don't you dare try to lie to me. I know what your last boyfriend did to you. I heard it, every night, the screaming and the crying. You'd turn the police away every time I called them. I wondered for the longest time why someone would be insane enough to do such a thing."

"Samantha," Will groaned, not having the time or patience for such a discussion.

"I'm not finished." This silenced him, but he folded his arms. "I figured it out, you know— why you didn't want him arrested. You wanted him dead."

"Is that so? And where do you get these wan theories?"

"I read about his accident in the paper. He didn't die from the crash. He was treated in the hospital for some time, and they said he was recovering. Then suddenly he dies one night? Why would he just die when they said he was starting to do better?"

Will hadn't even been asked these questions by the police, whom he always assumed suspicious, but perhaps they were letting him off easy for killing someone that was just a waste of tax dollars, as well as a waste of life. Samantha, on the other hand, had a son that was in love with him, and it was her duty to stand up for his rights. He didn't despise her for this, but she could have asked him at another time. "You'd have to ask the hospital those questions," he answered a little too casually.

"I don't need to ask them. Everyone knew, William." She was on a first-name basis with him now? He couldn't tell if that was good or bad. "*Everyone.* You got away with it, though. And now, who knows what you've done? Maybe you're trying to..." Tears formed in her eyes, but she blinked them away, and straightened her shoulders, standing taller. "...Trying to hurt my son because he looks like him."

What could he possibly say to comfort her? *Yes, it's true, I killed Ian, but I love Cory.* What good would that do? After all, he did love Ian, too. "I know you're afraid of me, and I know people like to talk about me, spread lies and things. I don't blame you for believing them. If I was rumored to do less threatening things, they'd be easier to ignore. But rest assured, and I swear this on the grave of my birth mother, that Cory means everything to me, and I didn't do this to him. I never would. If you could see how happy he is with me, you'd understand that."

"Please. My son means shit to you." Will felt sprays of her spittle hit his cheek, and he wiped it off. "You broke up with him so you could shoot yourself up with heroin, so don't play cheeky with me."

"You know of that, eh?"

"You think Cory wouldn't tell me?"

"I am a bit surprised. To be honest, Samantha, you coddle him and overprotect him. He's a grown man. He can make his own choices."

"*And he made the wrong one!*"

Will peered at the doctors and nurses now staring at them, and he lowered his voice. "Look, Samantha, I don't know what else to tell you. I *know* full well that you hate me. You don't have to remind me of that. And that's fine. You don't have to like me. You do have to accept, however, that Cory isn't your little baby anymore. You have to trust him, and trust that he's smart enough. I realize he won't tell you who really did this, but even I don't know why. I know who did it, and I'm going to settle it."

Saddened that Will didn't "come clean" like she hoped, the tears were harder to fight off. "I wish I could believe you."

"Do you believe Cory?"

Unable to answer honestly, she hung her head.

"Then how could you ever believe me?" He stopped arguing with her when a nurse passed them and entered the room with a cup of water. "I'm going to spend some time with him. Please, Samantha... even if you don't put your faith in me, put your faith in him."

She didn't acknowledge him in any way, but merely stared at the checkered floor. Will left her to sulk alone and went back inside to Cory, who was happy to see him return. Amanda and Erica were sitting next to his bed, holding his hand and arm. Erica looked at him with fear, but he didn't speak to her. He was sure Samantha told her many things that weren't very nice. Amanda on the other hand, didn't seem afraid, and she got out of her chair.

"You can sit down, William."

"I don't plan to stay for much longer."

Cory's cheerful smile dropped, and he moaned. "You're leaving already? Where are you going?"

"I have some very important tasks to tend to. I'll be back tomorrow."

His brow furrowed. "What tasks?"

"Forget about it."

"Will... tell me."

"I told you, don't worry. Everything will be okay." He stepped up beside the bed and gripped his hand, which was cold and shaking, the IV drip chilling his blood. He leaned down to his face and kissed his uninjured cheek. Then, he whispered, "Why didn't you tell her it was Derrick?"

Silence, for a moment or two. He seemed uncomfortable now, and it made Will even more nervous. "Let's talk alone for a second." Will nodded. After he dismissed his two sisters politely, he brought his pitch down to a near-whisper. "I know I'm young. I'm naïve and stupid. I still have a lot to learn, but I think I can easily read you. I know you more than you think I do, Will. You love me, and you respect me, and I know you do— but there's something bad inside you." Will was hoping he would never say that, that they'd spend their rest of their lives together without him bringing it up. It was only a matter of time before the truth reared its ugly head. He supposed that one day Cory would discover it, that he would see him for what he was, but he didn't expect it to come so soon. "When I told you what Derrick did, there was this look in your eye… it's like you knew exactly what you were going to do now that you found out, and whatever it is, it's not good. This isn't a new feeling, either. Your stalking, the tires you slashed at Hot Wire, your thieving…"

"How much do you trust me, Cory? Would you trust me with your life?"

"What? O-of course I would."

"Do you think I would ever harm you?"

"No. What are you getting at?"

"Would you ever do anything to hurt *me*?"

"You know I wouldn't." They both went quiet for a minute. Will had zipped his mouth shut. "I know you're hiding something from me. I told you before that if we're going to make this work, we can't keep secrets from each other. Tell me what's going on in your head. Tell me what you're thinking."

"There are some things better left unsaid."

"Don't give me that crap. You underestimate me, you know. You think I don't understand."

Will dragged his wiry fingers along the cheeks of his face, tucking them under his glasses to rub his sleepy eyes. "It's not that I think you won't *understand*. It's that I think you *can't handle it*."

"You killed Ian, didn't you?"

Time, sound, and light all seemed to stop instantaneously, and Will couldn't bring himself to look at Cory, who he was now picturing as a manifestation of a wrathful and unforgiving god about to shoot lightning and rain fire upon his head. "Whatever gave you that idea?"

"My mom mentioned it was once a rumor around the neighborhood. I didn't dwell on it much at the time. I thought she was just delusional. The police told me he died from a car accident, and I had no reason to doubt them. They're the police. Then I thought on it some more. If I had been you, I might have killed him, too. If I was beaten, abused, raped by someone who did nothing but drink his life away, and I had the opportunity to kill him, I *would have done it*. I remember how angry I was at you for what you did to me... and that was without you hitting me. I imagined how much worse it would feel if you *had* hit me, and raped me, and called me horrible things. Nothing would hurt worse than that— than being betrayed by someone you devote your life to."

The foundation of his spirit began to crumble, which was already built with decaying wood and misaligned bricks. This had been a conversation he only imagined on many restless nights, and never did he expect it to leap out at him so abruptly. "What must you think of me?"

"Will... I don't think anything is wrong with you. I'm just putting all of the pieces together now. Seeing how angry and, I'll admit, *vicious* you looked when I told you what happened to me, with you speaking in cryptic 'I'll handle it' terms. You want to kill Derrick, don't you?"

Slinking back into his chair, staring at the glistening, reflective tiles, he placed both hands on the armrests and tightly gripped them. "What would you do if it were me lying in that bed right now, Cory?"

He didn't find it an easy question to answer. "I don't know what I would do."

Crossing one leg over the other and folding his hands in his lap, he bobbed his foot up and down like an cat flicking its tail. "You wouldn't be furious at the one who did it to me?"

"Of course I would. That doesn't mean I'd be willing to kill someone."

"I would be willing to kill for you. I would do it in a heartbeat."

He adjusted the small tubes in his nose, squirming. He did look rather uncomfortable with those wires and hoses attached to him. "I don't think it's up to me to take anyone's life. It's not my responsibility."

Will continued to rhythmically rock his foot to the tune of a silent pendulum. "None of us truly believe we're capable of murder until a situation presents itself to us where we find there is no other alternative solution. Ian died in this very hospital, and I watched him. I watched him because..." He sighed. "I wanted to make sure that once and for all, he wouldn't live to hurt me any longer."

"How did you do it?" A speedy breath quaked out of his mouth.

"Pulled the plugs. He had a collapsed lung. The cutoff of oxygen caused respiratory arrest. He suffocated."

Cory grasped the oxygen tube that was placed in his nose as if someone were to steal it. Will's heart ached at his first sign of fear. "Did he die slowly?" Will hesitated, then nodded. It was hard to, as though the memory itself had prevented him from confronting just how much Ian suffered. "Did you feel better afterward? Were you happier?"

"I thought I would be. But no. I only felt worse. I just wanted to forget it ever happened, and kept wishing I could start all over. Then I met you one day, when you remarked on my lawnmower and asked why it was making that rattling sound. I never did find out. I stopped using it after that." He trailed off as he made an unscheduled stop to take a trip down memory lane. "I saw how much you looked like him, and it was like fate calling out to me. Do you believe in fate?"

Afraid that Will was coming somewhat unhinged, Cory swallowed in his now dry throat. "Not really."

"That's okay. You don't have to. I do, though. However, I don't believe in God or Heaven. Hell is something I've already lived through. It can't possibly exist beyond the realms of reality when life already involves so much pain."

"What did it feel like? To kill him, I mean?"

"It's been three years and it's only sunk in about thirty minutes ago, if that gives you any idea of how much denial I've lived in. The best way to describe it is concurrent bereavement and exuberance. I wanted to pretend it didn't happen, lie to myself. Hospitals were a painful reminder, like Death pointing his finger at me, telling me to repent. I wasn't ready." They breathed deep in unison. "I'm glad you know now. I wanted to tell you, but I didn't want to frighten you. I didn't ever want you to see that part of me. I planned to shelter it the rest of our lives. I think it's better that you know."

"I always felt like there was something you were holding back, something you didn't want me to see. I can tell how relieved you are." Will nodded, but didn't look at him. "What are you going to do now?"

"I think you know."

"You don't have to. I can have him arrested. Just because you once killed a man who abused you doesn't mean you have to kill Derrick."

"A man who beats on me, a man who beats on you... what's the difference? They both earned their punishment."

"The difference is that you could get caught. Luck eventually runs out."

"I don't think I will. It doesn't matter anyway. Think for a moment on Derrick's entire existence. What if you're not the first person he's brutally beaten? What if he abused previous partners? What if he hurts other partners in the future? What if he hurts your friend? Do you really want to give him that chance?"

"You don't see how hypocritical you're being. Aren't you pursuing violence, too?" Will smiled a bit, but didn't deny it. "Don't we have a judicial system for a reason?"

"The law isn't always concrete," Will snarled. "The law doesn't always solve problems. You know that. Just because Derrick gets arrested for assault doesn't mean anything. He'll be back out to do it again... and he *will* do it again. People don't just change because they spend a little time in jail. In my opinion, a cell isn't enough of a punishment. It's not required for us to agree on every point, just because we're in a relationship. There are some things we aren't going to like about each other."

"Will, I don't want you to turn into a killer. God damn it, it's not who you are. You're not that malicious. I want you to think about this. Don't be stupid."

"I have thought about it. I'm sorry you don't like it. I don't want you to be scared, but it's the only way I'll feel better. I'm afraid holding back would just make me want it more."

Cory was no longer able to fight away tears. "How are you any different from him? You're just as bad as he is, if not worse. I can't let you do this. You can't be this way."

"What are you going to do?" Will said with a chuckle. "Chase me in a hospital gown with a wounded leg and an IV stuck to your arm? I'm sorry. I've made up my mind."

Struggling against the restraints of his bandages, he shouted, "Will, please. Promise me you won't."

"I can't lie to you." He stood up out of his chair and buttoned his long coat, then kissed Cory's forehead. When he tried to sit up, he eased him back down. "Everything will be okay." As he turned and walked out of the room, he listened to Cory's wails of anguish.

He opposes it now, but in time, he'll forgive me. He'll see how much better off he is. How much better off we both are.

He checked his wristwatch. There was still time left in the evening to do a little shopping. If he worked fast, he could get it done swiftly and be back at his parents' house before too late.

There was a chance Cory would have gotten over the whole "my boyfriend is a murderer" thing by the time he returned. Then they could go back to their merry lives, however merry they might have been.

18. Hunt

Will found and purchased everything he needed at the hardware store: sheets of plastic, a tarp, rope, duct tape, and a shovel. The cashier who rang him up did so with tight lips and wandering eyes. He was surprised it wasn't followed up by nervous whistling.

Will passed her some cash after she tallied him up, and she refused to look him in the eye. He received his change, then left the store. He next made stops at a retail supermarket to purchase cleaning supplies, just in case he would need them. When he returned home, he left the items in his car to avoid his parents seeing them, and after some dinner, went out to Derrick's most commonly known locations. He wasn't surprised to see his car in the parking lot of Angie's apartment complex. Whether or not he was inside of it, he wasn't sure. It seemed that Derrick really hadn't decided to hide after all, but maybe he thought he didn't have to, that police wouldn't even believe Cory's story. Perhaps he knew Angie would lie for him.

When he was through tracking him, he went back home to have supper. Cory and his incident with Derrick never left his mind, and no other thought replaced it, even for several hours. He kept seeing Derrick's head exploding from the force of a bullet, and it repeated like a piece of broken film, even as he tried to sleep, unsuccessfully. He used this active time to paint, which helped clear his mind.

Early the next morning, Will took his first trip in many years to Detroit, where he scouted for abandoned and condemned buildings, mostly closed factories that hadn't yet been demolished. Many of them had asbestos warning tape over the shattered entrances, but it didn't deter him from his choices. He toured many of them, and found several of them too risky to do his business in because of the signs of homeless tenants, whom left hundreds of empty alcohol bottles littering the ground. Finally he found one that was perfect: cavernous, not too eroded, completely abandoned, no security, and no squatters. This was where he would bring Derrick to do the job. During his road trip, he jotted down notes, including addresses, in a composition notebook he brought with him. He circled the one he decided on.

Following that procedure, he went home to check the gun he stole from Derrick, and to be sure it was loaded and ready to go. After a long day's worth of work, he eventually grew sleepy enough to try to rest, but he wanted to pay Cory a visit first.

This time during his stopover, Cory was alone in the room and he didn't have to stand beneath those spiteful glares from Samantha. He showed up bearing gifts: a blooming rose and a faithful smile.

"Thank you, Will," Cory said with a scratchy throat. His neck brace had been removed, his arm now in a sling. "They did an X-ray, said my neck wasn't broken, so I didn't have to wear the brace anymore. I'm glad. It irritated me."

"I'm relieved to hear you're only fifty percent broken as opposed to seventy."

He smiled, but it only stayed for a fraction of a second. Will expected Cory to be sad, but his silence wasn't very reassuring.

"Penny for your thoughts?" Will asked, preening over his physical and emotional distance. He took a seat in the chair nearest the bed, but Cory didn't look at or touch him.

Staring up at the ceiling, he muttered, "I called the police."

Will's joints locked. He didn't move or speak. They could be watching him, right now, through glass, through cameras, spying and listening in on their conversation. He lowered his voice. "You... what?"

"I told them what Derrick did. They're going to be here in thirty minutes to ask me some questions and file a police report."

"I... w-what... *Cory!*" He slammed his hand onto the arm of the chair with great force. He jumped, then clutched his neck. "How could you?!"

"Will, I'm sorry! What did you expect?! For me to just let you do it?! I know you know me better than that!"

"Do you have any idea how much trouble I've already gone through to set this up?! I drove around Detroit for hours, and I *hate* Detroit! I bought all of the supplies, I found this one condemned high school to do the job in, and that took all night. I…" He calmed himself, drawing in a warm breath and closing his eyes. "All right. Okay. It's no big deal. I can still do it. I just have to get it done before they find him."

"What if I tell them what you plan to do?"

"You're not going to." It was much more of a demand than bewilderment.

"How do you know I won't?"

"Because I know you love me more than you care about the law. You have a good heart, but you're desperate to keep me. You wouldn't have reinstated our relationship so willingly had that not been true."

There was something lingering in Cory's broken heart—diminishing hope and fading future goals as the man he thought would be the love of his life stamped on them like mashing out a stubborn cigarette. He used the controls on the side of the bed to raise the back so that he was sitting up straight, and scolded Will with a look so powerful that it weakened his knees. "You assume a lot, don't you?"

It hadn't before crossed Will's mind that perhaps Cory was stronger than he gave him credit for. "It's not assumption. It's what I perceive as true, and I'm usually right, aren't I?"

"God," he sneered. "I almost wish you'd go back to shooting up. At least then you weren't so full of yourself."

He clenched his fists, but they only twitched. "*I'm* full of myself? Can you even hear how self-righteous you sound when you talk about how wonderful the law is?"

"Just because you pulled life support from a mortally wounded man doesn't mean you have what it takes to commit bloody, senseless murder. You can't possibly think it isn't selfish of you to try and involve me in this."

"Why not? If my father can do it to my mother, why can't I?"

Cory's cocked his head. The timing didn't seem best to discuss it, but on the other hand, no other moment would be perfect enough. "Your biological father?"

"I was born to a father that didn't want me. Didn't seem too much like he wanted a wife, either. Since I was born, he neglected me half the time, and beat me the rest of the time. Some kids get slapped around because they steal cookies from a jar. I got hit for everything, the kind of striking the breaks bones. If I looked at him, for just a second, he whipped out his belt, and I..." He stopped, thinking it might not be best to go on. He almost changed his mind. Was it really Cory's business what went on, even with the appropriate context? Then, he saw how attentive and quiet Cory was. He wanted to know. He *needed* to know, everything. "I'd run, and he'd chase me down. I'd hide, and he would find me. Eventually, my mother didn't even have the courage to face him. She let him do it. Didn't even call the police or let me go to the hospital anymore. Couldn't afford to, and she couldn't keep lying to them. Didn't want to keep saying that I fell down the stairs. What kid is stupid enough to do that twenty times?" He drummed his fingers on the plastic armrest. He really could have used a razor then. Then he wouldn't have to talk. He could cut it all out of him. "Until one day. The day she paid for her courage with a shot to the face, by a gun I didn't even know my father owned. He turned the gun on me, so I ran.

"I was terrified. I escaped out the back door, went to the neighbor's house. They called the police. When they arrived, they told me my father had shot himself before they got there." After a few rapid, tearful breaths, he went on. "I can still remember seeing my mother lying there on the floor as if she had settled down for a short nap. When I saw the blood..." He turned his palms up, gazing into them like they were crystal balls. "I... I didn't know what to do. Somehow or other, I knew she was dead. She was *dead*, and there was nothing I could do for her. I couldn't save her. I couldn't protect her. I let her die. *I let him kill her.* I shouldn't have ran. I should have let him take me, too." He brought his open palms to his eyes, silent and mournful.

Cory said nothing, not for a while. Will was grateful on some level. What *could* he say? Nothing, really. Regardless, Cory had been the first person since his foster parents to hear him tell this story, and it felt good to let him know, just as he had informed him about Ian's death. When he dragged his shaking hands down his face, he looked at Cory once more.

His reproofing stare threw him for a loop. He didn't understand what angered him so much, but he didn't appreciate being chastised after pouring his heart out. "Will, I'm sorry. What happened to you... *all* of the things that happened to you, were terrible. You have to live with those memories for the rest of your life. It shaped you into who you are. But does it really give you a free pass to commit crimes and hurt others? Is it supposed to justify you killing someone?"

"Justify?" His insidious glower chilled Cory's blood. "No. I'm intelligent enough to know right from wrong and good from bad. Lots of people get abused in early childhood and don't end up killing. Many children witness death and turn out just fine. My point is that 'good' and 'bad' don't really exist. They're just labels to help us better understand a situation, and to understand a person. There is no such thing as 'the right thing,' or 'the wrong thing,' just 'the human thing.' I'm securing my place, my rights, my family and my happiness. Who are you or anyone else to judge me for that?"

"Is it really going to make you happy, Will? Think of how you felt after you— after Ian died. You hated yourself for it."

"Don't you think that after he's gone, we would be allowed to be happy? After all, he's already intruded on my business, on my livelihood. I think it's my human right to snuff out those who do so."

"He's a person. He's not a very good person, but still, a person. He has family, friends, and I don't think it's fair to them to take something away from them. Human beings are what they are. I even told you once that I loved you, flaws and all. This can't really be what you want to do."

"You don't have to like it, and frankly, I don't care if you do— and I say that with respect." Cory, hurt, shut his mouth, his brow low. "If you plan to tell the police, at least let me know if you are. We might not agree on what I'm doing, but we're still in this together."

"I'm not *in* anything."

Will could at last see how serious Cory was. He thought at some point he might be able to crack through his steel exterior, but he didn't back down. He was ready to oppose him, despite everything they had been through together. Warmth spread around his neck and collar. "Why are you so intent on protecting someone that did this to you?!"

"I'm not protecting him! I'm protecting *you*!"

"You have a very strange way of showing me that you care. You want that animal running loose to beat any man or woman he wants, but you want to lock me up because I *don't* want him to? I might be a bit off my rocker, but I think your priorities are quite out of balance."

"I don't want him hurting people. But I don't want you out there plotting vengeance either."

It didn't matter what Cory said or believed. He wouldn't get a chance to speak on it much more to Will. His eyes lifted to the hallway outside of the room, and Will turned to see what he was looking at. Two police officers were strolling toward them, talking amongst themselves. Will faced Cory once again, and Cory said, "What are you waiting for? Get out of here."

"Setting me free, are you?"

"Giving you a head start. Just fucking go, Will." He didn't look at him, or say farewell.

He didn't need to be told twice, and he pushed himself onto his shaking, achy feet. He parted with Cory after kissing his cheek, a gesture that he only seemed to accept, rather than adore. Dodging the police, he slithered out of the room and maintained a casual posture as he found his way out. Cory didn't verify whether or not he would tell the officers what he planned to do, but at this point, he didn't care. Cory didn't know what building he was going to, and the police would have to send out a search party. By then, Derrick would be dead.

Will's first stop was Angie's apartment. He didn't see the foul young man's car in the parking lot as he had last time, so he decided to pay his ex-girlfriend a visit to ask a few questions. When she answered the door, she seemed both repulsed and concerned.

She didn't bother with pleasantries, and got right to the point. "Is Cory okay?"

Will shoved past her, into her apartment. Angie didn't object, but made affronted sounds. "He's in the hospital, actually. You didn't know this?"

"The *hospital?!* What happened?"

"Come on, Angie," Will groaned in exasperation, sitting on the arm of the couch while she stood fidgeting. "Don't act like you don't know."

"Did Derrick…?"

"Yes. Derrick did." As he stuffed his hands into his pockets, he watched her fall into a routine of pacing and biting her nails. She started smoking after a few circles around the room. "Where is he?"

"I have no idea. Probably at his parents' house. That's sort of where he lives now." She took a step away from his haunting glare. "Why? Are you going to hurt him?"

"That's my business." He scratched at the stubble growing on his chin. "Are you and Derrick back together?"

"No. Why would we be?" Her tongue traced the inside of her cheek and she stared at the floor.

"You're lying, but it doesn't matter to me either way."

"What do you want from me?" She inquired, her fingers shaking around the cigarette she was holding.

"You know you're at least partially responsible for what happened to Cory, don't you? I want you to understand that."

"Derrick makes his own choices! I didn't tell him to hurt him!"

He waved a scolding finger at her. "That he does, but you encourage him, don't you? You *want* him to fight for you."

Angie mashed out her cigarette, only to rip another one out of the packet and light it. "Slow down. I don't appreciate being looped into whatever Derrick chooses to do. He's his own person. Cory and I were talking the whole thing out before Derrick came over and saw him here. I'm not excusing Derrick for what he did." She puffed, popped the cigarette out and exhaled, then stuffed it back in. "But if you want my honest opinion, Cory should have known better than to come over here. He knows the way Derrick is."

"You're blaming the victim now? That's classy, Angie."

"Stop it!" She stamped her foot violently, stamping a print onto the carpet. "Do you really think that I'm not bothered by this? I'm really afraid for him! You just come barging into my house accusing me of guilt, and it's not fair! If I knew he wouldn't chew my face off, I'd go visit him in the hospital."

Will wasn't sure how to answer her. He wasn't going to change her mind or stance on the issue. Even when confronting her, she had no incentive to tell him the truth. There was a chance that she was right when she said she cared for Cory, at least to some degree, and he couldn't confirm or deny that. She might not have loved and cared for him as much as he did, but might have still loved him in her own way. "If you really want to help Cory, you'd tell me where Derrick is."

Angie deliberated, inhaling nicotine for several seconds. Billowing smoke trailed out of her nose as she gazed at her own shoes. "I'll call him." She walked to the entertainment shelf, where her cell phone was plugged in. Will strolled around the living room while she made the call, looking at photos of her and Derrick in tabletop picture frames. They both looked so happy together, and you would almost think they were married from the sight of their photo.

Even when things and people are at their worst, Will reflected, *we pull a veil over the atrocities and fake a smile. I'm sure the stories behind those photos are more grim than the photos themselves.*

"Derrick? Where are you right now?" She smoked between questions. He had to admit that she made cigarettes look like a delicacy. "All day? What time are you leaving?" She tapped her foot. "No, I'll just see you later. Uh-huh. Love you, too." She hung up, then looked at Will, who was buttoning his coat. "He's at his parents' house, like I said. He's coming over here later tonight."

"The police might stop by here," Will informed.

"For what?!"

"For Derrick. Cory called them, you know."

"Yeah... yeah, I don't blame him."

Will paused, shocked by her humility. Then, "Where do his parents live?"

She shoved the cigarette between her lips, puffing some more. "I'm not telling you that. I'll just explain it to the police when they come here looking for him."

"Except that I don't trust you to do that. I think you'd lie for Derrick."

"Lie to the *cops?*"

"To anyone, really. You're probably even lying to me."

"Look, I don't need to take this from someone who is a junkie. You can stand on your moral pedestal all you like, but you're twice the loser Derrick is."

Will was both intrigued and mystified at her switching the focus onto him. He meant to tell her he was clean now, but figured it was fruitless. She wouldn't believe him. He never believed Ian when he vowed to have quit drinking. In that case, however, he was correct. "It doesn't matter," Will answered. "I don't need to know." Brushing past her, he opened the door and took a final glimpse at her. "I'll send Cory your regards." She lowered her head, and he left before she said anything else, lies or otherwise. He would just come back at night, when Derrick would supposedly return, and if he understood Angie, he figured she would withhold information from the police about whether or not he'd come home.

For the time being, he went back to his own family home to get some much-needed sleep. Many things flashed through his mind: Cory's disappointment in him, Angie's defense of the man she still loved, but especially whether or not the police would capture Derrick before he could. He craved destroying Derrick and just as badly as his other addictive qualities, and no matter how important it was for him to do so, he couldn't stop feeling angry. *Should have killed him a long time ago*, a vicious voice berated. *Should have killed him the day you met him. Maybe after all is said and done, Cory will forgive you, then you could live happily ever after, perhaps in a beautiful condo, a place for your art studio and Cory's broken electronics and light fixtures and his other little gadgets. You could run away together, somewhere far away after you've saved up enough money.*

I hear England is beautiful. I'd even accept Brazil as an option. Somewhere… anywhere… just him and me. I just want to get out of this place. We'll escape, and won't look back.

The tranquil thoughts of him and Cory living together— owning their own isolated cabin on a solitary lake, or in a high rise on a bustling thoroughfare, laughing and loving, painting and fixing things, all day every day— made him blissful and drowsy. It was just a dream, but sometimes they came true. He yearned so badly for that happy life, where everything was perfect, and where there was no pain or anguish. He would never have to cut himself again, because the hatred, the rage, and emptiness would be gone, and he wouldn't have to be afraid of losing his confidence again to a shrieking madman with violent tendencies. He would just have Cory and their warm little home— the one where they'd grow old together. Maybe, if he gained the courage and finances, they'd adopt a child one day and extend their family. He never pictured himself as a father, but he was reminded of how loving his foster parents were when they took him under their wing when he needed it most. He would do that for his son.

But it wasn't a perfect world, and this was a truth that was hard to swallow. It was so removed from reality that it made him sick to his stomach. He would only be a successful artist if he was lucky. Cory might not even want to be with him anymore, let alone live with him in some happy-go-lucky fantasy. He could have turned back, changed his mind about avenging his beloved. After all, he was alive, and though he had a few scars, nothing was so permanently damaged where he couldn't go through his day-to-day life.

It was too late. He had already come so far, and the hatred was too deep to dig out now. He could admit that Derrick didn't *need* to die, but he didn't care. A shroud of blackness had coated his vision and soul, one wounded from loss, and he felt just as hollow of sympathy as he did when he planned to take Ian's life.

He would sleep on it for now. Come nightfall, it would be time to get the show on the road.

On his way back to Angie's apartment, he picked up some fast food to eat in his car while he sat in the parking lot of the apartment building. It was an enjoyable meal, a greasy, overstuffed hamburger and salty fries, food he wouldn't have thought so delicious years ago. He checked his watch on numerous occasions, despite having no clue as to when Derrick would arrive, or if he would even arrive at all. Though he had received enough sleep during the daytime, he was still exhausted. His eyes would not stop closing, no matter how much he rubbed them. He longed for rest. Just to rest, forever if he could. His days were so long now, almost endless. No. Can't pass out now. He had to stay awake. He had work to do.

Then, through the blanket of cloudy snowflakes, he saw Derrick's car pull into a parking spot. He leaned down in his seat, watching as he climbed out of the vehicle. This was it. There was no going back now. It had to be done.

As Derrick swaggered toward the front door of the building, Will slipped on a pair of rubber gloves, then snuck out of his own car, carrying the shovel in both of his hands. He begged the snow not to crunch beneath his feet, but it seemed relentless at giving away his location. He had to carefully plan his every step, had to practically caress the ground with his shoes before pushing his weight onto them. Every inch he grew closer, the further he lifted the shovel into the air, ready to bring it down across Derrick's head. It would be a swift blow if he didn't miss.

Oh, please, don't miss.

His chance had come, and he seized it. Just inches behind Derrick now, he raised the shovel high into the air.

"Shit," Derrick whispered, and halted, snapping his fingers. "Forgot the beer." He spun around back in the direction of his car, and stopped short.

Derrick stared at Will. Will stared at Derrick. Neither of them moved nor spoke, just gaped. Will was posed perfectly with his arms in the air, holding the shovel above his right shoulder, ready to swing, but he was as frozen as an ice statue. He had forgotten how to operate his arms. No matter how much he forced his muscles to obey him, they'd defy his demands.

"What the fuck?" Derrick, for once, wasn't angry, but confused. "What the fuck are you—"

Clang!

Will had not intended to swing at that moment, and it had been involuntary, his appendages finally waking to his call. It took for Derrick to collapse for him to truly understand what had just happened. Yes, that's right; he was there to knock him out and drag him back to his car. After wiping a sheen of sweat off of his forehead, Will took the shovel back to the car, then returned for Derrick's unconscious body, dragging him through the snow and to the backseat of his vehicle, which was tougher to manage than he estimated. Once he was in the car, he tied him up with the braided rope and taped his mouth shut, a mouth that was covered in a layer of several days' worth of facial hair.

With that out of the way, he sneaked back into his car and started the engine, then slipped out of the parking lot like nothing ever happened there. It was a long drive to Detroit, so he listened to the radio. The songs left something to be desired, however. It took several scans of stations to find one good enough.

After a good thirty minutes, Derrick roused, groaning. He rustled and twisted in place, knocking some of the supplies to the car's floor. Will snapped, "Careful, I'm going to need that stuff."

"Mmff!" Exclaimed Derrick, struggling against his restraints. His breathing quickened in approaching panic, and he whimpered.

"I didn't expect you to wake up so soon, Derrick," Will said in woebegone monotone. "I intended you to remain unconscious until we got to Detroit, but it's such a long drive. I trust you understand what's happening." Derrick only whimpered more. "I know, I know.

On your end, I imagine this feels a bit uncalled for. I did warn you, didn't I? You just didn't listen."

Derrick attempted to slip the ropes off of his wrists and ankles, but it was futile.

"Struggling is only going to exhaust you. I suggest you just enjoy the ride." Glimpsing at Derrick in the rearview mirror, he saw him give up after running out of energy. "I can really tie a knot, can't I? Ian taught me how. It's too bad you never got to meet him. You might have gotten along with him."

Derrick only panted through his nose in desperation.

"Why didn't you take my advice, Derrick? Why'd you have to make me do this? Do you think I like living with regret and guilt? I don't want to go another three years in solitude, snorting oxy and drinking myself to death, but I feel like I don't have a choice in the matter. I warned you and you didn't listen."

Derrick only heaved in and out, wrought with terror. He tried in vain to loosen the ropes again, but couldn't find the strength. He sobbed.

"Don't cry. We're almost there."

The abandoned high school Will had picked out to complete the "job" in looked, at first glance, to be an old military academy rather than a school. In the shroud of darkness, under the cloudy winter sky, its shadows gave it a foreboding appearance, and it seemed to have a life all its own. He pulled onto the dirt path leading up to the broken fence surrounding the property, which was as close as he could get his car. When he parked, he looked at his prey in the back seat. With Derrick struggling, he knew he'd have even more of a challenge getting him inside.

"Do I need to whack you in the head a second time, or are you going to cooperate with me?"

Derrick could only signal with head gestures and blinking. He nodded, his glazed eyes shining in the overhead bulb that Will had switched on. Will thanked him before stepping out, then undid the rope around his feet before yanking him out of the backset by the knots in the ropes around his hands. He gathered more rope and tape, as well as a small but bright pen light he clamped between his teeth, then pulled the gun out of his belt, sticking the barrel of it against his back. He nudged him forward, aiming the flashlight with his mouth.

Derrick shuffled to his imminent grave, his head drooped. For someone who was going to be murdered, Will thought his behavior was quite tame. It was possible that in some way, Derrick expected this moment in his near future, and there would be no fighting it when it came.

The old high school, one that was so old that Will didn't know the name of it, had a principal's office Will thought suitable for securing Derrick until he set up a killing floor. A heavy wooden chair sat behind a large desk made of decaying wood, and that's where he sat Derrick and tied him. After getting him snug in his seat, Will looked at his magnificent kidnapping job with pride, slipping the flashlight out of his mouth.

"Well, don't go anywhere. I'll be right back." He patted Derrick's fuzzy cheek, and he exhaled a sound of disdain.

Will stumbled back outside and followed the path back to his car. As he made the trip, he thought he could hear sirens in the distance. There was no way that they'd find him if he was indeed what they were looking for, but he still felt a tad paranoid. *Come on, William. It's good ol' impoverished Detroit, for fuck's sake. Of course you're going to hear sirens. You're going to hear them all night long. Don't have a heart attack every time.*

He relaxed, at least for now, and gathered his remaining tools from the backseat of the car. He listened to those distant wails over the horizon, a squad of speeding cars racing down Grand River Avenue. He listened carefully as they got farther away. They weren't coming in his direction, and once he was absolutely sure of that, he went back inside the rundown school.

Now that he had his items, he began laying out the tarp onto the ground by the glow of the small flashlight, Derrick all the while sniveling. Will didn't intend to speak to him much during this whole ordeal, but he couldn't stand those squeaking and sniffling noises. It was distracting him. "Are you really still crying? Derrick, please. You're making this tougher for me."

"Mmmff!" He howled. It sounded like a call for help.

"Oh, stop that. No one can hear you, and it's extremely annoying." Around the tarp on the floor, Will placed sheets of thin plastic on surrounding furniture. When finished, he approached Derrick, whose breathing sped up again. With a quick, merciless swipe, he tore the piece of duct tape from Derrick's mouth, pulling with it hairs of his stubble, and he screamed in pain. "I wasn't going to give you the benefit of speaking, but I have a very curious mind, Derrick, and I need you to enlighten me." He sat down in his lap like a child would on a mall Santa.

"Fuck... you..."

"Now, now. Play nice. There are worse things I could do to you than killing you, you know." Derrick tried to buck him off of his lap, but Will only clutched him around his neck to hold on. "What compelled you to hurt Cory after everything I've said to you? Was it impulse? You can tell me."

Derrick had to think about it for a second. Will guessed it possible that maybe even he didn't know. "I thought you were fucking with me with that story of yours about you killing that guy."

Will laughed, amused by the outcome. "Well, as you now know, I wasn't."

"Listen... Will, right?"

"Mm-hm."

He decided now was the one chance he'd get to bare his soul to another individual, and to seek guidance from them, even when under the assumption that he may soon die. "I've tried like hell not to be so angry all the time. My mom and dad are even tired of me, always costing them money because of someone's car I fucked up, or speeding tickets, or things I broke. Nothing I do works. *Nothing.* I can't stop it."

Though toying with Derrick was fun, he toned down the psychotic whimsy. "Why?"

"I don't know why. I couldn't tell you. It's just me. Everyone, even Angie, just pisses me the *fuck* off. I would never hurt her, though. I know the way that I am, but I would never hurt her. Not like that." He leaned his head back to move away from Will's. "Cory just got in my way. He came around and started destroying everything I worked so hard to build. Angie told me today that they never slept together, so you were right when you said she lied. Did I feel guilty then, for hurting Cory?" He shrugged. "I don't know the answer to that. Maybe I do. A little. But I've been living with that kind of shit since I was a kid. Cory actually fought back, you know. He clocked me right in the jaw, pretty good too." He turned his head and showed him the bruise. Will cocked a smirk at the sight of it. "But when I'm angry, I'm *angry.* I don't stop fighting until it goes away, and sometimes it doesn't for hours. You can't just turn it off. You must understand. I've seen you going through the same thing."

Curling his lip, Will growled, "I'm *nothing* like you."

"You are, though. Cory was fucking around with my life, so I attacked him. I fucked with your life, and you attacked me. Whether or not you like it, and I can see that you don't, we're exactly alike. We're just from different worlds."

"I am *not*. *Like*. *You*," Will barked, pressing the barrel of the pistol against Derrick's temple. His lower lip loosened and quivered. "I am doing this because you left me no other choice."

"If you let me go, I swear to you, I won't come anywhere near you or Cory again. I have Angie back, and that's all I need. That's all I'll ever need."

"I already gave you that opportunity to walk away, and what did you do instead?" This reminded him of the pain Cory was in as a result of Derrick's pettiness, and fueled his rage that was temporarily sedated in the corner of his mind. He slammed his hand around Derrick's throat, and he gagged and coughed. "I'm sorry, Derrick. Cory may be very forgiving, but I'm not like Cory. I can't stand scum like you. The world would be a much better place if you and everyone like you died horrible, painful deaths."

"That's not fair," he choked.

"It's *plenty* fair, you walking disease."

"So you're trying to be some purifier for humanity, huh?" Stammered Derrick, leaning his face away, but Will snatched it back, clamping his fingers and thumbs onto his cheeks. "Are you getting off on this?!"

"I think you misunderstand. I don't *like* to kill. I don't want to do this. However, I think in the long run, it will make me happier. I'll feel guilty, no doubt, but I'll feel even guiltier if I let you go. I couldn't just break up with Ian or send him to prison, because he could hurt someone else other than me. People don't change. They are what they are, from the day that they're born, from their first step into this dreadful world. Let's get down to business, shall we?" He ripped a fresh piece of duct tape off of the roll and stuck it back over Derrick's mouth, and he went back to his fearful crying. He leaned the rear of the chair back and dragged it along the dust and debris-covered floor, moving around large hunks of concrete and wood. He untied his victim from the chair, tossing aside the hunks of braided rope, then shoved him down on the tarp with the gun mashed against the back of his skull.

Derrick pleaded with him, but his every word was muffled. The second Will cocked the gun, Derrick's wails grew louder as his impending doom drew near. This was it. This was how his life would end. He would die from a gunshot to the head in a dingy, abandoned building in the ruins of Detroit. His body might go missing for months, maybe years. Angie wouldn't know what happened to him. His mother wouldn't be surprised at his going missing, but she'd also worry.

Will could only make out these final words from Derrick: "I'm sorry, dad."

He hesitated. He wasn't sure why. He had wanted this so badly for the past few days, and now Derrick was here, in his clutches, ready to meet his maker. No one knew they were there. They were hidden from the world, from everyone they knew. The chances of him getting caught were so slim. If he pulled the trigger now, no one would know. No one would hear. It was easy. It was quick. It was... difficult.

Is this me? A distant voice asked. *Is this what I've become? Is this who I am?*

Why does it matter? You're doing your job. You're doing what's right.

His index finger slowly squeezed the trigger. It creaked under the pressure. He released it, clutched it, then let go again.

Why is this so hard? Killing Ian was so simple, and he died slowly. Derrick's death will be instantaneous. I won't be causing him any pain. It'll just be instant blackness.

He flexed and re-clenched his hand on the gun's handle several times, sweat causing it to slip.

I'm protecting Cory. Protecting myself. Protecting my livelihood. Protecting everyone else Derrick comes in contact with. That's a noble cause, isn't it? I am doing the right thing... aren't I?

His trigger finger loosened. His palm was soaked with sweat, and the gun's handle slid down his hand.

He is your father. He is Ian. He is the embodiment of pain, rage he can't contain. This is his gun you're holding, after all. He might have used it on someone. It's better for it to be used on him instead.

I can't. It was easy to kill Ian. He made me feel powerless and weak. Derrick is the weak one, here.

Don't argue with yourself. Just fire. It's what Cory would want.
But Cory doesn't want it. He tried to tell me. He tried to explain.
JUST KILL HIM, YOU WORTHLESS SACK OF SHIT!

"Shut up!" Will screamed, dropping the gun and flashlight to the ground, putting his hands over his ears, silencing the powerful voice. He was drenched with gallons of reality, forced to face what was happening, and it overwhelmed him so much that he dropped to his knees and hugged his own waist. He had gotten himself into a horrible situation, and he couldn't decide whether or not to back down. He wanted to. He desperately wanted to. What on earth was he thinking? What was he doing? Had he gone completely out of his mind?

He heard the rustling of the plastic tarp, and raised his head. Derrick was now on his feet, and was moving slowly away from him toward a set of double doors. He had absconded with the handgun, which was now in the possession of its original owner. Instead of taking him out, however, Derrick opted to run, skittering through the doors and running off, possibly to hide. Will wondered then why Derrick didn't shoot him. It could have been for the same reason he couldn't pull the trigger. It was easy to fantasize about killing someone. It was tougher to carry it out. Will seized the shovel and rushed after him, pushing on through the doorway he escaped through, and could hear him ascending the staircase down the hall. He ran down the dusty, tiled floor, chasing him up the stairs.

Why am I chasing him? I don't know if I want to kill him.
Now you have to kill him. If he gets away, he'll tell the police.
Maybe he should. What am I doing? This isn't me.
He can't be allowed into the world. Remember what he did to Cory. What he does to Cory, he does to you. Through Cory's pain, he causes you just as much anguish.

Will jogged up the stairs to the second floor, passed old, eroding doors that were once biology and chemistry labs. The atmosphere was of death and faded memories, of lessons past that were long forgotten. In the dark corridors and chipped hallways, Will listened to the sound of his own voice speaking.

"He completely vanished."
Don't give up so quickly, William. He's hiding.
"Maybe I don't want to find him. Maybe Cory was right."
There's no time for that shit now. Find him.

Will didn't find him. He couldn't. After half an hour of searching, he began to give up, despite the chanting of infuriated voices in his head. The building was too immense, and Derrick could have been long gone by then.

"Should have listened to him. He tried to tell me. He tried to reason with me."

Will made rounds of the hallways, checking the abandoned classrooms and bathrooms. Then, he heard a distant melody, a sound of harmonious longing, of reckoning. It was a song so serene, and yet so frightening as it quelled the busy quarrelling inside of his head. It rose, so high, and fell ever-gradually, a comforting lullaby.

The song was the sound of sirens, sirens that were coming this way. The police knew where he was, and they were getting close.

Derrick must have called them! He had his cell phone! You didn't check that, did you?!

I'm glad he called them.

You go find that motherfucker right now and rip his god damned face off!

The police will stop me.

Find him and kill him.

They'll stop me.

They're coming to take you to prison for the rest of your miserable life, you idiot. What will you do then?

The front doors of the school wafted open with a harmony of metallic rumbles and squeals. He could hear it even from where he was standing. The police. They arrived. They found him. It was too late.

That's when he heard a familiar voice, a heavenly call. "Will!"

Cory?

19. Shepherd

Cory's flashlight was dying. No matter how often he smacked it against his palm, it wouldn't come alive. The thought of the light going out in a place so dark scared the living hell out of him, but not nearly as much as when he saw the plastic and tarp laid out on the floor. There was no blood, at least from what he could see with the blinking light in his hand, but there was no sign of Will or Derrick. Where had they gone? Was Will all right?

After getting released from the hospital, Cory had went straight for Will's home, which his parents willingly let him into. He went downstairs to his room in the basement and searched his things for hours, digging around in his desk. Will had written down the address for the high school on a page in a composition notebook he found tucked away in a drawer. Another page behind it was torn out, perhaps directions he had written down for the fastest route there. When he saw that the address was in Detroit, he hoped it was what he was looking for.

"Is everything okay with Will?" Anthony asked him when he saw him rummaging through his son's belongings.

"I don't know, to tell you the truth." He was indistinct with him on purpose. If Will made it out of this situation, he might have wanted to explain it to them in his own way. If he didn't make it out, on the other hand, he didn't want the last thing they heard about Will to be that he plotted murder. "I just need to go have a talk with him. He's really upset."

"Let me know if you need my help with it," he directed, but didn't push the matter further. Cory assumed he trusted him with Will. He hoped he wouldn't let him down.

By the time he had found the information he was searching for, night had descended, and he knew that if he was to go searching for Will, he had to do it soon before he could draw any blood. With no quick and hazardless way of contacting him, he had to go entirely on his knowledge of Will's behavior, and hoped like hell that his assumptions were correct. He didn't exactly want to go anywhere near Detroit, especially only on a whim that Will actually went there, but if it meant Will's safety, he'd have to.

When Cory did arrive at the address, one that took him quite a while to find, he noticed just how remote the location was, and could understand why Will chose it. As he parked outside of the chain-link fence surrounding the abandoned building, he saw Will's vehicle there. That was more than enough evidence he needed to go inside looking for him.

He supposed he should have called the police before arriving, but he didn't fear Will. What he did fear, however, was walking in on a gruesome murder site, to see Will consumed by malice and drenched in another person's blood. Even if Will was doing it in his name, it was something all too devastating for him to conceive, even in his imagination. Now that he was there, he realized he hadn't thought out the situation. What would he do when he found Will? Would he even be rational enough to speak to him?

Now standing alone in the cold, filthy corridor of the creepy remains of the dilapidated building, he wondered whether or not he would even find Will at all. The halls stretched infinitely in the darkness, and he couldn't see far beyond the guiding, however faulty beam of his flashlight. Will could be anywhere, hiding out, or moving from room to room. He called for him, but didn't get an answer. He tried again.

"Will! Will, it's me! Everything's going to be okay, just come out for me!"

"Cory," echoed a voice from above. "What are you doing here?"

Turning a full three hundred and sixty degrees, he tried to see him. Over his head was a balcony railing lining the hallway of the second floor and he aimed the flashlight upward. He couldn't see him, but he could hear him. "What do you think I'm doing here? I'm trying to get you out of this!"

"It's not safe here. You shouldn't be here."

"Where's Derrick?"

"Don't know. He ran." Footsteps crossed the creaking, old floor. Will leaned over the railing to see him, half of his body covered by shadows as Cory aimed the flashlight at him. "The police are coming, aren't they? You hear them?"

"I can hear them. Come down here, Will."

"Are you going to try to trap me?"

"You know I wouldn't! I just want to talk."

Will vanished from sight, his footsteps echoing, this time rushing down a set of stairs. Two chipped, steel doors flung open and Will beckoned him forth. "This way," he called, holding out his hand for him.

What was "that way," Cory wondered? Where was he about to take him? Did he even want to know?

Will might have completely lost his mind, and I'm alone in here with him. I don't know whether or not to trust him.

Will waved his hand a few more times, signaling for him to hurry. Cory never found a decision so challenging to make. His heart wanted to follow him, and his conscience wanted to stay there until the police arrived.

"Cory," Will summoned. "Cory, please. Don't be afraid."

At long last, Cory sprung forward with a slight limp and took his hand, clasping it tightly, and they headed up the staircase. "Where are we going?"

"Let's find a way to the roof."

"The *roof*? What for?"

"It'll buy us more time."

"Time for what? What are you planning to do?"

Will didn't answer him, only led him on down the grimy, crumbled halls, keeping at Cory's hobbling pace. As he searched the corridors and stairs for a way up, the sirens sounded only minutes away. The search for the roof went on and on, and Cory started to think Will was getting them lost, until they came upon a set of stairs labeled **STAFF ONLY**. Will kicked it open, and the thin steel dented as it swung, nearly coming off of its old hinges. The door seemed unlocked, so Cory knew it wasn't necessary, but it was one of those unexplained things that Will did he would never quite grasp.

The door to the roof was at the top of another staircase, and as soon as Will pried it open, gusts of snowy winds swept over them. Cory was pulled into the open by Will's taught hand, and he slammed the door behind them, barricading it with large five-gallon buckets of paint and cement cinderblocks left along the surface of the rooftop.

"Now what?" Cory asked when he closed up his jacket, the current of air biting his face and throwing his hair in all directions. "What are we doing up here, Will?"

"I didn't think I'd get a moment alone with you. I needed one." Brushing strands of hair out of his eyes, only for the winds to toss it back, he said, "I couldn't do it. I wanted to so badly, and I… I don't know what's wrong with me, Cory. I had the gun in my hand, ready to shoot…" He clasped Cory's wrists, nuzzled his frozen cheek and brought his lips against his ear, whispering, "I feel like two people are fighting inside my head. They want different things, and I can't decide which one of them is me."

Cory placed his one good hand on Will's shoulder and calmed him by giving it a tender squeeze. "But you didn't do it. I'm so glad you didn't."

Will embraced him, held him, tighter and tighter. "I was afraid you might never want to see me again. How did you even find me?"

He wrapped his uninjured arm around Will's neck, and Will wrapped the folds of his long coat around him to warm him up. "I found your notebook. The address was in it. I knew I probably only had one chance to find you. I'm glad I did."

"I love you, so much." His hug became even stronger, and Cory endured the pain in his broken arm.

"I love you, too."

For a moment or two, they were silent, holding each other, the winds howling around them, flakes of snow whipping against their skin. Then, Will spoke next, and he sounded determined. "I've never done right by you."

He tried to look Will in the eye, but he only turned his gaze away. "What do you mean?"

"Since the very beginning, I've done everything wrong. I've done nothing but hurt you."

"I don't think now is a very good time to be discussing our relationship." Just as he gave him this warning, three police cruisers pulled up to the fence around the old school. His grip on Will tightened.

"Please, Cory. It's important that I tell you now. I'll never get another chance to." Cory dreaded his implications. He didn't want to believe it when he said that. Still, he loaned him an ear, seeing how dire this was to him. "I've thought about it. For so long, I dwelled and pondered. I've looked back on my past, my life, my future with you, and none of it fits, no matter how I look at it or in what way. I wanted to be with you because you were a better person than me. I wanted you to show me what it was like to be human. When I held that gun in my hand, I knew I had turned out like the man who conceived me. It was always my worst nightmare. And, now, it's reality. I did the one thing I swore I'd never do."

"But, Will, you're not—"

"What if I turn a gun on *you*? Even if I don't pull the trigger, even if I just point one at you, what would you do? Would you cry, and forgive me? Would you accept that it's just the way that I am? What would happen then if you chose to turn and walk away from me? Would I... would I *shoot* you, Cory? Would I kill the only person that ever loved me? I've asked myself this. I don't know the answer. I don't know what I would do. And that horrifies me."

Never had Cory anticipated such a grim and dark conversation with anyone. He couldn't perceive that such a thing was being asked of him. Had they really come to this point? In truth, he didn't know Will well enough to argue with him. Perhaps there was a chance he would open fire on him if he left him, or fought with him. No, not Will, of all people. Not the man who held him on cold nights to keep him warm, the man who defended him when no one else was there, the very one who gave up a self-abusive life to start over with him. Such a man would never kill him. Such a man would never destroy his life so willingly. "You wouldn't." He said it with certainty, but his voice trembled.

"Don't say what you don't believe just to make me happy. I can hear it in your voice. You no longer trust me. You never will again. From now on you'll see me as nothing but a monster."

It wasn't true. Couldn't possibly be. Will was no monster. Will gave him something to work toward and someone to try for. He'd be damned if anyone took that way from him, even Will himself. However, in a way, he could see truth in his statement. Since Will confessed to him his murder of Ian, the thought never left his mind that Will might do the same to him one day. What if things didn't work out? Would he stay with Will, not out of devotion, but out of fear of death? Would Will become strict, demanding and possessive? Would he kill someone who flirted with him? None of these scenarios sounded so far-fetched anymore.

Will released Cory, as well as let out a moan of grief. "You've done everything in your power to be there for me, and I've done nothing but cause you anguish. If we go on like this, I might do something even worse to you. This whole situation proves that I have it in me. I am capable. You know it, too."

"That's not true!" Even the screaming breeze couldn't shield the fraudulence of his assertion.

"Yes it is. I know you can see it. You just won't face the facts."

"Will, we all make mistakes. You've just made really, really big ones."

"Mistakes? Mistakes are accidents, sweetheart. They aren't planned. They don't stew inside of our hateful brains for months, for years." When Cory shook his head, he went on. "Killing your life partner isn't a mistake. Almost shooting another man in the head… that is not a mistake. I *wanted* to do those things."

Cory was going to retort, but he heard the sound of doors opening and slamming, handheld two-way radios buzzing with the sound of officers swapping channels, discussing the "kidnapping situation." "Do you honestly believe you could hurt me? With a gun or otherwise?" He didn't ask because he doubted it anymore. This time, he asked for confirmation.

"I don't know. Every time I close my eyes, I see you in Ian's hospital bed. I see you suffocating, reaching for me. It brings me to tears, and yet, I feel nothing. There is nothing in me. Not anymore. I never meant for you to be exposed to it. I never meant for you to even see it. And now, here we are, about to walk off the stage. The curtain is closing. It's over."

The snow on the roof was so deep, and the feeling was leaving Cory's toes, as well as his fingers. "What do you want me to say? Do you want me to agree with you? I'm sorry, Will, I just don't. I admit we didn't have the happiest relationship. I admit that things could have gone better for us. In the end, you tried to change. I've forgiven you. I still would."

"I wish you'd stop. Just *stop* forgiving me, and just *accept* what I am. I've told you before, Cory… you can't fix me. I know you want to. You want to believe it's possible, because it gives you a purpose. You have to understand that it's not going to happen. You have to understand, underneath it all, I can't change."

"But you quit heroin. You don't think that's significant? I do. You've shown us both that you can do it. You have the ability to help yourself. You've chosen to hide from your regret and your guilt and chose to suffer because it makes you cope with it better. You don't have a reason to keep suffering. You have the chance to move on. You have the opportunity to be happy. You just won't take it."

"I don't deserve it. And damn it, neither do you. Must you continue pushing and striving for this? It's a wasted effort."

"I just think that you're—"

"*There is no future for me, or for us!* There is *nothing* to look forward to. I will never be normal. I will never be the man you want." He turned away from him now, his head hung.

The wind whistled, and Cory had to speak over it for Will to hear him. "You don't see how happy you make me, do you?" Will didn't answer. "You do, you know. I know you hide from me. I know that's what makes you comfortable. But you don't have to. You don't ever have to. I love you for who you are."

Silence, brief, but agonizing. Then, Will started to move away from him, his back still turned. Why wouldn't he look at him? That's when he saw he was walking toward the edge of the roof. "And when I go to prison, what are you going to do? Do you even understand how long I'll be in there? Premeditated attempted murder doesn't sit well with the court system. I could be in prison for twenty years. Could be thirty. Could be *life*. Are you going to wait that long for me? Are you going to be able to handle a relationship with a man who lives in a fucking *cell*?! Face reality, sweetheart." As he turned his head, the twirling red and blue lights of the cruisers below tinted his wet hair and face. "This can't go on."

Cory thought of saying that yes, he would wait for him, but he'd be lying. Twenty years to life was a very long time, too long to have a relationship with someone he'd only see during short visiting hours. They'd lack the intimacy and closeness of a real couple. On the other hand, he loved Will, and wanted to help him out of the mess he got himself in. "Then... what now? Where do we go from here?"

Will inched closer to the ledge. Cory's heart raced. Oh, God. He was going to jump. He started pushing through the mounds of snow to reach him, to pull him back to safety. Will put his hand up, motioning for him to stop. Then, he waved him back. Cory stopped, but didn't retreat.

"We?" He shook his head. "There isn't a 'we' anymore. I've corrupted a beautiful thing. I don't also want to corrupt a beautiful person. It's not too late for you."

"What are you doing?" Cory reached for him, waving his fingers. "Come on, Will, step back."

"They're coming inside now. We still have a little time left." He took a long look at the horizon, an expression of peace on his face, one Cory had only seen on him after a dose of heroin or making love to him. He seemed to be gazing at the lights on Grand River, even those of destitute liquor stores, ones he might have been familiar with. "So much graffiti," he mumbled to no one in particular.

"Will, would you listen to me?!"

"You should recognize a goodbye when you hear one."

He saw Will's foot slide onto the ledge, knocking dusty snow off of the building. "*Don't!*" Despite Will's gestures commanding him to stay back, he moved closer, tears of fright in his eyes now. "It'll be all right, I-I'll come and visit you every day, for as long as it takes. You might even get paroled! You don't know! B-besides, it's not even like they can prove you planned to kill him, right? It's Derrick's word against yours! No one said you were going to prison! Maybe the jury won't find you guilty!" Will only stared three stories down at the ground below. He seemed mesmerized by it. "I'll testify on your behalf."

Snow coated Will's hair and colored it half-white. Flakes seemed to speckle the lenses of his glasses, and he didn't mind it. "You know as well I as I do that the evidence is pretty devastating what happened here. I don't want you lying for me anymore. Don't do what I did. I'm setting things right."

Rivers of tears were flowing now, ones that Cory couldn't contain no matter how much they burned when the wind caught them. "We could run away together. That's what we can do, we can run."

"Cory…" He sighed with both adoration and impatience. "I'm tired of forcing myself out of bed every morning. I'm tired of living like this. I'm tired of hating, tired of running from my past. I'm tired of being me. I'm tired of turning away from mirrors because I hate who I see. Please. Let me do this."

"If you never want to see me again, fine. I'll do that if that's what you want, and I'll deal with it. Just please don't fucking kill yourself."

"It's my life, and my decision. You don't have to watch. You can pretend I flew." He smiled, but Cory didn't join him, but continued to weep. The smile fell, and Cory thought, even just for a moment, that he had changed his mind when seeing how much pain he was in. He retracted his foot and staggered a step backward. "It's not up to you."

Cory plummeted to his knees. It was so wet, and so cold, but his skin was already numb. Was there really nothing he could do to talk him out of it? He found that hard to believe, and yet, Will looked so prepared, as though he had been waiting for this moment all of his life. Even as he sat before him, pleading with him, Will could only tell him there was nothing he could say or do. The tears flowing down his cheeks had no effect on Will in the slightest. Maybe it really was the end. Maybe that was the final night he would see and speak to him. He bowed his head, mournfully and regretfully.

He felt the touch of a chilled, dry hand brushing his chin. He raised his eyes, blinking the blur away, seeing the silhouette of Will come into focus. Will kneeled before him, taking his cheeks in both of his freezing palms. This only made the tears run harder.

"*I'm sorry.*" His pressed their foreheads together, and they almost seemed to stick. "It's better this way." Something slammed against the roof door. Paint cans rattled and shook to the ground, and frustrated voices shouted from inside the building. "I know you tried. I want you to live your life." The slams continued, the top of the tall stack of cans dropping. "Don't think I'm doing this because I don't love you."

He flung his good arm around Will's neck and held him tight, hoping it might prevent him from escaping him. "Please don't leave me. Don't leave me alone."

"If I'm arrested, I'll be leaving you anyway, and I'd rather go this way. Try to understand. You have to let me go." He tried to get up, but Cory wouldn't release him.

"*I can't.*" He trailed off into a sob. Will pried his arm off of him, but Cory wrapped it around his hips.

"Let me go."

He didn't want it to, but his elbow weakened, and Will broke free. He went back to his perch, staring down at the ground far below them. The roof door screeched as it burst open, buckets and cans of paint falling over, spilling their contents. Three officers breached the doorway and invaded the rooftop, but halted when they saw Will on the ledge.

"Sir, step away from the ledge," one of the officers commanded.

Will took one last look at Cory. A faint smile spread on his lips. It was intended as comfort. He was telling him that it would be all right. He would move on. Life itself would go on. He wouldn't have to worry about whether or not he'd turn back to drugs. He wouldn't have to tell people his boyfriend was in prison for attempted murder. He wouldn't have to stitch his many wounds anymore. He could just be Cory, and Will wouldn't be around to taint that. Though he might never forgive Will for what he was about to do, and the scar might never heal, he returned the identical smile to him. They hadn't been together long, but he would never experience such a trial with any other person. Will was the one. There would be no other.

"Don't forget me," he made Cory promise.

He didn't think he'd be able to speak, since his throat had closed up. He forced out his farewell the best he could manage. "Never."

"Get back!" The officer warned, but it was too late now. Will took a step forward, as he would on any other day down a flight of stairs, and jumped. The only sound Cory could hear now was the hiss of the wind. Then, the still followed, silence as even the police were stunned to have seen it happen, and Cory hunched over his knees, his stomach in knots. It seemed so distant, but he heard his soul screaming in eternal pain. His voice became hoarse as it strained to heave the seething agony from his body. Nothing could force it away. His heart bled from an irreparable deep abrasion, bellowing from the depths of his chest.

One of the officers raced back down the stairs to inspect what happened to Will, and the other two helped Cory to his feet. One of them started asking questions. He had completely toned them out. Nothing mattered now. Will was gone, blinked out like a dead star, and he wasn't coming back.

I let him do it. How could I let him do it?

They brought him inside out of the cold, trying to snap him out of his shock and daze just to get an explanation out of him, but he didn't hear a word they said. Eventually they gave up for the time being, allowing him to grieve. Sitting down in the main hall of the school, he watched as one of them reentered the building, motioning for one of the other two officers to join him outside. Cory heard them calling a coroner. The wound in his heart grew to incomparable sizes.

He had experienced loss before. His grandfather died when he fourteen years old. It was nothing compared to this. He couldn't live with the fact that he allowed Will to jump off of the roof, and was beginning to loathe himself for it. He could have tried harder, in his view. He could have stopped him. He only sat down and watched him commit suicide.

Now alone with one of the officers, he heard him whisper, "Are you Derrick Holden?"

Cory blinked back his remaining tears, sniffed, and looked the officer in the face. "I-I'm sorry?"

"Derrick? Is that your name?"

Derrick. He had heard that name before. Wasn't it someone he knew? Someone's boyfriend? "No. Cory. Cory Anderson."

The officer asked him for identification. Cory passed him his wallet, not really concerned with what he found in it. He took a look at his license, then handed the wallet back, and relayed the information to the other officers via radio. Then, softening his voice, he asked, "What happened here, Cory?"

"Will," he whimpered. It was the only thing he could manage to work out.

"Is he the one that...?"

Cory nodded, covering his face, his shoulders twitching.

"We got a call from a Derrick Holden. He said he was kidnapped, that someone was trying to kill him. Do you know anything about that?"

It all came back to him now, the reason why he was there in the first place. "Derrick assaulted me a few days ago. Will's my boyfriend. He was... going to kill him for it. That's why he..." He couldn't bring himself to say it.

The officer sat down next to him in an eroded chair. "I'm sorry for your loss."

Cory was too hurt to show much appreciation, but he did nod to show it meant something to him.

The officer once again gave the others some information, and turned back to Cory. "There was a warrant out for Mister Holden's arrest for assault. We searched the building, but we can't find him. He must have got out before we came."

"Will brought him here. I can't imagine Derrick getting far on foot."

"Brought him here in his car?"

"Yes."

"Is Will's car silver?"

"No. That's mine. His is green. Forest green."

"There's no other vehicle out there. He must have stolen it."

Cory clenched his fists. They shook, as he did, with rage. The officer seemed to notice, because he lowered his voice.

"How did you find this place if he brought Derrick alone?"

He hoped he wouldn't ask, because it meant he suspected him of being an accessory. "Will had... told me prior to this that he planned on killing Derrick. I found the address and came here to stop him."

The officer was silent for a moment. "All by yourself?"

"I wasn't afraid of Will. He wouldn't have hurt me." When the officer gave him a suspicious look, he sighed. "I know how it sounds. Trust me. I wouldn't have come if I thought I was in danger."

After thinking it over, the officer said, "If Derrick called from a cell phone, it shouldn't take us long to track him down. We'll find him." It was the best comfort he could offer in the wake of the tragedy.

He nodded once more. As they walked toward the exit, hoping that by now he wouldn't have to see Will's body, he felt the need to ask: "What's your name?"

"Patrick." He took Cory's hand and shook it. Patrick's kind and gentle disposition made him wish he had met him under better circumstances.

Just as they stepped outside, the coroner and his assistant were loading the full black body bag onto a stretcher to place in their vehicle. Cory broke down all over again at the sight of it, and Patrick was kind enough to hug him and face him away from the scene as he walked him to his cruiser.

The only thought on his mind for some time was Will's parents. They hadn't yet known that they had lost their son, and they might even hold him responsible when they received the news. In a way, he supposed that he *was* responsible, but no amount of apologies would bring him back. The Shepherds were good people, and didn't deserve to lose Will in such a way, and he didn't want to inflict such pain on them. How would he ever explain to them that he didn't intend for Will's life to meet such an untimely end?

When he arrived home, he didn't explain to his mother or his concerned sisters why he had so many tears in his eyes and a shuffle to his step. He couldn't possibly find the proper words to describe his despair. Even simply saying "Will is dead" wouldn't be enough. The police were probably knocking on the door of the Shepherd house right now as he lied alone in his bed, and the thought of them breaking down just as badly as he was repeated in his mind for many long, sleepless hours.

So cowardly of you. So selfish of you. Why did you do this to them? To me?

It was a cruel prank. It had to be. This wasn't really happening to him. Things had just begun to work out between them. They were starting anew, cleansed of their earlier turmoil, and had plans for their life. He couldn't possibly be dead now, after they had been through so much together. He would show up at his door, yell "surprise" and explain how it was his plan from the start. Wouldn't he?

He hoped, for hours, that it was the case, but he knew better. Will wasn't pulling a prank. He wasn't the type to make such jokes. He was dead. He would never speak to him again.

None of the thousands of tears he shed would bring him back.

For three days, Cory didn't sleep. He began to have hallucinations where Will was alive. It all hit him much too hard when he attended the wake and funeral and saw Anthony and Maria Shepherd mourning their loss, crying over an open casket where Will now rested. It was the first time he saw him since his death, and interestingly enough, the first time he had ever seen him look so peaceful. Even when he slept, he looked twice as uncomfortable as he did now.

The funeral home was crowded full of people Cory had never met before, all of whom seemed indifferent and, at times, bored. They would help themselves to various snack trays and chat with family members like it was just another party. He wondered if their hearts ached as badly as his did, or if they might have even known the man he had spent so much time with the past few months. Feasibly, none of them knew Will very well, or cared for him. They yammered away, even laughed at times. He might have very well been the only one without dry eyes in the building. Either way, it made no difference to him. He was there for Will, not for them.

When he got a moment alone with Will, he peered over him with sleepless, purplish eyes. The suit they chose to dress him in wasn't really his style, and Cory had to amuse himself with a thought of him turning his nose up at the fashion sense. It only led him to shedding continuous tears. "I miss you," he wept. "I miss you so much."

Someone stepped up beside him and placed a gentle hand upon his shoulder. Without looking, he already surmised who it had been, and he didn't know what to say to Anthony now that they had seen each other for the first time since Will committed suicide. Still, despite his bereavement, his tone was friendly.

"We tried to call you," he soothed, a touch of fondness in his voice. Cory found it hard to believe he had no feelings of resentment toward him. "You wouldn't answer the phone. I don't blame you, though. Cory, I know you probably think that what Will did is your fault."

"You know that, huh?" He answered, avoiding eye contact.

"I want you to know that we don't blame you, and you shouldn't either."

"How could you *not* blame me? I was there. I let him..." He sighed, pushing back the threat of more tears. "I let him do it."

"Come outside with me for a moment. I want to speak to you alone."

He didn't want to leave Will, but he figured it'd be best to join Anthony. Outside was a small crowd of people massed around the entrance, possibly relatives of Anthony and Maria. Some of them were chortling. It disturbed him in ways that even Will's death didn't. Anthony seemed nonplussed, ignoring them for now, and he led Cory around the side of the funeral home, his thick jacket bundled.

He opened with a question that got right to the point: "Did Will ever tell you that we're not his biological parents?"

"Yeah. He did. He said his father..." Somehow, he couldn't bring himself to finish that sentence. It seemed like the wrong place to say something so gruesome, regardless of its truth. "Did something bad."

"When we adopted him, we knew he was scarred, though he was just fine for the most part. He went to a public school, he had friends, though not many, and he had boyfriends over the years. He coped. What happened with his biological parents was a thing of the past." He forced a pack of cigarettes out of his pocket and lit one with a shaking hand. "So I hoped, anyway. He could function just fine in the world without much trouble, but there was always... I don't know... this blackness in him. When he started cutting himself, I could see just how much he was hurting inside and how badly he wanted to hide his pain from us." He took a long drag off of the cigarette. "I sent him to a therapist, and... God, help me, Cory, I think I made it worse by doing that."

"Worse? How could it make things worse?"

"Because I don't think he wanted to open that wound, at least not all the way. He wanted to bury it, forget it, and try to move on with his life. I was always told that's the unhealthy way of handling things." He scoffed, dragging the back of his hand across his cheek, exhaling clouds of smoke. "When he was forced to remember it, he just got angrier, and sadder. He started cutting every day, to the point of where we needed to put locks on drawers and hide knives. He started confiding in me, telling me he wanted to kill himself. I didn't know what to do. If the therapy and medication wasn't working, what the hell else could I do for him? I felt helpless."

Cory knew just what he meant by that. "But he went so long without doing it. Why did he wait until now?"

"My guess would be that he didn't want to give up. Will was stubborn, you know that." Cory nodded. "He wanted things to get better. He tried, many times, but I assume he figured things would never get better. I feel... I *know*... how hard he tried to improve while you were in his life. For a while, he managed to solve some of his problems, and I was very grateful to you for that." He sniffed, but quickly smoked thereafter. "But I think, deep down, he wasn't strong enough. I feel terrible saying such a thing about my boy, but that's the way it is. It's not your fault. If it's anyone's fault, it's mine."

"It's not yours, either," Cory eased while patting his arm. "I think only Will had any control over it."

"He loved you. That much I know."

"I know he did. I'll always love him." He smiled as soon as Anthony's mouth perked, watching him put out the first cigarette and light up another. "About Ian…"

Anthony let forth a scratchy grunt of disapproval.

"Do you think they ever loved each other?"

"Will's concept of 'love' was once pretty tenuous. If you want my honest opinion, I believe Will *thought* he loved Ian. What I think he truly loved though, was putting himself into an abusive situation, trying to relive what happened so that he could make adult decisions in the same scenario. Many of his partners were abusive, but they eventually left Will for other men, or sometimes women. Ian stuck with him because he liked to belittle him. Will stayed because it was… I hate to say this… what he *needed*. No matter how often we tried to steer him away, he'd explain that Ian 'wasn't all bad.' Even after the fucker was dead, he'd make excuses."

If he didn't think he was all bad, why then did Will kill him? Cory wondered. *Maybe the same reason he wanted to kill Derrick. He wasn't getting revenge. He was putting him down, like euthanizing a rabid animal. It was just a fact to him that Ian needed to die.*

"You think he *needed* Ian?" Cory asked once there was a lull in Anthony's speech.

"I don't think he did, but Will certainly felt that way." A couple more puffs, and the cigarette was finished. He lit a third. "Even then, Will was smart enough to see the horrible mess he got himself into. Ian got so bad…" He shook his head, then his elderly palm over his wrinkled eyes, taking a moment to grieve. It reminded Cory of the reality of the situation— that they were speaking of Will because he was dead now. It reopened the scar over his heart, and it bled once more. "I'm glad Ian died when he did. I would have killed him myself." Wiping his nose, he sighed. Cory forewent the urge to divulge Will's secret murder. "When I saw how much you looked like him, I was instinctively ready to strangle you."

"I wish I didn't look like him," Cory stated. "To be compared to him even in looks is grotesque to me."

"But Will was drawn to you because of it, and his meeting you was a good thing."

"He's dead now because he met me."

"No. You didn't cause his death. You gave him life. I had never seen hope in him before, because he never hoped to have a happy existence. Will didn't kill himself because he was unhappy. That much I know."

At that, Cory couldn't think of anything else to do but hug him. Anthony's embrace was warm and tight, stronger than Will's, but just as loving. "He made me happy, too," he let him know. "I tried to see the best in him. When he was happy, he was really happy. It made me try for him."

"I only wish he hadn't been such a fool."

"Even the smartest of us make choices only we understand."

Just as he had at the wake, Cory attended Will's funeral, an event that was needlessly over-religious, an approach Will would have never chosen for himself. He imagined Will's spirit sitting beside him in one of the many chairs, leaning back with his leg crossed over the other in the way he often sat in life, his hands folded and fingers linked, shaking his head at him. *Can you believe these nuts?* He might have said, cocking that crooked smirk at him. The thought awakened a smile on his face. *You knew me better than any of them did. What is this drivel about me going with God?*

He even imagined Will beside him at his own burial, looking at the casket being lowered into the ground, telling him to get over him. Cory wouldn't, however. He couldn't. He would always be there. A ghost. A shadow. *His* shadow.

After a moving farewell, Cory placed his hand on Will's casket, the chamber of which he would return to the earth in, after kissing the surface of his palm. He left with his mother and sisters, who attended for his sake, though he informed them that they didn't have to. He didn't see his mother or Erica shed a single tear, but Amanda forlornly showed her condolences to her brother by weeping with him with sincere, heartfelt apologies. Cory knew that his relationship with his sister would from then on be a strong one.

When the service was over, and they returned home, Cory spoke little to his family about his intentions, but he started to pack his things. He was done now; done with his mother, done with Lansing, done with Michigan, done with it all. Staying there any longer would invoke thoughts of Will, thoughts of how much he hated his job, his life, and how meaningless it felt now. If he didn't leave, he might kill himself, too.

While packing his belongings in a series of suitcases and boxes, he reviewed each of Will's anonymous letters to him, only to induce more heartache. He saved a single box for Will's objects and tokens that he had kept, and in so doing, clutched them individually against his chest, close to his heart. His single greatest wish was to go back to the beginning, to start over, knowing what he knew, understanding that Will would leave him this way. He would stop him the second time around. He would do a better job of helping him. He would save his life.

Scott and Alex were happy to hear from him, though the call was no cheerful one. Scott especially expressed his sorrow for his companion's tragic loss, and his surprise at his admission of bisexuality. He welcomed him to return home, to New York, where he belonged, and Cory told him he had long been planning on it. What he hadn't been planning on was for his former friend Angie to show up at his house one afternoon, just a day before he planned to depart.

There was an unusual thaw that day, and the abundance of water from melted snow made it difficult to walk down the driveway without getting his shoes soaking wet. Regardless, he sloshed through it when he realized Angie wasn't going to. When he reached her, the cuffs of his pant legs were darkened.

At first, they said nothing to one another. Angie seemed to want Cory to speak first, but he had nothing to say to her. She sighed at the sign of his silence, and appeared perturbed at his glare.

"Derrick was arrested. I wanted to let you know that."

It was music to Cory's ears, better than his favorite song. *"Good."*

"Where is your boyfriend?" Her interrogation sounded accusatory.

Had Cory really neglected to tell his former companion that Will was now dead? When reviewing the choice to keep her in the dark, he understood why he had. He really thought she wouldn't have cared. In fact, he assumed she would have defiled Will's death by dancing with pom-poms.

"You should leave."

Disturbed, she stammered, "What? What do you mean?"

"Angie… there's no easy way to say good-bye to someone. We've been through a lot together." He released a heavy sigh, his lungs tightening. "I'm moving back to New York."

"You're kidding." Her eyes glazed.

"I'm not."

"Cory… you *can't*. I just lost Derrick, and I… I don't want to be alone here."

"You're going to have to deal with it. I won't stay here."

She broke down. He expected it to happen, in fact, he was counting down in his head to when she would burst. "You can't leave me."

"Angie, listen. I don't know if you knew about what Derrick did to me, and I don't care. He did it, and you… you let him. You *encouraged* him." When she took hold of his hand, he pulled it back, shaking his head. "We can't be friends anymore."

"You don't mean that." She breathed in. "You can't mean that." Her breath quivered out. "What am I supposed to do without you?"

"You don't need me. You'll be fine." He kissed her wet cheek, then turned his back to her, preparing to walk away.

"I'm sorry, Cory!"

He took one last look at her. "There aren't enough apologies in the world to make up for it."

Though she was stricken with grief, she grasped what he meant. She nodded, sniffling.

"Have a nice life." When he went back into the house, he didn't look back. Not anymore.

It was time to move forward.

20. Ashes

In the months following Will's funeral, Cory spent more time with Scott and Alex to make up for the years he had lost with them. They hadn't changed a bit, though Scott had gone back to school to get his associates degree. Alex still worked at that grocery store he always complained about. He was surprised he wasn't a manager there by now.

Scott had remained single, which Cory was surprised to learn, but Alex was still with that Jeff guy. Cory never liked Jeff, from the very day he met him. He always thought he was using Alex, and that Alex had never admitted to it. When he saw that Jeff had moved into the apartment to take his place when he initially left two years ago, Cory already knew they'd be clashing with one another. However, Jeff seemed to have improved since he last saw him. He was much more pleasant, and treated Alex better. He wondered what it was Alex did to encourage such a change, and if their relationship ever involved drug addiction like his did.

Following a few weeks of his moving in with his friends, he found himself a comfortable job in an electronics repair shop, one that came highly recommended and referred by Jeff. It was the one thing Jeff did that he could actually thank him for. Every day, even while at work, he thought of Will and how much he missed him. They had only experienced a few months worth of romance, but it was enough to know how much he cared.

One warm night in April, after leaving work, Cory made a choice that he would never have made years ago. He wasn't sure why he craved to do so, but he visited a bar: an upbeat, flashy place called **SLATE**. It had a marble-toned exterior and torches guiding the path to the front doors, which he slipped through after being carded by a bouncer. Inside, the music was loud, and the tables and floors were crowded, but it didn't stop him from heading over to the bar and finding a seat on a stool, which was black leather in color.

"Can I get you anything?" The male bartender said to him over the sound of blaring music. He had a cheerful smile full of bright white teeth, a bit too shiny and perfect for Cory's taste.

"Would you recommend something?" Cory asked, observing the customers from all angles.

"Well, not to brag, but I can make a damn fine manhattan."

He shrugged. "Sure. Make me one of those."

The chirpy barman nodded and started preparing his cocktail with that same toothy smile. While he waited patiently for his drink, someone took a seat in the vacant stool next to him, setting a bottle of beer on the bar top.

"Hey, there. I don't usually see such cute guys sitting at the bar alone."

Cory sighed, ready to tell him to buzz off, that he wasn't interested in company. He glanced at him, and their eyes met. His stomach sank to his feet. His lungs forgot how to draw in oxygen. The man before him, who was waiting for Cory to answer, thumbed a pair of wire-frame glasses up his nose. His irises were chocolate, like his chestnut hair. His complexion, his jaw line and face, as well as his body type were almost identical to Will's, the only exception being that he had a bit more meat on his bones.

Before Cory could properly react to such a sight, the bartender set his drink down before him. He wanted to thank him, but it was impossible to talk now. The bespectacled William Shepherd look-alike smirked, but only out of complexity. "Uh… are you all right?"

"W-what's your name?" Cory gasped, his eyes stretched wide.

"Austin." He still held that nervous grin, but looked ready to leap out of his seat and escape if things got too weird. "Yes, like Texas, and no, I'm not from Texas. Yours?"

"Cory," he said in a touch above a whisper. Austin slid off his stool a bit, reaching for the beer he set down after he muttered something like "cool" beneath his breath. When Cory saw he wanted to leave, he desperately talked him back. "I'm sorry, you just look a lot like someone I know... uh... *knew*. I didn't mean to get strange on you."

Austin eased back into his stool, chuckling. "That's okay, cutie. Sometimes people say I have a face that comforts them, so no hard feelings." Cory never took his eyes off of him. "This guy I look like... was he as good-looking as me?"

"He had different glasses."

"I see." He nodded, but continued to grin. It was beginning to look goofy. Will's smile was a lot more charming, in Cory's opinion. "So are you from around here?"

"Technically yes. I guess I am."

Puzzled by his vagueness, he cocked his head to the side. "Technically?"

"I moved here recently. Well, moved *back* here." He took a sip of his manhattan. The bartender was right. It was damn fine, indeed.

"From where?"

"Elsewhere."

Austin's laugh had an annoying snort to it. He had Will's looks, but unfortunately, not his finesse. "I'm going to guess from another planet."

"It feels like it sometimes."

"What are you doing in this bar? You don't look like the social type."

"I'm not. Not really." He shrugged, sipping more of his cocktail, becoming drawn to its delicious flavor. After smacking his lips a few times, he gulped more of it down.

"I guess I consider myself lucky you're speaking to me, then." Cory didn't answer him, only glanced back and forth between him and his drink. "You don't speak much, do you?"

"Who'd want to listen?" He finished his cocktail, feeling warmth wash over him. It was so good. He wanted another. He flagged the bartender down.

"I'm here, aren't I?"

"Okay. I guess don't want to talk about it."

"Would it help if I offered you a dance?"

He couldn't help but feel touched by this offer, even if his advances were likely selfish. "It might."

Austin held his hand out, and Cory only took it after he told him he wouldn't bite. He wondered how true this was. He followed him to the dance floor, which was packed with people, and danced to the best of his abilities, which were hardly practiced. Dancing was not something he commonly did, whether it was with men or women. On the other hand, when doing it with Austin, he liked it more than he thought he would. After all, he didn't see Austin, but Will, smiling and happy, enjoying his life, no longer in pain. It was what he always wanted to see, and what he needed to see.

After a couple of hours, and a few drinks, Austin asked if he'd like to return with him to his place. Cory obliged, wanting and hoping for at least one last night with Will, even if it wasn't technically him. He was drawn to who Will was, his problems, his seriousness, but all the same, it was relieving to see him happy. It helped him get the closure he needed.

The ride to Austin's place was awkward, but only because Austin was a chatterbox, and Cory wasn't. He didn't mind that he did all of the talking, since it saved him from saying anything foolish or insane. However, he spoke so quickly that it was hard to keep up.

When Austin parked, it was near a series of apartments. Cory recognized them. He drove past them every day on his way to work. Before he could say anything, he was being kissed and groped. If he didn't look so much like Will, he might have been a bit offended.

"You're cute as fuck," said Austin through steaming breaths of excitement. Cory didn't express his pleasure much, but he felt it, everywhere. Austin finally removed his hands and mouth from him, grinning. "Let's go." He hopped out of the car, welcoming Cory into the apartment building and up to his place.

Austin was an accomplished lover in bed, but Cory's joy lied solely in the thought that he was spending the night with his late partner. As soon as the short love affair was over, he yearned to experience it a second time. He wanted to feel Will against him again, to hold him, to soak in his warmth. He craved to hold him close, even in those moments of sadness. He found it impossible to fall asleep, though Austin was out like a light almost as soon as the act was over. He didn't hold him or speak to him like Will once did. He sank into a pit of depression. He even felt cheated out of his final goodbyes.

Things might be different in the morning.

When dawn broke, Austin awoke. When he stirred, he turned toward Cory, who was staring at him. He was a bit startled, as Cory could see from his wide eyes. "Uh, good morning." A nervous chuckle escaped his mouth.

"Couldn't sleep. Sorry." He wanted him to hold him again. Just once. Just one more time.

"That's okay." He sat up and rubbed his eyes, slipping his glasses on. "I'll drive you home."

"You want me to go?" Dread washed over him. Soon he'd have to say goodbye to Will a second time, this time forever.

Austin tilted his head, cracking his neck. He eyed the room for a bit, possibly searching for escape routes. "It's not like that. I just have some work I have to do and... stuff."

Even he couldn't understand why he felt the urge to cry. He couldn't lose him again. He wouldn't. "I could make breakfast."

There was an uncomfortable laugh from Austin as he moved out of the bed and away from him. "Cory, I had fun with you last night, but I really do have stuff to do. Maybe we'll do this again sometime."

"Please ..."

The young man that picked Cory up for a one-night stand now comprehended that in doing so, he may have made a poor decision. Cory wasn't just some meek young man surveying the bar for a good time. Something was wrong with him, and he was in the middle of a brewing emotional storm. "I'm sorry, Cory. I thought you understood what this was."

"What do you mean? What was this?"

"I didn't want the sex to continue more than one night. I thought that's what you wanted, too."

The reality of the situation, unfortunately, was that Austin wasn't Will. He was just a guy looking for a quickie, and he wanted to move on afterward. It reminded him of how much he had lost, and was losing once more, and he rushed out of the bed so that Austin wouldn't see the tears that started to flow. As he dressed himself, he felt his temporary escort watching him.

"You're right. Take me home."

"I'm sorry if I upset you."

Cory, facing away from him, shook his head. "It's not you," he sighed. "I had fun. Really."

Austin dropped the whole awkward matter, but Cory could tell he felt guilty. It only made matters worse to know that Austin was sincere and caring. It made it much tougher to walk away.

Just as he promised, he drove Cory home, but not without leaning in to give him a kiss out of generosity and appreciation. "Don't," Cory warned him, pulling his head away.

"Sorry," Austin apologized one final time. "Take care, Cory, okay?"

There wasn't much else Cory could say to him. After he was completely out of the car, Austin took off. He didn't blame him, exactly. He must have looked pretty crazy. He wished he had never met the man, because now, he only wanted to be near him again.

After an especially back-breaking day at work, he drove home with fatigued eyes. Halfway toward his destination, he was stalled by a train. Without really understanding why, he imagined throwing himself under it and getting smashed to unrecognizable pieces. It wouldn't have solved his problems, but it would end his depression and every other horrible thought that went along with it.

Once the railroad gates lifted, Cory didn't go straight home as he intended. Instead, he made a detour— to Austin's apartment. He knew it couldn't possibly go well for him to reintroduce himself. After all, he had been stalked before, and was very familiar with the concept of breaking boundaries. However, he thought that if he just saw him one more time, maybe tried to explain what he was going through, he might let him in for some coffee or a beer and talk it over. He did seem like a reasonable young man, as far as he could tell.

If I were him, I certainly wouldn't let me in. I look insane.

Still, he stopped at the apartments and parked, fixing his messy hair before he got out of his car. He remembered that Austin lived in apartment one-fourteen, despite being somewhat tipsy during his last visit. Before he did any knocking, he heard voices coming from inside the room. It was difficult to hear what they were saying, but they were elevated and irate. When he finally knocked, he did so with a shaking hand.

Austin opened the door. Cory didn't get a chance to greet him before he shoved his way into the hall, shutting the door behind him.

Cory thought he heard someone yell from inside. "What the hell are you doing here?" He asked when he caught his breath.

"I'm sorry," Cory quickly apologized, hoping it would prevent him from sending him away. Now that he was asked why he was there, he couldn't quite give a reasonable, rational answer. "I just wanted to see you and speak to you."

"What?" Austin, who had a chipper, friendly face when they last saw each other, was now glazed in sweat and apprehension. "What do you mean?"

"It's kind of important." He noticed Austin's hand was holding onto the door handle. Maybe he was ready to rush back inside, or he was barricading it so that whoever was inside wouldn't come out. Either way, it made him uncomfortable. "Um... do you have a minute?"

"Look, Cory, I told you." He sighed, closing his eyes. "It was a one-time thing, okay?"

"But, I..."

"I'm sorry. I'm sorry, I can't."

Cory expected such a thing to happen, but it still broke his heart regardless. He felt so foolish, so over-optimistic. What made him think that he would be interested in listening to his problems? Just because they had sex together? That was laughable, at best. "I didn't mean to disturb you. That was wrong of me."

As he walked away, Austin didn't retreat into his apartment right away. In fact, he cleared his throat and called him back. "Wait a minute." Cory halted and looked at him. "Please, understand. It's not that I don't like you or anything. I should have told you the truth last night."

"Truth about what?"

"I have a boyfriend."

Hearing him say that shouldn't have hurt as powerfully as it had. It struck him with such fierceness that he almost fell over. "Oh... I see."

"So, you get why I only wanted it to be one night."

"I didn't come back to have a relationship with you, or even fuck you. I just wanted to talk to someone."

There was a great amount of hesitation from Austin, then, "You're really nice, Cory, and, believe me, I feel terrible for hurting your feelings. I was drunk and stupid the other night. I should never have done what I did. I can't risk being seen with you. Please. I'm sorry, but you have to go."

There was no reason or use trying to force himself into the man's life. He backed off and nodded to show his demands would be met. He turned and walked out of the building without saying or signaling goodbye. Austin lingered for some time outside of his apartment, watching Cory as he left, likely to see if he would come back, but he didn't. He kept walking, and drove away almost as soon as he started the engine.

Cory might never speak to him again, but he felt a powerful desire to taste him, to embrace him, to be with him. Austin didn't have to know he was there. He didn't have to acknowledge him. He just had to live his life. Cory would keep his distance, but he wouldn't be far. He would stay away as he promised, but he couldn't leave him alone, not now.

This time, I won't let you go. I'm going do things right this time, and we'll be happier. I'll make it happen for us, Will.

Even if it kills me.